"Jessica Anya Blau's second novel is not only a wise and pitch-perfect depiction of family dynamics but also happens to be unrelentingly, sidesplittingly funny. I dare you to forget this family."
—IRINA REYN, author of *What Happened to Anna K.*

"If you took Jonathan Franzen, soaked him in Southern California culture, sprinkled him with biting insight and twisted humor, you would get a book that tasted something like *Drinking Closer to Home*. The Stein family is unlike any you've ever encountered, and yet the truth of their story is absolutely universal. Jessica Anya Blau is effortlessly hilarious and deeply profound. This is a stunning novel."
—KATIE ARNOLDI, author of *Point Dume*

"I have never encountered such exciting, eccentric, and lovably flawed characters as those Jessica Anya Blau creates in *Drinking Closer to Home*. This hysterical literary portrait of dysfunction makes me simultaneously grateful that my own family isn't this zany, and jealous of their close-knit ability to laugh even in the face of life's most difficult trials."
—ALLISON AMEND, author of *Stations West*

"If you think you've read enough novels about mixed-up families already, go ahead and read one more. Jessica Anya Blau's *Drinking Closer to Home* is a phantasmagoric, hilarious carnival ride."
—MADISON SMARTT BELL

"Jessica Anya Blau's *Drinking Closer to Home* is heartfelt and hilarious as it explores every nook and cranny of this wonderful (and wild) family. If you want to know why we love our parents and siblings even as they drive us to drink and distraction, you must read this book."
—RON TANNER, author of *Kiss Me, Stranger*

"Family agonies observed under plenty of sunshine with a sharp eye, an even sharper pen, and the forgiving heart of a wise writer. As perfectly pitched as it is comically painful, *Drinking Closer to Home* echoes a profound Tolstoyan truth about family. Many novelists have a sense for place; the gifted ones deliver life with such fidelity that the truth hits very close to home indeed."
—MARISOL, author of
The Lady, the Chef, and the Courtesan

"All families are eccentric in their own way, but this hilarious and heartbreaking novel introduces readers to one that exists on a plane all its own. *Drinking Closer to Home* is a testament to the impossibility of ever truly 'leaving home,' and the great triumph of this book is in Blau's skillful illumination of how that's both a blessing and a curse, not just for her characters but for all of us. This novel will stay with you for a very long time."
—SKIP HORACK, author of
The Southern Cross and *The Eden Hunter*

"The sharpness of Jessica Anya Blau's voice and wit never ceases to amaze me. From the first page this surprising novel takes a classic tale—adult children going home again—and turns it on its head. An absorbing, heart-wrenching read."
—KATIE CROUCH, author of *Men and Dogs*

"Jessica Anya Blau's emotional turf is kinship, from its betrayals to its bonds—and in her second novel, *Drinking Closer to Home*, she covers this territory with an honesty so raw and funny I wanted to read parts aloud to strangers. It's riveting and startling. It is not afraid of the dark. It has real heart."

—DYLAN LANDIS, author of
Normal People Don't Live Like This

"The hilariously irreverent sibling triad in *Drinking Closer to Home* had me laughing so hard at their gallows humor that I didn't realize how devastated I was until I was fully under their spell. This unconventional joyride of a novel is also an unexpectedly powerful and multilayered exploration of unbreakable family bonds."

—GINA FRANGELLO, author of *Slut Lullabies*

"It might surprise Jessica Anya Blau to hear that her stunning new novel struck me as old-fashioned, so maybe I'd better explain. She creates characters that have a lot more depth and more of a past than one often sees in fiction these days, and she never loses sight of the world they inhabit. Furthermore, she's of the school in which actions come with consequences and secrets bring surprises. She's lavished such attention on these people that I found it impossible not to care about them—and equally impossible to forget them. Blau is a magnificent writer, and this is one special novel."

—STEVE YARBROUGH, author of *Safe from the Neighbors*

"Chekhov knew that laughter and tears are only a breath apart. So does Jessica Anya Blau. The family in her marvelous *Drinking Closer to Home* is a raucous sextet—emphasis on the first syllable, please—unraveling its past in a Santa Barbara hospital room. They eat bad food, they take no prisoners, and they make beautiful, hilarious music through time and all the spaces in the heart. And spleen."

—JAMES MAGRUDER, author of *Sugarless*

"In *Drinking Closer to Home*, Jessica Anya Blau has created an unforgettably unique family—Buzzy, Louise, Anna, Portia, and Emery—and done them a great service by placing them in a compelling story that is alternately funny and sad as hell. I don't think I'd last twelve days in this family, but I could read about them forever. With this novel, Blau announces herself as a fearless writer, capable of anything and everything."

—KEVIN WILSON, author of
Tunneling to the Center of the Earth

"*Drinking Closer to Home* is as raw and heartbreaking as it is tender. Jessica Anya Blau has written an honest, haunting portrayal of a beguiling yet maddening family who together come of age amid the shifting morals of a country on the cusp of tremendous cultural change. With humor, compassion, and a keen insight into the human psyche, *Drinking Closer to Home* proves that despite the best of intentions, where we come from and where we end up are even closer than we could ever imagine."

—ROBIN ANTALEK, author of *The Summer We Fell Apart*

"Imagine a home with a nudist mother, a bird that perches on the living room curtain rod and shits on the couch, and an empty pool in the backyard filled with bikes. Imagine growing up in this home and then returning as an adult to the hospital bedside of this nudist mother. *Drinking Closer to Home* is a gloriously rich portrait of three adult children who discover that the tensions and hurts they still have between them are inextricably tied to their laughter and their love."

—SUSAN HENDERSON, author of *Up From the Blue*

"Jessica Anya Blau has written a very funny—but also deeply humane—novel. The central characters writhe in a particular kind of family agony. It might just remind you of your own family. (It certainly reminded me of mine.) Parental love and booze and drugs and all the complications of becoming an adult: this is a smart book—a book that makes you cringe and laugh out loud."

—PAULS TOUTONGHI, author of *Red Weather*

"Sadly, not a photo essay, but rather a witty account of the agonies and ecstasies of a girl coming of age in late-seventies California."
—*New York* magazine

"If books could be trains, *The Summer of Naked Swim Parties* would be a high-speed zephyr, traveling at great speed from California to Baltimore, providing great scenery and good company. To carry the metaphor further, this novel has energy and power and will be a great ride for everyone who reads it. Ms. Blau is a writer of wit, intelligence, deep feeling, humor, and imagination, and she gets into the head of a young person like almost nobody since J.D. Salinger. All aboard!"
—STEPHEN DIXON

"Reading this heartfelt and humorous coming-of-age story is the perfect way to spend a hot summer day. . . . Blau's writing style flows beautifully, so you will glide through this book and not want to put it down. So get out your crochet bikini, whack on your favorite Jimi Hendrix tune, and enjoy the ride." —*Cosmopolitan* (Australia)

"You're fourteen years old in 1976 and your parents throw naked swim parties. How the hell are you supposed to have your own private sexual awakening? Jessica Anya Blau creates a charming protagonist, her charismatic Santa Barbara family, and a summer of love, lust and confusion. You won't want summer—and this wonderful book—to end." —ELLEN SUSSMAN, author of
Dirty Words: A Literary Encyclopedia of Sex;
Bad Girls: 26 Writers Misbehave; and *On a Night Like This*

drinking closer to home

JESSICA ANYA BLAU

drinking
closer to home

A NOVEL

HARPER ● PERENNIAL

NEW YORK ● LONDON ● TORONTO ● SYDNEY ● NEW DELHI ● AUCKLAND

HARPER ● PERENNIAL

P.S.™ is a trademark of HarperCollins Publishers.

HarperCollins books may be purchased for educational, business, or sales promotional use. For information please write: Special Markets Department, HarperCollins Publishers, 10 East 53rd Street, New York, NY 10022.

FIRST EDITION

Designed by Fritz Metsch

Library of Congress Cataloging-in-Publication Data
Blau, Jessica Anya.
Drinking closer to home : a novel / Jessica Anya Blau.—1st ed.
    p. cm.
ISBN 978-0-06-198402-0
1. Teenage girls—Fiction. 2. California, Southern—Fiction. 3. Domestic fiction. I. Title.
PS3602.L397D75 2011
813'.6—dc22   2010019007

11 12 13 14 15   OV/BVG   10 9 8 7 6 5 4 3 2 1

With love for Bonnie Blau, Sheridan Blau, Rebecca Summers, Joshua Blau, and Alex Suarez. And for my grandparents.

1993: DAY TWO

Anna leans her head over Alejandro's plate, her black hair falling like a screen across her cheek. She sniffs, her head jittering above the gefilte fish that sits there like a rotten, battered sea sponge. Portia watches her and wonders how many chromosomes come between man and dog.

"Want some?" Alejandro asks. His hair is so dark it almost looks blue. And his eyes are like Anna's, circles of ink—like overly dilated pupils. Portia thinks that Alejandro and Anna look more alike than Anna and their brother, Emery.

"No fucking way I'm eating that stuff." Anna sits up straight and picks up the crossword puzzle she's been working on over dinner.

It is midnight. Louise—Anna, Portia, and Emery's mother—is in the hospital after having suffered a "massive" heart attack. No one knows if she will live. They spent the evening in Louise's room, watching her vomit, mopping up blood that spurted from her nose, breathing in the pissy smell from her leaking catheter bag and the sour odor of death mixed with medicine that seeps from her pores. Their father, whom everyone calls Buzzy, brushed her teeth and Emery rubbed scented lotion into her hands and feet, but the stink still remained, as if the air had been stained.

The gefilte fish is the fifth course of the birthday dinner Portia has prepared for Buzzy. The first course was quesadillas: *two flour tortillas with slices of Monterey Jack cheese stacked between them, fried in a pan of butter, then topped with cilantro and salsa.* Portia used the wrong pan, and the cheese melted out the sides of the tortillas and burned. Four tortillas were lost in the process. That left only enough for each person to have one quesadilla. Emery and Alejandro eat a lot. They would have had three each.

The second course was frozen tofu corn dogs. *Remove from package and microwave for two minutes.* Emery specifically requested them after the quesadillas were gone. Buzzy fetched the mustard from the refrigerator. The corn dogs were a hit.

The third course was salad. *Triple-washed for your convenience. Just open and serve.* Anna and Portia had bought the bag of greens at the store earlier that day. Portia dumped the contents into a wooden bowl and brought out a glass jar of Italian dressing. Everyone served themselves, using their hands to dish out portions.

The fourth course was pickles. *Chill before serving. Refrigerate after opening.* Anna opened the jar and passed it around the table.

And the fifth course was gefilte fish.

They are in Santa Barbara, where the days are so sunny you'd swear a nuclear reactor had exploded. Anna, Portia, and Emery grew up here, but no longer live here. They have each flown in from the East Coast, where they were still wearing weatherproof boots and scarves. Between them, the sisters have left behind two kids, both of whom they passionately love, but neither of whom they currently miss. Anna also left behind her husband.

Anna misses her husband the way you miss gloves on an October day only after you've seen a nice pair on someone else's hands.

When she was changing planes in Denver, Anna thought

about taking off her wedding ring. She finds airports stimulating, just like bars: strangers brushing by each other, a certain anonymity within the intimacy of a shared experience. Anna wanted the possibility of a flirtation or chitchat; or maybe she'd collect a business card that she'd throw away before flying home. In the end, she kept the ring on because more overpowering than her thoughts of men in suits, or a guy in jeans carrying a guitar case, were thoughts of her mother. It has been only recently that Anna forgave her mother for a litany of crimes Anna had been carrying in her stomach like a knotted squid. Now that the squid is gone, she is hoping she can enjoy her mother more, they way her sister always does, and the way her brother often does.

Portia brought a pedicure kit with her to Santa Barbara, because the last time she was here, her father warned her that women were getting hepatitis from pedicure instruments, even at the most exclusive salons. She plans to take the pedicure kit to a salon where she will pay a Russian woman who was most likely an engineer or physicist in her own country to use it on her feet. Portia is sure that the Russian will snicker at her fear and say something in her own language to the other overly educated Russian women who are slumped over other American women's feet. This will not bother Portia, she knows, because the severity of everything that happens these next few days can only be compared to the severity of her mother's heart attack.

In addition to the weight of Louise's heart, Portia is also laden with her own malfunctioning heart. Three months ago her husband of seven years, Patrick, left her and their three-year-old daughter to be with a childless, slim woman named Daphne Frank. Daphne Frank wears stiff white blouses and boots that reach her kneecaps. Portia is sure that when her husband yanks those boots off (like removing an épée from its shield) he sees perfectly pedicured toes. If she were to walk around with chipped toenail polish, Portia would feel that she looked like old leftovers, the ones that have been sitting in the fridge so long no one can identify the once-great meal they came from. Or maybe she'd look like mealy, blanched gefilte fish on a plate.

Emery packed very few clothes for this trip but brought Alejandro. He·does not think his mother will die—he feels too young to be someone with a dead mother. It is difficult for Emery to project bad news into the future. This inability is a gift that infuriates Anna. She once told Emery that she wouldn't believe he was an adult until he had learned to worry, until he had rolled some wretched thought around in his brain so many times that he'd altered the pathways of neurons and the length of telomeres. The truth is Emery did worry about things as a kid, but eventually grew out of it. Anna just never noticed.

Emery has no interest in revisiting worry and growing up on Anna's terms. His life is just starting: his career is flying forward like a high-speed train; he loves his boyfriend, and they've recently decided to have a baby. In fact, one of the reasons Alejandro has come to Santa Barbara with Emery is because they are going to ask Anna and Portia for their eggs to be implanted in a woman they've already met. Emery does not worry about his sisters saying no. He hesitates only because he wants to catch them at the right moment, when they're not fretting over Louise or their own lives, which they both seem to do with some frequency.

"Did you seriously like the gefilte fish?" Anna's pen is poised above the folded newspaper. She's staring at Alejandro's empty plate.

"It's not bad." Alejandro smiles, then glances toward Buzzy, who's leaned over his raised plate, scraping a fork against the last oatmeal-looking smears of fish.

Coyotes howl outside. They all freeze, their heads cocked like alert animals, and listen. Earlier today a bobcat ran in front of the car Anna was driving. It dashed out of the brush and silently bounced, like Tigger in *Winnie-the-Pooh*, from one side of the road to the other.

Buzzy and Louise live in an umber-colored Spanish stucco house with fresh blue trim on the windows and a red tile roof. There is a barn that is also stucco with blue trim. They are located on a stretch of eighteen mountain acres that abut the Los Padres National Forest. This is not the house Anna, Portia, and Emery grew up in. This is the house Buzzy and Louise bought only five months ago after selling the family home and unloading most of its contents into a giant, dented blue dumpster. The new house is a place that shows its non-family purpose in the same way as a convertible sports car. There are only two bedrooms in the main house and Buzzy and Louise each claim one of them. The barn with the guest quarters (and Louise's studio) is far enough away that nothing can be heard or seen from one structure to the other.

From Buzzy and Louise's property you can see the ocean spreading all the way down to Los Angeles, a hundred miles away. Louise loves it up here where, she says, the wind blows fiercer and the sun is more ferocious than in the town tucked at the base of the mountain. The house has a name: Casa del Viento Fuerte—House of the Strong Wind.

After Buzzy and the boys have gone to bed, Portia finds herself alone in the living room, where paintings are hung three-high and the fireplace mantle takes up an entire wall. She has the strangest sensation of being lost. Not lost like when you're trying to find a specific piazza in Rome, but lost like when you're a kid in the supermarket and you mistake the mother right in front of you for your mother who has disappeared down another aisle. Portia goes to the kitchen where her sister is, to moor herself, and has to sit to keep the floor from wobbling. She lays her head on the table and lets her thoughts move and gather like a cloud.

"You okay?" Anna asks. She is cleaning out the food in the pantry—throwing away the stuff that looks too old, or simply too disgusting, like a jar of crystallized jam that appears to have knife-scrapes of peanut butter glued to it.

"Do you ever feel sort of wobbly?" Portia asks. Since her husband left, Portia has been thinking that she is a faded, fuzzy outline of herself. And now that her mother may be dying, it seems that even that scant outline is evaporating, like a water painting on a sidewalk.

"No," Anna says. "Never." Portia could have answered this question for her sister. She knows that Anna is profoundly fearless compared to Portia's newborn sensitivity (startled and unsure at any sudden movement). Until her fifth month of pregnancy, Anna was a cop—the unusual kind who actually uses her gun. If their mother dies, Anna will be sad, but she'll be fine. Portia imagines her sister flying home to Vermont, making lunch for her son, driving to the grocery store thirty miles away, buying three hundred pounds of groceries (triple Anna's weight), trekking through the snow into the house carrying seven bags at a time, then putting it all away in less than ten minutes. Portia wishes she could be more solid, like her sister. When her husband left, he appeared to pull the bones out of Portia's body and take them with him.

"I just feel like it would be easier for Mom to die if I had a husband to help me," Portia says.

Anna puts down a jar of almond butter. "Who buys *almond butter?*"

"Dad buys it," Portia says.

"You need to appreciate the fact that you're not married," Anna says, and she turns her back to Portia, returning to the contents of the cupboard. "You're free to fuck whomever you want. You don't have to do some guy's laundry. Fewer dishes."

"Yeah, I'm really lucky." Portia clunks her head onto her folded arms. She thinks of Disneyland to stop herself from crying. It's an anti-crying trick she's been practicing since she was about seven years old.

"Ech," Anna snorts.

"What?" Portia lifts her head.

"Nothing." Anna opens a box of Wheat Thins and cautiously puts her hand in to pull a cracker out.

"Do you think this house is sort of scary?" Portia asks.

"No," Anna says. "Taste this and see if it's stale."

Portia takes the cracker, bites into it. It tastes like soft cardboard. "It's fine," she says, but really she is thinking about the last time she visited the house and the list she had made of the ten most likely ways to die at Casa del Viento Fuerte:

- **Death by mountain lion:** A neighbor's pony down the road was killed by one last year. And when Portia was eleven, a small boy hiking with his mother in the forest surrounding Casa del Viento Fuerte was snatched and killed by one. Their droppings are a frequent sight during hikes.
- **Death by rattlesnake:** Last month Louise deliberately ran over one in the car. She saved the carcass as a souvenir. When Anna and her son, Blue, were visiting three months

ago, Louise and Blue were rattled at by a snake outside the barn.

- **Death by falling:** Buzzy did fall recently. He was hiking with Louise when he slipped on some moss and tumbled over a precipice. Brushy chaparral bushes growing out from fissures in the side of the cliff broke his fall and he landed on a small sandstone ledge instead of plummeting to the stone bottom a couple stories below.

- **Death by drowning:** The stream that runs through the property is usually shallow with big jutting rocks like stepping-stones. But, occasionally, after a season of rains, it becomes surprisingly deep and rapid with a noisy foaming waterfall. Three months after Buzzy and Louise bought the house, a dead bear was found in the stream, apparently drowned.

- **Death by bear:** If one drowned, there must be others.

- **Death by earthquake:** When Portia was a teenager, she was lying naked with her boyfriend in a cave that was carved out of the side of a massive rock wall. Portia asked, "What do you think would happen if there were an earthquake right now?" Her boyfriend said, "This cave would collapse and we'd be crushed to death." A moment later the ground was sliding back and forth, as if they were sitting on a platform on wheels. The boyfriend scrambled out of the cave, abandoning Portia to her fate. The cave didn't collapse, but the ledge they had been sitting on a few minutes before they had crawled into the cave broke off and smashed to the ground a hundred feet below.

- **Death by bullet:** There's very little crime in Santa Barbara, but there's a rifle club in the nearby national forest. If one were to hike to the far end of Buzzy and Louise's property and someone from the rifle club wandered away from the target areas, it is conceivable that one could be hit by a stray bullet.

- **Death by fire:** Months go by in Santa Barbara with no rain, and in the summer the hot Santa Ana winds blow through town like spirits on a rampage. In the last three decades there have been three devastating fires in the vicinity of Casa del Viento Fuerte. Buzzy and Louise keep only two mountain bikes in the garage, to be used on the trails in case the road to the house is closed by fire.

- **Death by falling rock:** There are three yellow diamond-shaped signs on the drive up to Casa del Viento Fuerte, all with two simple words: Falling Rock. Often, a boulder the size of a Volkswagen will appear where nothing was the day before. No one's been hit by one yet, but Portia can't imagine it will never happen.

- **Death by sailing over a cliff in a car:** When Buzzy was teaching Emery how to drive, he said, "The key to driving is to be able to look at everything all around you while still keeping the car where it has to be." Buzzy is famous for noticing things as they pass, then turning and looking out the back window of the car as he zooms forward down the mountain road. When Portia imagines Buzzy driving her mother to the hospital, she thinks that at that moment Louise's chances of dying from a car wreck were probably equal to her chances of dying from the heart attack.

In fact, death by heart attack never even made it to the list.

This is what Portia remembers of the house in Ann Arbor: White clapboard colonial with green shutters set against the endlessly gray Michigan sky. Inside, everything was as neat and fresh as if it were brand-new, even though nothing was brand-new—the house had been furnished with antiques that Louise had polished or refinished or stripped and painted. On the walls were etchings and paintings Louise had found in antique stores or at art shows and matted and framed herself. The kitchen smelled like Pine-Sol and gleamed with light bouncing from all the flat surfaces. And Louise herself looked like she had stepped out of the Simplicity catalogue—in fact, all the clothes she wore were sewn by her own hands from patterns out of the Simplicity catalogue. Anna and Portia wore Louise's creations as well— and when she was particularly inspired, Louise would bend over the foot-pump Singer sewing machine, a cigarette dangling neatly from her red lips, and put together matching dresses for herself and her daughters.

Buzzy had friends at the law office and he and Louise often threw dinner parties. Louise complained that Buzzy always seemed to have more fun at their parties than she. He didn't mind if people stayed late, smoking in the living room, while Louise tended to the dishes in the kitchen, smoking her cigarettes alone.

Louise had two friends in the neighborhood, Lucy and Maggie, both of whom were fans of Louise's poetry, which had been published in the *Ann Arbor News,* and of her art, black charcoal sketches she'd work on in the kitchen once everyone had gone to bed. Lucy had heavy-hooded eyes and a slow, almost-Southern way of speaking. She liked antique shopping with Louise, and she liked refinishing furniture as well. She had two small children and was married to the man who was the father of the older child. The newborn was the child of the man with whom she was having an affair. Portia, who was often so quiet and still the adults forgot she was in the room, overheard Lucy tell Louise that whenever her husband played with the baby or held him, Lucy would watch them closely to see if either one knew he wasn't related to the other. And when the baby was asleep in his crib, she'd bend over and whisper in his ear, "That man is not your father. Your father is much kinder." This, of course, led Portia to wonder about her own father—a fear that was assuaged only when a neighbor pointed out that she and Buzzy had amber-brown eyes that were so similar you could swap them and neither one would look different.

And then there was Maggie. She was redheaded and smart. Portia heard her complain about doing housework with her Ph.D. in English while her husband, who only had a master's degree, taught at the local high school. Maggie wasn't good with her hands the way Louise and Lucy were, but she was a good talker, so while Louise and Lucy tried to repair a foot pump melodeon organ that Louise had found at a flea market, Maggie sat by and talked and talked and talked . . . about what she was reading, about what she had read, about what she would write if she ever had time to write. Portia had always thought Maggie's little speeches weren't nearly as interesting as Lucy's.

When Anna was seven and Portia was four and a half, just before Emery was born, the girls started spending time with the Cloud children who lived across the street. Aaron Cloud was

Anna's age, Gregor Cloud was Portia's age, and Sissy Cloud was younger than Portia. Sissy was always seen dragging her grayed, spit-shined blanket behind her as she followed her brothers.

Portia recoiled from the chaos of the Cloud house, while her sister thrived in it. The carpet in the living room scared Portia—there were smashed putty discs of old gum, and peanut-butter-and-jelly smears that changed color depending on how long they'd been there. Even the sounds of the house seemed chaotic. When the *Chitty Chitty Bang Bang* soundtrack played on the turntable and Anna, Aaron, Sissy, and Gregor sang at full voice, they would create a swirling, spinning world of daring, noise, and motion. Mr. Cloud often slept right through this ruckus—a fat, crumpled heap of a man who appeared to be part of the couch cushions he slept on.

A favorite game of the Cloud kids and Anna was to take a running start from one end of the room and leap over the couch and Mr. Cloud without waking him up. Anna and Aaron could both achieve this feat from the backside of the couch. Gregor and Sissy Cloud would approach from the cushion side, stepping one foot on the edge of the cushion before propelling themselves up and over. Sissy often fell and tumbled onto the pillow of her father, but even that rarely woke him. If Portia were there (whisper-singing with her head dropped, as if that would make her invisible), Anna often grabbed her, placed Portia at the proper distance, then pushed from behind to get her going on the couch-jumping game. Portia always took off running, then veered off around the couch. She feared landing on Mr. Cloud and didn't want to risk having to touch him: his chalky, elephant-skinned elbows, his gelatinous belly that pushed out above his pants, his wet-looking face that caved to the side like a fallen cake.

In fact, there were few things Portia was willing to try with her sister and the Clouds. She wouldn't shimmy down the rope that hung from the attic window to the tree branch that stood about two stories high; she wouldn't stand at the base of the tree and catch the *Playboy* magazines that were tossed down from the army trunk in the third floor where Anna and Aaron discovered them; she wouldn't eat the wormhole-pocked crab apples from the neighbor's tree; nor would she walk over to Steve Bologna's house and put a piece of bologna in his mailbox. She wouldn't light fires in the basement using bricks that were found in the backyard as a fire pit; she wouldn't sit in the windowless basement with the lights off so that it was pitch-black and listen to Aaron and Anna tell ghost stories; and she wouldn't run around the neighborhood after dark, climbing sharp-edged wire fences to cut through one backyard after another in search of phantoms and stray cats.

The winter Emery was born, Louise told her daughters she wanted them out of the house more, out of the way, so she could sleep when the baby slept. This was not a problem for Anna, who roamed the neighborhood in snow past her waist; in fact, if anything, it created a complication that made Anna's outdoor adventures more exciting. Portia didn't want to go out in the snow, so she hid in her room, silently reading or playing with dolls. She knew if she didn't ask her mother for anything, not even a glass of water, she could stay inside forever.

When spring came, Portia did, however, leave the house. She went on a picnic with the Cloud family. Louise had insisted.

"They were nice enough to invite you," Louise said, "so you should be nice enough to go." She was spread across an armchair like an elegant bird, holding a suckling Emery at her breast.

Portia went upstairs and changed into a red-checked puff-sleeved dress her mother had sewn for her. It reminded her of pictures of picnics, and girls in magazine ads for pies and pastries. It was what she imagined to be the perfect dress for a Sunday in the park.

As she had never been on an actual picnic, Portia's understanding of one was that it included a wicker basket to hold the food and a red plaid blanket to sit on. When the Cloud family loaded a giant green Hefty trash bag into the way-back of their station wagon, she realized that packaging was not what made an event.

Anna and Aaron shared the front seat with Mr. Cloud who drove, one hand on the wheel and one dangling out the window as if it were a prosthetic arm that had to remain straight. Mrs. Cloud, with her hair in a whorled hive on her head, sat in the back seat between Portia and Sissy. Gregor sat in the way-back with the Hefty bag.

"I'm hungry," Gregor said, and he tried to untie the garbage bag so he could start eating right then.

Mrs. Cloud, who had the reaction time of teenaged boy playing pinball, whipped around in her seat and slapped his arm. "You'll eat when we get there!" she said, and she stayed turned in her seat to make sure Gregor stayed put.

"I want fried chicken!" Gregor said, and Anna and Aaron, upon hearing his plea, began to clap their hands on beat and repeat over and over again, "I WANT FRIED CHICKEN, I WANT FRIED CHICKEN, I WANT FRIED CHICKEN . . ." When Sissy joined in, the noise was so loud and screechy that Portia began to feel a little nauseous. Then Anna upped the sound again, by lifting her knobby knees and stomping her feet on the dash with the beat. Aaron's legs were too long for him to stomp on the dash, so he pounded his feet on the floor, making the car vibrate so strongly it felt like the brake was being tapped. Mr. Cloud didn't seem to notice the uproar and Mrs. Cloud, who kept her eyes trained on her son, didn't seem to care.

Portia slumped against the door and let her mind go somewhere else as she waited for it all to pass: the fracas, the sense of danger that being with the Clouds always presented, the slapping machine of Mrs. Cloud.

When they reached the park, Aaron and Sissy burst out of the car, screaming, "FRIED CHICKEN, FRIED CHICKEN, FRIED CHICKEN." Gregor flipped over the seat from the way-back to the back, his foot grazing Portia's cheek and tangling momentarily in his mother's hair. "Get!" Mrs. Cloud screamed, slapping his legs as he slid across the seat and out the door. "GET OUT!"

Portia stepped out of the car and hovered nearby as Mr. Cloud unloaded the plastic sack from the way-back. She didn't know where her sister and the Cloud kids had run off to—it was a big park, with massive branchy trees obscuring the hilly vista—and she didn't want to get lost. The best course of action, Portia thought, would be to stick close to the people with the car keys.

They walked to a patch of thistly grass where Mrs. Cloud spread out a white chenille bedspread under a tree. Mrs. Cloud grunted when she kneeled down on the bedspread, as if it took effort to simply lower herself. Mr. Cloud sat beside her, then lay on his back, his stomach rising up like the landscape.

"Beer," Mr. Cloud said and he waved his hand around as if one would magically appear.

"Damn, I left them in the car." Mrs. Cloud stood and started to walk back to the car. Portia followed her a few steps behind. She had never spoken to Mr. Cloud before and didn't want to wait on the bedspread alone with him. Before she reached the parking lot, Mrs. Cloud turned and looked back at Portia. "Why don't you go play with the kids?"

"I don't know where they are," Portia said. She pulled on the hem of her checked dress, to straighten it over her white fleshy thighs.

"So find them." Mrs. Cloud clapped her hands like she was shooing a squirrel. Portia scurried back to the bedspread, then beyond it to the nearest large tree. She hid behind the trunk, peeking out on Mr. Cloud so she could be sure he wouldn't drive away without her.

Mrs. Cloud returned with a six-pack of Schlitz. She sat on the bedspread and ripped two beers off the cardboard cuff. She popped the metal tab off one and flicked it onto the grass. Mr. Cloud lifted his hand and kept it there until Mrs. Cloud put the opened beer in it. Portia was amazed that he didn't need to sit up to drink. Mr. Cloud simply tilted his weighty head forward and lifted the can to his lips, lapping at the beer without pause. When he was done, he dropped his head back and released the empty can on the bedspread beside himself.

Portia felt lonely and scared. She worried that she'd blink and her ride home would be gone. She wanted to sit down, but thought she'd need to take a running start to make it to the car should the Clouds suddenly decide to leave. More than anything, she wanted to be home with Louise, sitting beside her, reading a book or just nestling into the soft spot between her arm and breast.

Portia's heart fluttered with relief when she heard the cacophony of Anna, Aaron, Gregor, and Sissy, still chanting "FRIED CHICKEN" as they speed-skipped through the park, dodging trees, other picnickers, and small children. They skidded to a stop at the bedspread and surrounded the Hefty bag, whose neck was held tight in Mrs. Cloud's fist.

Portia ran out from the tree and stood beside her sister.

"FRIED CHICKEN, FRIED CHICKEN, FRIED CHICKEN," Anna screamed, stomping her scrawny, dark legs.

"As soon as you all settle down, I'll give you some fried chicken!" Mrs. Cloud said.

"*Order in the court!*" Aaron started, and all the kids, except Portia, who recited the words in her head, joined in. "*Order in the court! The monkey wants to speak! The monkey wants to speak! Let the monkey speak! Let the monkey speak!*" Portia had never tried to discern the meaning of this chant. It was just something the Cloud kids said regularly. Anna loved it and would often demand that Portia stomp her feet and say it with her when Anna and Portia were marching off to bed.

"Okay, okay, enough already!" Mrs. Cloud had a little smirk on her face. An idea shifted into Portia's mind just then, a discovery: wacko, smelly, loud children aren't nearly as wacko, smelly, and loud to their mothers.

"Dippity-do!" Sissy shouted.

"DIPPITY-DO, DIPPITY-DO," the kids easily slid into a new chant. Mrs. Cloud put Dippity-do in Sissy's hair after every washing. Everyone in the neighborhood knew her as the Dippity-do Girl.

"All right, now! I've really had enough!" Mrs. Cloud moved onto her knees as the kids settled in a circle around her. Portia squeezed in beside Anna, who elbowed her away.

Mrs. Cloud unwound the metal twisty that held the bag shut, opened the bag, and peered inside. "Goddamnit!" she yelled, and she turned and slapped her sleeping husband on his beefy calf. "You took the goddamned trash! I told you the food was in the trash bag on the counter! On the counter! But you took the godammned trash instead!"

Aaron, Gregor, and Anna scrambled onto their knees to look into the trash bag. Mr. Cloud sat up and rubbed his eyes the way little kids do when they awaken from naps. Eric pulled out a bloody piece of brown paper that had probably wrapped the chicken before it was cooked. He flung the paper in the air and it landed across Sissy's face, sticking there like an octopus. Sissy screamed and started crying; her mother pulled off the paper, then tossed it onto the grass. A stink was emanating from the bag—sour and foggy and unlike anything in Anna and Portia's tidy house, where Buzzy took the trash out to the alleyway can every evening after supper.

Sissy's crying was increasing in volume. Mr. Cloud raised his head. "Well, if there isn't any goddamned fried chicken, then let's go home."

Mrs. Cloud got up and shooed everyone off the bedspread with her foot. Mr. Cloud went through a series of grunting, stilted movements, and eventually he was standing. Once Mr. Cloud had stepped aside, Mrs. Cloud yanked the bedspread up from beneath the trash, causing the bag to tilt on its side and belch out a small pile of detritus. She picked up the remaining four beers and marched toward the car. Portia grabbed her sister's hand so she wouldn't be left behind, but Anna shook it off and quickly ran ahead to catch up with Aaron. Anna always made it clear that having Portia along was like trying to ride a bike with your foot pressed back on the brake pedal.

When they got home, Anna went into the Cloud house with Aaron, Gregor, and Sissy, while Portia went next door to Mrs. White's house. Mrs. White was a seventy-eight-year-old widow who looked like the old ladies in storybooks: gray hair in a bun, buttoned-up dress, crinkle-eyed smile. She was the only person on the block, other than Buzzy and Louise, who, Portia thought, was of reasonably sound mind. Mrs. White appeared to like her visits, as she'd make Portia tea with lots of sugar and milk and she'd get out her stuffed, knit monkey for Portia to play with. They usually sat on the screened front porch and watched Anna and the Cloud kids scramble by like a pack of wild dogs. But sometimes, Mrs. White would let Portia go into her extra bedroom upstairs, where there was a black antique dresser whose drawers she was allowed to explore. In one drawer were paper-wrapped soaps with different labels and smells. In another drawer were hand-crocheted doilies, and the blue cotton nursing cap Mrs. White had worn during the Second World War. In another drawer were clothes for the stuffed monkey—long and narrow like him, and even an array of hats that would fit over his round, knitted ears.

On the hottest week in August three events occurred in the neighborhood, each so startling it seemed impossible that they would overlap without somehow being a reflex of the same trigger: the oppressive humidity or the moon looking fuller than it had ever been.

The first event was that Maggie, Louise's friend, had a baby and decided it was the Messiah. When her husband took the baby away from her one night (he thought the presence of the child was causing her hysteria), she walked into the bathroom, picked up the bottle of Drano, and drank it.

The second event was that Gregor Cloud lit Sissy Cloud on fire when he was striking a match (for fun) after her hair had been slathered with Dippity-do.

And the third event was that Mrs. White died in her sleep (with a smile on her face, Louise told her daughters).

Everyone but Mrs. White miraculously survived.

Anna seemed unfazed when Louise told the girls about Maggie. This didn't surprise Portia, as her sister had always said that Maggie was a crazy lady whom their mother should never let in the house. But the Sissy Cloud tragedy had enraptured Anna, who liked to tell the story over and over again, each time embellishing the details (*Sissy's whole head was a giant fireball and the flames were leaping around her, lighting the trees on fire and burning off all her clothes so that she was standing there buck-naked when the firemen finally came!*) until Portia would start crying with fear. When it came to Mrs. White's death, Anna was sweet and gentle with her sister.

"It is weird that your best friend was an old lady," Anna whispered into Portia's ear as she lay in bed the night of the death. "But it's still sad." Portia nodded her head. She had stopped talking since she heard the news. It wasn't a deliberate, willful mutism; it was simpler than that. She felt hollow and quiet and no longer had an interest in talking.

"If you want to sleep with me tonight, you can," Anna said, and she pulled down the covers and helped her sister pad out of bed and across the hall to her own room where she directed Portia into the puddle of blankets at the foot of her bed.

Buzzy and Louise didn't worry much about Portia's silence, but Louise was kind enough to discontinue the forced play time at the Cloud house. And she allowed Portia to stay with her continuously, even bringing her along on the day she visited Maggie in the hospital (Portia had wanted to visit Sissy Cloud—now bald as a bare butt, according to her brothers—but she had been transferred to a hospital in Detroit). Louise brought Maggie a *Life* magazine and a box-wrapped red lipstick in a gold-ridged case.

Maggie was sleeping when they got to her room. She looked like a human appliance. Ropes and wires extended from all parts of her body and were plugged into machines that were plugged into the wall. Louise sat on the chair beside her bed, pulled a cigarette out of her snap-shut pocketbook, and lit it up. Portia sat on her mother's lap and stared down at Maggie's face and neck. Her flesh appeared surprisingly normal. And then she woke up, her eyes flashing at Louise, and she parted her lips and tried to smile. Her mouth, or what had been a mouth, was black and jagged, like a charcoaled cave. And she couldn't speak, she indicated, as she halfway lifted a wired-up hand and pointed to her throat. Portia wanted to point to her throat, too, to tell her that she, too, had stopped talking, but she didn't.

"I brought you lipstick," Louise said, and she held her cigarette in her mouth as she opened the package, took out the tube and twisted until the waxy, red fin rose up. "Should I put it on you?"

Maggie nodded, and so Louise nudged Portia off her lap, handed her the cigarette to hold, then leaned over and wiped lipstick on what Portia now saw were shredded, ripped lips. The lipstick caught in the nooks like plaster on lattice board. Louise tried to smooth it out with a second coat, then gave up, twisted the lipstick down into its tube, and put the lid on.

"We're moving to California," Louise said, taking back her cigarette. It was the first Portia had ever heard of this. "Buzzy has a job at a big up-and-coming firm in Santa Barbara."

A tear ran down Maggie's face.

"You'll be fine," Louise said. "We'll all be fine."

Maggie tried to speak but all that came out was a hoarse whispery bark.

"California," Louise said, with a puff of smoke, and Portia couldn't stop smiling.

There are six cats and two dogs at Casa del Viento Fuerte. Three of the cats live in the barn. The other cats and the dogs live in the house. Each animal is neurotic in some way. Emery suspects that his mother loves the animals more than she loves her children. Buzzy, who had allergies and asthma in his twenties and thirties, has apparently grown used to the animals Louise started bringing into the house once Emery left for college.

Anna continually yells at the black lab, Jasmine. She is so extreme that Emery feels embarrassed by her in front of Alejandro. He thinks she sounds like an abusive mother from a straight-to-video movie. When Jasmine slinks over to a bowl of cat food in the laundry room, Anna snaps, "Jasmine, you sick fuck! Get your binge-and-purge ass out of here!" Emery feels somewhat sorry for Jasmine, with her slanted trot and mucousy eyes. But he can't bring himself to touch her as each stroke lets loose weightless piles of black hair that smell like wet wool. Occasionally he'll lift his leg and pet her on the ass with the bottom of his shoe, but that's the best he can do. The yellow lab, Gumba, is completely ignored.

Emery and Alejandro are both cat people. At home they have a tiger-striped cat named Little Ricky. Little Ricky is far sweeter than Louise's cats, but Emery tries not to compare him to them so he can give whatever cat-love he has inside of himself to Louise's cats. He tries to love the dwarfed black-and-white cat whose name is Little Carl White and who lives under the stairs and won't let anyone pet him. And the slim gray barn cat, Fweddy, whose meow sounds like the word *Ma*, which Louise claims he's saying. And the old bony gray cat, Lefty, who climbs on laps and shoulders uninvited. And even Maggie Bucks, the fat, cross-eyed Siamese, who hangs out in the food cupboard and sleeps above the kitchen ceiling in the rafters. Maggie Bucks is Louise's favorite. Perhaps appropriately, she seems the most distressed by Louise's absence and has taken to pissing on Louise's bed, where Portia has been sleeping, and shitting on the couch, where Anna has been sleeping. Alejandro and Emery are staying in the modernized guest quarters on the second floor of the barn. They don't let the barn cats up there and so have not had their lodgings pissed or shat on; the first floor of the barn, however, has cat shit scattered across it like land mines, while the litter box remains clean and the miles and miles of surrounding mountains contain nary a shit from the Casa del Viento Fuerte cats.

It has occurred to Emery that maybe Maggie Bucks is tormenting his sisters because they torment her. Portia claims she hates Maggie Bucks because Maggie Bucks is a narcissistic brat. On the morning of Day Three, when Portia opens the cupboard and finds Maggie Bucks perched among the Grape-Nuts boxes and jars of gefilte fish and saltines that have been pushed back so as to give her a ledge to sit on, Portia begins speaking for the cat, saying what she believes Maggie Bucks is thinking. Emery, who is sitting at the kitchen table reading the paper, assumes that Portia is giving her a cartoon-like Asian accent because the cat is Siamese.

"What you do here, Connecticut Girl?! Smoker Lady no

here! Smoker Lady in hospital! You go home now! You go back to Greenwich! I no want you here, Connecticut Girl!"

Emery laughs.

"Sorry, bitch," Portia says, in her own voice, "I'm hanging around until Smoker Lady comes home." Emery's glad the cat can't understand his sister, as *bitch* seems far too harsh a word for this fat, velvety cat.

"No one want you here!" the voice of Maggie Bucks says. "I piss on you bed! I spray stinky piss-spray all over you pillow! Don't you know what stinky-piss spray mean?! It mean go away, snotty Connecticut Girl! No one want you here!"

Emery laughs again, then gets up and pets the cat in case the strength of his sister's voice scares her.

By the end of Day Three, Portia is so compulsive about speaking in Maggie Buck's voice when she sees her that Emery barely notices she's doing it.

The term "Smoker Lady," however, has caught on with the whole family, as a forty-year, two-pack-a-day habit is surely the single greatest factor in this heart attack. There are cigarettes, ashtrays, and cigarette butts everywhere in the house. There are burn holes like tiny craters scattered across the upholstery of Louise's car. In Buzzy's new car, a German luxury auto that he has finally given himself permission to buy (he always felt expensive cars were frivolous, and wouldn't even drive this new car for a couple weeks because he found it embarrassing), there is a cigarette tip–sized divot on the front corner of the leather passenger seat. Emery was fingering it on the way to the hospital one day, the way one might finger an acne scar or a scab, and noticed Buzzy visibly wincing, although his father would never complain about such a thing. Buzzy has continually tolerated Louise's smoking, just as he's tolerated her bossiness and insistence that he be home for dinner each night by five-thirty. Emery's always thought that Buzzy gives in to Louise too easily. Sometimes when he's home, he wants to take a side in his parents' arguments, and the side he always wants to take is his father's.

No one can figure out what to do about the cigarettes in the house.

"Smoker Lady will be furious if you throw them away," Buzzy says.

They are at the kitchen table eating dinner: Greek salad, pita bread, hummus, and microwave gyros that Anna and Portia bought on the way home from the hospital.

"But she can NEVER smoke again," Anna says. She is using her right hand to pick out cucumber wedges from her salad. They are lined up in an arc along the rim of her plate. Emery watches Anna and wonders if she is going to eat the cucumbers or eat everything but the cucumbers. Portia is shoving cucumbers and tomatoes into the pita and making a sandwich.

"She needs to decide that on her own," Emery says. "We can't make that decision for her." Emery and Alejandro also smoke, although now that Louise is not in the house, Emery's sisters insist that they go outside to do it. Emery is a grown person who owns his own apartment in New York, yet he listens to these women as if he's their child. And sometimes he feels like he is their child.

"Well," Anna says to Alejandro. "What do *you* think?" When Anna stares at Alejandro for too long, Emery wonders if she has sexual feelings for him. His sister seems to have no filter when it comes to whom she finds attractive. And Alejandro's exactly the type Anna has always fallen for: straight black hair, square face, a sexy, slim gap between his two front teeth.

They all wait for Alejandro's reply. He tilts his head, takes a deep breath.

"You don't have to throw the cigarettes away," he says, pausing. "Emery and I will take them."

"You two have GOT to stop smoking!" Anna says. She starts eating the row of cucumbers one by one. Emery puts his cucumbers in some pita, like Portia did.

"Jesus Christ," Buzzy says. "Look at your mother! Do you really want to continue smoking?"

"Actually," Emery says, "we're planning on stopping soon." He stares at Alejandro, but says nothing. Emery is not sure if this is the right to time to ask his sisters for their eggs. The woman who is going to carry the baby suggested he ask in the most matter-of-fact way possible, as if he were asking for the keys to a car. He trusts this woman; there is even a way in which he loves her, sort of like the way he loves his sisters. She is about Anna's age and already has three kids with whom she stays home. Her name is Lynn, and she is sturdy, healthy, and smiles when she talks. She doesn't drink or smoke and she doesn't really exercise other than stepping in and out of her Subaru and walking down to the basement to do laundry. Lynn lives in New Jersey; Emery's doctor introduced them. He and Alejandro are paying her fifteen thousand dollars to carry the baby. She says she's doing it because she and her husband need the money, but she also claims that she's doing it because it's her way of creating something good for someone else. Lynn says she enjoys her own children so much she wants everyone to have the opportunity to be a parent.

When Emery can't sleep at night he worries about children who need to be adopted. But two agencies that he and Alejandro went to would not consider gay men. And the one agency that agreed to take them would keep them at the eternal end of the list—so it wouldn't be until every straight couple had a baby that they would be in the running.

The fertility doctor in New York has no problem helping them make a baby. Emery suspects that the doctor himself is gay, although he mentioned his wife at least four times in their two meetings. He's handsome, a sandpapery beard on his face, forearms like bowling pins. The doctor said, "This is bigger than marriage." And Emery believes him. He imagines it's like getting his and Alejandro's torsos sewn together into a version of Chang and Eng, the famous Siamese twins. Emery loves Alejandro, he loves him the way people love breathing, or sleeping—Alejandro is necessary to Emery's life, and good for him. So Emery is not worried about the fact that they will soon be conjoined.

Alejandro kicks Emery under the table to nudge him about the eggs. Emery opens his mouth to speak, but the words won't come out. They are stuck in this throat like a lineup of golf balls.

"Well, when the fuck are you planning on quitting?" Anna asks, and she gets up and clears her plate. Her moods come on so strongly and quickly that sometimes it's hard to figure out what the trigger is. No one knows if Anna is upset right now because Emery smokes or because their mother has just had a heart attack.

"About nine months from now. Maybe forty weeks." Alejandro is dropping clues like a crumb trail and Emery is refusing to even look down and see that they're there.

"Nine months?" Buzzy asks. "Why nine months? Quit now! Quit tomorrow. Quit today."

"We definitely will, Dad," Emery says. "The timing has to be right." Emery drills his eyes into Alejandro. Now is not the time to ask for eggs. His oldest sister's in a bitchy mood and the other one seems spaced out and dreamy.

"Maybe the time will be right in about forty weeks." Alejandro won't give up. If they were alone, Emery would leap across the table and tackle him. Maybe he'd bite him on the neck. Just for fun. Sort of.

"I hope Mom's alive in forty weeks," Portia says. Other than speaking for the cat, it's the first thing she's said tonight. Emery wishes she'd start talking like Maggie Bucks again. He rather laugh than consider his mother's death.

Anna was profoundly disappointed when Portia started
talking again. She had enjoyed the silence, the absence of stupid questions about freckles, people with missing limbs, blind
people, dog dreams, why flowers smell, and was there a starting
point to infinity. Portia first spoke the day they readied the long,
blue station wagon for the drive to California.

"I'm sitting behind Dad," Anna had said. And then Portia
announced, as if she'd been yakking for days, "Fine with me.
I'm sitting behind Mom."

Emery's playpen was put in the way-back, loaded with stacking blocks, books, and a fire truck that he liked to bang against
the bars of the playpen and the windows of the car. At nine
months old, he had started walking and was balanced enough to
walk around the playpen even while the car was moving. Anna
thought Emery looked like a turtle. It was not because he was
slow; in fact, he was constantly in motion—rolling, climbing,
jumping. But his face had a sweet turtle look to it: a smooth gap
between his upper lip and his nose, big round eyes, and tufts of
blond hair sticking up that looked more like the hair on a turtle
(if a turtle ever were to have hair) than on a human.

The girls had coloring books, crayons, drawing pads, colored
pencils, books to read, and yarn sewing kits with big-holed mesh
screens in which they could sew designs and patterns. Neither
of them wore her seatbelt, and they slid around the bench seat

freely, often flipping around completely to play with Emery in his cage.

The few times Emery got carsick he was careful not to vomit in his playpen (like a dog who won't soil his kennel) and instead leaned over the top bar and hurled onto one of his sisters. It seemed that no matter how much Louise scrubbed and rinsed the car and her daughters' shoulders and hair, the smell of vomit remained, mixed with smell of cigarettes, indelibly staining the stale car air.

They sang for hours each day during the week of driving. Buzzy taught the kids songs from camp when he was a boy: "The Cannibal King," and "Dip, Dip, and Swing," a canoeing song that he would croon as if it were a love song. Anna and Portia choreographed hand motions for "If I Had a Hammer," and they were particularly fond of singing the theme from the *Romeo and Juliet* movie that had come out that year. But the song everyone liked best was "California Here I Come," a song that at once delighted and intrigued Anna. She wondered about those "Golden Gates" that were begged to be opened in the closing lines. In her imagination, California was some walled principality that could be entered only through a pair of towering golden-grilled gates, manned, of course, by uniformed men with gold, fringed shoulder pads, and hats with fur and a chin strap.

It was so sunny in Santa Barbara that it was hard to remember the dullness of an overcast sky. Everything looked fresh, clean, neatly outlined, brightly colored. It was as if the world in Ann Arbor had been viewed on a puny, grainy, black-and-white television, and now, in Santa Barbara, the world was broadcast in living color across a bright forty-two-inch screen.

The new house was in a recently developed suburb with three-car-garage houses and sidewalks as white as teeth. Like many of their neighbors, they had a kidney-shaped pool whose blue-painted bottom was as bright as the endless blue sky. Louise claimed they had the best house in the tract because they were at the top of their cul-de-sac, at the top of a hill, perched above the lemon orchard that abutted the development and went on as far as you could see: acres and acres of uniform round trees. When the pickers came they'd sing in Spanish. Anna and Portia both slept with their bedroom windows open and often woke up to the sweet sounds of harmonized Mexican folk songs. Small propeller planes would fly overhead and spray the orchard for Mediterranean fruit flies. Louise always said Anna, Portia, and Emery weren't allowed to swim in the pool for twenty-four hours after the planes had sprayed. That was an inconvenience, but other than that, no one complained about the spraying; they didn't even come indoors while they did it.

Buzzy and Louise had a bathroom off their bedroom with a double sink and vanity that were open to the room. With the plush, gold shag carpet leading all the way to the sink, the room looked luxurious to Anna, the kind of bedroom movie stars might have. The girls each had their own bedrooms on the second floor but shared a bathroom. They had walk-in closets that were deep enough to play in, and windows that slid sideways on a track, as opposed to the old, painted windows on the house in Ann Arbor, which only Buzzy had been strong enough to open. Emery had his own bedroom and bathroom on the first floor with a window that looked out to the long front porch framed with three stucco arches.

The neighborhood was packed with kids. Between their cul-de-sac and the two streets below it, there were two girls Anna's age and seven girls Portia's age. Both of Anna's friends had sparkling clean homes. No one had a mother or father who slept on the couch in the day, no one had gum or peanut butter in the living room carpet that would freak out her easily terrorized little sister. Anna quickly concluded that the people in Santa Barbara would never confuse a trash bag for a picnic basket.

In fact, it wasn't until they lived in California that Anna realized that Buzzy and Louise were unlike most people. Suddenly she saw her parents in sharp relief against the beautifully tanned, perfectly coiffed parents of her friends. Louise refused to go to coffee with the other mothers and talk about ironing (which she claimed was all they talked about), and she and Buzzy never showed up at neighborhood parties or ice cream socials at the elementary school. The walls in their living room were covered from floor to ceilings with bookshelves, whereas Anna's friends' living rooms had gold-framed paintings of ships, the ocean, and fields of flowers. None of her friends even had yogurt in the house, while Buzzy fermented his own yogurt using fresh fruit from the lemon trees, lime trees, guava tree, and banana tree in the backyard. (When their lemons weren't ripe, and if they needed one, Anna or Emery—Portia was too fleshy and slow—would hop the backyard fence and snatch one from the orchard.) Buzzy also threw pots on the kick wheel that sat near the pool on the back patio; he often left the house with splatters of dry clay on his forehead and arms. Both Buzzy and Louise meditated, attended aura-reading parties, and went to the nude beach. And by the second year in California, Louise was enjoying homegrown marijuana, which Buzzy farmed with the passion and sensitivity of an orchid grower.

In short, Anna thought her parents were total freaks.

The year Anna was eleven, Portia was eight, and Emery was three, Louise decided she quit being a housewife. Anna was playing Parcheesi with her sister on the family room floor when Louise told them.

"Portia, Anna," Louise said, and she began searching through the little piles of papers, mail, phone books, and pencils that covered from end to end the white tile counter that separated the kitchen from the family room.

"Yeah?" Portia asked. Anna looked at her freckle-faced sister, her white, hairless flesh, her wispy brown hair that shone like corn silk. As much as she often hated her, she could understand why her parents were always pawing at her with hugs and kisses: the girl was like a pastry or a sweet. She looked edible.

Anna was as small as Portia. But she was all muscle and sinew, as if she were made of telephone cables. No one ever wanted to pinch telephone cables. She rolled the dice and ignored her mother.

"Come here," Louise said. She continued to shift things around. Portia pushed her doughy rump up and went to the counter. She moved aside an empty box that had held ten Hot Wheels racing cars and handed her mother the pack of unfiltered Camel cigarettes she was most likely looking for.

"I quit." Louise tapped out a cigarette, then lit it from the pack of matches she kept tucked in the cellophane wrapper. She had grown her hair long at a time when mothers didn't have long hair. And she didn't wear makeup—a habit that made her look fresher and more alive than the other mothers. Anna hated it when Portia said that their mother looked like a movie star—she hated that her sister couldn't see the drop-out anarchist mentality their mother conveyed through her hippie clothes. And it really drove Anna crazy when she witnessed Louise opening the front door to the Fuller Brush Man or the Avon Lady and they asked Louise, "Is your mother home?" What kind of a mother didn't look like a mother?! One like Louise, Anna supposed, who only wore wide, drapey bell-bottoms, cork platform shoes, and flowing silk shirts with no bra. In her ears were always two gold hoops that hung almost to her shoulders. Anna knew that people in other parts of town dressed like Louise. But no one in their neighborhood did. They lived in a place of pantsuits, helmets of hair, waxy lipstick, sensible sneakers. Anna didn't know any mother who worked, or did art. At least her parents weren't divorced, Anna thought. The only person she knew who had divorced parents was Molly Linkle, a girl who was so fat she wore bras that made her breasts look like cones and shopped in the Ladies' Department at Robinson's.

"What do you mean you quit?" Portia climbed onto the orange stool. Anna wondered when her sister would stop asking questions.

"Your turn," Anna said. She looked toward her sister's back and watched as her mother pursed her lips and let out a slow stream of smoke.

"I quit being a housewife." Louise shook her hair and smiled.

"Can you do that?" Portia asked.

Anna was going to pretend she wasn't listening. There was something inside her that often led her to believe that if she ignored certain things they would cease to exist. She turned the Parcheesi board over and dumped the pieces on the rug.

"Of course I can. I just did. I quit!" Louise took another drag off her cigarette.

"Anna!"

Anna knew Portia was staring at her but she refused to look up.

"Mom quit!"

"I heard," Anna said. She could feel her face darkening, like a mercury thermometer.

"Does Dad know?" Anna asked. She crossed her legs and glared at her mother.

"I told him last night."

"What about Emery?" The idea that her mother wouldn't have the same occupation as her friends' mothers enraged Anna. Who would have the nerve to give birth to children, move them into a house, and then declare that she wasn't going to take care of them? A drug-addicted hippie, Anna decided, that's who.

"You girls are in charge of Emery now."

"Really?!" Portia's cheerful voice made Anna want to knock her off the stool. Portia was such a wannabe mother, she coddled Emery as if she owned him. In fact the only thing Portia had ever claimed she wanted to be when she grew up was a mother. She had a doll, Peaches, with whom she slept every night. When the family traveled, Portia always packed Peaches first in the bottom of her white, satin-lined suitcase. The current Peaches was actually the second Peaches, as the first Peaches had devolved into a repellent, floppy, dirty thing with a body like a lumpy mattress and arms and legs that were four different colors from dirt and stains. She'd gone bald from Portia's carrying her by her hair, and she smelled like spit. Anna didn't even like being in the same room with old Peaches. When Portia was seven, Louise had sewn Peaches a pink satin retirement gown with a matching satin-and-lace cap, and gave Portia a new, fresh Peaches who smelled like plastic and who, Anna thought, wasn't the embarrassing rag that was old Peaches.

"Yeah, Emery's yours," Louise said.

"Can he be mine alone?" Portia asked Anna.

Anna couldn't believe that her sister felt compelled to ask this question. It was like asking if Anna wanted to share old Peaches.

"What do you say, Anna?" Louise asked.

"I don't want him," Anna said. "He's dirty and he smells."

"He's adorable!" Portia said.

"Are we getting a maid?" Anna asked. Her friends' mothers cleaned their houses, but people on TV, characters with apartments and homes that seemed much smaller than theirs, had maids.

"No!" Louise snorted. "There are enough people hanging around here between your and your sister's friends. Besides. We don't have that kind of money."

"So who's going to cook dinner?" Portia asked.

"Anna will cook."

"Fine." Anna stood up and joined her sister at the counter. She could feel rage inside her like a team of insects crawling through her veins.

"And what about everything else?" Portia asked, although to Anna she didn't seem particularly concerned. And why should she be concerned? Other than giving Emery an occasional bath, Anna couldn't really name the things Louise did as a housewife. By all appearances, their mother did little other than swim naked in the pool and write poems or paint in her studio. On the rare day when Anna's friends came over (despite Louise's claims of frequency, Anna always tried to steer them to someone else's house), she had them wait on the porch on the pretense of having to ask her mother if it was okay if they came in when, really, she was checking to see that Louise was dressed. Anna preferred to hang out at her friends' houses, as even when Louise was dressed, she was an embarrassment.

Louise gave the girls a housewife's tour that started with the washer and dryer in the garage.

"This is where you put the dirty clothes. You open this up, put your clothes in, then pour in a bunch of this detergent." Louise picked up a green cardboard box and shook it.

"How much detergent do I put in?" Portia asked.

"A bunch," Louise said. "You know, a bunch! Shake some out, it doesn't really matter."

Anna rolled her eyes. There was a plastic scoop sitting on the shelf where the detergent was. Why didn't her mother measure it out like a normal person? Like the people who did laundry in the detergent commercials! Like all the other mothers in California!

"Then what?" Portia asked. Anna saw that Portia was getting nervous—more than one step in any set of directions was too many for her simpleton sister.

"Then shut the door and turn this dial to three o'clock."

"Three o'clock," Portia repeated, and when she rolled her eyes up toward her forehead, Anna knew she was envisioning a clock in her head.

"Yeah. Three o'clock," Louise said.

"Just turn it to the right, dingbat!" Anna said.

They took one step over and Louise opened the dryer. "Put the wet clothes in here and then turn the dial to nine o'clock."

"Nine o'clock." Portia looked back and forth between the washer and the dryer. Anna almost felt sorry for her; she knew Portia was trying to imprint in her mind which one would be on her left and which on her right. Portia had a horrible sense of direction and often she would state the landmarks they passed when she and Anna rode their bikes to the store or the beach. "Big white car with Arizona license plate," Portia once said, and Anna had hoped that the car would soon leave the driveway where it had been parked, only so she could see if Portia would then get lost on the way home.

"The washer is closer to the door," Portia said. "And the dryer is near the workbench."

"Yeah," Louise said.

"Duh," Anna said.

Upstairs, Louise showed the girls how to set the alarm clocks she had put in each of their rooms.

"Is this the only color they had?!" Anna held up the black clock and shook it. She didn't know anyone who had a black anything in her room. Everyone had pink or blue or yellow, or even green. But black? Black was a color for drug addicts and psychotics.

"You're going to have to get yourself up a little earlier than I've been getting you up," Louise said, "so you have time to feed Emery and get him dressed before you go to school."

"Okay." Portia stared at the back of her boxy alarm clock. Anna knew she'd already forgotten how to set it—there were too many knobs for her sister to keep track!

In the downstairs broom closet Louise showed her daughters the vacuum, the dust mop, the Lemon Pledge, and the dust rags. She also pulled out a bucket and sponge mop that the girls had never seen used in the house before.

"Do you do that?" Portia asked.

"Of course," Louise said.

"Really?" Portia said. "You do that with that thing?"

"MOP!" Anna said. "Don't you know what a mop is?! Are you a retard or something? And no, she never mops, because I didn't even know we owned a mop!"

Portia and Louise both looked at Anna without responding. They were used to her outbursts in the same way that they were used to Louise's cigarette smoke.

"When do you do it?" Portia asked.

"When you're at school," Louise laughed. "It's a lot of work being a housewife! That's why I quit." Anna rolled her eyes and slumped against the wall.

Anna was certain that the kitchen would be impossible for

Portia. She was afraid of the gas stove, of flames that would burst out and lick at her thin, sun-frayed hair. And there were too many dials on the wall oven with nothing that differentiated the broiler dial from the bake one.

"Just stay out of here," Anna said to Portia. She already had full control of the kitchen. Anna liked to bake when she got home from school, using recipes from the back of *Sunset* magazine.

The yard and gardens, Louise said, were Buzzy's concern, a concern the kids had heard them fighting about in recent days. Buzzy wanted to hire a gardener. Everyone on Abelia Way had a gardener—illegal Mexicans who always smiled and often liked to whistle while they did the quieter jobs like planting and weeding. Louise didn't want any strangers in the yard. She claimed it wasn't safe to have anyone, even an illegal alien, know about the marijuana orchard in the backyard.

"We'll get Esteban who does the Dixons' yard!" Buzzy had argued. "He takes care of their marijuana plants as if they were his goddamned children!"

"Well, what about swimming!" Louise had said. "How am I going to swim in my own pool with strange men lurking nearby?!"

"You think Esteban hasn't seen tits before!" Buzzy had frantically begun to pace the family room, waving his hands in the air. The black curls on his head bounced as he walked. "He's from Mexico, for God sakes, they nurse their babies till they can talk, there are tits everywhere—"

"They're Catholics!" Louise had shouted back. "The only tits they know are covered with a drape and the head of baby Jesus!"

Esteban was never hired.

There was no system to oversee the care the girls took of the house and Emery. So by the time Anna was thirteen and Portia was ten, the house had grown so dirty the once-white kitchen floor was the color and texture of sidewalk gum. Emery's cockatiel, Ace, had permanently fled his cage and taken refuge on the wrought iron curtain rod that hung above the couch, and so the back of the orange family room couch was encrusted with gray and white bird droppings. Anna was not surprised that no one minded the usually hardened, stiff splatter of shit behind their head. Portia was a slob whose hair was often so tangled that a little pod of snarls the size of a robin's egg sat at the nape of her neck. And she wore the same clothes every day—brown cords that were rubbed smooth at the knees and were shredded like lace at the hems that dragged on the ground. Emery's brain seemed to have not developed any ability to discern between filth and nonfilth: a Life Saver candy plucked from the gutter was every bit as good as one taken from the roll.

As far as she knew, Anna was the only person in the household who bathed daily, ironed her clothes, and kept her room neat. She was the single child with linens on her bed, as she dutifully pulled off her sheets each week, washed them, and returned them to the bed. Portia's sheets were kicked down into a greasy bundle at the bottom of her bed. Her mattress was slick and shiny-gray from body oil and dirt. Sometimes Anna went in Portia's room just to make sure it really was in the decrepit state she imagined. Emery's sheets were tangled up in the eucalyptus tree where he had tried to make a canopy in case it ever rained (which it rarely did; California was in the midst of a years-long drought). His mattress was almost black because he was as dirty as a feral guinea pig—and he smelled like a guinea pig, too: earthy, pissy, with an astringent echo of eucalyptus.

Anna didn't like touching Emery because of his filth. But

Portia didn't mind. Sometimes Anna would sit on the closed toilet seat and watch as Portia gave Emery his Sunday bath in the bathwater that she, Portia, had just used. Next to the tub were kept two dented aluminum pots and two thick gas station glasses that Buzzy or Louise got for free when they filled the car at the Esso station. The glasses had Daffy Duck and Goofy on them; Emery often spoke to them as he filled the glasses up and poured them out while Portia scrubbed him with a washcloth. There was always a black crescent moon of dirt behind each of his ears, and a necklace of dirt around his neck, swooping down to his clavicle. Often Anna would jump off the toilet and rush to Emery to examine his neck before Portia started scrubbing. There was something about the before and after images that thrilled her. As long as he had pots to fill, pour, and refill, Emery would sit relatively still while Portia scoured him clean until he shined as pink as a tongue. Later, when Anna saw the movie *Silkwood* in which Karen Silkwood is abraded with wire brushes to remove the radioactive material on her skin, she thought of her sister giving Emery his vigorous Sunday scrubbings.

When Emery was out of the tub, Anna would watch her sister bundle him in the same black towel Portia had used, which was never washed and simply dried between uses. Anna hid her towel in her bedroom. She washed it almost daily and never left it in the bathroom where her brother and sister could wipe their sticky paws on it. Anna washed Emery's clothes every now and then, so after his bath he was often dressed in pajamas that had holes in the knees and at the neckline but were clean nonetheless. In fact, with the exception of Sunday, the pajamas were usually cleaner than her brother.

Buzzy and Louise seemed to neither notice nor care about the derelict state of the house. When an earthquake cracked the pool foundation, Buzzy bought a sump pump, connected it to a long garden hose, and drained the pool down the hill into the orchard. Louise did her sunbathing at the nude beach while weeds began to grow out of the crack in the pool. Emery liked to play in the empty cement basin—he rode his big wheel around the oval like he was on a racetrack and when he got his first skateboard he ran straight to the backyard, dropped it into the shallow end, and took off. Even Anna and Portia liked to roller-skate in the pool from time to time, sliding down the slope toward the deep end where the drain had a leafy branch darting up through its slats like a bony arm through a prison grate.

Buzzy and Louise's bedroom was as forbidden to the children as Louise's art studio off the garage but, unlike the studio, there was no padlock on the door to keep them out. Anna and Portia liked to dig through the room—excavate it as if it would answer the questions they had about their parents. Portia always went into the jewelry boxes that were stacked on top of Louise's dresser. She would stand on the small padded stool that sat at the vanity and bring them down one by one, while Anna spread the bedspread over their parents' unmade bed. One day, when Portia questioned Anna's reasons for always making the bed, Anna explained to her sister that if she didn't cover up the sheets, Buzzy's loose sperm would crawl up their legs and impregnate them.

"Why is his loose sperm on the bed?" Portia asked.

"It slips out of his penis," Anna said.

Portia stood back and watched as Anna pulled up the comforter and tucked it under the pillows. When Portia didn't get on the bed, Anna grabbed her arm and pulled her toward it. There was no way she was going to sit there if Portia wouldn't. "It's safe now!" she said, yanking Portia into place.

Anna assumed it was Portia's low intelligence that led her to only the jewelry boxes. Portia seemed content trying on rings with giant glittering stones in them, or bracelets that jingled when stacked on her arm. Louise never wore any of this jewelry and the girls couldn't understand why. She didn't even wear a wedding ring, although she seemed to have several—some with diamonds, some with lace-like patterned gold, and one with a simple, round rock sitting like an offering.

Anna preferred to go through her parents' drawers, particularly the drawers in each of the black nightstands that stood on either side of the bed. She'd flip through the notes, receipts, and stacks of loose papers in Buzzy's drawers. At Louise's side of the bed, Anna would look through her mother's silky underpants and nightgowns and examine the beige, ridged vibrator that had an on/off button on the bottom. Anna often turned it on, held it up in her hand, and watched it buzz.

"Gross," Anna said, every time, as she rotated the vibrator in her hand. At thirteen she had a fairly clear picture of how it could be used and imagined that if hadn't belonged to her nudist mother who always smelled like armpits, she might want to try it out.

"Yeah, gross," Portia always said, but Anna could tell from her face, skin as smooth as a polished stone, that Portia had no idea what she was looking at.

One day, as Portia was stacking a cuff of bracelets up her thin arm, Anna found Buzzy's diary. She sat back against the black, shellacked headboard and started on page one.

"Boooring," Anna said, as she flipped through the pages. She thought her father was an overly sensitive whiner—*I feel this, and I feel that, wah wah wah wah.* And then she landed on something that made her gasp.

"What?" Portia asked.

"Mom might have an affair." Anna felt like she had just swallowed a handful of tacks. Her stomach was pinging with pricks that made her eyes burn and water. The affair was proof of Louise's shortcomings as a mother and a wife. Her mother should put on a wedding band, a bra, and a headband. If her hair weren't swishing across her face like a teenager's, and her nipples weren't showing, people would understand that Louise was married, had three children, and was unavailable.

"Who's she going to have an affair with?" Portia asked. Anna wanted to whack her across the head with the diary. Portia was smiling, flopping her hands around to make the bracelets clink. It was obvious that she didn't see herself entwined in anything Louise or Buzzy did; she simply skipped around them the way one skipped around mossy, glistening rocks when hiking up a stream.

"Dad caught her flirting with another poet," Anna said, and she felt the tacks pierce into her belly. Unlike Portia—dashing from one dry rock to the next—Anna parked herself in the center of every treacherous, slick stone she found—sitting there with a scowl on her face and her arms crossed until someone listened to her protests.

"So," Portia said.

"SO?" Anna said. "Dad wrote that if something happens, he hopes it's just a *one-fuck deal*."

"What?!"

Anna was thrilled that Portia was shocked by the word. Of course, their parents used it frequently: *fucking Nixon, fucking schmuck, fuck you and fuck you and fuck you, too!* But they never used it like *this*. They never used it as a verb, as an action, as something dirty, and nasty and forbidden. *Now* she had her sister's attention; finally Anna could get Portia to understand how serious this all was.

"He hopes it's a one-FUCK deal." Anna leaned toward Portia, she was almost smiling from the grittiness of the word. It felt like she'd taken her bellyful of tacks and thrown them at her sister's face.

"What's a one—"

Anna loved that Portia couldn't get the word out. She felt older (which she was) and more powerful (which she wasn't always). "One-FUCK deal! Get it? One-FUCK deal!" She turned the diary and pointed at Buzzy's slanted, tight script on the page of the black leather-bound book. Anna wanted Portia to understand how demented their parents were, how perverted and disgusting. It was as if Portia's head were made of soft cheese with no holes for any of this information to enter. Portia was happily oblivious, roller-skating through the streets with her friends, never thinking about the sick state of affairs in the house. Sometimes when Anna was flipping through the Diane Arbus photo book that sat on the coffee table in the living room (there were photos of freaks in nudist camps in the book, more proof of her parents' perversions), she would pause at the pictures of the retarded people at the end of the book. They were happy, holding hands, shuffling through the fog with veiled hats on their heads and dopey gap-toothed smiles on their faces. *That's like Portia,* Anna thought, *blissfully stumbling in a fog.*

"What does that mean?" Portia shook her wrists. The bracelets sounded like wooden wind chimes.

"It means that if she has sex with the poet she's been flirting with, he hopes she only does it one time." Anna stared at Portia's small, freckled face. She wanted to insert worry and outrage into her sister the way you'd put stuffing in a turkey.

"Why doesn't he just hope that she doesn't do it at all?" Portia asked.

"Because he figures she will. Mom is a slut."

"She is not. She just likes to go to the nude beach." Portia looked down at the bracelets and deliberately clinked them.

"She's a slut." Anna said the words as if they were a karate chop. "She's a married woman who flirted with a poet and might have sex with him."

"I like Mom," Portia said. "She's fun and she's pretty."

"She has hairy armpits and wears patchouli oil that stinks like gym socks!" Anna said.

"She doesn't stink," Portia said. "And she doesn't follow us into the kitchen, like all my friends' moms do. We eat whatever we want and do what we want."

Anna imagined grabbing Portia's head and knocking it repeatedly against her own until the stuff in her own brain poured out like sticky lava and flowed into her sister's cheesy head.

"She wants to have sex with a poet!" Anna said.

Portia slid the bracelets off her arm and examined them. Anna stared at her, not blinking, willing her into submission.

"Is it the poet from that party?" Portia finally asked.

"Probably. Dad just calls him 'the Poet.' That's what it says here: 'the Poet.'" Anna thumped her pointer finger against the words.

The girls had heard their parents talking about a famous poet who was living in Santa Barbara that spring. They had been invited to a party where he was the guest of honor. Louise had told the girls that he had stood in front of the fireplace and read some of his poems and she had almost cried. Anna thought her mother must be stupid or simple, to almost cry at a poem. It was ridiculous, like when Cathy L. cried at school because she heard John Denver was going to do a concert at the Santa Barbara County Bowl.

"Mom likes his poetry," Portia said. "It doesn't mean she's going to have sex with him."

"That's not what Dad thinks!" Anna said, and she slammed the book shut and replaced it in the drawer.

"Dad's a worrywart!" Portia said. Anna could see that even Portia didn't believe that to be true. Buzzy never seemed to worry about anyone in the family. If he was worrying, it was about work, or trying to decide if he should put coffee grounds in the compost pile or not.

"Mom's probably in her studio right now with the poet having a *one-fuck deal*! And when he leaves I bet some other guy will come in and do it with her! There's probably a sign-in sheet, like at the doctor's office, and every guy has to wait his turn!"

"Where are they waiting?" Portia asked. "In the front yard?"

"And," Anna continued, "Mom might even have diseases like syphilis or gonorrhea! In fact, she probably has them now and that's why she's so crazy because that stuff affects your brain, too, you know!" Anna's speech had the wrong effect: instead of making Portia cry, it made *her* cry. And the calmer Portia remained, the more frustrated and teary Anna became.

"You're so gross," Portia said, casually. She gathered up the bracelets and returned them to the jewelry box. "And you're such a liar."

"Don't believe me," Anna said, her voice stuttering with grief. "See if I care." She sat with her back against the headboard, crying in little jags. Anna wished she had more control over herself. She didn't want to be anything like her mother, who cried at poems, or like moony Cathy L. who cried at even the idea of John Denver. But emotions were like a runny nose for her—there was nothing she could do but wipe them up as they poured out.

When Portia had finished putting the jewelry away, and had returned the boxes to the top of her mother's dresser, she crawled up next to her sister on the bed. There were tears in a continuous stream down Anna's cheeks; her mouth felt as if it had been pulled shut like a drawstring bag.

"I believe you," Portia said. Anna knew she said it just to make her happy.

"Get ready for divorce," Anna said.

"Don't you think it would be kind of fun if they divorced?" Portia asked.

"Do you even know anyone whose parents are divorced?!" Anna thumped her back against the headboard to make her point.

"No," Portia said. "But in *The Courtship of Eddie's Father*, Eddie lives only with his father and it looks like they always have fun together, walking on the beach, finding shells. And in *The Brady Bunch*, Bob and Carol married each other after . . . I don't know, maybe a divorce, and their kids each got new, fun, supercute siblings. If Dad remarried and Mom remarried, we could have two new homes with lots of kids running around, and maybe even a playmate for Emery so he wouldn't have to spend so much time wandering the outdoors alone."

"It would be awful if they got divorced," Anna said. "Dad would have all the money and Mom would be poor. And maybe someone would marry Dad because he's got a good job and he's not very bossy or anything. But no one would marry Mom because she's a slut and she has three kids and no one wants a used-up lady with three kids."

"But she's so pretty," Portia said. "Everyone thinks she's the prettiest mom ever."

"No one wants other people's kids." Anna thought that only

someone who was mentally ill would want kids who looked like orphans and smelled like a compost pile.

"They wanted each other's kids in *The Brady Bunch*," Portia said.

"You're dumb and Emery's dirty," Anna said. "No one would want us."

"Let's go listen at her studio and see if she's having a one . . . a one-time deal right now!" Portia appeared to be on the verge of laughing. She hopped off the bed and went toward the door. Anna hurried off the bed and pushed herself ahead, out the bedroom, down the stairs, and into the garage to their mother's studio.

They stood with their ears pressed against the door, Anna's head stacked above Portia's. The radio was on, a talk show of some sort with a woman who was taking calls. Louise mumbled something then laughed. Anna pulled her head away from the door, wiped her eyes, then mouthed, "See." Her heart flipped around with grief and joy. She so wanted to prove to her sister that she was right that it was worth the horror of catching her mother in the middle of a one-fuck deal.

"I bet she's talking to the radio," Portia whispered.

"She's not talking to the radio! What she said didn't have anything to do with what that lady on the radio said!" Anna had no idea what Louise had said, but she wanted Portia on her team and was willing to color in the blanks in the story.

"What did she say?" Portia asked.

"I'll tell you later. Now don't move!" Anna gave her sister the open-palm *stay* sign, then ran into the house.

Moments later Anna returned to the garage holding two empty gas station glasses, like the ones Portia used in the tub when she washed Emery. Anna handed her sister the Road Runner glass.

She had Bugs Bunny. They each put the open end against the door and placed their ears against the bottom. It was a trick Louise herself had taught the children in a hotel in Boston one summer when she was convinced the men in the room beside theirs were planning a robbery.

"Quit moving!" Anna said as her sister squirmed beneath her. Once Portia had stilled they could hear the radio more clearly. A woman was asking for advice on how to persuade her husband that she should be the one to balance the checkbook since he seemed to mess it up every month.

"Oh, shut your fucking mouth!" Louise said, and she laughed again.

Anna pulled her head away and rapidly pulsed her finger at the door as if pointing at the proof.

"She's talking to the radio!" Portia whispered. Anna knew she was probably right. Louise talked to the radio in the car, she talked to books and magazine articles, she talked to the TV on the rare occasion she sat in front of the small black-and-white one in the family room. Once, Louise gathered the family together to watch a movie she had read about in the *Los Angeles Times* called *A Girl Named Sooner*. There was a scene in which a retarded boy was pushed into a pond by the local kids. "Big boy push me in the water," the boy cried, "he hurt me!" Louise laughed, and each time that kid came on screen again she'd shout in the muted boggy voice of the mentally disabled, "Big boy push me in the water, he hurt me!" Later, when Anna was visiting Portia in Berkeley, and they went to see *Blue Velvet* at a movie theater in nearby Oakland, Anna discovered a whole culture of people who talked to objects that couldn't hear. She knew her mother would have loved it when the guy sitting right in front of them shouted at the screen, *That's a BULLSHIT bird, that ain't no real bird!* (Although the idea of her mother joining in and publically vocalizing her thoughts during a movie still horrified her.)

But just because Louise was talking to the radio didn't mean that someone else wasn't in the studio. So Anna stayed where she was, ear posted against the glass on the door, for at least another hour while her sister went inside and finished the game of solitaire someone had laid out on the family room floor.

Shortly after that, when summer started and Louise spent less time in the studio and more time at the nude beach, Louise decided that Buzzy was having an affair with one of three women she collectively called the Gorgons and individually called Lompoc Lucy, Tits-N-Ass McCoy, and Bitty Royce.

Lompoc Lucy was a lawyer who lived in the small inland town Lompoc. She was consulting with Buzzy on a case she was working on. Tits-N-Ass McCoy was Buzzy's receptionist, a soft, dough-faced woman who was always friendly with the kids, and who gave Christmas presents to Anna, Portia, and Emery every year. Anna hated the presents and thought they weren't worth the work of the thank-you note that had to follow. And she was disgusted when her sister gushed over her gifts: ladybug compact perfumes from Avon, bubble bath with a lid shaped like a flower, boxes of stationery with paper that folded around itself to make its own envelope you could seal with a sticker.

The third gorgon, Bitty Royce, was the paralegal Buzzy had hired to help out in the office that summer. She was younger than Buzzy and Louise, a child and an embarrassment—according to Louise, who could spend an entire dinner discussing the disadvantages of doing business with a girl who wore lipstick two shades too pink.

Buzzy usually rolled his eyes and grunted while Louise went on verbal tangents attacking the Gorgons. Every now and then he'd throw up his hands and yell—like a dog with a sudden startling bark—"For chrissakes, I don't give a shit about any of them!"

But Louise would not relent, and by the end of the summer the children were so accustomed to listening to the anti–Bitty Royce, –Lompoc Lucy, and –Tits-N-Ass McCoy rants that if Louise didn't bring it up at dinner, one of them would.

"Did you see Bitty Royce today, Dad?" Portia would ask. "Take her to lunch?"

Buzzy would openly laugh, while Louise smiled and shook her head.

"You girls have no idea," Louise said to Anna and Portia one night, when Buzzy had a dinner meeting and wasn't at the table. "Your father has done horrible things. Horrible, awful things!"

Anna silently gnawed on her hamburger and watched Portia who seemed not to have heard what Louise had just said. She was decorating her open hamburger patty with a smiley face made of peas.

"Does he love Tits-N-Ass McCoy instead of you?" five-year-old Emery asked.

Louise threw her fork onto her plate, picked up her glass of wine, and left the room.

The following evening, when Buzzy had yet another dinner engagement, Louise decided she'd had enough.

Portia was setting the table while Anna finished preparing dinner. Anna was shouting to her sister from the kitchen, "Put soup spoons out!" She was serving homemade matzo ball soup from a recipe their paternal grandmother in New Jersey had mailed to Louise. Portia went back to the kitchen for spoons when there was a thunderous bang, somewhat like the boom from an earthquake. Anna stopped stirring the pot on the stove and stared at her sister. More thumping and banging followed. It was coming from the stairway.

The girls ran to the entrance hall where they found their father's lumbering antique wardrobe stuck like a dead wooden whale on the stairs.

"Mom?" Anna called up toward the second floor. A drawer from Buzzy's night table came flying down the stairs, over the wardrobe, and splattered on the marble landing. Papers, receipts, and Buzzy's diary flew out of the drawer as if they were running for their lives.

"MOM!" Anna yelled. "What are you doing?!" Anna was convinced her mother was suffering from syphilitic brain damage. She clicked back into her mind to the chapter she had read about syphilis in her health book (it hadn't been assigned but Anna had read it before bed one night). The primary symptoms were canker sores and, indeed, her mother often had canker sores on her mouth. Surely the one Louise had a few weeks ago, that she was dabbing with Campo-Phenique so often that the whole house had that eucalyptus-alcoholic smell, was the start of syphilis from her one-fuck deal. The syphilis would have then gone into the secondary stage, a rash. But Anna wouldn't have seen the rash since every time her mother walked around the house naked Anna turned her head or left the room so she wouldn't be affronted with Louise's naked body—her jiggling square butt, her long nipples, her feathery brown pubic hair. The quiet latent stage of syphilis would have followed, and maybe her mother had a short latent stage considering her one-fuck deal couldn't have been more than a few weeks ago. But now, clearly, she was in the final stage, Anna thought. This was the brutal end to what could have been an easily treatable disease. From here on out her mother would have brain damage, delirium, insanity. Vincent Van Gogh-style.

"OUTTA THE WAY!" Louise yelled down, and the two girls jumped back as three cologne bottles hit the ground and exploded, sending a small fireworks of green glass up toward their heads. The musty, spicy smell was so strong it was almost nauseating.

"It's irreversible brain damage," Anna said, and she began crying.

"WATCH YOUR HEADS!" Louise shouted, and the remainder of the heavy black night table came down, bouncing once off the wardrobe, before tumbling into the glass and landing against the front door.

Buzzy's suits, shirts, and ties were next. They slicked over the wardrobe, making a blue-and-gray ribbon that led to the crowded entrance hall. Louise must have been aiming when she tossed down Buzzy's shoes, as each one seemed to nail the door with a quick, solid thump before falling to the ground.

Then there was a brief respite of silence. Anna stood crying while trying to figure out how many weeks they had until Louise died. The silence was cut open by a tinkering of Buzzy remnants: a shaving brush, razor, toothbrush, and a shoehorn.

"Our mother is permanently crazy," Anna wept.

"She's just angry," Portia said, and she put her hand on her sister's shoulder.

Anna shrugged Portia away. Portia never believed anything Anna said; she was stubbornly stuck in her glowing, happy vision of their world where no one was having affairs, and the family wasn't a bunch of backwoods, slovenly freaks.

"It's contagious," Anna said. "If you kissed Mom when she had that sore on her mouth a few weeks ago, you could have it, too. That sore was syphilis, you know."

"That was a cold sore," Portia said. "And Mom's not crazy.

She's mad at Dad because he had another late dinner with one of the Gorgons and Mom had asked him to only have business lunches."

"There's no way she's this mad about the Gorgons!" Anna said. "Dad didn't make such a big fuss over her one-fuck deal!" Anna wiped her nose with the base of her palm. "She needs to get to a doctor! She's probably going to die of this!"

"Mom didn't do that one-time deal," Portia said. "She just flirted."

"You are SO stupid!" Anna's voice screeched like the brakes on a speeding car. "You don't know anything about medicine and venereal diseases and affairs! Dad is probably having sex with the Gorgons now and he's probably giving them syphilis, too! Don't you understand? Our parents are out of control and the affairs aren't even the worst of it! The worst of it is that that Dad's going crazy next and eventually they'll both die!"

"He's not having sex with the Gorgons!" Portia actually started to giggle. Anna wondered if Portia even heard what she had said about *both their parents dying soon*. It was as if those words hadn't even entered her sister's daisy chain of a brain.

"Mom told me he's sleeping with them." Anna peeked her head up toward the stairway to see if anything else was coming down. She heard the fast clicking of Louise's clogs against the wooden floor.

"Coming down!" came from the top of the stairs, followed by a flying lamp that used to be on Buzzy's nightstand. The lamp ricocheted off a couple of suits and the wooden drawer before landing on some scattered papers with a hollow *thunk* sound.

The barricaded front door rattled. "Portia," Emery called, "let me in!"

"GO AROUND!" Anna yelled. "IT'S DANGEROUS!"

"Mom couldn't have been serious if she told you Dad's having an affair," Portia said. "She's just jealous. It's stupid. That's why she sometimes laughs when I bring it up."

"She laughs because you're her favorite," Anna said. "And because of the brain damage." Anna was smoldering with rage; the tears in her eyes magnified and distorted everything she saw. She turned toward her sister and could see in Portia's pale worried face that she was more afraid of Anna's rage than of the furniture heaped in the entrance hall, their father's having sex with the Gorgons, and venereal disease running rampant in the family.

"I'm getting Emery," Portia said, and she turned away from Anna.

"I'll get Emery!" Anna said, and she pushed Portia aside and rushed toward the family room.

"I shampooed my hair!" Emery said when his sisters walked in the room. His blond head was covered in mucky gravel; streaks of mud ran in lines down his face. His striped Charlie Brown–looking shirt was black with dirt.

"Where'd you shampoo your hair?" Portia asked, and she picked him up. Anna shivered; she wouldn't touch anyone that dirty even if she were going into anaphylactic shock and they were handing her the epinephrine pen.

"In the street!" Emery said. "Mr. Kluck was washing his car and the shampoo was going down the gutter, so I washed my hair!"

"He's so proud of himself!" Portia said, and she laughed and pulled her brother against her chest.

"Wash him. He's revolting," Anna went to the sink and began loading the dinner prep dishes and the lunch dishes into the dishwasher to clear a space in the big basin sink where Portia could plant her brother. Emery's bathroom, which was downstairs, had only a shower, and there was no way, save climbing a ladder and crawling in a window, to get upstairs to the bathtub.

Emery was barefoot, as usual; Portia simply slipped off his T-shirt and elastic waist shorts (he had outgrown his underwear a year earlier and no one had bought him new underwear to replace the old stuff) and dropped him into the sink.

"Let's pretend this is a boat," Emery said, "and you're a mermaid named Willomina Portia Ernie Bert Oscar Stein."

"Willomina Ernie Bert—"

"Willomina PORTIA Ernie Bert Oscar Stein!" Emery said.

"That's me," Portia said, "you know who I am."

Portia turned on the water, pulled out the extendable faucet, and rinsed Emery's face, laughing as he lapped at the water like a dog at a hose.

Anna leaned against the counter and watched. She hated them both even more than she hated her syphilitic-adulterating parents. Why did she have to be the only child in the family not blessed with an idiot's ignorance?

The morning of the heart attack, as they were en route to the hospital, Louise had choked out a single sentence: "If you tell the kids, I'll kill you." Had she died that night, those would have been her last words. Buzzy put off calling his children for a day, but finally he broke down and sheepishly phoned: "You know, I promised your mother I wouldn't tell you, but, well, she had a little heart attack, and . . ."

When "the kids" showed up on Buzzy's birthday, Louise was too bleary to know they were there. Today, Day Four after the heart attack, she is alert enough to speak, and she's pissed.

"I told your father not to tell you." Louise speaks uncharacteristically slowly and slurs her words, as if her lips are numb. Anna sees this as a bonus to being hospitalized (and drugged): the blurriness of time, being taken out of the overly needy world, your only job to lie around in a pool of smeary consciousness.

"He couldn't *not* tell us," Portia says.

"I'm fine," Louise says. "Go home."

"Mom," Anna says, "you had a *massive* heart attack."

"Says who?"

"Says everyone!" Anna shouts. "They thought you were going to die."

"Well if that's dying," Louise mumbles, "dying's not so bad."

No one tells her that she's still in critical condition. The doctor comes in and confirms the story. "Your husband saved your life," he says. "Twenty minutes later and you would have died."

"If he saved my life, what do I need you for?" Louise's eyes are closed as she speaks, as if she doesn't have the energy to see and talk at the same time.

"It was a joint effort," the doctor says.

"Thank you," she says, and she rolls her eyes under closed lids. Anna thinks they look like marbles under folds of ashy tissue paper.

Louise is fifty-four years old. Anna thinks that at this moment she looks eighty-four. Her face is as gray as her hair, and her eyes are puffy flesh donuts. She has melted somehow.

"How do I look?" she asks. It is late afternoon and she has finally forgiven her children for flocking to her in this time of crisis.

"Like you just woke up from a nap," Anna says. She has no intention of telling her the truth. Anna wouldn't leave the house if she ever woke up looking that bad.

"You look beautiful," Buzzy says.

"Yeah, yeah," Louise groans. "I'm so beautiful, Arabs are going to burst in here any second and kidnap—" Louise appears to fall asleep midsentence.

"What?" Alejandro straightens in his chair.

"Dad's always been worried that Mom would be kidnapped by Arabs," Anna says, and she flips the page of the *New Yorker* she's reading. Or barely reading, as she finds herself focusing on *who* the writers are of each article rather than *what* they've written.

"Arabs?" Alejandro laughs. Anna is glad that Alejandro finds everything in this family funny. Her own husband seems confounded by her parents and siblings. "Why not Asians, or Aryans, or Jews?"

"Fuck the Jews . . ." Louise is suddenly awake. Before they were married, Louise converted to Judaism. In her older age, however, Louise claims she hates the Jews. She refuses to see Woody Allen movies or read Philip Roth books. She has even said that if Buzzy insists on being buried in a Jewish cemetery, she'll never visit his grave. Her Jewish children know this is Louise's way of doing battle with Buzzy (the super-Jew) for crimes none of them care to know.

"Jews wouldn't kidnap her!" Buzzy says. "But Arabs . . ." Buzzy shrugs as if it's a real possibility.

"You two need to travel more," Emery says. He is the least tolerant of his parents' eccentricities. Once, Emery told Anna that he thinks their parents are borderline crazy. Anna pointed out to him that they are no crazier than she, and her brother didn't disagree.

"Arabs are sexy," Anna says. "I love Arabs." The article she is reading is written by a guy with an Arab-sounding name. Anna has a fantasy that this guy is some smarty-pants New Yorker with a cool apartment somewhere in the Village. She imagines herself going to chic parties with him where lots of famous and semi-famous writers show up. Anna and her Arab writer would come home from the party and fuck like mad after being inspired by all the women who flirted with him and all the men who wanted her.

Anna looks up from the magazine; everyone, except Louise, is looking at her. She assumes they're waiting for her to confess to an affair with an Arab lover.

"What?" Anna asks.

"What sexy Arabs do you know?" Portia asks. Her face is wooden.

"Random ones," Anna says. "Strangers I've seen." Anna won't tell them (although maybe she'll tell Portia later, if she remembers), but in fact she has had one Arab lover, a coke dealer in Jackson, Wyoming, who was astonishingly sexy.

"Your not having another affair, are you?" Portia's eyes are shiny now.

"Fucking relax," Anna says. "I'm not having another affair!" Anna hates that Portia's unfaithful husband has given her seismographic sensitivity to the world's transgressions.

Anna's marriage has survived two affairs that her family and even her husband know of. She has had three other affairs that, as far she is aware, only she and her lovers know of. Her husband is as faithful and immoveable as boulder. He is also profoundly forgiving. Anna looks back down at the magazine and reenters her fantasy about the New Yorker writer.

"I had a Persian boyfriend in college for a while," Portia says. "Maybe I should have married him instead of Patrick."

"Good thing he never met your mother," Buzzy says. "He might have kidnapped her!"

"Persians aren't Arabs." Emery's voice is stiff.

"They're not," Portia says. "They're Persian. But I would have dated an Arab if I had met one I was attracted to."

"I fucking love Arab men," Anna says, and she can feel everyone staring at her again.

"How do I look?" Louise groans, as if she has just woken up for the first time and hasn't already asked how she looks.

"I think you look awful," Portia says. "You don't look like yourself." She is the most direct with their mother and this usually makes Louise laugh. Sometimes Anna wishes she could be like that with Louise, but it never comes naturally.

For years Anna was angry at Louise for what Anna believes was a chaotic and messy childhood. But recently Anna realized she is no longer angry; in fact, she has not been angry since she was in her early twenties. She was just in the habit of being mad. Sometimes when Anna is talking to Louise she sees words coming out of her mouth like fistfuls of stones. But she doesn't intend to spew stones; it's simply the only way Anna knows how to talk to her mother.

"She doesn't look awful," Emery says. "She looks like she just woke up." Anna completely disagrees, but won't let Louise know. She is holding the stones in her mouth.

"Give me a mirror," Louise says.

"No way," Portia says. "It would be too depressing."

Louise gives a breathy, weak laugh, and the nurse—there is usually one in the room—looks at Portia askance.

In addition to *The New Yorker*, they have brought the *New York Times*, the *Los Angeles Times*, and three books that were sitting on Louise's bedside table at home. Louise cannot hold her head up or keep her eyes open long enough to read. And it doesn't feel right to read this stuff aloud—it requires a strength of concentration that no one (including Anna, who can't even silently get through a paragraph of the maybe-Arab-authored *New Yorker* article) currently possesses. Anna goes to the gift shop and returns with the *National Enquirer* and *Star* magazine. They pass the tabloids around, reading out headlines and the captions under pictures.

"Hillary hired a private detective to follow Bill," Anna says, "and found that he has been having affairs with a string of women . . . all kinds of women." Anna imagines that Bill Clinton would be a fabulous lover. She wonders how she can get herself to Washington to meet Bill Clinton. What could be sexier than a man who's running an entire country?

"Good thing Bill Clinton never met you," Buzzy says to Louise. "He would have been all over you."

Louise is too weak to open her eyes at the moment, but she rolls them anyway. This time, the roving eyes remind Anna of bodies tumbling beneath a sheet.

"Tell me how I look," Louise says, for the third time today. She bats her eyes open, then lets her lids drop shut. She is so silent and still that Anna thinks her mother may have died. She studies her closely, is relieved to see that she's breathing.

Louise has wrinkles that radiate out, framing her mouth like a drawing of a radio signal. Her skin is like lumpy gray papier-mâché. Below her chin is a small shawl of fat. Her lips are like two desiccated slugs. Anna hopes she dies before she ever looks this bad. She is far more fearful of a withered face than of the possible side effects of plastic surgery.

Buzzy is holding Louise's hand, lifting it to his mouth every few minutes and kissing her knuckles. If Anna were to have a heart attack, her husband would be like Buzzy, Anna thinks, sitting by her side like a Seeing Eye dog. Poor Portia. It is doubtful that her husband would sit by her for anything.

The end started coming three years ago; Anna saw it in Patrick's muddy-clay eyes when Portia was swooning over their new baby. Anna figures that if Portia hadn't walked into Patrick's office when he was working late one night and caught him *in flagrante delicto*, she never would have noticed how distant and dispassionate her husband was. Her sister was too far gone with baby-love.

On the last day of her last visit before Patrick moved out, Anna looked at Portia with the bull's-eye milk stains on the nipple-points of her old T-shirt, and five extra pounds rolled like a sweatshirt around her hips, and knew that Portia wasn't in the marriage she thought she was in. Patrick was trim, lime-smelling; he was wearing a crisp pressed shirt that was whiter than the flash on a Polaroid camera. Two weeks later, when Portia told Anna about finding her husband, pants pooling at his ankles, ass machining in and out of a slim woman whose skin was as unmarred as a brand-new bedsheet, all Anna could think about was the shimmering fish of a caesarean scar that sat under Portia's belly fold, or her unshaven legs that were the texture of an old, half-bald dog.

Nothing is fair in love and romance. Anna knows this for sure, as she has exploited her own husband's devotion many times. But it wasn't until she heard her sister on the phone wailing over her loss that Anna realized how cruel these things can be: how vicious and shallow-minded it is to discount a woman battered by child-bearing; how cunning and slippery it is to use a sleek female body to seduce a man. Anna hated herself for being a person on the winning side of lust and affairs. But that's exactly where she was. Just like Patrick.

Portia decided that Emery had to scrape the hardened cloak of bird shit off the TV room couch. The bird, Ace, who liked to perch on the iron curtain rod above the couch, was Emery's, after all. They were cleaning the house for the annual December visit of their grandparents, Harry and Yetta Stein, whom they called Zeyde and Bubbe. Even Buzzy and Louise were helping out—a fact that made the chores seem festive, like the Friday after Thanksgiving at Portia's friend Denise's house where the whole family decorated for Christmas. At Denise's, they tacked thick layers of cotton to the porch rails and called that snow. It occurred to Portia that if her family suddenly were transformed into people who decorated for Christmas, they could leave the bird shit on the couch and pretend it was snow.

Portia handed Emery the paint scraper. He was seven now, had skipped second grade, and seemed old enough to do some cleaning. Anna helped Portia chase Ace around the house, trying to catch him with a metal trash can and a cookie sheet. When he was finally captured, they locked him in his cage, where he silently batted against the bars with a painful persistence that drove Louise to put him on top of the washing machine in the garage.

After banning the bird, Louise took on the kitchen floor with a wire brush and bucket whose water Portia changed for her every five minutes. The revelation of the white linoleum under the putty-gray of the kitchen floor was like a magic act, or the miracle of finding a Picasso under the amateur painting of a silo one has bought at a garage sale.

The Saturday morning of Bubbe and Zeyde's arrival, the family was quietly occupied with the final acts of preparing the house. Buzzy was sitting on the stuffed green chair in the TV room, leaning into the white kitchen trash can he had dragged in there as he rummaged through the latest stuff Anna had thrown away. Portia was cleaning the sliding glass door in the family room with Windex and newspaper and Anna was dusting the newly empty surface of the black driftwood coffee table with Lemon Pledge. The room smelled fabulously, chemically sterile. Emery was organizing the board games in the family room and Louise was sorting sheets she had purchased for the beds (the old sheets hadn't been laundered in a year and were almost waxy with dirt and oil). As in other years, Emery would sleep with Portia, or on a nest of blankets on her floor. Bubbe and Zeyde would sleep in Emery's first-floor room on his bed and a foldout cot, which was kept in the garage between their visits.

Louise gathered up the sheets, a burning cigarette dangling from her mouth. She stared down at Buzzy, who was reading a crumpled piece of paper. Louise shifted the sheets to one arm, pulled her cigarette out, and pointed it at Buzzy as she spoke.

"Buzzy, fuck the trash, get the plants."

"She may have thrown out the receipt from when I had the oil changed on the car last week, I can't find—" Buzzy dropped his head back into the trash can.

"GET THE FUCKING PLANTS!" Louise lifted her cigarette hand and pushed a sweaty strand of brown hair out of her eyes. Portia was stilled by the suddenness of her mother's anger.

"Dad," Anna said, "you *have to* chop down the marijuana

plants." She was the only one bold enough to insert herself into their parents' arguments.

Gardeners had been called in to bring the front yard under control, but the backyard, with the bursting fruit trees and chipped tile deck, had been ignored. The empty pool had been transformed into a giant junk container that reminded Portia of the drawer most people have in their kitchen that holds all the odds and ends that have no other place. Only larger. There were bikes in the pool, unused lawn tools, skateboards, old terra-cotta planters, even shoes, towels, and a few bathing suits.

"They never go in the backyard," Buzzy said, "and chances are they won't even recognize that they're marijuana plants."

Emery looked up from the Masterpiece Game; he was separating the painting cards from the value cards.

"We have marijuana plants?" he asked. His eyes were oversized brown grommets; his hair was a blond rag mop.

Portia, Anna, and their parents looked down at him, squatting like a monkey in front of the game.

"No," Louise said, calmly, "we don't have marijuana plants."

"Marijuana's against the law," Emery said. "It's illegal."

There was a certain oddness to any moment when Emery spoke while the entire family was present. What Portia thought of as the original family—Buzzy, Louise, Anna, and herself—was such a noisy, bickering group that there never seemed to be room for Emery's tiny voice. He was like Ace, his bird, a vision of constant movement, chaos, and mess, but not a vocal part of the family.

"How do you know it's illegal?" Buzzy asked.

"We talked about it in school."

"You talked about marijuana in school? What the hell kind of a school are you in that you talk about marijuana in third grade?" Outrage at his children's schooling was a common theme for Buzzy.

"We talked about drugs. Marijuana is a drug."

"Jesus fucking Christ," Louise moaned and shifted the weight of the sheets in her arms. "Marijuana is harmless! And yes, we have marijuana plants because I smoke marijuana!"

Portia turned from the sliding glass door and leaned toward her brother. "Don't tell your teacher or your friends, okay? Or Mom will go to jail."

"For chrissakes, Portia!" Louise snapped. "Nobody's going to fucking jail— why put that thought in his head?! Now come help me put sheets on the beds, and Buzzy, cut down the fucking plants!"

Buzzy stood from the trash can. "But the buds are only a few days from being fully ripe—"

"You don't even smoke them!" Louise said. "Portia! Take these!"

Louise dumped the sheets in Portia's arms, then circled the room with her cigarette butt, searching for the abalone shell ashtray that usually sat on the coffee table. There was a perfect cylindrical ash sitting atop the clean white sheets. Portia walked to the trash can, tilted the sheets toward it, and blew the ash off. It left a streak of gray, like a cartoon drawing of movement beside running legs.

"Where are the marijuana plants?" Emery's mouth was pulled into a worried little scowl. Portia imagined the picture in his brain of a drawing by his favorite illustrator, Richard Scarry, whose dog-police would pull up in a black-and-white paddy wagon and haul off their parents.

"They're surrounded by lemon trees," Buzzy said. "No one can see them."

"Dad," Anna said, "I know you like to grow the best plants

you can, but you have to admit that if it doesn't matter to Mom, it's much safer to chop them down than risk that Bubbe and Zeyde see them and—"

Emery stood and slid open the glass door. He ran out into the backyard toward the lemon trees.

"You think he's going to pull off the buds and sell them at school?" Anna asked. Portia laughed, although she didn't quite know what the buds were.

"Poor little guy," Louise said, and she walked out after him. Buzzy got up and followed, so the girls went, too, the pile of sheets still in Portia's arms.

Emery was in the middle of the stand of six-foot-high marijuana plants, pulling one down to the ground and trying to break it at the base of the stem. The plant bent and bounced as he pushed on it with his dirty brown bare foot.

"Okay, okay," Buzzy said, and he took Emery by the arm and directed him away from the plant he was attacking. "Don't worry, I'll pull them out. Okay?" He tugged on Emery so that he faced him. "We're going to lock them in your mother's studio where Bubbe and Zeyde will never see them."

"IT'S AGAINST THE LAW!" Emery wailed, and fat tears began to fall down his face. He broke free of Buzzy's grip, ran to the eucalyptus tree, and scaled it to the platform perch before anyone could even reach the base.

"Hey," Anna called up the tree, "Noble Citizen, come on down! Dad's taking care of it!" Louise and Portia laughed. Buzzy sighed and went to the marijuana plants, where he dug each one out at the roots.

They all piled into the long, blue station wagon to pick up Bubbe and Zeyde from the airport. Even the car was clean—Anna and Portia had picked up all the old, nearly petrified McDonald's

French fries, the mysterious hairballs fuzzed with dust, the gum wrappers, and other detritus off the floor of the car before Buzzy took it to a car wash, where the workers vacuumed and wiped down the inside as well as scrubbing the outside. The car smelled like pink bubblegum—a change from the usual cigarette and gasoline smell that, strangely, in Portia's mind, equated with the smell of vomit.

At the airport, they stood at the low stucco wall that separated the grassy courtyard from the runway. Emery scaled the wall and walked along the top of it, his arms extended like the wings of an airplane.

"Hey, Noble Citizen, get down from there," Louise said. The name Noble Citizen had stuck since Anna first used it; Louise, Anna, and Portia had since completely abandoned Emery's proper name. Buzzy took Emery's hand and held it while Emery leapt from the top of the wall to the grass.

Bubbe and Zeyde's plane came roaring in. Portia put her hands over her ears; Anna squinted toward the plane, her eyes crinkled up like black raisins. Buzzy picked up Emery and held him near his shoulder so he could better see the plane touch down, then roll along the runway until it stopped not far from where the family stood.

They gathered near the wall, their bodies still in anticipation as the moveable stairs were pushed by a small tractor-like vehicle to the white, looming airplane. Movie star–looking people—men in sports jackets, women in owl-eyed sunglasses—effortlessly glided down the stairs and onto the runway. And then came Bubbe and Zeyde.

Bubbe was the size of kids a grade lower than Portia. She wore a pink skirt-suit with shiny square-heeled pink shoes. Her curled white hair had a glossy sheen that could be seen from the distance. She stopped on the stairs, smiled, and waved. Emery jumped up and down, waving his arms. Buzzy groaned and waved.

"There she is," he said. The only person who dreaded Bubbe and Zeyde's visits more than Louise was Buzzy. He claimed his parents were loony: his mother a meddler, his father a braggart.

With one hand on the handrail and her face directed down at her feet, Bubbe slowly stepped down the stairs one foot at a time, as if she were doing the wedding march. Zeyde was right behind her. He was the shape of a penguin and wearing his usual bow tie. (After retiring as an accountant for the post office, Zeyde had taken up sewing and painting. The only thing he sewed was bow ties. He claimed that his attention to detail was greater than anything one might find in a bow tie from Boscov's department store.) Zeyde's hair was black, slick. His nose looked like a crow's beak. His skin was darker than Buzzy's, as dark as Anna's.

"Cookalah!" Bubbe shouted as they crossed through the open arch into the courtyard. Bubbe grabbed Portia and gave her hollow smacking kisses on the cheeks and the forehead. Then she pulled her granddaughter's head down to her sloping bosom and rocked her back and forth. Zeyde was kissing Anna all over her head. He was taller than Anna, but not as tall as Buzzy and not much taller than Louise. When that was done, Portia was passed to Zeyde and Anna was passed to Bubbe, where the process started all over again. Buzzy, Louise, and Emery stood by waiting. Emery was open-mouthed smiling and bouncing on his toes—Portia knew he thought just as much love and affection was about to come his way.

"Look how these girls have grown!" Zeyde said, and he laughed in a sharp, whining rhythm that sounded like a boat engine working to turn over: AH heh heh heh heh, AH heh heh heh heh. It was a sound that belonged to Zeyde in the same way that the bubbly rumble belongs to a Harley-Davidson motorcycle.

At last Emery was kissed, with far less enthusiasm and barely a grasping hug. Portia hoped he'd think that Bubbe and Zeyde had run out of kissing energy because they were so old. She didn't want her brother to know that Bubbe and Zeyde had never taken to him. It was as if having Anna and Portia were enough and Emery was one child too many for their tastes.

On the drive home, Bubbe and Zeyde sat in the backseat with Anna between them and Portia on Zeyde's lap. Emery asked if he could sit on Bubbe's lap, but she said no, he'd wrinkle her skirt, and so Emery was tossed into the way-back, where he stuck his head over the edge of the seat and watched his sisters, like a dog.

Portia stood in Emery's room as Bubbe unpacked the two hard blue suitcases. She moved quickly, humming and smiling, like a little windup toy. Propped against the mirror on Emery's dresser were two paintings, done by Zeyde, that he had given Buzzy and Louise for Hanukah a few years earlier. One was a bald baby in a bath. When they had unveiled the painting, Zeyde put a fat brown finger on the canvas and said, "Can you believe I got the water to look exactly like water?!" When he opened the next painting, Louise gasped.

"Oh, I like that pirate!" Portia said, and her parents and grandparents laughed.

"That," Zeyde said, his finger pointing to the ceiling in a gesture of erudition, "is Moshe Dayan."

"Is he a pirate?" Portia asked, and her grandfather chugged with laughter.

"HE"—Zeyde paused to give weight to his words—"was a great leader of the Jewish people."

"A great leader of the Jewish people!" Bubbe had repeated.

They kept *Baby in the Bath* and *Moshe Dayan* behind Emery's dresser between Bubbe and Zeyde's visits. Anna was the one who always remembered to pull them out. She remembered *things* in general: where the tape measure was, how much gas cost, what day Bubbe and Zeyde were arriving. Portia, on the other hand, remembered details: what Bubbe and Zeyde were wearing when they stepped off the plane last year (she was in a peach dress with a matching cardigan, he wore a satin peach bow tie), what Louise said to the dinner guest she thought was an obnoxious flirt who was trying to seduce Buzzy (*You know, why don't you just leave? Why don't you just get the fuck out of my house?*), who Emery's favorite characters were on Sesame Street (Ernie and Bert).

"Cookalah, Cookalah," Bubbe said, and she grasped Portia's hand with her pointed, bony fingers and slipped a twenty-dollar bill in her palm.

"Thanks, Bubbe!" Portia shoved the bill down into her shorts pocket.

"Use it in good health," Bubbe said, and she smacked some kisses on Portia again. "Now, where's your sister?"

"I'll get her. Do you want Emery, too?"

"No, no, shhhhh . . ." Bubbe raised a crooked finger to her lips and looked around as if she were a spy on a mission. Knobby gold rings tilted on her hand, as if the rocks were too heavy to sit upright.

Portia brought her sister back to Bubbe the moment her grandmother was about to change into her housecoat. She had removed her bra and stood in the middle of the room with her giant, plummeting breasts sitting below her waist.

"Cookalah, Cookalah, shut the door!"

Anna and Portia stepped in and closed the door behind

themselves. Portia thought Bubbe wanted it shut for reasons of modesty, when, in fact, she later realized, her grandmother was no more modest than their mother, who never wore underwear (even when she was in a skirt) and didn't even own a swimsuit. Portia thought about her own breasts, which had just started to grow and had no fold; her mother's breasts, which had a fold but faced forward, staring the viewer in the eye; and then her grandmother's breasts, each like an orange sitting at the bottom of a net bag. She decided then that she would never go braless: she would bind her growths so tightly against her chest they would never stray, bounce, accordion-fold, or release.

Bubbe tucked a twenty into Anna's palm, then went to her suitcase for more goods.

"Do you want your housecoat?" Portia held out the pink shapeless shift that was hanging on a wire hanger on the closet doorknob.

"Yes, yes, but first I have presents for you girls!" Bubbe clapped her hands together and flashed her gold teeth at her granddaughters. Portia stared at her teeth as a way not to stare at her grandmother's hipline breasts. Her sister had completely turned her head and was facing the door as if waiting for someone to enter.

Bubbe lifted some shirts from Zeyde's suitcase then pulled out two white plastic grocery bags.

"One for you," Bubbe said, and she handed Anna a bag, forcing her to turn to accept a kiss on the cheek. "And one for you!" She handed Portia the other bag, kissed Portia on the cheek, and, at last, reached for the pink housecoat.

The two girls moved to the bed. They sat side by side, opened their bags, and peered in.

"Use them in good health! God bless!" Bubbe said, as she buttoned her housecoat. "And share!"

In Portia's bag were white pens, perhaps a hundred, with Bank of Trenton printed on the side. In Anna's bag were about fifty plastic rain caps that appeared to be little more than Saran Wrap with a string. They also had Bank of Trenton printed on them. Anna unfurled a rain cap and put it on. Portia thought she looked like she was wrapping her head for refrigerator storage.

"They fit in your purse, see?" Bubbe said. "I never walk out the door without one."

"That's cool," Anna said.

"Yeah, really cool," Portia said.

"Use them in good health!" Bubbe said, just as Emery burst into the room.

"Your grandmother's getting dressed!" Bubbe turned to Emery and, with a hand on each shoulder, pushed him out the door and shut it tightly behind him before reaching up and pushing in the last button on her housecoat.

"I don't have anything for him," she whispered. "He's a little boy! What can he do with a pen or a rain cap?!"

"Yeah, he likes getting wet in all our rain," Portia said. Anna nudged her fiercely with her knee. California had been in a drought for so long, rain was an event—like the Santa Ana winds or a big earthquake. The last time it had rained, all the neighborhood kids ran out into the street, heads tilted toward the sky, tongues out, screaming and jumping around. Everywhere Portia looked, people were adjusting their lives for the drought. The Fletchers, at the end of the cul-de-sac, dug up their grass and replaced it with gravel and fire hydrant–sized cacti. At Portia's friend Denise's house, she had to turn on the water in the shower, get wet, turn off the water, soap up and shampoo, and then turn the water back on and rinse. And Anna told her about a girl at school whose entire family showered together in order to save water. They also had a saying written in brown ink and taped to the inside of the downstairs toilet lid: *If it's brown, flush it down; if it's yellow, let it mellow.* In Portia's home, the marijuana plants were watered regularly, Anna took daily forty-minute showers, and there were no demands for when one could and could not flush the toilet. It was as if Buzzy and Louise were too preoccupied to notice the drought. In fact, the one time Portia heard her parents mention the drought was when she and Denise performed a rain dance they had choreographed one Saturday afternoon—leaping and clapping in synchronized fashion over a tin bucket they had decorated with grimy little feathers they had found in their yards and in Portia's family room (the latter thanks to Ace).

"Wait," Buzzy had said, after he and Louise gave slow, weak applause. "So is the rain dance to stop rain in flooding areas or to bring rain?"

"It's to end the drought, asshole," Louise had said, and she got up and walked into the house.

When they had shown Denise's family the dance, her parents and little sister stood from their lawn chairs and gave the girls a standing ovation. Then Denise's dad fetched his home movie camera, which was the size of a saxophone case, and asked Portia and Denise to perform the whole thing over again so he could get it on film.

Once Bubbe finished unpacking, she went into her purse to give her granddaughters even more gifts: silverware from the plane that had Pan Am engraved on the handle (she had wiped it clean with the cloth Pan Am napkin she had also taken from the plane), sugar packets that said Pan Am on them (she kept the pink Sweet 'n' Low packets for herself), and a folded soft copy of *LIFE* that had a subscription sticker on it addressed to Ralph Castle in Ridgewood, New Jersey.

"Who's Ralph Castle?" Portia asked Bubbe, while flipping through the magazine.

"Who's Ralph Castle?" Bubbe said.

"Yeah," Portia said. "Who's Ralph Castle?"

"I don't know Ralph Castle," Bubbe said. "Is he a friend of yours?"

Anna tapped Portia's shin with her toe.

"Thanks for this stuff, Bubbe," Anna said. "We love *LIFE* magazine."

"Your Aunt Rose," Bubbe said, "may she rest in peace, also loved that magazine!"

Once the presents were fully distributed, the girls followed Bubbe into the family room. Zeyde had already taken up his usual spot on the big green chair in front of the TV.

"Sweethearts, come here, come here!" Zeyde slapped both his knees with his palms.

Anna went to the couch and sat in the corner closest to Zeyde. Portia collapsed on his lap, and tucked her head under his neck. At twelve she was still a snuggler, somehow both aware and unaware that her body was no longer a potbelly-centered ball of flesh. She had slimmed out, flattened in the middle, widened at the hips, and had outgrown her training bra of sixth grade, yet she still moved through the world like a child.

Zeyde shifted Portia onto his left knee as he dug into his right front trouser pocket. He slipped a twenty-dollar bill into her hand and kissed her on the cheek.

"Use it in good health," he said, then he leaned over, shot a glance at Emery, who was sitting on a stool at the kitchen/family room counter, and, through a fake handshake, passed off a twenty to Anna. It was a gesture Portia later recognized in the *Godfather* movies, and even later, in *Goodfellas* and *The Sopranos*. Bubbe had set out a plate of Tastykakes and a glass of milk for each of the children. Tastykakes weren't sold in California, so she loaded her suitcase with them each year, doling out butterscotch to Anna, chocolate to Portia, and whatever there was an excess of to Emery.

Buzzy and Louise came in through the garage. They looked guilty, Buzzy with his black curly hair looking like broken springs, Louise with a dark fan of sweat under each arm of her magenta silk shirt. Portia guessed they had been wrangling the marijuana plants in Louise's studio, roping them upside down like bodies hanging from their ankles. That was how the marijuana plants had been stored all the previous years—it was one of the many reasons the kids weren't allowed to bring their friends near their mother's studio.

"Sarah," Bubbe said to Louise, "they love the Tastykakes! You want to try one?"

Bubbe was the only person Portia knew who called her mother Sarah. Sarah had been the name Louise had adopted when she converted from atheism to Judaism. There had been a three-year period of Shabbat dinners, Yiddish bandied about, and regular attendance of services at the Hillel temple while Buzzy was in law school and Anna was a baby. Buzzy often spoke of that time with a yearning. By the time they moved to Ann Arbor for Buzzy's first job and Portia's birth, Louise had abandoned "Sarah" but maintained the dinners and services, even sending Anna to Hebrew school. When Portia was five and Emery was born, the only remaining Jewishness in Louise was her frequent use of Yiddish, mostly to crack herself up and to baffle Anna, Portia, and Emery. Hers was an Orthodox conversion, however, indelible in the eyes of Jewish law, a one-way street, rendering her permanently Jewish whether she liked it or not and making her children indisputably Jews.

"It's Louise," Louise snapped, "L-O-U-I-S-E."

"Yes, yes." Bubbe was still smiling, clapping her hands together, pacing behind the three kids who were all at the counter now devouring Tastykakes. "Sarah, sweetheart, you want to try a butterscotch one?"

Louise ignored her and walked into the kitchen where she began pulling out food, knives, and a cutting board to prepare dinner. Anna, who normally cooked dinner, didn't know the laws of keeping kosher, so Louise was reinstated as the cook each year during Bubbe and Zeyde's three-week visit.

"Yetta," Louise said to Bubbe, "I put your fleishig dishes over here and your milchig dishes here—" Louise pointed to two sets of plates, bowls and silverware stacked up on the counter—one set for dairy foods and one for meats. Zeyde was willing to abandon his kosher diet when he ate outside of his home, but Bubbe stuck to it like a zealot, each year trapping the kids' friends in the kitchen and explaining to them what Kosher meant, and holding hostage the non-Jewish waitstaff of Santa Barbara when she placed her orders in restaurants, describing the reason for the tin foil she carried in her purse and handing it to them for use when cooking her food. Of course, she never divulged to them the reason for the plastic sandwich bags in her purse, which by the end of a restaurant meal were always filled with sugar packets, sweeteners, and salt and pepper shakers if Buzzy wasn't paying close enough attention.

"I'm making fish tonight and baked potatoes—"

"Half a potato for me, dear," Bubbe said, wandering into the kitchen and clapping her hands, "and you can use butter with fish—"

"I know," Louise said, "I know, I know." Louise was a good

student. Portia thought that there wasn't anything about being Jewish that her mother didn't seem to know.

Bubbe hovered over Louise and watched her cook, clapping her spindly, bejeweled hands as the tunes she hummed reached a rousing chorus. At one point she started singing *Beso Me Mucho*, and Zeyde leapt up from his chair in the family room, shuffled into the kitchen, and sang harmony with her, one arm around her miniscule shoulder, his long dark head pressed against her little white head as they held the last note, both mouths open— his a cavernous, sunken cave; hers a bed of gold jewels among ivory stones. Louise leaned against the counter and stared at them as she tapped out an unfiltered Camel, lit it, and exhaled slowly, releasing a cloud that settled over Bubbe and Zeyde.

While Louise prepared dinner under Bubbe's supervision, the kids gathered around Zeyde in the family room. He had a quarter in his hand that he was tugging out of their ears, finding in their pockets, pulling out from between Emery's near-black-with-dirt toes.

"Do the math for us!" Emery said, jumping around Zeyde's knees.

"Not yet . . . not yet." Zeyde brushed off his trouser leg where Emery's little hands had been.

"Can you do the math, Zeyde?" Portia asked, and he laughed and pulled her onto his knee.

"Okay, sock it to me!" Zeyde said.

"A hundred!" Emery shouted.

"To the third power," Anna added.

"That's a million!" Zeyde was nose forward to Anna, waiting for the next step.

"Divided by six," she said.

"Got it!"

"Times eleven point five," Anna's voice got higher the more complex the directions.

"Got it!"

"Divided by two . . ." Anna's voice slowed when she was ready for the answer.

"Nine hundred and fifty-eight!" Zeyde's finger pointed upward as he gave the answer. Portia and Anna cheered. Emery went to the middle of the family room, stood on his head, and fluttered his feet in applause.

When they challenged his answer, which was rare but had been known to happen, Zeyde told the kids to get their calculators. Anna and Portia each had a book-sized Texas Instrument calculator that they used in school, but by the time they brought them out to double-check, everyone had forgotten the sequence of the problem. Sometimes Anna would punch numbers in the calculator while she shouted instructions at Zeyde. He took a lot longer on those problems but, invariably, he got them right. The kids had seen his routines many times before—they were identical every year, each feat punctuated with his signature laugh at the end—but they loved them nonetheless. There was something about the ritualization of them, the fact that these acts seemed honed just for them, that made them happily soak up his shtick.

The house blissfully remained clean during Bubbe and Zeyde's visit, as Bubbe, who didn't like to go outside, spent most of the day wiping up after the family and doing laundry that she would sort and fold on the couch in front of the TV. She watched soap operas that everyone, including Zeyde, called *her shows*, as if she had actually produced or written them. Zeyde would watch with her, but unlike Bubbe he was willing to miss *her shows* to go to the beach or for a walk on State Street.

One morning, as Portia was eating a bowl of Grape-Nuts at the counter, Bubbe came downstairs carrying a laundry basket filled with the family's dirty clothes. Zeyde came out of the bathroom carrying a *Playboy* magazine that he waved in the air behind himself. Buzzy and Louise didn't have magazines like that in the house, although Denise's dad had stacks the height and width of a coffee table beside his orange chair in the living room. Zeyde settled on a stool beside Portia and slapped his magazine onto the counter, cover down. There was an aged scotch ad on the back with a woman who looked like she could have been in the magazine holding the bottle. Portia looked down at the ad, blushed, and turned away.

Louise walked into the kitchen wearing a red chenille bathrobe. She poured a cup of coffee and before even taking a sip pulled a cigarette out of her robe pocket and lit it.

"Want some coffee?" Louise asked Portia over the counter. Louise's eyes were always puffy in the morning, little fleshy life preservers that sat like glasses on her face.

"I don't drink coffee," Portia said.

Zeyde laughed. "In Europe," he said, lifting his pointer finger, "children often drink coffee!"

"I've been trying to get her to drink coffee," Louise said, "but she refuses."

"It's yucky," Portia said.

"Then how 'bout a cigarette?" Louise tilted her pack toward Portia and winked to let her know she was kidding.

"In Europe it's very fashionable to smoke cigarettes," Zeyde said. "But not at age eleven!"

"I'm twelve now," Portia said, and Louise grinned, popped a cigarette out of the pack, and tossed it across the counter, where it rolled into the side of the bowl of Grape-Nuts. Zeyde looked down at it but he didn't even smile.

Bubbe was at the couch sorting the colors from the whites. Emery came into the room wearing cotton pajamas with red dump trucks on them. His blond hair stood up in choppy little tufts. He went to the TV, turned on *Sesame Street*, and sat on the floor, cross-legged, his face only inches from the tiny black-and-white screen. Anna and Buzzy came into the kitchen. Buzzy didn't drink coffee but Anna did on occasion, so she poured herself a cup and stood beside Louise, cigarette smoke snaking across her face.

"Where are the Grape-Nuts?" Buzzy asked.

"Ask her." Louise pointed at Portia with the cup of coffee she was balancing in her cigarette hand.

"Here," Portia said, and she handed her father the small box.

"Harry!" Bubbe shouted to Zeyde from the couch. "Look!" Bubbe came to the counter where they were gathered: Portia, Zeyde, and Buzzy on the family room side of the counter; Louise and Anna on the kitchen side.

Bubbe was holding a pair of Portia's pink floral underpants, the crotch turned out and pulled taut.

"Look at this!" Bubbe said. She held the underpants under Zeyde's face and pointed at the white streak across the center of the crotch.

Portia hoped that she was really pointing at the weave of the cotton, the color of the flowers, the thick bands of pink elastic around the leg holes. If anyone asked whose underpants they were, she decided, she would tell them they were Denise's—left here the last time she had slept over.

Buzzy stopped pouring his Grape-Nuts and leaned his head over to see what Bubbe was fussing about. Anna darted her eyes between Portia and Bubbe, then landed her stare on Portia as if she had done something wrong.

Portia wanted Anna to stop looking at her, indicting her.

She turned toward her cereal, spooned in a mouthful, then swallowed barely chewed Grape-Nuts that scraped against her throat like fish-tank gravel. Zeyde slowly pulled his glasses out of his shirt pocket, put them on, and stared down at Portia's underpants.

"Those are Portia's underpants," Anna said sharply.

"So!" Portia's head was instantly clogged with a scorching fuzziness. She couldn't think clearly enough to deny the fact.

"She has discharge!" Bubbe said to Zeyde. "Portia's maturing now, God bless. She's in puberty!"

Louise laughed so hard she had to lean over the sink and spit out a mouthful of coffee. Portia felt as though she were a tiny, burning fire ant, hanging from the ceiling, watching her mother from afar.

"What?" Buzzy said. "You have to examine the laundry before you wash it?! You gonna show him the shit stains in Emery's underpants?!"

"Yetta!" Zeyde said, removing his glasses. "You don't need to look at her underpants to see that she's in puberty. Look at her breasts!"

Portia remained suspended on the ceiling. She could see her body sitting at the counter: motionless, blank-faced, skin flushed from an internal fire that beat away at the outward calm.

"Yes, yes!" Bubbe leaned in and grabbed Portia's cheeks with the underpants still clutched in one hand. She kissed Portia once, smack on the lips. "She's been blessed with breasts that, God willing, will grow bountiful like her grandmother's!"

Louise was still laughing over the sink. She stood up straight and poured herself another cup of coffee. Anna's mouth was a thin, stern line, a knife-cut across her face. She put down her cup, went to the laundry basket, and began digging. Portia assumed she was removing her own underwear in case there was something that might implicate her in the public puberty fiasco.

When Anna left the room, her underpants secured in her fists, Portia dropped back into her smoldering body and casually followed her sister out, as if she happened to have just finished breakfast and needed to go upstairs for a shower. Her pose fooled no one; she could hear her father scolding his mother as she headed up the stairs.

In her dream that night, Zeyde called Portia to snuggle with him on the chair in the family room. She went to him, as usual, and sat on his lap, her head tucked under his chin. Bubbe's shows were on and she was talking to the characters: "Don't listen to him, he's meshuggener!"

Portia looked down at her grandfather's lap and saw a crispy, blackened, coiled sausage whose starting point was somewhere in his pants. His fly was open. As soon as she realized that it was his penis and not a sausage, it began to uncoil, like a snake, undulating its way toward her.

Portia startled awake, horrified and nauseous.

The next morning when Zeyde called Portia to sit with him, she plopped herself down on the corner of the couch nearest his chair.

"I'm too old for a lap," Portia mumbled, but he didn't seem to hear and continued to pat his knees, beckoning her.

"ZEYDE! I'm too old to sit on laps!"

Her grandfather cocked his head to one side, like Ace, the bird. He reached into his breast pocket and pulled out his glasses.

"Sock it to me," he said, punching his fist in a gung-ho arc.

"Nine hundred divided by seven . . ." Portia started, but her mind was elsewhere—on the beach, with her friends—and she wasn't following the answers as he gave them.

The whole family filed into the station wagon to escort Bubbe and Zeyde back to the airport. Bubbe and Zeyde sat in the back seat with Anna in between them; Emery and Portia were loose in the way-back, tumbling into one another each time Buzzy took a turn too quickly. At the airport, Emery climbed the wall again and Anna and Portia limply waved their arms in the air as Bubbe and Zeyde ascended the steps to the sleek Pan Am jet. When they reached the top of the stairs, Zeyde put one arm around Bubbe, lifted his hat, and waved it. They looked sadly off-color in the blaring Santa Barbara sun, like a Polaroid picture that would eventually fade into a ghostly fog.

7

DAY FIVE

On the morning of Day Five the doctor comes to speak to the family. Everyone stands encircling Louise's bed as in a Christ scene from an Italian painting.

"She should never smoke again, right?" Anna asks. She is saying this only so her mother will hear the words from the doctor.

"No," the doctor says.

"No?" they all say, except Louise, who has her eyes shut and is wincing with nausea.

"I mean yes." Then, as if to explain the mix-up, the doctor says, "I was dyslexic as a kid. I sometimes get things backwards."

Anna envisions him opening up the wrong side of her mother's body to get to her heart, or sending a Roto-Rootering tube up the wrong artery and hitting her brain.

"Just a minute ago, a funny thing happened," the doctor says.

Louise begins to retch a little. Anna motions to Emery, who is standing closest to her head, and points at the kidney-shaped dish that is used as a vomiting receptacle.

"There was this ninety-year-old woman in, and she seemed malnourished—"

Emery doesn't seem to know where to put the dish, under Louise's chin or near her shoulder, so he waves it around a bit. Anna is about to snap at him to put it *near her mouth* (dumbass!)

but the retching stops, nothing has surfaced. Alejandro takes the dish from Emery and parks it near Louise's mouth. Anna is glad he has better sense about these things than her brother. How hard was it to figure out where to place a barf-dish?

"I took her to the nurse who was standing near the scale," the doctor says. "And I said, 'Nurse, this woman needs to get laid.'"

Everyone laughs, except Louise, who vaguely smiles.

"You meant she needed to get weighed?" Buzzy asks. He had a 4.0 grade average all the way through college and law school, yet often has trouble following the simplest ideas. When she spends too much time with her father, Anna begins to imagine his head as a coconut. She often wants to take that coconut and crack it against a rock.

"Yeah, she needed to get weighed," the doctor says.

"She probably needed to get laid, too," Portia says, and now her mother actually laughs.

Anna wants the doctor to leave so she can eat the twenty-four-pack of red licorice she has in her purse. She ran an extra forty-five minutes this morning just so she could eat the licorice. Anna realizes that if she simply pulled out a single strand of licorice and nibbled, it wouldn't look strange. But she doesn't want to nibble. She wants two ropes in her mouth at once, she wants to fill herself with sugar, and food coloring, and the taste of *red*. Her family is accustomed to her eating habits, but she knows that, beyond her family, a thirtysomething woman's shoving double sticks of neon licorice in her mouth and eating straight through the box in about fifteen minutes would be seen as odd.

But the doctor won't leave. Buzzy is asking questions as if there's going to be an exam at the end of the day. He wants to know the names of the different medications Louise is on, the exact dosing, the possible side effects, how long she'll be on them. Anna is feeling the coconut-crashing urge. She is growing furious at the pace of this conversation. If the doctor doesn't leave shortly, she herself will leave—she'll sit in the grubby little carpeted waiting room, hold a *Time* magazine up as if reading, and get to it with the licorice.

By the time the doctor walks out, the nurse reenters. Anna doesn't care if the nurse thinks she's loony. She rips open the box and starts eating.

Portia is sitting on a chair with *People* magazine, her feet tucked under her rump. Her eyes tick across the page in a way that lets Anna know she's only reading the captions beneath the pictures. She hopes Portia is engaged enough not to notice the licorice. Anna wants the entire box for herself.

Portia looks up, puts her hand out for a piece. Anna reluctantly lays it across her palm.

"What's for dinner tonight?" Anna asks.

"Baked ziti," Portia says, and looks back to the magazine. Portia always serves ziti when she's with the family—a simpleton concoction made by cooking pasta al dente, throwing it in a pan with a jar of red sauce and piles of cheese, then sticking it in the oven for forty minutes or so. Everyone complains about Portia's meals. But Buzzy doesn't cook, and for Anna this time away from her family is a vacation from cooking. When they're home in New York, Emery and Alejandro only eat in restaurants. Anna doubts either one even knows how to make tea.

In spite of their griping, everyone eats Portia's meals as if they are ravenous, as if they have never tasted anything better. They are like that when they eat in the hospital, too.

A social worker pauses at Louise's room during a moment when the nurse has stepped away. Buzzy, Anna, Portia, and Emery are surrounding Louise's lunch tray, which has been pushed as far from her bed as it can go. They are busy eating Louise's grilled chicken, steamed vegetables, dinner roll with I Can't Believe It's Not Butter, and Jell-O cup. Alejandro sits on a chair accepting the morsels Emery hands him.

Anna looks up and says hi to the social worker, then gets back to eating before everyone else finishes the tray. Louise's heart alarm is dinging. It has been dinging off and on all day and they have grown immune to it: Louise sets it off every time she bends an arm or leg, kinking the small hose that has been connected to her heart.

"What seems to be the problem here?" the social worker says. She is thick, long-headed, and tall: a human rectangle.

"She's constantly setting that thing off," Anna says. "It would take handcuffs or a rope to keep her still." She has a bite of roll in her mouth and the remainder of roll in her hand which she waves as she speaks. There is no way she'll put down the roll because Portia will grab it. Her sister's always been a pig when it comes to breads.

"Oh, I see," the social worker chirps, "you've got to put your arm down." She tucks Louise's arm into her side and remains there, next to Louise, who seems only half-conscious, as the family continues on with the meal.

"Well, then," the social worker says, "I guess I'll check back later."

"Oh," Buzzy says. "Did you want to talk to us?" A booger of red Jell-O quivers at the corner of his mouth.

"I really wanted to talk to your wife," she says, "talk about how she feels now, see if there's anything she needs."

Louise shuts her eyes and either instantly falls asleep or feigns sleep. If Anna were betting, she'd put money on the fake sleep.

"I'll come back later," the social worker says, and she quietly squirms out of the room as if she were leaving a viewing in a funeral home.

Moments later, the nurse returns and tells the family that the social worker did not approve of their behavior.

"She thought you were an uncaring family," the nurse reports.

Louise opens her eyes, suddenly awake, and laughs in a big, open-mouthed way. It is the most vociferous she has been all day.

Buzzy is insulted. "I don't understand," he says. "What are we doing wrong? What do other people do?"

"Most people sit quietly in the room," the nurse says. "I told her you weren't like most people."

"She probably didn't like us because you talk too fast," Portia says to Anna. The teachers in elementary school wanted Anna to go to speech therapy because she talked too fast. She never went, of course, as Louise and Buzzy only snickered at the suggestion. She still speaks quickly and has an acute intolerance for slow talkers.

"Maybe she's upset that we were eating Mom's lunch," Emery says.

"Well, she's not eating!" Buzzy says. "Why shouldn't we eat it?"

The nurse finishes writing on Louise's chart, smiles pointedly at the family, and leaves. Anna wonders if the nurse hates them, then she decides *fuck it*, who cares if the nurse hates them. They don't need her love. They have each other.

"Listen," Louise says. "The next time the social worker comes, shut up and sit down . . . but Buzzy, you've gotta come over here and stroke my head or something."

"I'll stand on the other side of you and stroke your forearm," Anna says, and she gets into position.

"Maybe I should pray," Portia says.

"Yeah!" Louise laughs so hard that she snorts. "And tell the social worker that I don't need to talk to her because our family pastor—"

The word itself, *pastor*, is so foreign to them—like block parties and Christmas caroling and other civic-minded activities that they as a family have never known—that everyone breaks down laughing.

"Tell her the pastor," Louise continues, "is on his way here to see me!"

They are almost in tears at the idea of Louise being visited by a pastor. Buzzy is hooting. Alejandro claps his hands. Portia leans into Emery as if she's going to fall down from laughter.

"He needs a name," Anna says. "You have to give him a name."

"Ken," Portia says.

"Yeah," Louise says, and her voice weakens as she runs out of energy. "Pastor Ken. Our family pastor."

8

1976

Buzzy and Emery were both wearing blazers—Buzzy's was navy blue and Emery's was sky blue—because, as Buzzy told Emery, one should never board an airplane without looking respectable. The family was standing outside the white rental car at the Burlington, Vermont, airport. It was four in the afternoon, almost ninety degrees, and they were going to drive to Fulton Ranch to visit Billie and Otto.

"Take your blazer off and fold it over the seat like this," Buzzy said, and he draped his blazer over the velvety console behind the back seat. Emery leaned into the open car door, did as he was told, then paused and stared at the two blazers, big and small. He liked getting dressed up. He enjoyed feeling like he was a grown up, maybe even important. Anna was standing outside the car waiting for Emery to sit down. He would be in the middle, as he always was; Portia and Anna both refused to sit in the middle seat.

"Get in!" Anna said, and she pushed Emery lightly on the shoulder.

"How long will it take to get there?" Emery asked. Buzzy was adjusting his seat, fixing the mirrors, looking for the blinker and lights.

"Not long." Louise began rummaging through her shoulder sack; she was probably looking for cigarettes. She, and about a hundred other people, had made full use of the smoking section on the Pam Am flight. Anna, Portia, and Emery were the only children in the smoking section and, other than Buzzy, the only people who weren't smoking. Emery's lungs felt like they'd been roughed up with a nail file and his throat felt like it was wrapped in sandpaper.

"How long's not long?" Portia asked.

"As long as a piece of string." Louise lit her cigarette from the car lighter, then rolled down her window as Buzzy pulled out of the rental car lot.

Emery looked out the window and wished the people in his family could give a straight answer every now and then. He decided to try a new angle. "How many miles away is it?" he asked.

"Around seventy," Buzzy said.

"Back roads or freeway?"

"Half and half."

Emery guessed they'd be there in ninety minutes. He couldn't wait to see if he had figured correctly.

About an hour into the ride Louise asked Buzzy to pull over so she could pee. Emery looked at his watch so he could deduct the minutes from his estimated travel time.

"Go far off into the bushes, Mom," Anna said. "Make sure no one can see you."

Emery was certain that no one peed as often as his mother. Louise had peed at the airport in Los Angeles before they took off, peed on the plane, peed at the airport in Burlington. And now, only an hour away from the last toilet, she had to pee again. Emery thought maybe his mother's bladder was damaged from having had kids. Or venereal disease. A few years ago, when Portia fell asleep reading to him, Emery corralled Anna into telling him a story until he fell asleep. Anna had refused to read Portia's book, but stood next to Emery's bed and told him the story of syphilis: its symptoms, how it spreads, and the very real possibility that their parents would eventually die from it. The supposed pending death didn't worry Emery; other than his parents' outlaw behavior, he had never noticed insanity in either one of them, and insanity, according to Anna, was the final stage of the disease.

"Don't worry," Louise said, "no one will know I'm peeing."

Louise stepped out of the car, her burning cigarette in hand. She stood no more than arm's distance from Portia's open window, lifted her gauzy skirt to her knees, and, with her legs stepped out into second position, she simply peed. It suddenly occurred to Emery that this might be the reason his mother often wore skirts and dresses.

Buzzy laughed and clapped his hands. Anna lifted her hand over her eyes as if she were shielding them from the sun, turned, and looked away out her window. Portia laughed along with her dad as she leaned out the window and watched. Emery crawled over his sister's lap and looked out the window, too. The stream of urine trailed toward the car, then separated into two streams as it hit the front tire.

"Mom!" he yelled. "That's probably against the law!" Emery had three chronic fears: 1. The law and what it would do to his family if they were caught for any of their numerous infractions. 2. His sisters' moving out, running away, marrying early, or otherwise leaving him alone to fend for himself (wake himself up in the morning, pack his own lunch, etc.). 3. Not being the best and smartest kid in school. His father was convinced he was a genius and so far he seemed to be able to perform to the level expected of him. But what if he really weren't that smart? What if his school happened to be the easy school, and what if they moved and he was suddenly in the smart school and what if, then, everyone found out that he was only average?

"Don't worry, Noble Citizen!" Louise said, laughing. "We're in Vermont! There's only one cop in the state and he's your second cousin Randy, so we'll be fine."

Louise wiggled her hips a little, as if she were trying to drip-dry, then let her skirt drop. She lifted her cigarette to her mouth and got back in the car.

"How do you know my second cousin Randy won't arrest you?" Emery asked. Surely Randy had taken some kind of oath that would require him to stop any lawbreaker even if she were his cousin.

"Because I know everything."

Anna rolled her eyes.

"If you know everything, then tell me what's going to happen in the future," Portia said. Emery thought that was a pretty good question.

"For one," Louise turned in her seat to look at Portia, "your brother will outgrow this fucking pain-in-the-ass upstanding citizen phase he's in!"

"Don't say the F-word and don't say A-S-S!" Emery knew you couldn't be arrested for swearing. But swearing seemed like a Slip 'n Slide to him. One step on that slick platform and you couldn't stop yourself from swooshing to the bone-breaking end.

"Ass!" Portia and Anna both said, then Anna leaned across Emery and tapped Portia's knee to jinx her.

"Mom!" Emery said. He knew there was no one in the family who would help him bring the swearing under control, but sometimes his mother would take pity on him and spoil him in a way that she never spoiled the girls. Like when she'd make him cocoa and toast for a snack (his favorite), even though she wouldn't pour a glass of water for his sisters or Buzzy.

"They're just words, Emery! Besides, sometimes you have

to say *ass* and *fuck* to get your point across. Sometimes people won't listen to you unless you use those words," Louise said.

"Fuck yeah," Anna said.

"Listen to your fucking mother!" Buzzy said, in the screechy voice he used only when he was teasing the kids.

Anna, Louise, and Portia laughed and hooted. Emery crossed his arms and dropped his head, pretending not to look at them. There was no chance of winning against the force of all four.

"Oh, read your book!" Louise pulled *James and the Giant Peach* out of her sack-purse and tossed it over the back seat toward Emery. Then she stubbed her cigarette out in the ashtray, reached for the radio dial, and cranked up the volume.

The last time the family had seen Louise's parents was five years earlier, when Emery was four and Buzzy and Louise had taken the kids on a tour of the East Coast from Maine to Rhode Island. When Emery had asked his mother why Billie and Otto never came to California, Louise said, "Otto thinks there are too many weirdos and freaks in California and Billie does what Otto wants just to make him happy." Emery thought that one day he'd like a wife who did what he wanted just to make him happy.

The rental car turned onto the long drive that led to the house. Emery closed his book and read the double-posted sign aloud: "*Fulton Ranch. Private Property. Trespassers will be shot.*" Emery gasped. He didn't remember the sign from the last visit. Were they trespassing, he wondered? Or was it not trespassing when you were related to the person who posted the sign?

"Do they know we're coming?" Emery asked. "Otto won't shoot us, will he?"

Louise lit up another cigarette. "Not if you stay out of his way."

No one spoke during the ten minutes it took to drive from the trespassing sign to the shingled house overlooking the lake. Buzzy pulled the plain, dull car up behind Otto's convertible sports car. When he cranked up the emergency brake Emery checked his watch. He was thrilled that he'd correctly guessed how long it would take to get there, but knew better than to announce this feat for fear of being teased about his wonkish attraction to schedules, timing, promptness.

"Porsche," Buzzy said, aloud.

"What?" Portia said.

"No, the car," Buzzy said. "Otto's got a Porsche."

"He's always had a Porsche," Louise said, opening the door. "You know that."

"Not when you were a baby. *That* convertible couldn't have been a Porsche, they weren't making them then."

"Tell that story again!" Portia said.

"Yeah, tell it again!" Emery said, although his mother had never told it to him. Portia had told him one night, lying cozy in his bed, her voice slurring as she tried not to drift off to sleep.

"You guys are so rude!" Anna said. "How could you even bring that up right before we visit Otto and Billie?"

Louise appeared not to hear. She pushed her glowing cigarette into the ashtray, then stepped out of the car.

"Mom doesn't have to tell it!" Emery said. "Portia will tell it!"

He was referring to the story of Louise's infancy. When Louise was three months old, Otto and Billie drove thirty minutes out of town for a drink at a tavern owned by Otto's cousin. Otto didn't want his mother to watch baby Louise; he thought she spoiled her by holding her continually and coddling her when she cried. So, they tucked the baby into a basket that was placed on the opera seat of Otto's convertible.

The top was down, as usual, even though it was early spring and only about forty degrees outside. Louise's parents went into the tavern, leaving baby Louise asleep in her basket, bundled like a worm in a cocoon. After many drinks, Otto and Billie seemed to forget that they had a baby, but they did remember that they were fairly far from home. They checked into one of the rooms upstairs, had what Otto called a *rollicking good time*, and passed out. In the morning, Billie woke up, looked out at the snow falling like miniature fairies outside the window, and suddenly remembered her child. She ran, barefooted and without a coat, to the car where she found Louise purple and frosted, like a sugarcoated plum.

Otto came out, dressed and carrying his wife's extra clothes, which Billie put on in the car while they raced to the hospital. Of course Otto didn't tell the hospital that they'd simply forgotten about the child—he claimed she'd been left by an open, screenless window where the snow blew in.

It was assumed that Louise would die from her night in the snow, making her a perfect test case for penicillin (*It's hard to further harm the imminently fading,* one nurse had said). Penicillin was then a new drug that the government was stockpiling in case Americans were sent to the war overseas. The doctor claimed that Louise was one of the first humans, and *the* first infant, to receive it. At the time, her survival seemed like a true miracle.

At the story's end, Portia had said to Emery: *Otto always said that the lesson he learned from that calamity was always to go drinking closer to home.* Emery loved when his sister said the word *calamity*. It reminded him of Western movies, shoot-'em-ups, order instilled through chaos. And, as usual, Portia had allowed for questions after the story. This was Emery's favorite part of Portia's stories because his sister would answer anything, no matter what, even if it were impossible for her to actually know the answer. When he asked Portia what their mother's frozen skin felt like, she said, "Like a hot dog straight from the freezer." And when he asked her what it felt like to be frozen, she said, "It feels like you're moving in slow motion and the air is made of clay." And when he asked if Otto and Billy were mean old people, Portia said, "They weren't old then, they were forgetful."

Louise forbade the kids ever to speak of the event with Billie and Otto. But Portia, Buzzy, Emery, and even Anna, at times, liked to bring it up to Louise—it was like a handicap she had overcome, something they could joke about simply because she'd survived.

Buzzy followed Louise out of the car. The three kids slid out of the back seat. They stood there, all five faces turned toward the solid, looming house. Emery checked for movement behind the windows, three stories up, but everything looked dark and still, as if there weren't a single light on. It was dry and calm out—the lake as flat as a sheet of slate. The empty dock stuck straight into the water, an exclamation point without its dot. A giant gray bird appeared to plummet from the sky, then landed gracefully on the end of the dock.

"Where are they?" Emery asked. He couldn't even remember what they looked like. The one picture in the house of Billie and Otto had been taken during World War Two. In it, Otto was wearing a cloth soldier's hat not unlike the paper hats people wear in fast-food restaurants. He looked bulky and tough, which Emery knew to be true. Otto had been hit by lightening three times and, obviously, survived each strike.

"They probably forgot we were coming," Louise said.

Buzzy laughed. "They tend to forget about your mother."

"Don't they want to see their grandchildren?" Emery asked.

Because he was so adored and beloved by Portia, his parents, and even Anna at times, Emery expected all relatives to adore him. Even the ones who had accidentally left their baby in the snow.

Everyone looked down at Emery. Louise messed his hair with her hand and pulled him up against her hip.

Portia leaned over and whispered in her brother's ear, "Otto believes that only the firstborn kid should be given any attention. Everyone else is a spare in case the first one dies."

"A spare?" Emery was astounded that children could be thought of in the same way as tires. But he saw that it had worked out well for his grandparents, as his mother's older brother, Rex, had been killed in the Vietnam War before Emery ever had a chance to meet him. It was funny to think of his mother as a spare.

"That's why Anna's the only one to get birthday cards—'cause she's the firstborn."

"They send birthday cards?" Instead of explaining, Portia took Emery's slick, sweaty hand and pulled him to the front door behind Anna, who was leading the family. Louise came up beside them and took his other hand.

"I'm the firstborn son," Emery said, and he tugged his mother's hand. "Does that count?"

"In China," Louise said, and she laughed. Emery couldn't believe this; it seemed impossible to him that anyone would favor a firstborn. Maybe his parents would tell his grandparents that even though he was only in fourth grade, he had to go to the advanced sixth grade reading and math classes. Or maybe they'd tell them about the Corny Kids Variety Show that he and his best friend Josh had written and starred in. The principal at school was so impressed, he had Josh and Emery tour the school, giving performances to each grade. Emery was a celebrity at Fairview Elementary.

Anna knocked on the door, then Louise scooted in front her and opened it. "Billie? Otto?" she called. There was no answer.

Louise walked in and the family followed behind. The stone-floored foyer had bookshelves from the baseboard to the ceiling on two full walls.

"Your grandfather's a great reader," Louise said. Emery didn't doubt this. He thought everyone in their family was a great reader.

"OTTO!" Buzzy shouted, his hands cupped around his mouth.

"Let's go in the kitchen," Louise said.

They shuffled into the kitchen, which looked out over the lake. There wasn't a dish in the sink, or on the counter, or anything, really, on any flat surface.

"I wish our kitchen were like this," Anna said.

"But there's no food around." Emery thought it was like the mausoleum the family had once visited in LA. Were there dead bodies behind the closed cupboard doors?

"If you put down your keys on the counter," Anna said, "they'd be right there. On the counter. You'd see them."

She had a point, although Emery sort of liked the Hidden Object feel of their own kitchen counter. Often when Louise was looking for something, Emery would race Portia to see who could be the first to find the missing thing in the piles and piles of stuff that littered every flat surface in the house. It was like finding the emerald among the heaps of jewels spilling out of a treasure chest.

"Look!" Emery pointed out the window. A rowboat was pulling up to the dock. Otto was rowing. Billie jumped out and tied up the boat. She was lean, short-haired, and moved like a girl and not an old woman. There were two large speckled dogs in the boat. Otto gave each dog a push on its backside to scoot it out and then hopped out himself. Even as an old man he was broad, muscled, and flat-stomached. He wore khaki pants rolled at the cuff, a white T-shirt, and boat shoes. Billie had on similar khaki pants and a short-sleeved blouse.

They walked the short dirt path up to the house, pausing when they noticed the rental car in the driveway.

"They're here!" Emery said and he jumped up into Portia's arms. "Let's go outside and see them!" He had a plan. When Billie and Otto walked into the house, Emery would break out into the Corny Kids opening theme song. Surely they couldn't resist him then! Emery practiced the song in his head: *We're the Corny Kids! I'm John-John* (that was Emery), *I'm Miller* (that was Josh). . . .

"Wait here," Louise said. His mother sounded angry. Emery wondered if he was squirming too much.

"Louise?" Otto's voice shouted, seconds later, and then he and Billie were there, standing in the kitchen staring at the family.

"Heeeey," Buzzy said. Emery noticed that his father's voice was suddenly huskier.

Buzzy walked toward Billie and gave her a hug and a kiss on the cheek. Billie patted Buzzy's back stiffly with both hands and quickly pulled away from the hug. Emery jumped from Portia's arms, ran to Billie, and gave her a hug.

"Emery," Billie said, firmly, as if reminding herself who he was. Emery had never felt a woman who was so hard. Even Anna, as skinny as she was, felt cushier than his grandmother. There was something about her hug that made Emery think of the lice-check the school nurse had done a couple months earlier.

When Emery approached Otto with both arms extended, Otto said, "Boys don't hug other boys, sissy. Give me your hand." Emery dropped one hand and stared up at Otto. He couldn't believe that a grandfather would call his own grand-son a sissy. Wasn't there a law against things like that? Emery watched as his fingers were fisted up and down a few times, forcefully, in a way that reminded him of Annie Sullivan pumping water onto an astounded Helen Keller. The idea of breaking out in the Corny Kids theme song fell through Emery's stomach like a sinking stone.

"So," Otto turned to Anna, "you graduated from high school, I hear."

"Uh huh," Anna said. "Did you get the invitation to the grad-uation ceremony?"

"Oh yeah, we got it," Billie said, and she turned to the sink, turned on the tap, and poured herself a glass of water. "We got you a present."

"Thank you!" Anna said. She had wanted presents for gradu-ation. She had wanted someone to come to the ceremony. It was all she talked about in the days leading up to the event. The night before the ceremony, Emery had awoken when he heard crying. He wandered into the family room and found his sister sitting on the floor, sobbing at their mother's feet. Anna turned to Emery and told him that Buzzy and Louise refused to go to her graduation and that she would be humiliated by being the only kid there without her parents. Emery offered to go, but Anna didn't want him there. Emery didn't count in these things, and neither did Portia—Anna claimed they both were an em-barrassment. In the end, Buzzy went, dragging Emery along. Louise showed up about thirty minutes late, waved at Anna on stage so that she'd see that she was there, then snuck out again ten minutes later.

"You won't ask me to go to yours, will you?" Louise had asked Portia and Emery, later that day.

"We won't ask," Portia had promised. Then she put her arm

around Emery and whispered in his ear, "Don't worry. I'll go to yours."

"What about you?" Otto nudged Portia's cheek with his fist. "You still in Dummy School?"

Emery looked up at his sister curiously. Why, he wondered, was he always the last to find out the happenings in the family? Portia in Dummy School? No one had told him about this!

"I'm not in Dummy School," Portia said, and she looked down at Emery, who felt a great surge of relief.

"Yeah you are. Dumb girl like you. You're in Dummy School!" Otto laughed in quick, deep barks. Emery looked at Portia to see if she was hurt by this mean joke. She seemed unbothered, but still, Emery thought it was cruel to tease Portia about being dumb. He hoped Otto wouldn't quiz his sister about politics, as even Emery was recently surprised to find that Portia didn't know the names of the heads of state of any country other than the United States. Not even Canada!

"Let's go get your present," Billie said to Anna, and they left the room together.

"So, are you in second or third grade?" Otto asked Portia. Emery couldn't believe he was carrying on like this. He was as bad as Ron Stinson at school who tormented wormy Doug-Doug Finney so ceaselessly that Emery felt it was his duty as a living, breathing fellow human to visit the principal, Mr. Devereaux, and inform him of Ron Stinson's word-torture.

"I just finished ninth grade," Portia said.

"Nah!" Otto laughed. "I don't believe it. Dumb girl like you. You're in fourth grade in Dummy School!" Emery wasn't worried that Otto would pick on him in the way that he was picking on Portia—his sister often did things that could be seen as dumb. In fact, he couldn't wait for his grandfather to ask about him—there was so much to tell. He could start with academics, move on to soccer, then end with Corny Kids. Maybe Otto would want to see a performance with Emery doing both his and Josh's parts.

"How are the dogs?" Louise asked.

"Bentley, that big motherfucker, knocked up Belle and we had nine goddamned pups here last week."

"Can I see the puppies?" Portia asked.

"Yeah, if you jump in the lake about three hundred yards out. I stuck them in a burlap bag with a bunch of rocks, rowed out and let them drop."

Emery pushed in toward's Portia's leg to steady himself. He felt a little queasy.

"Oy!" Buzzy groaned.

"And if that's not bad enough, the cat, who just lies on the porch like a fucking socialite in Palm Beach, had six kittens last week."

"Are they in the lake?" Buzzy asked. He had his sturdy voice on again.

"Nah. I just let them run free. There've gotta be enough goddamned field mice out there to feed an army of cats." Otto looked out the window. Emery followed his gaze to see if he could find any little kittens running around with mice hanging out of their mouths.

"Look!" Anna said, running into the kitchen. She extended her right hand to show off a glamorous diamond ring that looked odd on her short-nailed, boyish hand.

"Two fucking karats," Otto said. "It was my mother's."

"That's nice." Louise didn't seem impressed as she leaned over the ring.

"Lemme see it." Emery put his hands up toward Anna.

"Don't touch!" she said, batting him away. "Your hands are gross."

"Look at those little hands!" Otto said, staring down at Emery. "He's got sissy hands!"

Emery looked at his own hands. His fingers were squared at the tips, sort of large for his frame, flopping on the end of his arms like a puppy's paws. They didn't appear to be sissy hands to him, and he was fairly certain his sisters would agree.

"What are you going to do with a two-karat diamond ring?" Buzzy asked. He, too, seemed unimpressed.

"She can save it for her wedding," Billie said. "When Mama gave it to Otto, she told him to give it to his firstborn daughter for her wedding."

"So why didn't you give it to Louise?" Buzzy asked.

"Louise!" Otto said. "She's already got a wedding ring! The one you gave her! You want her to have two?!" Otto laughed, went to the cupboard, and got down a low, thick-bottomed glass. "Who wants scotch?"

At breakfast the next morning Louise announced that she had gifts for her parents.

"What is it?" Otto asked. "A seashell we can put to our ears to hear the California ocean?" He laughed and gave Emery a little punch in the shoulder. Emery took the punch the same way Portia took being called a dummy. He now understood that you had to steel yourself against Otto like a cement wall, hold yourself up against his constant butting.

They were at the oak, claw-footed kitchen table. Diagonally cut toast sat on one plate, a softened stick of butter sat on another. Louise had made scrambled eggs that lay wet and shiny in an orange plastic bowl. There were only six chairs at the table so Emery shared a chair with Portia, each of them on half the seat. Billie drank Sanka that she spooned out of a glass container into a thin, brown coffee cup. Otto, Louise, and Anna drank coffee.

"She brought you some of her etchings," Buzzy said, and he spooned more eggs onto his plate.

"Etchings?" Otto said. "Etchings? Hippies do etchings! You a hippie now, Louise?"

"Yeah, yeah." Louise stood from the table and adjusted the waist of her batik skirt. "I'm a hippie."

Louise asked Anna and Portia to clear the table while she showed Billie and Otto the etchings she had brought for them. Emery's sisters did as they were told, silently moving the dishes from the table to the sink while Louise untied the black portfolio she used to carry her work. Inside were three etchings, each precisely matted by Louise. Emery had been allowed in her studio that day. He had stood at the edge of her worktable watching as Louise, with a cigarette burning in her mouth, penciled out the interior cut using a long silver right angle. The exterior cut was done on a paper cutter. Louise worked so quickly that Emery imagined her snipping a fingertip off. It would tumble into the wire trash can that sat waiting below the edge of the paper cutter.

"This one was in a show." Louise pulled out a magazine-sized etching with a moss green matte board. It was a picture of a fat naked woman whose entire being, cheeks, chin, breasts, and belly, drooped toward the ground where a sheet lay puddled at her feet.

"Oh my." Billie pursed her lips and handed the etching to Otto.

"Who is this woman?!" Otto shouted like he was angry, although he was smiling.

"She was a model," Louise said. Louise had been attending night classes at City College where they had live models she could draw.

"Why'd you use such an ugly model? Couldn't you get a pretty girl or at least a sexy girl to model for you?!" Emery had to admit, it might be a nicer picture if the model were a prettier girl. Or a boy even.

"It's not about being pretty." Louise took the etching from her father, lay it on the spot on the table where Anna had cleared Buzzy's plate, and pulled out another one.

"Ach, Louise!" Otto looked at the etching of a naked, bony woman standing on a stage. Her giant, arched big toe hung off the edge of the stage where a man in a baseball cap had his mouth open, poised to bite it.

Billie shook her head, stood up and cleared the coffee pot and the trivet it had sat on.

"Wait, there's one more." Louise pulled out the third one, then turned and watched her mother return from the sink. "There's one more." She was almost whispering.

"This one's my favorite," Buzzy said. "It won an award!"

"No, this isn't the one that won the award," Louise said, and she handed the etching to her mother.

"Yes it is!" Buzzy stood halfway from his chair and peered down at the etching in Louise's hand. Emery stood and worked his way in front of his father so he could see. It was a picture of a dying, naked man, floating down a river with fish biting chunks out of his flesh.

"No it's not," Louise said firmly, glaring at Buzzy.

"Well, it's still my favorite!" Buzzy said.

Billie said nothing and handed the etching to Otto.

"Jesus Christ, Louise!" Otto said. "What the hell is wrong with you?! Why would you make such ugly depressing shit?! Why don't you paint flowers or something beautiful! Or if you're going to do naked people, do a pretty girl, for God sakes! Who needs to look at this shit?! This is nothing but shit!"

Emery felt his mouth drop open. He was afraid to blink. Anna and Portia were poised beside the table. Buzzy dropped his head in his hands, then lifted his head for a second as if to say something, but said nothing and let it drop again.

"It's art," Louise said, firmly. She pulled her cigarettes and matches from her skirt pocket. When Louise held the lit match to the cigarette in her mouth, the flame quivered like a strobe light. Emery watched it, thought about strobe lights, thought about his mom, and decided that now was not the time to ask if he could have a strobe light in his room.

A passel of relatives showed up at the ranch on the final night of the family's visit. Many of the men were similarly named, as if there were only four names in the world and each one had to make the name his own: Jimmy-Scott, Jimmy, Jim-Jim, James-Ray, Ray-Boy, Ray, and James. There were women who had names that Emery guessed were nicknames, none of them seeming to reference any given name: Sis, Lennie, Flossy, and Skipper. Anna claimed she remembered everyone. Portia remembered all the odd-named relatives from the last visit. Emery's most acute memory was of the one aunt who was so fat Emery imagined her flesh layered like the wooden, colored stacking rings he'd had as an even smaller kid. Most of the relatives poked at or hugged the kids with genuine, enthusiastic affection of the sort Emery had expected from his grandparents.

On the basement floor of the house was a bar with two sets of double glass doors that opened up to a patio and a steep uphill of grass. This wasn't a bar like neighbors and friends often had in the rumpus rooms of their California houses: a small stainless steel sink with a mini fridge tucked beside it; two or three barstools facing the mirror above the sink. This was a bar like the ones on TV where the sheriff hangs out with townspeople.

Wood shavings were scattered across the flagstone floor. Neon beer signs hung over the glossed, wooden bar that ran long enough to hold ten stools. Three different beers poured from a tap, and there was a full glass-shelved wall of what looked like a hundred different liquors. The cash register sat at the end of the bar—Otto punched in random keys and let the drawer shoot out making a noise that sounded like coins hitting bells. Six high tables were arranged in two rows across the room. In the center of every table was a bowl of peanuts and a thick two-sided menu that listed drinks on one side and food on the other. There were no prices on the menu, but the bar's name was written in bold black letters across the top: A Clean, Well-Lighted Place. There was even a neon Open and Closed sign in the window with a small off/on switch by each word.

Louise laughed uproariously with all her cousins and aunts and uncles. It was clear that even though Billie and Otto hadn't had much use for their spare child, the rest of the family adored her. Buzzy nursed a beer and wandered from group to group. He gave people healthy back slaps and seemed to puff up a bit, like a pigeon, as he listened to stories of rifles backfiring, a golf ball nailing a bird and knocking it dead and, then, The Stinkies.

A Stinky was what all the married, male relatives in Vermont called their girlfriends. Of course, everyone at the party insisted that they were content with their wives and they themselves didn't have Stinkies. The Stinkies who were mentioned were always those of whoever was missing from the party. Portia and Anna remembered hearing about Stinkies five years earlier. Portia leaned into Emery's ear and explained that the last time they were here everyone was talking about Jimmy-Don's Stinky, as Jimmy-Don and his wife Vicky had been vacationing in South Carolina at the time. Jimmy-Don's Stinky was mad,

Otto had told the crowd, because Jimmy-Don didn't take her to South Carolina instead of his wife. And now, here was Jimmy-Don, regaling the crowd with a story of absentee Uncle Linus's Stinky. Anna and Portia moved in closer to hear. Jimmy-Don was on a stool at a table and the crowd was two-deep in a circle around him.

"This girl must be six feet tall," Jimmy-Don said, raising his hand so it was even with the top of his own head. "She's got hair down to her ass and fingernails like a fucking eagle—" The crowd laughed. "So Linus comes home the other day with fucking bloody zebra stripes on his back—" Jimmy-Don shouted so even people at the table beside him could hear. "And Sharon says, 'Linus, what the hell happened to your back?' He told her he'd been golfing, see?"

"He WAS golfing," Uncle James shouted from another table. "He was with me, I swear!" James put a bulky arm around his wife and a roaring laughter ensued. Emery was fairly certain that Uncle James was making this up. But he wasn't worried about that—he was trying to figure out how the bloody zebra stripes got on Linus' back.

"Of course he was with you!" Jimmy-Don said. "So Sharon asks what happened, and what does the fucker say?"

"I was hit in the back with a rake!" someone shouted from the bar.

"I was fucking a sewer grate!" Otto yelled from behind the bar. Emery flinched at the F-word. These people cussed as much as his parents!

The laughter was so thick, Jimmy-Don had to pause before finishing. "He says, '*You* did that to me!'" Laughter rang out like a sonic boom. Jimmy-Don continued, "And Sharon says, 'What do you mean I did that to you?' Sharon with her stubby fingers, says this. So he says, 'Last night, after all that goddamned scotch, you did this to me when we were making love—" The term *making love* threw the crowd into hysterics. Emery knew what it meant, but he had no idea why it was funny. "And, guess what?" Jimmy-Don waited until everyone had silenced enough to hear him. "She had had so much fucking scotch the night before she didn't even know that Linus had fallen asleep on the sofa watching TV that night and had never even come to bed! And now she thinks she's some kind of tiger between the sheets!"

Jimmy-Don's last lines brought a rousing round of applause. Then Uncle Jim-Jim started up with another story about Linus's Stinky.

Emery could see that there were two types of people in this side of his family: the ones who told the stories and the ones who laughed at the stories. No one had a normal conversation where you might tell someone how you were, or discuss what you had been doing. And they teased, too. They teased abundantly, the way his parents and Portia kissed him (Anna refused to touch him), teasing as an endless source of affection. Emery decided that if you got teased, or if they told you a story, it meant you were a part of the family. He was glad that two different people had told him stories: one about the guy at Aunt Sis's office who died on the toilet, and one about Uncle James's nipple getting rubbed off on an innertube when he was nine years old.

Food was brought out on great big serving platters that were set on top of the bar. A stack of paper plates and plastic forks and knives were at one end and everyone lined up and went down the bar, like a buffet, gathering up all they could pile on a plate without it dipping down heavy and wet in the middle. The line moved slowly as most people ordered a drink from Otto or Uncle James, who tended bar together. When the girls and Emery finally made it to the food, Emery found it strangely comforting to see that everything that was on the menu had been brought out: chicken wings, tater tots, green salad, three-bean salad, coleslaw, hot dogs, and barbeque potato chips. There was something about his grandmother, her stringiness and upright posture, her empty white kitchen, and the way she had patted his back when they first arrived, that made Emery believe she had nothing to do with feeding the crowd.

"Who made all this?" Emery asked Louise, when she stopped by the table where her three kids sat eating.

"Your aunts," Louise said. "Billie will only cook for Otto and Otto doesn't cook."

"And our aunts happened to make everything that's on the menu?" Emery asked.

"No!" Louise laughed. "They make the same greasy food for every party—so Otto had that printed on the menu knowing that no one would ever bring anything different."

"Wouldn't it be fun to feed them California food," Portia said. "We could make them tacos or falafels." The most popular fast food in Santa Barbara was from the falafel stand where people lined up to pay a dollar for a fried chick-pea patty in pita bread. Emery loved falafels.

"You hate falafels," Anna said, to Portia.

"Yeah, but wouldn't it be fun to watch everyone eat them? They wouldn't even know how to pick them up," Portia said.

"You're so nasty," Anna said. "This is our family. Why would you want to shock them with falafels?"

"Do you think Otto told everyone that you're in dummy school?" Emery asked. Portia shrugged.

"Probably," Anna said. "But that's what she deserves for wanting to feed them falafels just to freak them out."

"I just want to show them how different we are," Portia said.

"I'm not different," Anna said. "I'm exactly like them." And Emery thought that she was sort of right. Anna was the one who never told anyone she was Jewish. And she didn't like to be touched and often paid Emery a quarter to sit at least one cushion away from her on the couch. She knew the exact acreage of Fulton Ranch (5,476) and at least three times Emery heard her say that she wished Buzzy were a little more like Otto: outdoorsy, sporty, not a complainer. And she was planning to go to college in Vermont, as she thought the whole state suited her better than New York, New Jersey, or Connecticut, where Buzzy had suggested she go to college. Even the boys Anna talked about seemed to be more like Otto than Buzzy: Johnny Brownstein, who played baseball and was a waiter at the Charter House steak house; Kirk Nintzel, whom Anna told Emery he should grow up to be. Kirk was president of the Key Club, had been voted Luscious Lester, and had a football scholarship to USC. Surely neither of those guys would go to the falafel stand.

The party had thinned out and calmed. A few people, including Buzzy and Louise, had gone out in the rowboats. In what Emery thought was one of the coolest things he'd ever seen, Uncle Ray-Boy had tried to do a wheelie on the lawn mower and flipped it, rolling down the hill toward the lake. Uncle Ray-Boy and the lawnmower both survived.

Anna and Portia were standing at an empty bar table eating peanuts. Emery was hovering nearby, hiding himself from Otto, who had publically called him Sissy Boy at least three times in the last hour. Emery thought that if only his grandfather could see the singing and dancing extravaganza of the Corny Kids Variety Show, he'd never call Emery a sissy again.

Otto was behind the bar. Uncle Jimmy-Don was holding

court at a bar table nearby. In a moment of silence Otto lifted his scotch glass and shouted out across the room, "Jimmy-Don, did you see the tits on these girls?"

Portia looked from Emery, who was staring at her with his mouth in a hard O, to her grandfather, to her uncle. Anna turned away, as if she were examining the horizon out the glass door. Jimmy-Don lifted his drink and winked toward Anna and Portia.

"Can you believe the tits on these girls, Jimmy-Don!" Otto shouted, louder.

Jimmy-Don laughed. "Yeah, Otto, you got some pretty grand-daughters with mighty big tits."

Then Otto looked at Anna and Portia, pointed at them with his drink, and asked, "Do all the girls in California have tits like that?"

"Uh . . ." Anna said. Emery had never seen his sisters like this: silenced as if they'd had thick blankets thrown over their heads, their bodies as stiff and still as if they'd been left in a snowstorm while sleeping in the back of a convertible.

Emery put his hand on Portia's leg and leaned out to face Otto. "Hey Otto!" he shouted. Everyone looked at him. "YOU'RE A FUCKER!"

Emery grabbed Portia's hand, Portia grabbed Anna's hand, and the three of them ran out of the bar and up the hill scream-ing with laughter. When they could no longer hear the roaring hysterics from the bar, they dropped hands and collapsed onto the grass looking down at the bar. Emery lay back and kicked his feet in the air. He was laughing so hard that he was losing sound. Every time Anna and Portia looked at him, they laughed harder. It was a spiraling laugh-chain that didn't let up for minutes. Eventually they had to look away from each other so they could turn the laugh-motor off long enough to return to the party.

By the time the kids got back to the bar, most people had left and their parents had returned from the lake. Louise smiled when her children walked in. Buzzy looked up from the bowl of peanuts he was hunched over and grinned. Otto wasn't around but Billie was washing glasses behind the bar.

"I hear you called your grandfather a fucker," Buzzy said.

Emery looked over at Billie and saw that she was smiling. Her smile warmed him like drinking cocoa did—he could feel it in his belly, feel things changing inside him.

"Yeah." Emery sidled next to Buzzy, who rubbed his hair and kissed him on the top of his head. Louise beamed down at Emery.

Emery had never before felt so proud.

The next day, as they were driving to Maine to visit Louise's best friend from college, Portia retold the story of Emery's calling Otto a fucker. Emery laughed so hard his eyes closed up into little slits of eyelashes. He loved hearing the story as if it were an episode of a TV show—he loved seeing himself as the mighty, brave, and fierce character Portia created.

"Tell it again," Emery said, when he had finally stopped laughing.

"Don't you dare tell it again," Anna said. In spite of her joy at the moment of Emery's rebellion, she seemed to be sticking to her fantasy of Otto as the guy Buzzy should try to be.

"Well, what if I only tell the part about Otto telling everyone to look at our tits?"

"Don't say that word!" Anna said.

"You sound like your brother now!" Louise said.

"*Tits* is not such a bad word," Buzzy said. "You just don't want to hear it coming out of your grandfather's mouth."

"Tits!" Emery said, laughing. Now that the language hatch

had been opened, Emery was flinging bad words hither and yon. He was batting them around like crumpled paper balls. Yes, indeed, it felt good to act out, to break free from the restraints of public order.

"Well, at least he didn't call them oranges," Louise said.

"Do we have to keep talking about this?" Anna asked.

"What do you mean, 'oranges'?" Portia asked. Emery scooted up from the center of the seat so his head was leaning into the front seat between Buzzy and Louise.

"When I started puberty, Otto kept a running track of my breast size and that's all he ever said to me. 'Ach, you got little grapes there, Louise!' Then, 'Ach, look at her strawberries popping out!' Then, 'Ach, the girl's got plums in her shirt!' "

"Wait!" Portia said. "Don't tell me the next one, let me guess . . . nectarines?"

"Gross. Will you shut up?" Anna asked.

"I love nectarines," Emery said.

"No, we didn't eat nectarines," Louise said. "I think it went from plums to oranges and then it was oranges until I left for college." Louise laughed.

"I think Anna's are more grapefruits than oranges," Portia said. Emery turned around and looked at his sister.

"You people are sick." Anna turned toward the window, her back to the family.

"We're not sick," Emery said. "We're funny."

"No, you're sick!" Anna turned to Emery with wet eyes. "Sickness runs in this family, like freckles and wide feet. None of this is funny. It's plain, pathetic sick."

"Fucking sick," Emery said, with a sly smile. And everyone but Anna, of course, laughed.

9

DAY FIVE

They have been watching cartoons for at least an hour every night after dinner. Emery is a television producer; before he
flew home for the heart attack, he was developing a new cartoon
series. He is searching for animators, so he watches the most
popular shows to see what works. Everyone watches with him.
They are so compelled that they don't talk unless the commercials are running. Emery has seen all the shows many times; he
has a television in his office that has been tuned to cartoons for
the past six months. When a cartoon starts, he sings along with
the opening song. Often, when Emery is watching cartoons, he
imagines himself sitting with his and Alejandro's kid. He doesn't
care if they have a boy or a girl; he just wants a kid with a sense
of humor. A kid who can appreciate a good cartoon. And a kid
who will love roller coasters. He and Alejandro both still love
roller coasters; it was one of the first things they talked about
when they met.

It is the evening of Day Five. Emery has promised Alejandro
that he will ask his sisters for the eggs tonight. He imagines toss-
ing confetti in the air as he throws out the question.

"Alejandro!" Emery calls toward the kitchen. "Will you come
in here?"

By the time Alejandro joins them in the TV room, the show
is back on. Emery will ask his sisters during a commercial.

They are watching *Pickle Man-Boy*. The animation alone
makes them laugh: one guy has a nose hanging down like a

penis in the middle of his face. Alejandro, who is sitting between Anna and Portia, allows Lefty, the cat, to crawl across his shoulders, but the cat continually runs his tail across Alejandro's eyes, and he is trying to watch the show. Emery picks up the cat and settles with him on the floor beside the big cushioned chair where Buzzy sits. The dogs have joined the group, too. They lie on the floor between the chintz couch and the oak blanket box that serves as a coffee table. Like a litter of puppies, everyone is huddled, it seems, into the smallest possible area.

"I don't get this," Buzzy says during a commercial. "Is he a pickle?"

"It's *Pickle Man-Boy*," Emery says. "He's a cucumber who lives in a saltwater pond." Emery's stomach bumps around as he prepares to ask the question. In order to give eggs, one of his sisters will have to take shots that will at first put her in menopause, followed by other shots that will cause hyperovulation. It's uncomfortable, there are some health risks, and it fucks up the balance of your hormones for a couple of months. Emery imagines it's like sitting on a teeter-totter, a flying/falling sensation that lasts for weeks.

"So is he pickled yet?" Buzzy asks.

"He's Pickle MAN-BOY," Anna says. She has always had little tolerance for questions. As a kid, Emery would save up his questions until Portia got home from school.

"But is it a pickle?" Buzzy says.

"Dad," Anna says, "didn't you listen to the opening song? He's a cucumber who lives in a cantaloupe in a saltwater pond."

"Who wants purple plums?" Buzzy asks, and he gets up and goes into the kitchen.

"Do you ever wonder how Mom can take it day in and day out?" Anna whispers. She's facing the TV. Emery isn't sure whom she's speaking to.

"Take what?" Portia asks.

"Dad!" Anna says, louder but still whispering. "His curiosity is endless—like three-year-olds when they go through that *why* phase: *But why?* Because. *Because why?* Because I said so. *But why are you saying so?* I mean, I fucking wanted to put Blue up for adoption when he started doing this." Blue is Anna's son; Emery now thinks of him as the cousin of his yet-to-be-conceived child.

"Buzzy's funny," Alejandro says. Emery is glad that Alejandro isn't intolerant of questions. He thinks it will be fun answering endless questions from some curious kid.

Buzzy returns with a bowl of purple plums soaking in syrupy juice. "Does anyone want some purple plums?" he asks.

"Dad," Anna says. "You've been offering us canned purple plums since we were born, and *no one* has ever wanted them. You are the only one who eats purple plums."

"I'll have some purple plums," Alejandro says, and he gets up and goes into the kitchen for a bowl. Emery wants to call him back and tell him to sit so he can ask the question, but he does nothing. By the time Alejandro returns the show is back on.

Emery can't concentrate on what he's watching. Instead, he is gathering the courage to ask his sisters to risk their lives (very small chance, the doctor said), mess up their equilibrium (guaranteed), abstain from sex (might not be too hard for Portia—who's she going to fuck, anyway?), cut out vigorous exercise (ditto Portia), stop drinking and smoking (ditto ditto Portia encore), so that he can have a baby that is biologically related to him. By the time the next commercial is on, Emery has decided that merging this question with these two women could be like steering a cruise ship into an iceberg. Maybe it would be safer to ask in the morning, in daylight, when everyone's still dopey with sleep.

"So he's under the water?" Buzzy asks.

"He *lives* in a cantaloupe *deep in a pond*," Anna says. "He's in a pond."

"Ooooh," Buzzy says, "so a moment ago when he was up in that alternate universe, that wasn't an alternate universe at all, that was land above the pond, right?"

"Well, yeah," Emery says. "What'd you think it was?" Emery wants to laugh but doesn't. He senses his sister's impatience and doesn't want to gang up on Buzzy.

"I thought he was in heaven or something, because the colors were so bright."

"But Dad," Anna says, "how could you have missed the opening theme song? You were sitting right here. *He lives in a cantaloupe deep in a pond.*" She actually seems pissed. Downright angry.

"Why does he live in a cantaloupe?" Buzzy asks. "Is it a metaphor for something?" Now Emery laughs.

"Do you think they make mute buttons for people?" Anna asks. "You could put it on the remote control and mute either the TV or the people sitting near the TV."

"Maybe he feels safe in a cantaloupe," Portia says. "Protection from the murky pond." She's laughing, too.

"This dog is so fat she looks like she's *pregnant*," Alejandro says, peering down at Gumba. Emery gives him the shut-up head nod, but Alejandro won't look up and acknowledge it.

"She looks fine," Emery says. Maybe he should ask now and get it over with. What's the difference between tonight and tomorrow morning?

"Did anyone feed these pregnant-looking dogs?" Alejandro asks. He's rubbing both dogs' bellies with his bare feet.

"I still don't understand the cantaloupe," Buzzy says.

"The cantaloupe's his house," Emery says. Just ask for the

eggs now, he thinks. No, don't. Do. Don't. Do. Do it. Say it. Quick.

"Most people feel safe in their house," Portia says. "Although I was a little spooked in this house when I first got here."

"Somebody's gotta feed the dogs," Buzzy says. "They never eat this late."

"So why don't you feed them, Dad," Anna says. Emery thinks she's still pissed about the *Pickle Man-Boy* questions. It definitely wouldn't be good to ask Anna while she's angry.

"I'm watching *Pickled Man*," Buzzy says.

"*Pickle Man-Boy!*" Anna says.

"I like *Pickled Man* better," Portia says.

"I'm never feeding these dogs," Anna says. "They're obese."

"Yeah," Alejandro says. "They look like they're having babies!" He glares at Emery.

"I'll feed them when *Pickle Man-Boy* is over." Emery refuses to meet Alejandro's eyes. "It won't kill them to wait." It won't kill him to wait, either. Besides, Alejandro's pissing him off now, so there's no way he's going to ask tonight. Maybe tomorrow. Tomorrow will probably be a better day for things like shots, hormones, eggs.

"Your mother would die if she knew the animals weren't fed in time," Buzzy says.

"She'd die if she knew you were making fun of Maggie Bucks all the time," Anna says to Portia. She's smiling as she says this; everyone knows that Anna laughs the hardest when Portia makes fun of Maggie Bucks. Anna claims she hates all their mother's animals.

"She'd die if she knew that you were using one of the antique quilts on the couch," Portia says to Anna. Emery agrees. He thinks his sister is pretty nervy, taking the delicate antique quilt Louise was planning to hang somewhere instead of using one of the many comforters that are folded and heaped in the linen closet.

"She'd die if she knew that Little Carl White barfed on the stairs," Emery says.

"What d'you mean?" Buzzy asks. "She doesn't care about the carpet on the stairs."

"No," Emery says, "she wouldn't die because of the carpet, she'd die because she'd be so upset that Little Carl White had actually barfed." Emery feels bad for Little Carl White—he thinks LCW is a sweet, neurotically shy cat who needs to be pitied.

"She barfed?" Buzzy asks.

"I cleaned it up!" Anna says. "And I'm not cleaning up anymore! I'm sick of fucking cleaning up after this family!" Emery guesses by her smile that she's no longer angry and is now pretending to be angry because she knows that's what the family expects of her. So maybe he should ask now.

But the show is back on.

At the next commercial Portia asks Buzzy about Little Carl White. She claims she has only seen the cat as a streak, a shadow, something that flashes past when she goes up or down the stairs. Emery's had more contact with her, but he agrees that catching sight of her is sort of like seeing a mouse or a cockroach when you step into your kitchen in the middle of the night. Turn on the light, and *surprise!*

"So is he a boy or a girl?" Portia says.

"He's fucking Pickle Man-Boy!" Anna says. "Man-Boy! Boy! Boy!"

"No! Little Carl White. Dad called him a she. Relax. Freak," Portia says.

"Yeah, he's a she. He's a girl. She's a girl," Buzzy says.

"Little Carl White is a girl?" Alejandro starts laughing.

"Louise named him after some man she met at a party. He was playing guitar or something and she hated him."

"So she named the fucking cat after him?" Anna asks. Emery thinks it's interesting that his sister, who named her son Blue, would criticize anyone for what they've named their animals.

"Was the man's name *Little* Carl White?" Emery asks. Something about Little Carl White makes Emery crave a joint. For a second he wishes his mother still smoked pot so he could find a roach to kill.

"No, his name was Carl White. And then Louise got the cat and she was little so she named her Little Carl White."

Emery watches Alejandro crack up. People in Alejandro's family don't name animals after people they dislike. They don't have animals as pets. His mother doesn't speak English and likes to talk to him about food. Alejandro told Emery that he will never tell his mother he's gay because he fears the grief might kill her. He did tell his brother and two sisters, however. They have never brought it up since and never ask about Emery. Emery thinks Alejandro's siblings look at gayness as some embarrassing disease you can catch from being careless or from drinking too much at a naked swim party. Emery is not pushing Alejandro about telling his siblings about the baby. He figures Alejandro will deal with that when the baby is actually here.

"Has anyone called Otto and Billie?" Anna asks.

"Your mother insists that I don't tell them." Buzzy shifts in his seat and reaches for the bowl of walnuts in shells on the coffee table. Emery looks at the nuts and thinks that he has never been home and not had nuts within arm's reach.

"What about Bubbe and Zeyde?" Portia asks.

"Absolutely not," Buzzy says. "They'd want to come out here."

"Can you imagine Portia trying to cook kosher?" Anna laughs.

"Shhh!" Emery shushes with his finger in front of his mouth as if he is blowing out a flame on the tip of his nail.

The show is on again.

When Anna was applying to colleges, Buzzy was happy to go through the process with her. In fact, after he and Anna ran into a father-daughter team at a USC open house and the father, whom Buzzy had met professionally before, claimed that his daughter would probably get into every place she applied and would simply have to pick a school in the end, Buzzy became competitive about it.

"If that asshole can get his kid into a good school, then Anna's going to go to an even better school!" Buzzy had told the family at dinner that night. Portia felt relieved to know that she'd have Buzzy on her side when it came time for her to apply.

After Anna was accepted to Bennington College in Vermont (her first pick), Louise took her shopping at Robinsons, where they bought wool plaid skirts, cardigan sweaters, and a navy blue wool peacoat. Anna put on one of her new outfits for her flight to school. Portia thought her sister looked like she was playing the role of an East Coast private school girl in some high school production.

That Christmas, Anna came home thirty pounds heavier and with razor-chopped hair. She had traded her plaid skirts with a cross-dressing Asian boy for tickets to a David Bowie concert in New York. Her preppy sweaters had been cut into parts— the sleeves sewn into fingerless gloves by her Italian roommate, Giovanna, and the bodies resewn to make tiny miniskirts that Anna wore until she could no longer fit them.

When she was alone with Louise one day, Portia told her mother that she thought Anna looked like a thrift store hooker. Louise cracked up. And for the next few days she snickered every time Anna walked in the room. Portia hoped her sister didn't know why her mother was behaving like this.

Three years later, Buzzy had lost his competitive interest in college. Portia mentioned application dates to her dad several times in the fall and he brushed her away each time, saying, "It will work out, don't worry about it." Finally, Portia forced the conversation at dinner one night.

"Dad," she put down her fork and leaned toward Buzzy. "You need to help me find a college."

"Sweetheart"—Buzzy had a wad of mashed potatoes in his mouth—"why don't you go to junior college for a couple years, figure out what you want to do, and *then* go away to college if you're up for it."

"Yeah, okay," Portia said, realizing she would never get Buzzy interested in her college application process. Secretly, she phoned for the application to the University of California, Berkeley. They had driven through Berkeley on a family road trip to San Francisco once and Portia had found what she saw through the car window fascinating: hordes of people who looked like they rarely bathed, coffee drinkers, clove cigarette smokers, readers.

Portia sent in the application without telling her family, friends, or boyfriend (of her two best friends, one thought she'd be joining her at the junior college and the other was going off to the East Coast because her mother, who filled out the applications for her, didn't apply to any West Coast schools). The only people who knew of Portia's plans were the three teachers who wrote her letters of recommendation. One was a philosophy teacher, an odd robotic man named Mr. Vasquez, whose lectures Portia found so interesting that she easily soaked them in and spat them back up in their entirety on every test. The other was the Health & Sexuality and English teacher, Mr. Gates, who showed the class how to use condoms by rolling one onto a banana (he later ate the banana). He also taught Carlos Castaneda and, by extension, everything anyone needed to know about peyote buttons. And the third recommendation came from Portia's French teacher, Madame Dick, whose very name was the source of endless jokes, and whose sheer blouses managed to spotlight her magnificently cantilevered breasts. She was probably in her thirties, looked like she was in her twenties, was as skinny as a paper doll, and liked the prettiest girls best (Portia was not in that group) and those who received straight A's in her class second (Portia's group).

Around the time that she would be hearing from Berkeley, Portia confessed at the dinner table that she had applied.

"You applied to Berkeley?" Buzzy asked.

"Good for you!" Louise said, and she ladled out more lentil soup into her ceramic bowl. Buzzy had bought a kiln and was glazing and firing all his clay works; item by item, the painted blue china was being replaced with brown, gray, and beige ridged pottery. The soup bowl set was complete, however, and for that reason Buzzy frequently requested soup. Also, once Anna had left for school, Louise became the cook again and she often made soup whether Buzzy requested it or not, as she could prepare it in the morning and let it simmer all day while she was in her studio or at the nude beach.

"Sweetheart," Buzzy said, and he laid his big hand on Portia's, "you'll never get in. It's a very competitive school." Because she was the least competitive child in the family, Portia was often taken as the least intelligent. Anna let all her feats be known and insisted that everyone witness her every achievement. Emery, who was known to be the smartest, was watched by everyone above him. But Portia was like wallpaper—it was easy to forget she was in the room. Easy not to see her.

"I know I won't get in," Portia said, although she didn't know. She didn't know anything about the place other than that there were a lot of interesting-looking people walking the streets and few of them appeared to be over the age of thirty. Her stomach felt rocky; she was embarrassed by how foolish she had been. She couldn't eat any more soup.

"How do you know she won't get in?!" Louise asked. Then she turned to her daughter and said, "Don't listen to your father. He's an asshole."

Emery's eyes went large as he ticked his head from side to side, following the conversation.

"She's a *beach bunny!*" Buzzy said. "She's not an academic!"

Buzzy was right. Portia had spent her high school years as what her parents called a beach bunny and what the kids at school called a surfer chick. She was the color of a nutshell. Her hair had streaks of gold in it. She and her friends dated only surfers, and she had a hardened layer of beach tar on the bottom of her feet like a surgically attached shoe sole. But she hadn't blown off school. It hadn't occurred to her that she could blow off school. Indeed, Portia did her work in a haphazard way— writing papers the morning they were due and finishing home- work during lectures. But she turned everything in on time, received A's and B's, and didn't seem to get penalized for things like writing an essay on a ripped-flat brown grocery bag when she was at the beach and couldn't find any lined white paper in her boyfriend's truck or anyone else's car. Buzzy and Louise never asked for her report cards, so she never even thought to show them to them. Although, once, when Portia got straight A's, not even an A-minus, she stuck the report card on the refrigerator. The refrigerator was littered with scraps of paper, business cards, photographs, postcards. Portia's report card remained uncovered for about three minutes; Louise came home from the grocery store immediately after Portia had gotten home from school, pulled out a postcard that she had bought, and said, "Look at this!"

She picked up the magnet that held her daughter's report card, put the postcard on top of it, and replaced the magnet.

"*This house is clean enough to be healthy and messy enough to be happy,*" Portia read off the card.

Louise laughed, "That's us, all right!"

"I'm not sure it's clean enough to be healthy," Portia said. "I mean, there's animal poop all over the back of the family room couch."

"Bird shit?" Louise had said, and she started unloading groceries. "Bird shit is sterile. The dumb thing only eats seeds— what could be unhealthy about shit from pure seeds?"

Louise seemed to have faith in Portia's intelligence, in spite of her complete disinterest in her education. She paused while ladling more soup into Buzzy's bowl and said, "Well, just 'cause she's a beach bunny doesn't mean she's not smart!"

"She doesn't even know who Agnew is!" Buzzy was referring to the dinner conversation the night before when Buzzy had compared someone in his firm to Spiro Agnew. It was the Spiro part that had tripped Portia up. She *did* know who Agnew was, as years earlier Louise had clipped out every *New York Times* article about Watergate and shellacked them on the downstairs bathroom walls. After several months, each wall was covered, the empty patches filled in with articles about Mark Spitz when he won seven gold medals and the Japanese playing baseball. Anna, Portia, and Emery had the headlines memorized.

"'Agnew Quits Vice Presidency,'" Portia recited over her soup. "'And Admits Tax Evasion in '67. Nixon Consults on Successor.'"

Buzzy and Louise laughed. It was a relief. Portia was happy to veer the subject away from Berkeley and her ridiculous inspiration to apply.

"See!" Louise said. "She knows who Agnew is!"

"Besides, Dad," Portia said, "that whole Agnew vice-presidency thing was like a decade ago. You should be impressed that I know who he is—I was younger than Emery when he was vice president!"

"I was three," Emery said.

"And you know who he was?" Portia asked.

"The vice president!" Emery said, and he started laughing. Sometimes Portia pretended she didn't know things Emery knew only so she could see him crack up like this. But the Agnew thing last night had been all real.

"Of course he knows—he knows everything!" Buzzy said.

"I know, too," Portia said.

"Okay, so who became vice president when Agnew quit?" Buzzy asked Portia.

Emery smiled and looked at his sister. He reminded her of a jester; his hair was sticking up as if it grew in an atmosphere without gravity. He mouthed the name to her. Portia knew he wanted her to get it right if only because it seemed like their father was picking on her. Otherwise he would have reveled in being the only of them who knew.

"Leave her alone!" Louise said to Buzzy. Then she turned to Portia and said, "Don't answer him."

"I know who it is," Portia said. "I can answer."

"Well?"

"Vooor."

"Who?"

"Vord?"

Emery started laughing. "FORD!" he shouted. "And Ford became president and then Jimmy Carter became president and now we have Reagan. The actor. Married to Nancy. His son's name is Ron and he has a daughter named Maureen."

Buzzy and Louise laughed.

"I know who Ford is, I just forgot! And I know all about Reagan, I swear!" But the truth was, she couldn't even recall who Reagan's vice president was. Portia wasn't interested in politics and was never at home to overhear her parents discussing politics. Once Emery was old enough to raise himself, the only thing that was asked of Portia was that she show up for dinner every night. And eventually, when she eased her way into living at her friend Sarah's house, Portia only had to be home for dinner on Sunday night.

Sarah's mother had moved out to the hillside town of Summerland, so her giant cement-and-glass home was occupied only by Sarah and her dad, Clint. The house sat on a cliff overlooking the beach and there was a pool house that the maid slept in. The kitchen had stainless steel before stainless steel was in fashion—it was odd then, reminiscent of restaurant kitchens more than high fashion. The girls often hung out in that kitchen, staring at the ocean, eating cheddar cheese melted on tin foil. Sarah's dad loved when she had lots of friends over. He liked to talk to them about their boyfriends and sex lives. And once, when he and Portia were alone in the house (Sarah was out picking up a couple friends who were stranded on Cabrillo Boulevard after having run out of gas), Sarah's dad reached over and put his hand on Portia's knee. She was sitting on the stainless steel kitchen stool, her elbows slapped onto the tile counter, slouched recklessly.

She straightened up and looked at him.

"Portia," Sarah's dad said.

"Clint," Portia said, and she laughed because he suddenly seemed so serious.

"Tell me. Are you having good orgasms with your boyfriend?"

"Uh . . ." Portia laughed again. The truth was she had never had an orgasm with her boyfriend, although they'd been having sex for three months.

"You should be having beautiful, amazing orgasms," Sarah's dad said.

"I'm trying!" Portia said, earnestly.

"Does he perform oral sex?" Sarah's dad stared into her eyes. He was the best-looking dad of any of her friends. He wore leather coats, and drove a convertible sports car, and had muscles carved into his body as if he were made of stone. But Portia had never thought of him as someone who would be interested in her or her friends. He could date movie stars (and they did live in his neighborhood), or Madame Dick.

"Well . . ." Portia wasn't sure if she should answer. It seemed dangerous to answer. But, then again, Portia had been living at his house. She had to trust him. In fact, Sarah's dad had seen her naked, as the two girls always went naked in the pool when they were home alone, which was almost always. And whenever he got home from work, Sarah's dad would come outside and talk to the girls. Portia did think it was odd that Sarah wasn't uncomfortable being naked in front of her dad, but he was her dad, he had changed her diapers. So Portia never believed that Sarah's dad was thinking of her, his daughter's friend, in sexual terms.

"Well," Portia shifted her leg a little to remind him that his hand was on her bare knee. "He licks me and it feels good, but nothing really happens."

"Where exactly does he lick?" The hand on Portia's knee flickered, like a cat's tail.

"All over. Down there." Portia pointed to her crotch.

"He needs to focus the pressure on your clitoris," Sarah's dad said. "Tell him to keep his lips fairly close together and to use his tongue as a forceful nub."

"A forceful nub." Portia breathed in and reminded herself to breathe out. What she didn't want to happen was anything that would compromise her tenancy in the house. She liked the pool with clear blue water in it. She liked the food that the maid bought—twenty different kinds of crackers and cheeses that ranged in color from white to black.

"Yeah. Forceful. Focused. Remind him that he's not a labrador. He's a man. And you're a woman. And you should be treated as such."

Portia was as still as a trapped animal, nervously waiting for what would come next. If his hand moved closer, she thought, she'd have to make a choice about actually doing *something* with Sarah's dad (whom she'd admittedly had fantasies about). If he let her go, she'd be freed to live in the world where people like him were so beyond realistic expectations that they were entirely safe.

Sarah burst in the kitchen door, Susie and Donna behind her. They were carrying brown grocery bags filled with oranges that Sarah, her father, and Portia had picked at an orchard that morning and had left in the backseat of Sarah's dad's convertible. Sarah's dad took his hand from Portia's knee, stood, and gathered the bags from Donna and then Susie.

"I was just asking Portia if her boyfriend was good at oral

sex," Sarah's dad said, and the girls started to laugh, Portia the hardest, harder than she should have been laughing.

"Daaaad," Sarah said. "He asks me that all the time. I swear!"

"So, is he good?" Donna asked. She looked like ripe fruit—everything bursting, juicy, round.

"I guess." Portia couldn't stop laughing, but it was wire-edged. A breath's width away from tears.

After that, whenever Sarah left the house Portia went with her. But at night, alone with her thoughts, she let the image of Sarah's dad slither in: hot, grown-up, knowing.

When she didn't sleep at Sarah's house, Portia often slept at the beach with her boyfriend, or in the rumpus room at her friend Lucy's house. Lucy lived around the corner from Portia, so it was easy to walk home and get clothes. Although it appeared to be a somewhat degenerate life, Portia kept things in control through a reasonable fear of death and limb loss. She refused to get in a car with a drunk driver, never stole anything from anywhere, took vitamin C every day, didn't eat sugary foods, and never rode on the back of a motorcycle without a helmet. She rarely drank, smoked pot only a few times (in spite of its abundance in her house), and never, *ever* did hard drugs.

Until she got into Berkeley.

The acceptance letter came on a Friday and sat on the kitchen counter with other assorted mail until Sunday, when Portia came home for dinner. It was Portia's usual practice to sift through the piles of objects and papers on the counter every Sunday to see if there was anything she needed or wanted. The white Berkeley envelope was the size of a magazine, barely hidden under the unopened gas and electric bill, a Robinsons catalogue, and an unopened letter from Anna. Whoever had brought in the mail clearly hadn't looked through it before scrambling it into the junk heap.

"Mom, you got a letter from Anna." Portia handed the letter to Louise who was at the stove frying meatballs in a skillet. She watched Louise open Anna's letter while holding the envelope from Berkeley on her lap. Once Louise was immersed in reading Anna's letter (it looked like it was about seven pages long, not unusual for Anna), Portia opened the Berkeley envelope and gasped.

"What?" Louise was still reading Anna's letter.

"I got into Berkeley." Portia looked up at her mother.

"I *knew* you would!" Louise raised a triumphant hand in the air, Anna's yellow lined pages flapping around, then came to the other side of the counter and wrapped Portia in a hug. "I just knew it. You're way smarter than anyone gives you credit for." Portia couldn't speak. She felt like some vague idea of herself as a person who could possibly *do* something in her life was suddenly starting to materialize.

Through a friend of her father's, Portia was introduced, via phone, to a girl two years older than she who would be a junior at Berkeley and was leaving the dorms for a vine-covered four-story clapboard house three blocks from campus. The girl, Beth, called Portia one day in the spring right after Portia had been accepted, told her that one of her planned roommates had recently checked into a mental hospital, thus opening up a bedroom in the house she was renting, and that she needed the cash and commitment of a new roommate *that moment* in order to keep the lease. Did Portia want to be their housemate? Yes. Did she want to drive up to school with her in the fall? Yes. Did she need to check over any of this with her parents before it was a done deal? No.

On August 25, Beth pulled into the driveway in a lumbering white Buick she had inherited from her father. Her stuff took up most of the trunk, so Portia's boxes and Hefty trash bags of clothes were stuffed onto the back seat and the floor of the passenger side seat. Beth couldn't see out the rearview mirror as she tried to back out of the driveway. Buzzy ran out into the empty street and directed by shouting, "Turn your wheel now," even though she was already turning.

"Turn some more," Buzzy said, and he swirled his hand in a circle.

Beth turned the car and faced it down the cul-de-sac. Louise came out of the house wearing a halter top she had sewn from a blue-and-white handkerchief, cut-off jean shorts, and no shoes. Her hair was blowing across her face. She had a cigarette in her right hand.

Portia rolled down her window. "Where's Emery?"

"I couldn't find him," Louise said.

"I don't want to leave without saying good-bye to him." Emery was the only thing Portia thought she'd miss. Her friendships throughout high school had been so intense she'd needed a divorce from them. And Portia's last boyfriend had accepted a blow job after karate class from a soft, sweet girl whom Portia had thought was a friend of some sort. Portia didn't feel attached to anyone or anything, except Emery, who had been somewhere in her peripheral vision since he was born.

"Who's Emery?" Beth asked. They had met in person only two hours earlier. Beth was shockingly beautiful, with long dark hair and a face that seemed to be poised for a kiss. She was also about six inches taller than Portia and much cooler, Portia thought. Beth was like a grown-up—giving off an air of independence Portia both admired and coveted.

"Emery's my little brother," Portia said, then leaned closer to Beth and whispered, "I think he might be gay."

"EM-ER-Y!" Buzzy shouted, wandering to the center of the cul-de-sac with his hands cupped over his mouth.

Beth turned off the engine, shrugged her shoulders, and said, "Well, let's go look for your gay little brother so you can say good-bye."

They got out of the car and roamed outside the house, Buzzy following and hollering Emery's name. Louise meandered behind, smoking her cigarette and absently poking into the magenta-flowered bougainvillea bush as if they'd find Emery there. When no one could find him after several minutes, they returned to the car. Emery was sitting in the passenger seat, examining the gearshift on the steering wheel. He was thirteen and, like Portia and Anna had been, small for his age. His blond hair grew straight down around his ears. He was browned from the sun and wore no shoes or shirt.

"Where were you?!" Emery asked as they walked toward the car. His front teeth were as jutting and crooked as a seaside fence.

Louise laughed and flicked her cigarette into the street. Buzzy opened the door, took Emery's hand, and led him out of the car.

"I gotta go," Portia said, and she wanted to cry.

"Bye," Emery said, and he leaned into his sister, his head barely reaching her breast line.

"I love you," Portia said, and she kissed the top of his head. He smelled like the earth and rain and sun.

"I love you!" Emery said, and he pulled away and waved at Beth.

"Hi," Beth said.

"Hi!" Emery said.

Louise came to Portia, wrapped her in a hug, and gave her kisses on each of her cheeks. Then she passed Portia off to Buzzy, who kissed her like he did when Portia was younger, from ear to ear and on each of her eyes. "Okay," Louise said, "get on out of here, your dad and I've got work to do."

Portia and Beth got in the car. Portia rolled her window all the way down and stuck her arm out. "I love you!" Portia waved to her parents as the car started to roll away.

"We love you!" Louise shouted.

"I love you all, too!" Beth shouted from her window. And then they drove off.

"Your brother doesn't seem gay," Beth said, once they were cruising on the freeway.

"I know," Portia said. "He doesn't *do* anything that's gay. It's just this weird feeling I get. Like I know it somehow. Sort of like how you know you're you and I know I'm me. You know?"

Beth laughed. "I know! Whatever you say!"

Somewhere around Bakersfield, Beth pulled into a gas station with a little market attached. Portia gave her five dollars to buy some Fiddle Faddle and Diet Coke and waited in the car, as the locks didn't work and they didn't want to leave everything unattended. When Beth returned she had the Fiddle Faddle but no Diet Coke.

"I got beer instead," Beth said.

"Really? How?" Portia peeked into the bag as Beth slid into her seat and started the car.

"Fake ID."

"You're going to *drink and drive*?" Portia asked.

"There are hardly any cars between here and San Jose," Beth

explained. "And by the time we reach San Jose, we'll be totally sober."

"Okay," Portia said, and she popped open a Heineken. It felt good not to care or worry. Like she had just unlaced some god-awful corset she'd been wearing for years. And it wasn't as if Portia had simply tucked away the list of thoughts she normally had about alcohol, cars, drugs, speeding, and anything else that could possibly kill her. It was as if she had torn up the list—tossed it out the window and let it blow onto the freeway with bits and pieces slapping themselves against other people's car windows. Portia was done parenting herself. She was done making sure she did the right thing. She had gotten herself into college, and so it seemed, in a sense, that her job had been completed. Now it was time to simply fuck up.

DAY SIX

There is a saturation point during each hospital visit. Every day, a moment comes when someone can no longer take sitting in the beeping, stinking room. It usually hits Anna first. She stands, paces, eats the candy that she keeps in her giant backpack-purse (Skittles on the days she doesn't have licorice), and then she says, "Let's go run an errand." Anna feels that if she stays in the room even a second longer she might do something inappropriate, like stand on a chair and start peeing, or unplug Louise's machines to see how long it will take for a doctor to show up.

Sometimes it hits Emery first. He walks to the doorway where there is a curtain (almost always open) but no door and says, "Okay, I'll be back in a couple hours." Anna is sure that Emery would never do anything inappropriate. He probably needs air, room to breathe. Anna, Alejandro, and Portia rush toward Emery when he says that; no one will let him take a break without them, it would be entirely unfair. Buzzy stays behind. His entire being, since the heart attack, seems wholly devoted to Louise.

These breaks last two or three hours, no longer. One day they went shopping. One day they went to a park on the beach. One day they sat in an outdoor café. One day they walked— simply walked—down residential streets and along the main shopping street with terra-cotta tile sidewalks and a fountain on every third block.

Today, Day Six, Anna has hit her saturation point earlier than usual. It's only eleven o'clock. She can feel currents run-

ning through her forearms—the sensation reminds her of cocaine. Not doing it. Wanting it.

Louise is sleeping. The machinery that frames her like an
electronic headboard is quietly humming.

"Let's go to the club," Anna says.

The family belonged to the tennis club years ago. Buzzy and
Louise joined for the kids: to clear them out of the house, to
give their mother some room, they were told. Buzzy and Louise
had no interest in the place; they never even walked up the long
wooded driveway. Anna went daily for tennis and swimming.
Emery swam on weekends and hung around the clubhouse with
friends. Portia went swimming, sometimes, although she always
preferred the ocean, which Anna was glad for. She didn't need
her sister hanging around in her knit bikini with her waist that
was so small you could close two hands around it and her hips
that exploded out on either side.

Anna spent so much of her childhood at the club that her
connection to the place is stronger than her connection to high
school (which she never enjoyed), or the mountains surrounding
Casa del Viento Fuerte (which have never interested her), or the
studio where she took gymnastics twice a week (she hated most
of the girls there). At the club, she is still in contact with the tennis pros, the club manager, and the Australian man and his wife
who run the café.

"Are we still members?" Emery says.

"Of course not," Buzzy says. "You think we'd pay all that
money when none of you even live in town?"

"I go every time I'm in town," Anna says. "They always let
me in."

The boy at the front desk is about eighteen. He is cute in a
tennis-y way—tan, tousled hair, lean. Anna imagines him

naked—the solid cleanness of his body, the lack of excess anything: fat, hair, skin.

"Can you tell Jerry that Anna Stein is here, and I'm with my brother, his friend, and my sister." She looks at him a beat too long, wonders if he'll read her eyes.

The boy picks up a phone and speaks to Jerry. He barely enunciates, almost as if it takes too much effort to speak. Anna instantly loses all sexual interest. She wants to grab the phone out of his hand and speak for him.

The boy hangs up the phone and says, "Jerry says you're all welcome to spend the day here."

"Do you have loaner suits?" Portia asks.

"I'm not wearing a loaner," Emery says.

"Well, what are you going to wear?" Portia asks.

"We only have loaners for men," the boy says.

"Why?" Portia asks.

"I dunno."

"They sell suits in the shop," Anna says. "Buy one." She can't believe she has to wade through this bumbling suit business just to get to the pool.

"I'll buy one," Alejandro says. "I need one anyway."

"But they only have ugly Speedo shit," Portia says. "I'm not spending money on that ugly swim team stuff."

"Fucking buy it," Anna says. "I'll wear it and you can wear my bikini." Now that a fling with the desk boy is out of the question, Anna could care less what she looks like.

"I can't believe you brought your bikini to Mom's heart attack!" Portia says.

"Well, you brought a fucking pedicure kit!" *Fuck you!* Anna thinks.

"That's because my husband left me and I can't walk around looking like some woman whose husband left her!" Portia is staring at the guy behind the desk. Anna looks at him, too. He's clearly listening, mouth half open like he's watching a fight scene in a movie and is waiting for the next blow.

"Then put on my fucking bikini, and you won't look like a woman whose husband left her!" Anna thinks the bikini won't really make any difference. Portia has been looking like a woman whose husband left her since before her husband left her, since the day she had a baby and stopped thinking about things like sex, flirtations, possibilities.

"You know it won't fit me," Portia says. They have never been able to wear the same clothes. Where Portia is slender (her middle), Anna isn't. Where Anna is slender (her limbs), Portia isn't. They are endomorph and ectomorph; a yin-yang of body shapes.

Anna sees her sister focusing on not crying. Portia's obviously at the breaking point where all she'll have to do is open her mouth and she'll cry. And then, stupidly, she does it. She opens her mouth. "And I haven't even gotten my pedicure yet!" Now she's sobbing. Anna looks down at Portia's raggedy red-chipped toes and wonders if her sister sees them as a metaphor for her raggedy, chipped-up heart. Maybe the bikini will help after all—maybe it will make her sister feel put back together. It *will* be too small, but it's the idea of it that matters now.

Alejandro and Emery are watching Portia. Anna can tell that they don't know how to proceed. Anna has to be the one to end this public display of grief and she better end it quickly if she wants to get in any time by the pool.

"You're going to be okay," Anna says, hoping that she sounds sympathetic and not impatient.

Portia sniffs and wipes her eyes. "Your suit won't even cover a quarter of my ass."

"Your ass doesn't look that much bigger," Alejandro says,

and he leans back and checks out Portia's ass. Everyone laughs as a form of relief.

"Are all the suits in the shop that ugly Speedo swim team stuff?" Portia is asking the desk boy square on as if she doesn't care about what he's just witnessed. Her eyes are baby-flesh pink, puffed into little slits. Her face is all freckles.

"I dunno," the boy says.

Everyone pauses for a moment, looking at the boy. Then Anna turns on her heel, takes her sister's hand, and pulls her to the shop.

Portia is wearing a navy blue Speedo suit that covers her from her collarbones to her thighs. Anna thinks she looks like a mentally disabled person: an adult who has been dressed by a mother. Anna's suit is minimal. She has giant breasts that are tan and bulging outside the lines of her suit. Her legs are thin and toned from her ten-mile daily runs. Anna is fully aware of her baffling combination of self-loathing, insecurity, self-love, and adoration. From puberty on she has been jealous of Portia's shape, of the way boys looked at her. But now, when Anna can sit up in a chair and not have a single fold in her stomach, when she can walk around a pool without her flesh even rippling or shaking, Anna is glad that she has her own body and not Portia's Marilyn curves.

The few men and women around the pool look up at Anna and watch as she settles herself. A Mexican boy rearranging the lounging chairs eyes her closely. With her black hair, black eyes, and dark skin, she is often mistaken for Mexican when she's in California. She hated it when she was a kid, but now, as she senses the energy from being stared at, Anna understands the exoticism of her looks, the small advantage it gives her over the endless blondes who crowd the beaches here.

Alejandro dives into the pool and swims laps. Emery is sitting at the edge of the pool with his feet hanging in the water, hesitating to jump in. Anna watches them for a moment before picking up the *Star* magazine she took from the hospital room. She flips through the pages quickly, then tosses it on the tiled ground. After so many celebrity magazines in so few days, she has memorized the celebrity news—what they're wearing, who they're dating, who's in rehab, who's had a baby, who's gained weight and who's lost it.

Portia applies sunblock that she's pulled out of her purse, then lies on the chair next to Anna. She appears to fall asleep, although Anna thinks she could simply be checking out of reality after her public bawling.

Anna gets up and wades into the pool, slowly, from the shallow end. There is an overly tan, overly hirsute, barrel-bellied fiftysomething man standing in the pool, running his hands through the water as if he were a human mixer. Anna imagines what it would be like to have sex with him, someone his age. Not the body of the desk boy, but certainly he'd be more articulate. Highly skilled, perhaps.

Anna dives down and disappears under the water. Everything goes silent. Her legs kick once as hard as they can, her eyes are shut—she feels like a blind seal. When Anna pops up, she is no longer the seal, she is Pickle Man-Boy in the alternate universe of life above the pond, heaven beyond the cantaloupe. At first the air sounds like empty noise; an impacted hollow space. Then all grows quiet and the sky seems hushed and still, like the sky before an earthquake or a solar eclipse.

The pool is surrounded by hills that are covered with eucalyptus trees. Everywhere you look there are tall, scabby-barked trees whose finger-slim leaves shine with astringent oil. The sky is bright blue, like the sky out the window of an airplane. There is nothing in this setting that is stressful, or tense, or treacherous. Anna wonders if this is how people who don't need to do drugs normally feel. Is this the way the nonantidepressant-pill-popping people see the world? To Anna, this moment is almost miraculous. She has never before felt such calm without being on something. And maybe it's because her mother could die any second now. Or maybe it's because her sister, who's normally so ridiculously happy, has fallen apart. Perhaps when everyone else is fucked up, or fucked, Anna can actually hold it together and live in a quiet peacefulness.

For an hour, no one speaks. They swim, and stand, and lie, and sit, and read, and look up at the trees, the sky, the water. And then they get hungry.

Anna orders and pays for food for everyone—she is feeling generous in her newfound (although certainly temporary) peacefulness. Also, she figures this will make up for her not having cooked dinner any night since they've been here. For herself, Alejandro and Emery, she gets the most interesting foods on the menu: an avocado-and-chicken salad, a honey-mustard chicken sandwich, and a baked mushroom-and-pepper polenta. For her sister she brings a grilled cheese sandwich.

Portia loves the grilled cheese sandwich. She is actually smiling as she eats it.

"You have to taste this," Portia says, and she hands the sandwich to Anna.

"It's amazing," Anna says. The bread is perfectly salty and crisp; the cheese gushes out with every oozy bite. She hands the sandwich to Alejandro.

"Oh, my God," he says. "That's way better than gefilte fish."

"Lemme try," Emery says. He takes a bite and smiles. "That is *so* good. Why is that so good?"

———

Back at the hospital they smell like chlorine and sun. Anna looks in her compact mirror and sees that she is so dark, the whites of her eyes pop out like moons on her face. Portia's long hair is wet and her cheeks appear to have new constellations of freckles. Emery and Alejandro are like two brown squirrels. Louise is still sleeping, or asleep again, as she probably was awake at some point during their absence. Buzzy looks up from his book and examines his children.

"You had your suits with you?" he asks.

"We had to buy them," Portia says. "I bought this really ugly Speedo that made me look like a housewife."

"But aren't you a housewife?" Buzzy asks.

"I guess," Portia says, and she yawns and looks away. Anna watches her sister for a second to make sure she doesn't start bawling again. She imagines connecting Frankensteinian wires between their two heads, flipping a giant Y-shaped current paddle, and transferring her own emotions into Portia so that Portia could have a break from herself. Anna has never felt undone by the end of a relationship; it's as if she has always known there would be someone else lined up to take the last person's place. But Portia, who sees herself as having been replaced by Daphne Frank, is simply standing at a dead end, refusing to turn around and walk the other way.

"Did you buy a suit, too?" Buzzy asks Emery.

"Alejandro bought two of them—"

"I lost my suit," Alejandro says. "I needed new ones, anyway."

"I had mine," Anna says.

"I'll pay for the new ones," Buzzy says. "Let me give you the money."

They all wave him away. No one will let him pay, even though it might make him happy to pay, it might relieve something for him, the way tension is relieved through a fight, nervousness through a jiggling foot.

Louise is suddenly awake. She mumbles, "Let your father pay for the suits."

"Mom, the suits were nothing," Anna says. "It's the plane tickets that set us back."

"I'll pay for those, too!" Buzzy says.

"I was kidding," Anna says. "I used miles. The ticket didn't even set me back."

"I used miles, too," Portia says.

"We got one of those companion-fare specials," Emery says.

"I'll give you all plane tickets to pay you back," Buzzy says, "or I'll give you money to cover the tickets."

"Forget it," Anna says. She'll need money later for something, she always does; it wouldn't be good to blow his generosity on this.

"Let your father pay for the tickets," Louise groans. "Don't be silly."

"Mom," Anna says, "why don't you take another shot of morphine and check out for a while."

Louise laughs. The nurse, whose presence in the room seems somewhat like the machinery, smiles at her.

"I had this grilled cheese sandwich at the club," Portia says, "that was so good, it was like I was on drugs or something."

The nurse leaves.

"It was as good as drugs," Anna says.

"It was like being on Ecstasy," Emery says.

"What do you mean it was like being on Ecstasy?" Buzzy asks.

"The degree of pleasure," Emery says.

"I thought *she* had the sandwich?"

"We all tasted it," Alejandro says. "It was amazing."

"You ever done Ecstasy?" Anna asks Emery. Ecstasy became popular after Anna went to rehab. She's always wanted to try it, although her psychiatrist has warned her against it.

Alejandro laughs as a way of saying yes, they've done it plenty.

"You shouldn't do it," Anna says "My shrink says it will mess up the serotonin balance in your brain." If she ever goes off Prozac, Anna thinks, she'll start taking Ecstasy. If you're going to be addicted to something, it might as well be something that makes you peacefully happy, rather than manic and needy.

"We do it, like, twice a year," Emery says. "Nothing major." Anna continues to be surprised at how far the most uptight, law-abiding member of the family has come.

"Don't do drugs," Louise groans.

"Not sure you should be heading the 'Just Say No' campaign, Mom," Emery says. They all laugh. Alejandro laughs hardest, which makes Anna wonder what stories Emery has told him. She doesn't really care what he's been told about her: she is who she is and that's that. But she is curious about how much of her past is in his mind.

"And," Louise tries to lift her finger as if to make this point more powerful, "be careful about who you have sex with."

"Mom," Anna says, "don't you think we should have had this talk years ago? Like, before any of us went away to college?"

"Yeah," Portia says. "Think how different our lives would be now if you had actually warned us against drugs and sex!"

Buzzy picked up Anna from the airport when she flew home for Christmas break. He waited in the brown four-door sedan in front of the terminal. When Anna approached the car, she could tell her father didn't recognize her at first. She was thinner than she'd been last summer, and she had a row of hoops running up the side of one ear.

"Get in!" he shouted. All the windows were down. It was December 5 and about seventy degrees outside.

Anna rolled her eyes, opened the back door, and shoved her giant suitcase on top of the newspapers and the empty shopping bag that sat on the seat. She slammed the door shut and got in the front seat. Her father was so erratic—one day smothering her with affection and then today yelling at her to get in the car when the last time he had seen her was the middle of August. Not that she missed his hugs and kisses. They were over-the-top, in her opinion.

"I have a shrink appointment in ten minutes," Buzzy said, and he roared away from the curb.

"Then why didn't Mom pick me up?" Anna asked.

"She's locked in her studio. She wouldn't open up for me."

"Are you in a fight?" Anna asked. If they were fighting, she'd rather not be home.

"No, we're getting along fine. She's busy. Trying to finish some series of something . . . I don't know if it's etchings or poems."

"Is Portia home?"

"She's on her way."

"Where's Emery?"

Buzzy shrugged, changed lanes, and cut someone off.

"That guy's honking at you," Anna said. She put her hand against her right cheek so the angry driver wouldn't see her. She was embarrassed to be in her father's dirty, swerving car.

"He's not honking at me!" Buzzy adjusted the rearview mirror and looked in it. "There's no one even back there."

"He's fucking next to us, Dad!" Anna slunk down low in the seat. Buzzy ignored her and zoomed on.

At the house, Buzzy kept the car running while Anna tugged her suitcase out of the backseat. He opened his door, ran around the front of the car, and gave Anna kisses all over her head.

"I'm glad to have you home, sweetheart," Buzzy said. "I'll see you when I get back from the shrink." Buzzy got back in the car and sped away.

When Anna walked into the house, the lights were off and the orange, nubby curtains were drawn.

"Hellooooo," she called out. The house was still as air.

Anna stepped past the piles of shoes and books on the stairway and went up to her room. She had the eerie feeling of being in the wrong house. The mod, striped wallpaper Anna had picked out at nine years old remained, but everything else that signified her was gone.

Buzzy's leather armchair was in the corner where Anna's blue beanbag chair and record player used to sit. On the bed (no bedspread, only a single white sheet) were stacks and piles of papers and books. The desk held more of the same. The bulletin board over the desk had notices and receipts having nothing to do with Anna.

The room smelled of Buzzy—distinct and profound as any animal smell, musky but clean. Buzzy had taken over Anna's room.

She had been erased.

Anna went to her sister's room and saw that it was now Emery's junked-up room with Portia's old pink-flowered wallpaper on the uncovered bits of wall. Her sister's pink desk was pushed in a corner and Anna's blue beanbag chair sat beside Emery's dark oak bunk bed. Taped to the walls were maps of Disneyland and Magic Mountain—there was even a map taped on the ceiling over the bed. Along the floor, Emery had lined up his shoes according to height (high-tops to flip-flops) and color (darkest to lightest). It seemed that Emery had tried to create some order within the mishmash. He was searching for an aesthetic, although Anna didn't think he had quite found it yet.

Downstairs, in the room that used to belong to Emery, was Portia's bed, properly made up, and the cot that Bubbe and Zeyde had used. (The kids had been told that Bubbe and Zeyde's annual December trip had been rescheduled for summer, as Louise couldn't take the sudden accumulation of so many people.) Anna's old, fuzzy white blanket and patchwork bedspread were folded on the cot with a pile of mismatched sheets from various years. Lined against the wall were cardboard grocery boxes, each with Buzzy's nearly illegible scrawl on the sides: "Anna's Stuff" or "Portia's Stuff." There was also a giant open crate, like a miniature boxcar from a train, filled with toys and stuffed animals that Emery had given up. Sticking out of the top of the crate was Emery's sock monkey, Laird. He had loved Laird, carried him everywhere, sucked on his foot. Anna poked at Laird with the toe of her boot. He was brown and shiny, filthy. She couldn't believe anyone would actually save a thing like Laird.

The room felt small: the two beds, the numerous boxes, and

the circus animal wallpaper were closing in on Anna. She noticed that Emery had drawn on the wallpaper animals, giving black ink penises to some, and hanging-nippled breasts to others. The elephant had the biggest penis of all, dragging on the ground like a fifth leg.

"This is disgusting," Anna said. Like her mother, she was prone to speak aloud to herself. Anna left the room and retrieved her suitcase from the entrance hall. She hauled the luggage into Emery's old room and plopped it in the middle of Portia's bed. There was no way she was going to sleep on the cot.

The front door banged open.

"Hello?!" Anna called out.

"Me!" Portia said, and Anna rolled her eyes. How was it possible that her sister was so happy all the time, even when surrounded by the muck and mire of their home and their parents?

"Anna?!" Portia called.

"In Emery's room!" Anna said.

Portia popped open the door and looked in.

"Dad took over my room as a second office and Emery moved into your room."

"Really?" Portia asked.

"Really."

"I've only been gone three months!"

"We're out now," Anna said. "We're like Bubbe and Zeyde visiting."

Portia looked down at the bed and the cot pushed side by side against the wall.

"It's like we're in a dorm!" Portia said, and she stepped in and threw her backpack onto the cot. Anna couldn't understand why her sister wasn't distressed by their sudden, intense proximity. They had rarely spoken since Anna went away to college.

Only recently had the girls been exchanging letters. Anna's letters were usually cartoon strips with drawings of the people sitting around her in the cafeteria eating, or of a group gathered in a closet-sized room passing around a bong. She would write single-sentence captions underneath, things like, "This guy and I made out one night after doing shots at some alky-towny bar near school." Portia's letters rarely had drawings, and were mostly detailed character descriptions about her housemates, classmates, and the people she met at the café at the end of her block. Anna's favorite letter from Portia detailed her friendship with the bearded quadriplegic who spoke by banging the pointer strapped to his head onto a lettered Ouija-like board that straddled the arms of his wheelchair. It turned out he directed porn movies and he spent fifteen minutes one day banging out, "Will you star in one of my films? You'd only have to have sex with my wife and me. And maybe some of her friends."

But with all the details, the minutiae the two girls revealed, they rarely actually talked about themselves. Portia was, in a way, a stranger to Anna; Anna could only think of her sister in memory: daffy Sally, from *Peanuts*, or Pigpen, the slob, who would sit on the floor of the family room watching TV and making the most infuriating popping sounds when she breathed. Anna walked to her sister and gave her a quick hug.

"Where are Mom and Dad?" Portia asked, and as if on cue, the girls heard their mother's wooden clogs tapping against the kitchen floor.

Louise was tending to the dinner she had set to simmer hours earlier.

"Hey, Mom!" Portia said, and she went to her mother and hugged her for a long time. Louise rocked her daughter back and forth, as if she were a little girl, then pulled Portia away and kissed her on the forehead. Of course their mother would kiss Portia first, Anna thought.

"I missed you!" Louise said.

"Did you miss me?" Anna said, and she approached for her hug.

"Of course," Louise said.

"No, you didn't. You only missed Portia." Anna smiled. She figured she better at least act like she was joking.

"Yeah, Mom only missed me!" Portia said, and Louise laughed.

"Come to the store with me," Anna said, to Portia. She had to get out. Just being in the house made Anna's mind feel as cluttered and muddled as the kitchen counter.

Anna picked up Louise's car keys that were sitting on the counter.

"What do you need?" Louise asked.

"Tampons," Anna said.

"Use mine," Louise said, and she lifted a spoon to her mouth and slurped the steamy gravy from the pot roast she was making.

"Yours are too big," Anna said.

"You've got a big vagina, Mom," Portia said, and Louise and Anna laughed.

"Portia, come with me. Mom, I'm borrowing the car." Anna headed down the hallway toward the front door as Emery came running in.

"Hey!" he said, and he leaned in and hugged Anna. Emery had grown about six inches since she had seen him last. Anna thought he smelled like moldy bread. Louise had written Anna a letter that chronicled Emery's current interest in taking a pitchfork, standing on the hill-sized compost pile Buzzy had fenced off with redwood planks, and turning the fusty, steamy pile. Maybe this accounted for his smell.

"Emery!" Portia said, and she ran down the hall and grabbed her brother.

"Portia, let's go. Now. Emery, we'll see you when we get back." Portia was slow in everything she did: she moved slowly, walked slowly, said hello slowly. If Anna didn't push her sister out the door this second, she'd never get her out.

"Can I come?" Emery followed Anna.

"No!" Anna said.

"Take your brother!" Louise shouted, from the kitchen.

Anna was practically running toward the blue station wagon in the driveway. Emery and Portia followed her, jumping into the car as if they were making a getaway.

"Listen," Anna said, and she tilted the rearview mirror so she could see Emery in the backseat. He was skinnier with his new height, and his voice was starting to crack.

"Listen what?" Emery asked. He scooted up and put his hands on the back of the bench seat. The rims under his finger-nails were black as tar.

"Whatever you see me and Portia do, you are not allowed to report to Mom and Dad. Get it?"

"What are you going to do? Rob a bank?"

"Yeah," Portia said, "what are we going to do?"

"I don't know what we're going to do. I mean *anything*. Anything I do or say cannot be reported back to Mom and Dad."

"Are you doing drugs?" Emery asked.

"Noble Citizen wants to know if you're doing drugs?" Portia asked, and she alone laughed. She knew from the letters Anna sent that she was at least doing some kind of drug on occasion.

"Portia, reach into my purse and get me a cigarette, will

you?" Anna could hear Louise's voice in herself when she said that.

Emery jumped in his seat. "YOU SMOKE!?"

Portia handed her sister a cigarette and a lighter, then stuck a cigarette in her mouth, too.

"NO WAY!" Emery said. "You smoke, too?!"

"You smoke?" Anna asked.

"I thought I'd try it during finals a couple weeks ago," Portia said, "and then this really hot boy told me it looked sexy, so . . ." She lit her cigarette.

"You're smoking because a boy thought it was sexy?!" Emery said. "That's the dumbest thing I've ever heard."

He was right, Anna thought, but Portia was dumb in just that way.

"I'm smoking so I don't eat and barf," Anna said. "But I seem to be drinking more calories than ever, so it sort of evens out."

"You drink alcohol?!" Emery said.

"You eat and barf?!" Portia asked.

"I'm twenty-fucking-one now!" Anna shouted.

"But eat and *barf.*"

"Everyone at Bennington does it. We keep a big black Hefty bag in our room and barf in it."

"Your roommate barfs with you?!"

"It's no fucking big deal! And anyway, I told you, the smoking helps me not do it!" Portia was such an alarmist, Anna thought. Everyone at Bennington was doing everything: free-basing cocaine, barfing, cutting themselves with razors. Why did Portia have to act like there was something wrong with all this? This was college. Shit happens.

"Fine!" Portia said.

"Fine really? Or fine, and now you're going to run home and tell Mom and Dad that I'm barfing?"

"If it's no big deal to you it's no big deal to me," Portia said.

"But it is a big deal!" Emery said.

"You can think it's a big deal, but don't say anything about it, okay?" Anna asked.

"Okay," Emery said, and he bounced back against his seat. Anna glared at Emery in the rearview mirror until she was sure he would submit.

Anna drove past the grocery store and the drugstore.

"I thought you needed tampons," Portia said.

"I needed a cigarette," Anna said. "And now I need a drink."

"It's five o'clock in the afternoon!" Emery said. "And Portia's not twenty-one. And I turned fourteen only two days ago."

"Happy birthday to you . . ." Anna started singing and then Portia joined in. They were laughing and singing so enthusiastically that Anna almost missed the turn for Jasper's Saloon. She had to slam the brakes and skid into the driveway.

"Do you have a fake ID?" Anna asked. Portia nodded but she looked nervous, like she was carrying some Girl Scout ID that might not work.

"Do you have a California driver's license?" Portia asked.

"No, a Vermont one." Anna turned off the car, pulled up the emergency break, and tapped an ash out the window.

"Cool," Portia said.

"But before I turned twenty-one, I had an Alaska driver's license. They sell them at the back of this restaurant in Chinatown."

"Chinatown?" Emery asked. "There's a Chinatown in Vermont?"

"There are Chinatowns everywhere!" Portia said to her brother. "Even Vermont."

"There's no Chinatown in Vermont!" Anna said. "There

aren't any Chinese people in that state. Just snow and white people and some Canadians with French-sounding names." Anna got out of the car. Emery and Portia got out, too. No one locked their door.

"Well, then where'd you get the fake ID?" Portia asked.

"Chinatown, New York," Anna said. "My friends and I have been taking the train there since freshman year."

"You never told me that," Portia said.

"You never asked." Anna heaved open the heavy wooden door of Jasper's. From the outside, the bar had always reminded Anna of Noah's arc: it was built with horizontal slats of shellacked wood, like an old boat. Neither she nor Portia had ever been inside.

Jasper's was long, narrow, and as dark as a closet. Against one wall was the bar with wooden stools against it. The other side of the room had a row of two-seat tables. No one was at the tables. A smattering of men in plaid work shirts and a couple of coifed smoky ladies sat at the bar. Emery tugged Portia's arm anxiously.

"I'm too young to be in a bar," he pleaded.

"We'll pretend you're a midget," Portia said.

The girls sat at stools and Emery stood half-hidden between them.

"Sit down!" Anna snapped at her brother.

"No!" Emery hissed, then whispered, "I don't want the bartender to see me, and if the police come in, I want to be ready to run." Anna and Portia cracked up.

The bartender was younger than Buzzy and Louise but older than Anna and Portia. He was appealing in that he had even, smooth features and hair that looked streaked from the sun. He leaned toward the girls across the bar and raised his eyebrows.

"Whiskey sour," Anna said.

"I'll have the same," Portia said. The man turned his back to them as he fixed the drinks.

"What's a whiskey sour?" Emery asked.

"No idea," Portia said.

"It's good," Anna said. "You can share Portia's with her."

"I'm not drinking!" Emery said.

"IDs," the man said. He slid the two drinks in front of the girls, then reached out a sturdy, veined forearm.

Portia pulled her license from her wallet. Anna whipped her license out from her back pocket.

"Anna Stein and Anna Stein," he said, looking from one ID to the other. Anna looked at Portia with hard, fast eyes.

"We're twins," Portia said, smiling.

The bartender winked, handed back the IDs, and went to the end of the bar to help an old woman who was singing "Funny Valentine."

"Twins wouldn't have the same name!" Emery whispered. It was clear he was disgusted with Portia's lack of insight into this matter.

Anna grabbed the driver's license.

"What the fuck?" she asked. "How'd you get a real driver's license?" She was both angry and impressed. A genuine matte, ribbed California driver's license was so much more masterly than a plastic Alaska license that looked like the IDs you get when you drive a go-kart.

"I used your birth certificate." Portia took the license back and shoved it in her wallet as if she expected Anna to confiscate it. "Mom sent it to me accidentally when she sent my passport and a bunch of other papers."

"Do you realize how many laws you're breaking?!" Emery asked. Anna and Portia looked at Emery and laughed.

"He's like the cartoon angel that sits on the guy's shoulder and tells the guy not to do the bad thing," Portia said.

"Yeah," Anna said. "Exactly! Except he needs a little devil-red twin who will tell us to go ahead and do it." Anna took a sip of her drink. She thought that she was her own who-gives-a-fuck devil. The good angel inside her was an anorexic waif who was too weak to give a voice to anything. That was fine with her. Life was more fun that way. Easier.

Anna huffed as she pulled over the station wagon on the way home from Jasper's so Portia could vomit. Why did her sister have to be such a lightweight? Louise always said that Portia had a "delicate system." What kind of bullshit was a delicate system?! Anna thought the girl simply needed to build up tolerance, be braver, buck up. She needed to be more like Otto and Billie and less like Bubbe and Zeyde.

"I think I'm allergic!" Portia yelled as she ran to the soft, plush grass and leaned into the bougainvillea bushes along the front walk of the Smyths' house. Emery crawled out of the car and stood behind Portia, his dirty little paw rubbing her back. No one was worried about the Smyths' finding Portia barfing on their lawn. It was clear they were gone for Christmas—there were no cars out and the curtains were closed. The house looked dead.

"Hurry up!" Anna shouted out the window. "Mom's going to freak if we're not back in time for dinner." She wasn't really worried about their mother, but she was tired of waiting for the lightweight to heave up her drinks.

Portia stumbled to the car. She looked deflated and soiled. Emery opened the door for her, helped her get in, then climbed over her lap and did a flip into the back seat. He was too big for the move, legs and tennis shoes banging against the ceiling.

"You okay?" Emery asked. Anna looked in the mirror at her brother's tiny face. With his crinkled brow, she could imagine him a grown man with worries.

"Yeah, it's no big deal," Portia said.

"I can't believe you're barfing from three drinks! What's wrong with you?" Anna jerked the car backwards out of the driveway.

"I dunno," Portia said. "That's what happens every single time I drink."

"Then WHY do you drink?!" Emery asked. "If I threw up every time I drank Tang, I would stop drinking Tang!"

"But drinking's fun!" Anna said, and she reached for her purse on Portia's lap, swerving the car, as she tried to get her cigarettes.

"Watch the road!" Emery shouted.

"Hey, Father Junior," Anna said, "don't worry about the road. We'll be fine!"

Portia took the cigarettes from Anna, pulled out two, and lit them both before handing her sister one.

"This cigarette makes me feel like I have to vomit again," Portia groaned.

"THEN PUT IT OUT!" Emery said. His eyes were as big and round as his mouth. It was clear he had never before witnessed such imbecilic behavior.

"But I really like smoking," Portia said, and she laughed and coughed at the same time.

"You know what the best thing is about being in Santa Barbara?" Anna asked.

"The ocean," Emery said.

"All the hot surfer guys," Portia said.

"No, dumbasses!" Anna drove half-way up on the curb as

she aimed for the driveway. "Oops," she said. She put the car in reverse and tried landing it once again.

"What's the best thing about being in Santa Barbara?" Emery asked.

"This town is so fucking small, no matter where you're drinking, you're always drinking closer to home." She pushed down the emergency brake with her foot and cut the engine.

"I guess Otto would be happy here," Emery said.

"Nah," Portia said. "Otto wouldn't be happy here. Too many freaks and weirdos, remember?"

The girls stubbed out their cigarettes in the open car ashtray that was heaped with cigarette butts and ash. Most of the butts had a blot of red on them from Louise's lipstick. Portia tucked her butt under others so that it wouldn't be the one to fall off the pile. Anna set hers down and watched as it toppled two other butts onto the floor in front of Portia's feet. They both stared down at the butts and saw that there were plenty others down there, along with gum wrappers and a balled-up oily paper wrap from a McDonald's run.

"I hope Mom doesn't notice that there are a couple of Marlboro butts in with her Camel butts," Portia said.

"Mom's such a slob," Anna said. When she owned a car, there would never be so much as a cellophane wrapper from a pack of gum on the floor.

"Yeah," Portia said. "You know, I keep my room clean in Berkeley. It's weird. I'm, like, the cleanest person in my house."

"Everyone who comes from a messy house becomes clean when they go away to college." Anna declared this as if she'd already thought it through, had had the conversation a thousand times with a thousand different people, when in fact such insight had only come to her now.

"Does that mean you're messy now?" Emery asked.

"No. Clean people are always clean people." Anna got out of the car and shut the door. "But people who come from messy houses are so relieved not to have to deal with other people's messes that they become clean people. It's true. I swear."

As they were walking toward the house, Anna grabbed Emery by the neck of his T-shirt and pulled him toward her.

"Listen, Father Junior," she said. "Everything we just did is our secret, right?"

"Got it!" Emery said, and he squirmed out of her arms and ran ahead into the house.

"Do you think he's gay?" Portia asked, and she steadied herself by clutching Anna's forearm.

"Emery?" Anna tugged her arm away. Everyone in the family touched her too much.

"Yeah. I just get this weird feeling that he's gay. I don't know why."

"He probably is. He did draw penises all over the wallpaper in his room." Anna opened the front door and rushed inside with Portia stumbling somewhere behind her.

Louise was carrying the pot roast to the dining room table, a cigarette dangling in her mouth. Anna grabbed a trivet from the kitchen, then placed it on the table as her mother waited. The ash from Louise's cigarette dropped into the pot, melting into the sauce. Louise put down the pot, stuck her finger in where the ash had landed, and quickly swirled it until it had thoroughly dissolved.

"It's like pepper," she said.

Anna tried to keep track of where the ash swirl was in the pan. Portia walked into the room, stood beside her sister, and stared into the pan.

"Don't have a shit fit," Louise said.

"Who shouldn't have a shit fit?" Portia asked.

"Your sister! Who has all the shit fits around here?"

"You have shit fits, Mom," Anna said.

"Why do you think Anna's going to have a shit fit right now?" Portia looked at her sister. Anna thought Portia's eyes looked funny, wobbly, and wet.

"She dropped ash into the pot roast," Anna said. She tilted her head as she tried to remember the ash spot.

"I think Father Junior might have a shit fit over that," Portia said.

Louise laughed. "Father Junior? Is that his new name?"

"He's one uptight little poindexter," Anna said.

"Well, at least he's over the pot thing," Louise said.

"So Emery's hitting the bong now?" Anna grinned. She figured he'd probably die an old man, never having tried pot.

"Of course not!" Louise said. "But he's fine with the plants in the backyard and he doesn't leave the room when I'm getting high."

"What about when you're shooting up, Mom? Or freebasing?" Portia asked.

"Oh, please!" Louise tittered. Anna looked at her mother's face, her long center-parted hair hanging in front of her shoulders, and thought it wasn't hard to imagine her shooting up.

Anna saw herself and Portia as cartoon characters: Anna spinning up dust like the Road Runner as she whirred around Portia, the slow moving, overly mellow Dumbo. As Portia cleared the table, Anna did the dinner dishes, cleaned the stovetop, cleaned the sink, ran the garbage disposal, and took out the trash. Then she asked her mother for the keys again.

"Where are you going?" Louise was lying on the couch, a *New Yorker* magazine in one hand, a tightly rolled joint in the

JESSICA ANYA BLAU (168

other. Buzzy had the ironing board out and was watching the
news as he ironed a pile of dress shirts. Emery was kneeling on
the floor with a giant pad of paper covering the coffee table in
front of him. He had an open flat of colored pencils and was
drawing a roller coaster that did loops, traveled backwards, and
shuffled from side to side. He had shown his sisters the drawing
earlier, and had also shown them the thirty or so other roller
coasters he had designed.

"We're going downtown," Anna said. "Portia's going to meet
up with her friends and I'm meeting up with Alice." Neither
Portia nor Anna had called their friends since they got home.
Anna's impulse was to lie even when it was unnecessary.

"Okay. Don't stay out too late."

Anna picked up the keys and Portia started to follow her,
then looked back and yelled, "Bye!"

"Where're you going?" Buzzy asked, as if he had only then
noticed his daughters.

"OUT!" Anna yelled.

"To meet friends," Portia said. She tugged on her sister's
shirt to slow her down. Anna stopped for a second, then pulled
away.

"Don't stay out too late," Buzzy called after the girls.

Anna drove to Flapper Alley, a disco on State Street near the
beach. She parked by the railroad tracks, next to the only gay
bar in town.

Portia was wearing lizard-skin pumps she had found in her
mother's closet with a button-down dress shirt, taken from her
father's closet, as a dress. Her sleeves were rolled up, her legs
were bare. Anna was already sick of hearing her complain about
being cold.

"Hurry," Anna said, and she took her sister's hand and

pulled her along the dark, gravelly alley. Anna was wearing lace-up flat black boots that looked almost like boxers' boots, black silk boxer shorts, and a lace camisole top. She looked over at her sister and realized that Portia, with her three-inch pumps, appeared much bigger than she. People often commented on how small Anna was, but she never saw herself that way. She felt enormous: a high-speed giant whirring through a world of lumbering dwarves. She did notice that most people, once they knew her for a while, forgot she was small. This was especially true after her breasts grew in.

When they got to the line up at the door, Anna put Portia at the back, then cut two people ahead, lessening the chance that the repeated name would be noticed. Her plan worked, and they met up again at the long, open stairway up to the bar. It was so crowded inside, you had to move up the steps and through the room sideways, choosing whom you'd brush against as you walked past.

"Do you have money?" Anna had to shout in her sister's ear to be heard over the throbbing music. "I spent all mine at Jasper's."

"This is all I have for my entire Christmas break." Portia pulled a twenty-dollar bill from her breast pocket and handed it to Anna.

Anna wormed her way toward the bar, checking out everyone near her on the way. The men seemed fully grown, filled out, confident. Her eyes lingered on the ones who stared. It was like clicking through a file cabinet looking for exactly the right thing. Anna could sense Portia behind her like a tucked tail.

"Don't leave me alone here," Portia said, and Anna pretended not to hear.

At the bar, Anna handed Portia a milkshake-sized glass filled with icy pink-and-yellow swirled slush. "It's a zombie," she said.

"About seven kinds of liquor in there and enough shots to make you trashed after only one."

Portia took a sip, then pulled her head back as if she'd been shocked. Anna took the straw out of her own drink, tossed it to the ground, and chugged from the side of the glass.

"Don't barf," she said, when she paused for air.

"I'll try not to." Portia slurped up tiny bits of the drink. Anna suspected she was letting it slide down the straw and not really drinking it.

"Are you drunk already?" Anna asked, smiling, leering.

"No. But I can feel it already. It's like a buzzing, fluorescent light's been turned on in my head."

"Let's dance," Anna said.

The last time Anna saw Portia, she was being twirled by a smooth-dancing guy on the dance floor. Anna watched as each spin pulled her sister in closer and closer. But then she stopped looking because she couldn't turn her head away from the tall, skinny, surfer dude who was whispering in her own ear.

The next time Anna saw Portia was when she and the skinny dude pushed the bathroom stall door open to find Portia barfing up clean, virtually odorless Slurpee-looking foam into the bathroom sink.

Another stall door popped open and a girl the size of a radio antenna walked out wearing strappy high heels and a flirty dress.

"Gross," she said, and she left without washing her hands.

Portia remained hunched over the sink. She appeared to be waiting to see if more would come out.

"What the fuck?" Anna said. The girls looked at each other in the mirror. Anna thought that if she weren't so fucked up, she might be embarrassed by Portia. But now, Anna felt sorry for her. Poor Portia was a boneless blob of a human: couldn't drink, walked at the speed of melting glass, talked in the slow drawl of a surfer who'd smoked a blunt.

"I got sick," Portia said.

"I don't know what her problem is," Anna said, and she wiped her nose with her palm.

"Coke?" the guy asked, and he held out a vial toward the back of Portia's head.

"Nobody barfs from coke," Anna said, and she laughed.

"I know," Portia said. "But I don't like coke. It makes my heart beat in my stomach and I feel like I'm getting electric shocks in my jaw."

Portia turned on the faucet to wash the vomit down the drain. Once it was gone, she rinsed her hands and washed her mouth out, gargling. Anna turned her face to the tall surfer and they made out against the open stall door. Whoever was in the third stall wasn't coming out—a pair of scuffed black pumps sat in view under the door waiting, watching, still.

"Here," the guy said when Portia turned around. He lifted a tiny spoon from the vial and held it under her nostril.

"I don't like it," Portia said.

"Come on!" Anna said. "Don't be such a lightweight!"

Portia leaned her head down and took it up one nostril. The guy dipped the spoon again and she took it in the other nostril. Anna and her guy were already kissing again. He had one arm extended, holding the vial out as they stumbled—still attached, still standing—into the stall.

"Thanks for the coke," Portia said.

"No problem," the guy mumbled. Anna ironed her lips into his.

"I'll see you out there," Portia said. She sounded so far away and small; Anna imagined her as a mouse about to exit through a crack in the wall.

The coke-carrying surfer's skin was hot. His body was as solid and flat as a sidewalk. And his hands were like giant vibrating paddles roaming Anna's flesh. Everything beyond her body and the surfer's body was a blurry, impotent background. Sometimes Anna thought of herself as an appliance. She was never fully operating unless she had the electrical charge of another body plugged into her. When someone was plugged into her, especially when she was high, she found a beautiful, dreamy timelessness where nothing was ahead and nothing was behind. Her life was only in the pulsating here and now: sensation, excitation, elevation.

The guy had slipped Anna's boxers down to the mucky half-wet bathroom floor and was sawing into her now—a fabulous, wet oblivion.

And then he was out of her. And Anna was cold and the guy was pulling tufts of toilet paper off the roll and wiping his dick like it was a dusty piece of silverware he was about to lay on a table.

"Can I have some?" Anna asked. The guy looked at her and she tried to focus on his face. She liked his nose—it was a perfect triangle. He handed her a few squares, then slipped out to the other side of the beige, metal door.

"I'll see you outside," he said, and he was gone.

Anna stood in the stall for a moment and watched as a white, almost-opalescent drip of something plopped onto the floor between her feet. She looked down, saw her boxers like a black hole near her right foot. Anna pulled the boxers up, stopped them at her knees, and then used the toilet paper in her hand to wipe herself clean. She yanked the shorts up the rest of the way, stood in the stall a moment, and thumped her head against the back of the door. There were two girls chatting at the sink— laughing, squealing. Anna tilted her head and spied on them through the crack. They were lithe, long, fresh-looking. Anna felt like a smudge of muck. She didn't want to walk out and see herself beside them—a dark, viscous stain of cum and sweat and oil.

The girls left, and Anna staggered out of the stall. She paused at the mirror for only a second. She needed to move on, to find the tall surfer, to plug him in again so she could glow and feel powerful once more.

The music was thumping. Anna could hear it in her skin and it gave her small charges, pushed her forward, pumped her up again as she darted through the crowd.

She found her sister dancing with a shirtless guy. His body was ridged, taut, sinewy. He was mouthing the words of the Kim Carnes song that was playing, snaking his arms around, fingers pointing alternately at himself and at Portia. Anna couldn't bear standing there alone while her sister was uniting with someone who looked like energy and strength. She flipped around, scanning for her bathroom lover. He was at the bar, leaning on one elbow, the first finger of his free hand hooked in the back belt loop of a girl with brown hair as thick and shiny as a waterfall. Anna felt a chill screaming inside her. She felt her body shredding away like burning newspaper. And then she saw someone new. A boy with eyes like cameras on her. He moved closer and closer, bouncing with the music.

"Hey," he said, and he placed a hand on Anna's hip.

"Hey," Anna said, and she waved her pelvis toward him.

"Wanna go to the beach?" he asked. "It's so fucking hot in here, I need a swim."

Twenty minutes later Anna was naked, breaststroking along the shoreline with the new guy. It was so dark out the water looked like ink. The guy appeared as a splashing shadow. Most of the bar crowd had tumbled out to the beach at two a.m. when drinks were no longer served. Anna saw the people more by the sounds they made than any outline she could decipher. Echolocation, Anna thought. Portia was probably out there somewhere with the shirtless guy she had been dancing with.

Anna's guy snatched her foot mid-kick. He pulled her toward him in one water-ballet motion. Anna's legs wrapped around his waist—he could stand, but it was too deep for her—and he plugged himself into her, as if they both knew that that was the single purpose of their union. Anna wanted to pull her head back and see what he looked like—she remembered he was good-looking, but couldn't recall a single feature.

Anna slipped out of coitus and, with her legs still knotted behind the guy, she lowered her back like an ironing board against the water. She squinted and focused.

"How old are you?" Anna asked. It seemed like an age might help bring his face in focus, might fine-tune the details she couldn't make out.

"Eighteen," he said.

"Me, too," Anna lied, and then she did a sit up so she was upright once more. Anna kissed the boy and he slipped inside her again as if she were the nesting spot for his dick; penis memory. It wasn't hard to cleave together but it was hard to create friction, as there was nothing against which either of them could gain purchase. So they fucked like sea turtles—weightless, without thrust—until they drifted closer to the crowd, at which point he pulled away, took Anna's hand, and led her to a dry, flat rock underneath the base of the old pier.

"Why don't we go on the sand where it's softer?" Anna asked. The boy's hands seemed to have multiplied. He was somehow touching her everywhere at once.

"Too sandy," he mumbled, and he pushed his mouth against hers. "Lie down."

Anna lay down for a second, then sat up. The rock felt as jagged as glass against her back. She and the boy traded positions so that he was on his back and she was straddling him, holding on to his dick as if it were a stick shift.

"You're so sandy," Anna said. She hopped off, got down on her knees, and tried to brush the grit off his dick. Even when she was high, Anna still had the impulse to clean.

The boy grunted and tried to nudge Anna on top of him again.

"What is this?" Anna leaned closer and tried to see what was growing on the sides of the boy's dick. She was thinking of tide pool creatures: a sea cucumber with tiny crustaceans all over it.

"They're scabs," he said. "I got them from jerking off too much."

"Really?" Anna laughed, and mounted him once more. She imagined all his tiny scabs scraping against her insides and cleaning her out, like a bottle brush.

Anna could make out the murky form of people approaching, but she didn't slow down until she heard her sister's voice.

"Anna!"

"What?"

"We gotta go!"

"Who's with you?"

"I'm Tim! I love your sister!"

"You don't love me!" Portia said. "Anna, let's go." They were close enough that Anna could see them now. She dismounted the boy and he ran off. The night was so dark it looked like he had actually dissolved.

"Patricia, you are the love of my life," the guy said. Anna and Portia laughed.

"I'm Portia, not Patricia," Portia said.

"Man, and I was already comin' up with all these nicknames for you based on the fact that your name's Patricia."

"Do I look like a Patricia? What are the nicknames?"

"Patty O' Furniture, Patty Wagon, Party Patty, hamburger Patty, Pitty Patty, Patty in my mouth—"

"And everyone's cumin'?" As soon as Anna spoke, she remembered she was naked, but didn't really care.

"Yeah." Tim laughed.

Anna's guy was suddenly back. He held both their clothes. It looked like he was on his way to do laundry. He tossed Anna her clothes and then he put on his own.

"Can we give Tim a ride home?" Portia asked.

"Buddies left without me," Tim said.

"Yeah. Anyone got any coke?" Anna asked.

"I know where we can get some." Anna's lover buttoned his jeans and reached a hand out for Anna.

Anna drove, swerving on the road so much that the boy grabbed the wheel a few times. Portia was in the back seat with Tim. All the windows were open. Strings of Anna's hair darted in front of her eyes, then away again. The boy directed them up the hills, to a Spanish-style house that had a wrought-iron security gate in front. It was four-thirty in the morning. Anna cranked down her window and the boy reached across her and finger-punched the buzzer.

"Yeah," a scratchy voice came over the speaker.

"Joe, it's me."

"Me who?"

"It's Roy, you fucker!" Roy gave the finger to the speaker box and the gate slowly swung open, bouncing a bit before stopping. Anna was glad he had said his name as, even in her current fucked-up state, she was aware that they were too deep into it for her to ask.

Anna pulled the car up the driveway and parked with the front bumper resting against the bumper of a sturdy, low sports car. Joe came out in boxer shorts, black dress socks, and no shirt. His body was shadowed with muscles; there was no hair on his chest but his legs were nearly black with fur. He leaned in the station wagon window.

"Nice car," he said, and he grinned.

"No one has any money," Roy said, "but we need some coke."

"I'll give you each a line," Joe said, and he opened the door and held his arm out for Anna.

"My brother," Roy said.

"My sister!" Anna said, and she pointed at Portia and lost her balance so that she went, knees down, onto the tiled driveway.

"Fuck." Joe chuckled and picked Anna up.

Joe, Roy, and Anna were chattering like a bunch of mating birds. Blood dripped down one of Anna's knees from where she had scraped it on the driveway; every few seconds she stopped talking, bent over, and licked her wound. In her peripheral vision she felt her sister sitting there, right beside her, with Tim, like two lumps on the couch.

"Do you love this house?" Anna said to Portia, trying to pull her in from her spacey orbit. Anna looked around at the Mexican and African carved sculptures, the black-and-white poster-sized photos of children with dinner-plate-sized eyes and dirt on their faces, the furniture that smelled new but looked lived-in. The half-gallon bottle of tequila on the table.

"What do you call this style?" Anna felt like she was shouting from inside a glass block. No one seemed to hear her.

"Celebrate Poverty?" Portia said.

"Celibate poverty?" Tim said.

"Line?" Joe held a small silver straw out to Portia and nodded toward the two pencil-length thin lines spread on the polished rock coffee table. Portia passed the straw to Tim, who passed it back to Portia, then gathered her hair in the back. Anna thought of herself and her Italian roommate at Bennington each holding their own hair back while they barfed in the black plastic trash bag.

Portia leaned down and took half a line in one nostril and the other half in the other. Then she handed the straw to Tim, who did the last line.

"I hate this," Portia whispered to Anna.

"Why?" Anna thought her sister stupidly and ignorantly rejected some of the greatest pleasures in life: cocaine, runny cheeses, Dijon mustard.

"It feels like my muscles are going to burst out of my jaw." Portia turned to Tim. "Do you hate this?"

Anna leaned down, licked up a drip of blood from her knee, then sat up and did a shot of tequila to wash it down. She shifted in her seat so her back was to her sister. Portia's total lack of virility was pathetic and embarrassing. Luckily, Anna was so high she didn't feel embarrassed for long; time had suddenly accelerated and she was instantly ten moments past her embarrassment.

Anna opened her eyes and saw she was arm wrestling with shirtless Joe. She wasn't sure how it started but she was certain that's what she was doing. Her bony elbow was grinding into the stone table. Roy was the referee.

"Winner gets another line!" Joe said, and he punched Anna's arm to the coffee table.

"Again!" she said, and she slid off the couch and propped herself up on her knees. She wasn't sure if her sister was still in the room. After uncountable lines and many shots of tequila, her vision had closed in like a curtain and she could only see three feet directly in front of herself.

"Yes," Anna said, although she wasn't sure what question had just been asked of her. She was fully plugged in. Anna had done enough coke to silence all the dithering, piddly, bullshitty little squeaks in her brain: the squeak about being inadequate, the squeak about not being pretty, the squeak about not being cool enough.

She and Joe and Roy were in the master bedroom that had a bed as big a boat. And the bed was rocking like a boat, too, as she and Joe and Roy rolled from one end to the next. The brothers had arm-wrestled for her—a match that ended in a tie. Together, they were a mess of flesh and muscle; Anna could not find the outline of either brother. She looked at an arm, a hand, a knee, and didn't know whose it was—it could be hers, even, as the lights were dim and everything was muted and gray. If she could roll like this forever she would, Anna thought. This was the highest form of living. It was an endless, glorious, body-charged freefall.

And then Portia was there, standing in the doorway as stiff and hard as a broomstick.

"I'm going home," Portia shouted.

"You're going home now?" Anna sat up, fully naked, and stared at the upright line that was her sister. What was wrong with this girl? Did she not enjoy fun? Did she not think that these were the two hottest coke-holding guys she'd ever seen? Was she a moron?!

"Join us!" Joe said.

"Call me in the morning if you want a ride home!" Portia turned and vanished. Anna was glad—getting rid of Portia was like taking off her collar and leash. She was totally free now.

Anna opened her eyes to the bright daylight. Her body was throbbing, as if she were a single, purple bruise. She looked to her right and saw the sinewy, naked body of . . . Roy. Yes, Roy. She was almost certain of it. On her left was Joe.

Joe opened his eyes. He sat up and stuck a hand on Anna's breast, which lay fallen to her side. "Coke?" Joe asked.

Anna blinked. Yes, she thought. She felt exposed in the daylight, as if her skin were made of cellophane. "Yeah, sure," she said.

Anna followed him, naked, downstairs to the living room.

"You doing any?" Anna bent over the line on the stone table, her bare ass raised toward Joe.

"Nah," Joe said, and he put his hands on her hips and motioned forward.

DAY SEVEN

Every morning, before they leave for the hospital, Emery calls his office, Alejandro calls his office, Anna calls home, and Portia calls her three-year old daughter, Esmé, at her pending ex-husband Patrick's apartment in New York City. It's not really his apartment; it's his girlfriend Daphne Frank's. Esmé didn't even know about Daphne Frank until the heart attack. Portia did not want Esmé to stay in Daphne Frank's apartment with Patrick. She wanted Patrick to stay in Portia's house (what used to be *their* house) with Esmé. But Esmé is in nursery school, nursery school ends at one-thirty, and Portia couldn't find any-one in Greenwich to watch her while Patrick was at work. The search for childcare took place in the two hours after Buzzy told Portia that her mother had had a heart attack, after Por-tia had insisted on speaking to a doctor because Buzzy was be-ing so evasive, after she finally spoke to a nurse who told her she needed to take the next flight possible, as every minute her mother was alive was a miracle. During this time Portia was also trying to find a plane ticket and a ride to the airport. Before she had come up with anything, Patrick found an old Filipina woman, Jo, the caretaker for an even older German woman in Daphne Frank's building, who said she could watch Esmé until Patrick got home from work. But she had to do it in the apart-ment in New York, so that she was only a floor away from her main charge. Portia had worried for a moment that Esmé would be ruined somehow by staying in Daphne Frank's apartment.

But then she remembered a Swedish study she had read that said the first three years are the most formative years in a child's life—after that, everything's more or less set. Since Esmé was a few months past her third birthday, Portia rationalized that Daphne Frank's sixteenth floor cool-girl apartment at Seventy-second and Broadway couldn't change who her daughter was, wouldn't turn Esmé into a short-skirt-wearing knee-high-boot chick like Daphne.

"Don't make out or anything in front of her!" Portia whispered in Patrick's ear, when he picked up Esmé to take her back to New York with him. "And don't let her know that you're sleeping in the same bed as Daphne!"

"Come on!" Patrick said, and Portia realized she was wrong to worry about that. Patrick had never been very demonstrative, and was almost a prude when it came to the things Esmé was exposed to. Portia knew he'd sleep on the couch or the floor with Esmé.

Every morning, Jo has answered the phone. Portia has asked the same questions each time: what is Esmé eating, are there are enough books in the apartment for her, is she getting outside every day, and have they been to any parks or museums? It is lunch there when they talk and Jo tells Portia what she has prepared, where they have been, where they plan to go and what books they have read. She was calling her "Miss Portia" and it made Portia feel guilty and uncomfortable, a reminder of the inequalities in the world and her place within them. When Portia told her not to call her "MISS Portia," Jo corrected herself and said "Mrs. Portia." Portia didn't have the heart to correct her again.

When Esmé gets on the phone, Portia asks the same questions over again and gets different versions of the day's events.

Yes, they went to Barnes and Noble for story hour, but the boy next to Esmé smelled like pee so it wasn't that much fun.

Today, on Day Seven, Daphne Frank answers the phone. Portia is startled into silence. Her stomach flops over, her face feels inflamed. She forgets where she is, then looks around the kitchen and places herself at Casa del Viento Fuerte.

"Hello?" Daphne Frank says again. Her voice is as dull as a spoon.

"Can I speak to Patrick?" Portia asks. Her own voice sounds odd to her, as if someone else were speaking for her.

"Who's this?" Daphne Frank asks.

"His wife." There is a drumbeat in Portia's belly as she speaks.

Patrick answers the phone.

"What are you doing there?" Portia watches Maggie Bucks walk across the stone counter. She wants to push her off but finds herself unable to move.

"The old woman Jo takes care of is sick today, so Jo has to stay with her."

"So you *both* are staying home?"

"Daphne got last-minute tickets to a matinee of *Stomp*. We're taking Esmé."

"You BOTH are taking off work to go to *Stomp*? You know you can't afford to get fired! You have a lot of people to support and I don't have a job. You really can't fuck up your position right now." This is not what Portia intends to say, and it is not even what she is thinking. She knows that Patrick won't get fired, he is invaluable at the firm. And she doesn't care if Daphne gets fired. These are simply words that fill in for what she is really feeling, for what she really thinks: *I am lost. I'm afraid I'm not going to have a mother soon. I no longer have a husband. I am afraid that I won't be able to manage myself without the people to whom I am attached.*

"The job's fine," Patrick says.

"If Jo gets sick, don't let her in the apartment." *I am afraid. I am afraid. I am alone.*

"She'll be fine." Patrick is short with Portia. It is like he doesn't want her to exist, doesn't want to take her, or anything she thinks or feels, into account. Portia imagines he is overloaded, like a bubbling chicken stock, and she is the grayish-white fat that floats to the top and gets skimmed off with a wooden spoon.

"Make sure Esmé eats something before the show. Like string cheese or something with protein in it." *Everything is out of my control. I feel like I'm swimming in a rip tide. I want someone to swim out and save me because I don't think I can do this alone.*

"Yeah, yeah. I'll give her string cheese. Do you want to talk to Esmé?"

"Well, I want to hear everything from you first so I can have the adult version of what's going on before I get her version." *We have a child together. We have known each other since college. Why do you treat me like I am your jailer?*

Emery walks into the kitchen. He is wearing an old, soft T-shirt and knit boxer shorts. Alejandro walks in behind him wearing something similar, only he has a beanie cap on his head. Portia waves at them. She is trying to make the moment seem normal and light, as if there isn't a stew of rocks and bile churning through her empty body. Alejandro and Emery wave back.

"I don't have time for this," Patrick says, to Portia. "Esmé can tell you everything."

"Don't you want to know about my mother? Your mother-in-law." *Don't you see that even when you eliminate me, I still am here?* Portia stutters as she holds back tears. She looks over at Emery and Alejandro and sees that they are oblivious to the turmoil inside her. Emery is making café au lait for the two of them, pouring milk into cups and heating the milk in the microwave. He loves café au lait and he loves breakfast, he always has. Alejandro is rummaging through the fridge, pulling out different things and asking Emery what he wants. Emery looks at each thing and considers it.

"Will you make me cinnamon toast with butter soaked through and an almost hardened layer of cinnamon and sugar?" he asks Alejandro. He's so lucky to have someone who makes him breakfast, Portia thinks.

Alejandro rolls his eyes, but he's smiling. He starts making the toast. Emery picks up Maggie Bucks, kisses her on the nose, and places her on the ground. She runs to the open cupboard and jumps up and in.

"How's your mother?" Patrick asks after a long, empty pause.

"I don't know." *I am so afraid.* Portia starts crying. Her nose is running. She picks up the paper napkin she had used this morning when she had toast and blows her nose in it. Toast crumbs rub against her nostrils like sand.

Emery and Alejandro continue making breakfast, only they're doing it slowly now. Portia can feel them each keeping an eye on her. She pulls in and tamps down her cry; she knows that the only thing her brother wants right now is to sit on the bench seat by the window, drink his café au lait, eat his cinnamon toast, and read the paper. Alejandro probably wants the same thing— who wants to deal with a crying woman?

Patrick says nothing. There is absolute silence on the phone.

"Hello?" Portia says. "Patrick?" *This is what's so awful about the breakup. This is what's so painful: you were there. We were*

*together. And now no one is there. It is just air on the other side
of me, as if a scab has been picked off my entire body and nothing
beneath is ready for exposure.*

When she hangs up the phone Portia looks at her brother.
She feels like she is balancing on the edge of a cliff—if she falls
forward she'll splatter into a thousand drippy pieces. If she
maintains her footing, Portia might survive this moment.

"You okay?" Emery asks. He's holding a piece of toast in
front of his mouth but hasn't bitten into it yet. Portia knows he
wants to take that bite and move on.

"I'm fine," Portia says. She's stepped back from the cliff. Portia ordinarily doesn't like to expose her emotions like some open,
runny sore, although she feels like she's been doing exactly that
with some frequency since her husband left. The crying-at-the-
club scene tapped out her tolerance for her own public displays
of grief.

Emery bites into the gooey center of his triangle-cut cinnamon
toast. It looks delicious. It is almost cracking in the center, exactly
as Emery had asked. It is painful to watch her brother eat his love
toast. Emery has the very thing Portia had until the interference
of Daphne Frank. And yet, when the toast is all gone and Alejandro gets up to make more for Emery (who gets up to make more
café au lait for them both), Portia tries to remember what exactly
in her marriage resembled this toast-making scene. It occurs to
her that the thing she thought she had lost may have never really
been there. Patrick never, ever, not even in the spoony beginnings
of their relationship, even thought of making toast. She offered
the love toast, she made the love toast, she served the love toast.
Patrick merely ate it. And there was no café au lait.

This thought is like dirt on Portia's hands, fudgy grime stuck
beneath her short, unpainted fingernails. She wants to take a
shower and wash this grime away.

"Well." Portia stands and looks at her brother and Alejandro. They are side by side on the bench seat, each with a plate of toast, cup of coffee, and a section of newspaper folded beside the plate.

"Well?" Emery says.

"Well, I think I'm going to shower," Portia says, and she walks away from the kitchen.

"Have a great shower!" Alejandro calls out, in an upswing voice that actually makes Portia smile.

Emery took his time driving from his Junior Statesmen
meeting to his girlfriend Katie's house. They were going to
have sex for the first time, a decision they had reached together
after dating for four months. He was a senior in high school,
president of the class, president of the Santa Barbara Chapter
of Junior Statesmen, and owned his own car (a used red Buick
bought with bar mitzvah money and McDonald's earnings).

Emery looked out the window and watched the lemon orchard blur by. He pushed a button and the window went down.
This act, using the power window, never failed to make Emery
smile. He was the first person in his family to own a car with
power windows, a luxury he quickly grew to think of as a right.
The last time he rode in Buzzy's car, after struggling with the
sticky window crank, Emery snapped his hand away, turned to
Buzzy and said, "I could never live like this!"

The air outside smelled like lemons. It was a gorgeous sunny
Thursday, a perfect day for Emery to lose his virginity to the
smartest, most beautiful girl in school.

After Emery's partner in the Corny Kids Variety Show, Josh,
had moved away, Emery had gone through a series of useless
friendships with boys who never really seemed like complete
humans. There was Adam: too dumb, loved to plant farts in
public that would be blamed on other people; loved to blow
things up. Randy: too restless, couldn't even watch TV; loved to
blow things up. Geoff: too sporty, only wanted to kick things

or throw things. Or blow things up. Mike: usually smelled like pork chops, except when he smelled like the burning remains from the things he had blown up (pumpkins, lizards, kelp, etc.). And then Emery discovered the magic of girls. They were calm. They liked to talk (Emery's favorite girls would talk about politics, or the economy, or films). They weren't interested in blowing things up. And although Emery loved adventure and wanted to travel, and live on a boat, and hike Machu Picchu, and go heliskiing in Switzerland, he didn't want to blow things up.

Emery turned left, away from the orchard, and pulled onto Katie's street. She was at the house waiting for him; her parents wouldn't be home until seven.

Emery and Katie were a perfect couple. They had already planned their lives together. They would have two kids, a girl named Matisse and a boy named Piet (both after the painters). They would live in Paris at first, but then would raise their children in Barcelona where the weather was more temperate. Katie would be an international lawyer, defending women in third world countries against all the inequities women in those places suffer. And Emery would be an ambassador, maybe, or an architect. Something both creative and commercial. There was no way he'd be like his mother, suffering in her studio alone with the radio all day, making etchings that reflected a nightmarish inner life. And he certainly wasn't going to be like his father, working in an office the size of a hotel suite with one secretary and one receptionist. And his sisters, well, who knew what was to become of them. The only stuff Portia reported from college was whom she was hanging out with, whom she was in love with, and how she spent her weekends. As far as Emery could tell, she wasn't even taking classes. Anna had graduated from college and was living in Jackson, Wyoming, where she skied in the winter and waitressed all year. Who would allow her parents to spend all that money on an education and then become a waitress? Not even a restaurant manager, but a waitress!

Emery pulled into the driveway of Katie's house. He cut the engine, turned the rearview mirror, and poked his hair up with his fingers like a rake. He had used so much gel that his hair felt like rubber. But he liked the volume the gel gave him, the upward thrust of his head. Sometime around puberty Emery's blond hair had turned brown. Louise had colored it for him the first time. She bought a box of Nice 'n Easy at the grocery store, lit up a joint, and brought Emery back to his original color. Buzzy never even noticed. Now Emery colored it himself, every four weeks or so. The white made his tan look even deeper, made his brown eyes more profoundly brown.

Emery turned the mirror back in place and looked toward Katie's looming house. The grass was like a green shag rug. The giant windows reflected like mirrors. The red door had a floral wreath on it with a little wooden clog in the center on which was painted "Velkommen, Friends."

"Go in," Emery said aloud. Why was he hesitating? Shouldn't he be running for the chance to have sex with this five-foot-nine-inch California Amazonian goddess? At five-eleven (this week, he seemed to be growing an inch a week), Emery was barely taller than Katie. And they weighed exactly the same—both of them lean and sinewy, with perfectly tawny skin. Vicky Smathers in their English class had pointed out that Emery and Katie looked like twins. Everyone laughed and a few kids at school had taken to calling them the Twins. Katie liked that; she called Emery "Twin" and signed her notes to him, *All my love, Your twin.*

Emery pulled the key out of the ignition and got out of the car. He felt like he had the lead role in a play and just now realized, moments before the curtain was to open, that he didn't know his lines. Well, at least there wouldn't be an audience.

Emery walked to the door, knocked, and then opened. Katie was in the kitchen dipping Oreo cookies into a big glass of milk. Emery pulled out some Oreos, stacked them in front of himself, and started dipping, too.

"Okay," Katie said, "we better do this if we're going to do it before my parents get home."

They were in her bedroom on the big copper bed. The bed's rails and knobs reminded Emery of plumbing or a factory. Katie removed all her clothes and got under the covers before Emery had a chance to see her totally naked in the bare, bright light. A guy in calculus, Toby Robitzer, had gone on and on about seeing his girlfriend totally naked in the bare, bright light. Emery had realized then that he'd never even wondered about Katie in bare, bright light. He didn't know it was something he should want.

"Okeydokey." Emery peeled off his clothes and slipped under the covers. He and Katie held each other, face to face, kissing with little birdlike pecks. Emery slid his hands down along Katie's body; she was as smooth and flat as he was.

Katie put her knees up and nudged Emery on top of herself.

"Okay, I'm ready. I already put the sponge in." She smiled and Emery smiled back. And then he started laughing. He was imagining a giant yellow kitchen sponge, maybe speckled black from coffee grounds on it, sitting in her vagina.

"You put a sponge in?" Emery couldn't stop laughing.

"A contraceptive sponge!" Kate giggled and slapped Emery on the shoulder. Emery laughed harder.

"If it were a sponge from my house," he said, "it would smell like curdled milk and be as thin and nonabsorbent as cardboard."

"Gross!" Katie laughed some more, then got serious. "Okay, we *have to* do this."

"Put your knees down," Emery said. He felt like he had mounted a balance beam. Katie dropped her knees and Emery put his legs outside of hers. He placed his hand on his penis and tried to push it inside Katie. It felt fairly smooth and snug; he figured he was in. Emery bobbed up and down a little, tentatively, like he was dancing.

"I don't think that's right," Katie said. "I think it's going in between my legs."

"Really?" Emery stopped bouncing and looked at her. "It feels like it's in."

"No. That's the pressure from my thighs." The sheet was tented over Emery's back. The two of them looked down toward their crotches as if a clear visual could somehow help them make this work.

"How do I get it in?" Emery asked.

Katie put her hand on Emery's penis and tried to feed it into herself. Emery felt like he was a sweatpants drawstring that had come out in the wash and was being threaded back into the tiny hole.

"It's not working," Katie said. They both stared some more: at each other, at their own bodies.

"I know!" Emery said. "Your legs go on the outside and mine go on the inside!"

"Oh yeah! DUH!" Katie choked out a little snigger.

They rearranged their legs. Katie threaded Emery again, only this time he went in. Emery thought she felt warm, and slightly damp and strange. Like he had wrapped his penis in a piece of cooked bologna.

"Now I think you need to move again," Katie said.

"Oh, yeah." Emery did his bouncy little dance and Katie started giggling.

"Am I doing it wrong?" Emery couldn't not laugh—Katie's giggles were like bubbles of alcohol popping in his throat.

"I don't know!" Katie was still laughing. "I think we need to focus."

"Okay, I'll focus." Emery contained himself and shut his eyes. He tried to concentrate, but there was a buzzing in his ear, like a mosquito you can't find in a dark room. The mosquito was buzzing that something was wrong with him, something was amiss. This was sex. He was a teenager. This was the thing he was supposed to want more than anything. But Emery felt like he was watching a boring TV show with characters he didn't really like. He was doing it until a normal amount of time had passed. He was waiting it out.

"Are you done?" Katie tapped Emery on the shoulder. He opened his eyes.

"Yeah. Are you done?"

"Yeah," Katie said. She sounded like she might start giggling again. Emery didn't look at her face as he pulled his penis out and collapsed on top of her. Then he did look at her and they had a chugging, hard laugh for a couple minutes.

When the laughing stopped, Emery rolled off Katie and lay by her side. They held hands under the sheet.

"So, I guess we've lost our virginity," she said.

"I guess," Emery said. "What did it feel like for you?"

"It felt like a big giant tampon that I was starting to pull out but then decided to leave in, but then decided to pull out. You know. The in and out."

"Maybe it starts to feel good the more you do it," Emery said.

Neither of them said anything for a while. Then Katie squeezed Emery's hand. "Hey Twin, would you care if we didn't try again for a couple weeks or something? My vagina feels sort of inflamed—I think it needs to rest."

"No, I don't care." Emery smiled. He was so relieved she didn't want to do this every day. It was ridiculous and uncomfortable and . . . well, who needed it? He and Katie were the ideal couple—why did they have to ruin everything with strange, giggling nudity and the penetration of different body parts into different holes? Who even said a penis had to go into a vagina? Why not a toe, or a nose? Emery wouldn't have felt any differently about the interaction if it had been his toe or his nose!

At home, Emery saw Portia's duffle bag in the entrance hall and remembered that today was the day she was coming home for the summer. Emery walked right past the bag and straight upstairs to the bathroom. He wanted to shower and wash Katie off himself. It wasn't that he didn't love her; she was the greatest person he knew, and wasn't that love? And it wasn't that he was particularly a neat-freak or afraid of germs; he had spent a good couple of years playing in the compost pile in the backyard. But suddenly, Emery was aware of and feeling jittery about Katie's dead skin cells shedding; the exchange of oils and microbes; the millions of microscopic parasites that lived on skin and hair jumping from her body to his. And then there was Katie's vagina. What was in that vagina, anyway? It was a landscape that never saw open air, never smelled a lemon orchard. He wanted it off him, gone, his skin all shiny and new again.

After his shower, Emery walked into the family room, his hair freshly regelled, his body smelling of citrus. Buzzy was on the phone; he was speaking in that low rumbling of emergencies and secrets. Emery's mother and sister were on the couch, qui-

eter than normal. Portia jumped up when she saw Emery and
ran to hug him.

"Baby brother!" she said. "I miss you." Emery shrugged.
He didn't not miss his sister, but he hadn't thought about her
much.

"What's going on?" Emery nodded toward Buzzy.

"Your sister's suicidal," Louise said. Portia took Emery's
hand and pulled him toward the couch. She dropped down next
to Louise. Emery sat in the chair.

"Anna?"

"Well, not me!" Portia said.

Buzzy hung up the phone and started pacing the room. "You
don't have a drug problem, do you?" Buzzy asked. He stopped
walking and scratched behind his ear like a dog.

"Who, me?!" Emery smiled. Of course he didn't have a drug
problem! He was president of the Junior Statesmen, for crying
out loud!

"Not you!" Buzzy waved his hand. "Your sister!"

"No," Portia said. The last time she and Emery had talked on
the phone she told him that she had quit doing drugs, quit having sex with strangers ("Too many fingerprints on my body"),
and even quit smoking cigarettes because her teeth were now
the color of wet tea bags. Emery had no interest in details like
this when it came to his sisters' lives, but he couldn't help but
remember them and file them away in his long-term memory.

"I'll call Dorey and ask her for a recommendation," Buzzy
said, and he went to the kitchen counter and picked up the wall
phone.

"Are you STILL seeing Dorey?" Emery asked. Dorey was the
psychiatrist Buzzy had been seeing since they moved to California. Anna had seen her during her period of retarded physical

development when she loathed Portia because Portia had her period and breasts before Anna did. Emery saw her the year before his bar mitzvah when he was questioning the purpose and intent of religion. Louise saw her on and off over the years when she and Buzzy did couples therapy. Portia had only seen her once when Buzzy felt they should try to do family therapy.

"Of course I'm still seeing Dorey," Buzzy said, and he dialed her number, which he clearly had memorized. "Why would you ask such a question? Why would you say such a thing?!" Buzzy glared at Emery as he waited for Dorey to pick up the phone.

"Your father's upset about your sister," Louise said to Emery. Then she looked at Buzzy and said, "Don't fucking snap at Emery! He just walked in the door—you haven't even said hello!" Louise went to the chair, leaned over Emery, and gave him kisses that he didn't feel he needed. He could handle a little snapping from Buzzy; it wasn't going to crumble him into bits. Louise pulled away and flopped back onto the couch. The coffee table in front of them was crowded with magazines, the newspaper, and two ceramic bowls, one with nuts and three silver chevron nutcrackers, and one with oranges. Emery watched as Louise rummaged through the litter and pulled out a clamshell ashtray that held a half-smoked joint. Louise shifted the magazines, felt along the table, and finally came up with a pack of matches. She lit the joint, then held it out toward her daughter. Emery rolled his eyes. The only thing worse than his mother's smoking pot was the fact that she tried to get his sisters to smoke with her.

"No, thanks," Portia said.

Louise pulled the joint back to her mouth and inhaled deeply, holding the smoke for a few seconds before blowing it out. Buzzy was leaving a message with Dorey's answering service.

"So what'd Anna say?" Emery asked.

"I don't know," Portia said. "I only got here a couple minutes before you did."

"Oy, *gut*," Louise said in a fake Yiddish accent, and she took another hit off the joint.

"Did she really try to kill herself?" Emery asked.

"No!" Louise said. "She won't kill herself. She's too selfish. She's like your dad."

"But she's threatening it?" Portia asked.

"She's been calling all week, wanking into the phone, *waaa waaa waa, I'm going to kiiiill myself, I hate myself, I hate my liiiiife!*"

Emery was so startled by his mother's whiny, nasally imitation of his suicidal sister that he started laughing. Portia laughed, too. Louise tittered and continued. *"My life is poooooooointless, I don't want to liiiiiive! Tell Portia and Emery that I loooove them!"* Louise laughed so hard she choked and began coughing up smoke.

Portia imitated her mother imitating her sister: *"Tell Portia and Emery I looooooove them!"* Emery could feel his eyes squint as he cracked up. He couldn't help himself in spite of the fact that he truly, honestly, sincerely believed it was wrong to mock the suicidal.

Louise howled, shaking her joint in the air. She took a hit, then picked up where her daughter had stopped. *"I've been doing coke every day, I can't even see straight, I sold all my clothes to buy coooooooke—"*

"She really sold her clothes?!" Emery asked. "What? Her thrift-store clothes?"

"I'm naaaaaaaked," Louise whined, *"and now I'm going to kill myself because I haaaaaaate myself!"*

"Is she really naked? Is anyone with her?" There was a funny feeling in Emery's stomach, like a small animal was swimming there. Emery realized the feeling was his reaction to his desperate sister. The nudity had made it all seem entirely serious, and even a little scary.

Buzzy walked over to the couch, leaned over to kiss his daughter a couple times on the forehead, kissed Emery once on the forehead, then sat next to Louise.

"Oy," he said, and he slapped his hand against his head.

"*Tell Dad I loooooove him!*" The couch shook with Louise's hysterics.

Buzzy looked at Louise and Portia laughing. He looked at Emery, who gave a worried shrug.

"I don't understand what's so funny about this?" Buzzy said. He didn't seem upset; he was genuinely curious.

"Oh, she's not going to kill herself!" Louise said. "She's just a pain in the ass. She wants us to prove that we love her by flying all the way out to Wyoming and bringing her home."

"She says she's addicted to drugs. She says she's going to kill herself. Why would she say that if it weren't true?" Buzzy leaned forward, picked up a nutcracker, and opened an almond.

"She's being ridiculous. So she did coke a few times! That doesn't mean she's an addict! Portia's probably done it and she's not wanking on the phone and asking for help."

Buzzy, Louise, and Emery looked at Portia. Emery knew she'd done it, but he wasn't going to rat her out.

"I did it, but I didn't like it," Portia said.

"Anna always takes the simplest thing and makes it a crisis."

"Like when she barfed twice a day," Buzzy said, mocking Louise. "That wasn't bulimia—that was a simple diet that she turned into a crisis!"

Louise chortled. "Right. A diet! The girl goes on a diet and suddenly she gets all this attention, gets to go to the shrink three times a week, go to the hospital for a couple weeks—"

"She went to the hospital for bulimia?" Emery asked. No one had ever mentioned it to him. Maybe she was legitimately insane.

"Before she moved to Jackson Hole," Louise said.

"So she was *hospitalized* for it?!" Emery had been living in the house with Anna at the time. How could he not have noticed that she was missing?

Buzzy's shoulders shook as he laughed. "Yeah, and now she does a few little snivels of cocaine—"

"Snivels?" Portia said.

"Snorts. Whoofs. Whatever. She does some of it, sells her clothes, sells her high school graduation diamond—" A scrap of nut meat hung off Buzzy's lip.

"She sold my grandmother's ring?!" Louise sat up straight and stubbed out her joint. "I'm going to fucking kill her!"

"Well, if you're patient enough, Mom, she'll do the job herself," Portia said.

Buzzy and Louise laughed so hard that Emery decided his fears about Anna were probably groundless. The phone rang and they quieted. Buzzy went to answer it. It was clear by the way he was talking that it was Anna.

"What's going on in your life?" Portia tapped Emery's shin with her toe, and Emery knew the questions had begun. Portia always wanted to know *everything*. But really, other than the fact that he had lost his virginity in his girlfriend's brass bed only an hour ago, there wasn't much to say.

Before Emery could start being evasive, Buzzy cupped his hand over the mouthpiece of the phone and shushed them. Saved by the shush. Emery sat quietly and watched his mother smoke a cigarette while he listened to his father calmly tell his sister that everything was going to be fine.

Anna flew home the following day. She claimed she weighed a hundred pounds, but refused to get on a scale in front of her parents. Louise started calling her Anna Rexia, which made Emery wonder if all of her problems did stem from the family, as she claimed.

During meals, Anna sat at the counter or table staring without touching her own food. Emery imagined she was watching lips move, the viscous gunk of food churning through and behind teeth, stains on shirts, black specks and green leaves stuck in the crevices of receding gums. Eating really was disgusting when you focused on it the way Anna seemed to.

Anna claimed she couldn't share a room with Portia and insisted that she be allowed to stay in Emery's room, her old room, alone. So Emery was moved to the cot beside his sister in his old room—the cot that he could think of only as Bubbe and Zeyde's bed. He thought it was interesting that the more messed up you were, the more you could demand. Emery figured that if Anna had asked for a brand-new car in exchange for quitting drugs, Buzzy would have bought her one.

Anna rarely came out of Emery's room, and she always kept the door closed. The second day she was home, she called Emery into the room and insisted he eat everything on the tray of food Louise had brought up. There was a giant bowl of spaghetti with tomato sauce and lots of parmesan cheese. There was also a wedge of white garlic bread and four Lorna Doone butter cookies. Emery was starving and ate it all. No one had cooked dinner that night, as all his parents' efforts were going into trying to feed Anna and arguing about which rehab center to send her to (Buzzy wanted her to go to the inexpensive place in Camarillo;

Louise wanted to send her to a holistic rehab center in Phoenix where celebrities went and which Buzzy claimed was really an expensive spa and who the fuck wouldn't get over their suicidal thoughts while lounging by a pool and getting massages for a month?!).

Her third day home, Anna called Emery into the room again.

"Yeah?" Emery leaned into the doorway, holding on to the doorknob. Anna was on the bed in shorts and a tank top. Her folded-up brown legs reminded Emery of broken matchsticks.

"Come in and shut the door!" Anna hissed.

Emery stepped in and shut the door behind himself. He looked down at the tray. It held meatloaf, potatoes, carrots, and another stack of Lorna Doones. It was Saturday, noon, seventy-eight degrees outside. Emery was about to go pick up Katie and take her to the beach. He didn't want to fill up on meatloaf.

"I can't eat that for you," he said.

"Come on! I'm going to rehab tomorrow morning, so it's not like you're threatening my health or anything!"

"I'm going to the beach. It's hot out. I can't eat meatloaf!"

"I'll give you some coke." Anna opened her palm. She held a magazine-paper square with a small pile of glittery white coke on it.

"You're *still* doing drugs?!" Emery wondered if there were no end to his sister's ravenous appetite for everything that was bad for her.

"Oh, for fuck's sake, Emery! I'm going to fucking REHAB tomorrow! This is it for me! This is the last day I can do this stuff! The final hurrah!" Anna scooped a little pile with her long pinky nail, lifted it to one nostril, and sniffed.

"I don't do drugs," Emery said.

"What do you do?"

"Homework," Emery said. It sounded way more uptight and smarty-pants than he intended, but it was the truth.

"Jesus," Anna said. "Have a little fun sometimes."

"Okay. I gotta go." Emery wanted to get the beach, put baby oil on his skin, and deepen his tan while finishing the book he was reading about the life of Walt Disney.

"Wait. You *have* to eat this meatloaf!" Anna's eyes were huge circles on her face. She looked like a poster child from the Christian Children's Fund.

"I can't help you," Emery said. He realized this was the first time in his life he didn't feel that he had to do what his sister wanted. Everything was upside down.

"Seriously! Emery! Dad is going to come up here and force-feed me unless this plate is empty!" Anna took three rapid hits of coke off her fingernail.

"Go on the roof and dump it into the bushes or something." Emery was half-kidding, but Anna's panic subsided.

"Great idea. Help me." Anna put the coke down on the night-stand, stood on the bed, and opened the window. She popped the screen out and laid it down on the wood-shake roof. Like a tree monkey, Anna climbed out to the roof, then turned around and faced inside the room. "Okay, hand me the meatloaf."

Emery picked up the plate with the meatloaf and handed it to his sister. She stood, walked out of his line of view, and returned with an empty plate.

"Now hand me the Lorna Doones." Anna passed the plate out to Emery.

"I'll eat the cookies," he said, and he snatched them up, dropped them into his shorts pocket, and left the room. The only good thing about Anna's being a frantic drug-addicted an-orexic was that she was so stuck in her downward-spiraling self that she didn't have any interest in what Emery was doing or thinking about. As far as that stuff was concerned, he had to deal only with Portia.

Emery wanted to check out from all the emotion in his house, and he was uncomfortable on the cot, so he spent the next couple nights in the guest room at Katie's house. Katie had told her parents about Anna, and they took pity on Emery, responding as if his sister's addiction were a contagious cancer from which he needed to be protected. No one in Emery's family called to check on him. Emery suspected they hadn't noticed he was missing. On Monday, instead of going back to Katie's after school, Emery finally went home. Portia was sitting at the kitchen counter reading a book.

"What are you reading?" Emery asked. He dropped his backpack on the floor at the base of the counter.

"I don't know," Portia said. "It was sitting here and I flipped it open and started reading and haven't been able to stop." Portia closed the book and looked at the title. "*The Anatomy Lesson*. Philip Roth."

"Must be Dad's. He loves Philip Roth."

"I think dad thinks he *is* Philip Roth and this life with us is some dream he has every night when he goes to bed." Portia slid the book down the counter. Emery sat on the stool next to her.

"Where've you been?" Portia leaned onto an elbow and stared at Emery.

"Nowhere," Emery said. "Did Mom and Dad notice I was gone?"

"I don't know. But I noticed you were gone. Where were you? You had to have been somewhere."

"I was at my girlfriend's house." Emery both wanted and didn't want this fact to be known. He knew it would elicit more questions. But he also thought his sister should know that he was a guy with a girlfriend now. A sort of grown person who liked girls.

"You have a girlfriend?! Who is she? What does she look like?"

Emery tried not to groan, even though he knew he had started this. "I don't know," he said.

"You don't know? You don't know?! Come on!"

"She looks like a girl. I know her from school. She's nice." He had little hope this would work, but the urge to keep his private life private pushed ahead of logic.

"Oh, please! What are you, some undercover spy? *What* does she look like?" Portia peered into Emery's face.

"People say she looks like me. Blond, tall, thin." Emery slumped onto two elbows, his palms holding his face.

"Are you guys fooling around?" Portia was grinning now.

"I'm not going to tell you."

"Come on! I changed your diapers! I bathed you! I fed you! I have a right to know if you're still a virgin!"

"I'm not going to say." *No, he wasn't a virgin! Although, okay, yes, BARELY not a virgin. His penis had been between her legs, mostly. But it had been officially in her for two minutes or so, so he was officially NOT a virgin!*

"Okay, fine. Then at least tell me what's up with all that shit in your hair." Portia got off the stool, went around the counter into the kitchen, and turned her attention to the refrigerator as if she hadn't even asked about his hair. She began opening every tin-foiled wrapped bit of furry food to see if it was still any good. Watching her was like watching an assembly line: open, sniff, toss, open, sniff, toss. With the refrigerator door open, the kitchen smelled like dirty underpants.

"Will you make me something to eat?" Emery hoped that feeding him would be enough for Portia, that she wouldn't have to probe into his mind like some sci-fi flea-sized robot that crawls in your ear, luge-runs through the folds of your brain, and reads your thoughts as they pop up. Emery tried to control his thoughts. He didn't trust that his sister couldn't read his mind anyway. But the more he tried to restrain certain phrases and words—*I always feel vomity when my girlfriend wants to make out*—the more they persisted. *Yeah, I'm coloring and spiking up my hair! But don't you think I look better like this, cooler, handsomer? I look like people in LA, people on soap operas, actors. And, no—all actors aren't gay!*

"Sure, I'll make you something. Gruel?" Portia said. Gruel was dense, and sweet, and felt like a lump of sand in your belly. The lump-in-the-belly feeling lasted for hours, so it was a good thing to eat if you knew there wasn't another meal coming soon.

"Yeah, gruel would be great," Anything but questions about his hair, his girlfriend, his life! Emery pushed up his T-shirt sleeves as if preparing to eat.

"You're as skinny as Gumby. Does Mom give you money for lunch at school?" Portia closed the refrigerator and went to the cupboard for the Grape-Nuts.

"I take money out of her wallet every day," Emery said.

While making the gruel, Portia quizzed him with variations of the questions he had anticipated. It was like being interrogated by the KGB—just the asking of the questions made Emery feel like he had something to hide. He grunted, stuck his head in his gruel once it was served, and refused to answer.

"All right, have it your way." Portia said. "You know, you used to be so connected to me. Now it's like you're some vestigial limb that just cracked off and floated away."

"Vestigial limb!" Emery smiled. "Is that my new nickname?"

"Naw," Portia said. Emery could tell she was genuinely distressed about not being able to enter his brain. He felt it coming out of her like a mother-sadness. "Your new name is Secret Agent Man."

"Secret Agent Man," Emery repeated. He sort of liked the sound of that.

"*C'est toi,*" Portia said.

Louise walked into the kitchen, an unlit cigarette stuck in her mouth. She turned on the stove burner, held her hair back with one hand, leaned over, and lit the cigarette. "I just got off the phone with the rehab people," Louise said. "Anna should be out of detox in four more days, then they'll put her in the sex addicts unit." Smoke puffed from Louise's mouth as she spoke.

"Why are they putting her with the sex addicts?" Emery asked. He set his spoon on the counter, picked up his bowl, and began licking up the last smears of gruel.

"Can you have styled hair like that and still lick the bottom of your bowl?" Portia asked.

"Yeah." Emery kept licking. "I thought Anna was a drug addict and anorexic; I didn't even know there was such a thing as a sex addict!"

"Well, there is," Louise said. "And your sister is one."

Anna was way too heterosexual, Emery thought. Carrying the hetero genes for the whole family and leaving him deficient and not hetero enough. Here she was flinging herself against everyone who didn't have a vagina, while he had no desire to do *things* with the vagina that was coming at him.

"Hey, Mom," Portia said, "if they put the sex addicts together, won't they all sleep with each other?"

"I suppose, but they have more restrictions on them—"

"I still can't believe that there's such a thing as a sex addict!" Emery said. "Maybe all the guys at school should go to sex-addict rehab." Why was he the only one who wasn't trying to get laid by everything on campus? Jeremy Groning told him at lunch one day that if it was pink and it moved, he wanted to fuck it. If those weren't the words of a sex addict, what were?!

"She's got a lot going for her right now," Portia said. "Suicidal, drug-addicted, anorexic, sex addict."

"How come no one told me she was a sex addict?" If Russia were sending the nuclear bomb to Santa Barbara, Emery wondered, would his family remember to tell him to get out?

"You haven't even been home." Louise picked up the wooden spoon from the pot of gruel and nibbled at the bits hanging off it like semidry paste. Emery was glad she had noticed he was missing.

"So what kind of restrictions are there in the sex-addict wing?" Portia asked.

"They're not allowed to wear anything revealing or clingy or fitted or short."

"So what's she wearing?" Portia asked.

"Baggy sweat pants and T-shirts. And she has to wear a one-piece bathing suit in the pool."

"They have a pool?" Emery asked.

"Yeah," Louise said, "and yoga classes and pottery classes and meditation and acupuncture—it's sort of like going to Esalen." So, Emery thought, Louise had won the argument about where to send Anna.

"What's Esalen?" Portia asked.

"You know, that yogi-meditation-rebirthing place up near Big Sur."

"Wow." Emery sat up straight. "I have a sister who's a sex addict."

Buzzy walked into the kitchen. It was five. He was wearing his jacket and tie and carrying the soft, slouchy briefcase he'd had for at least ten years. There were two pockets on the outside of the briefcase, like back pockets on cargo pants, and they always bulged as if they'd been stuffed with rolled-up socks. Emery thought that if he ever carried a briefcase it would be a flat, slick, hard one. Maybe lizard-skin or snakeskin, even.

Buzzy leaned in and kissed Louise on the lips, then Portia on the cheek. He walked to the other side of the counter, put his hand on Emery's head, and kissed him on his forehead.

"What kind of shit do you have in your hair?" Buzzy asked. He set his briefcase on the floor, then went to the sink and washed his hand.

"It's gel," Portia said.

"What's the point of that shit?" Buzzy asked.

Emery shrugged. Portia said, "Secret Agent Man doesn't tell his secrets, Dad."

Emery and Katie decided that the only proper way to pay respect to Anna while she was in rehab for sex addiction was to abstain from sex until she came home again. The following month was, in Emery's opinion, the best month of their relationship. They graduated from high school and were free to spend days at the beach, where they debated politics and read the same books, taking turns reading aloud to each other. At night they went to the movies. Three times they saw *The Killing Fields*, which made Emery wonder if he should be a war reporter for the *New York Times*. Some days they organized each other's rooms, sorting through old yearbooks and clothes as they tried to decide what they had to take with them to college (Katie was off to Smith, Emery to Haverford). Emery thought that without all that time wasted kissing and having sex, they were so much more productive. It was, by far, the best way to enjoy each other in their final days before college.

Four weeks went by too quickly. The night before Anna was due home, the ban on sex was lifted. Katie and Emery were lying together, face down on her bed, flipping through *Interview* magazine.

"So," Katie said, and she hooked her foot around Emery's. "I guess now that your sister is cured, the ban should be lifted."

"Oh, yeah," Emery said. "It's definitely time to lift the ban." Emery felt a whorly convulsion in his stomach.

Katie leaned her head in for a kiss. Emery kissed her for as long as seemed possible, then pulled his head up and turned the page of the magazine.

"What do you think of Boy George?" he asked.

"He's okay," Katie said. "Should I put in a sponge?"

"We should wait until tomorrow," Emery said, "when Anna's officially home." Emery wanted to flee the bed, the room, the house. He thought maybe this was a sign that he should break up with Katie. But he didn't want to break up with her. She was his best friend, the only person he knew who could discuss both apartheid in South Africa and the latest episode of *Dynasty*.

Instead of breaking up with Katie, Emery called her the next morning and told her that his parents wanted him to stay home for a few days to help Anna acclimate. The whorly feeling returned during the phone conversation, making Emery think that maybe staying home with his incessantly interrogating sisters would be worse than trying to have sex with Katie again. As soon as Anna was home, however, Emery knew it wasn't worse. Being home was way, way better than trying to have sex.

It was like Anna was high those first few days back: nothing got to her—not Emery's bare feet on her legs when they sat on the couch together, not the way Portia breathed when she watched TV, not the way their father internally scratched his throat so that it sounded like someone was frantically rubbing a spoon against a balloon, not the way their mother made a slight popping sound when she took a suck off her cigarette, or the way her knees cracked when she bent down, making the sound of walnuts being cracked open under a boot, not even the mess on the family room coffee table. And when Anna called Emery "Secret Agent Man," she said it with a tenderness she'd never shown before—as if she'd formerly been too busy to notice what a kind, skinny, spiked-hair guy he was.

With the twenty-five pounds she had gained at rehab, Anna looked like her own, more attractive twin. And Anna even talked slower during this time. She was like a battery-operated toy that was now running on the silent thrum of solar energy.

In this same period, even Portia, who was already calm, seemed more peaceful to Emery. She was riding her bike to the beach every day, napping on the family room couch in the afternoons, staying in many nights and avoiding the mania of her old high school friendships. And Buzzy also seemed to have caught the contagion of peace. He was spending his free time farming marijuana, wearing a wide-brimmed bamboo hat that Emery thought made him look more Asian than Jewish. Louise passed her days at the nude beach and her evenings cooking dinner as if she had never quit being a housewife and had always been someone who fed her children. And, unlike any other time that Emery could remember, his parents had miraculously stopped fighting about the things they usually churned over and over again like a butter that would take a lifetime to make.

In their nightly phone calls, Emery told Katie about the strange, calm joy that was floating in the household. Katie agreed that he should spend his last few weeks before college at home, now that everything was so harmonious. Emery was grateful to her for being so understanding. He made it clear to her that the shroud they were currently living under was totally unique in his life. For the first time ever, the sun was shining down on his family. Everyone was glowing in the beautiful yellow heat.

DAY EIGHT

Anna runs each morning, usually starting off before everyone else has awoken. If she didn't run she swears she would be doing drugs, or starving herself, or eating and then barfing. Portia believes her. She can tell that running keeps Anna's itching at bay. She doesn't even like talking to her sister (on the phone or in person) before Anna's had her run, as she finds her much too steely and sharp.

Emery and Alejandro go to a gym when they're in New York, but neither of them feels the need to exercise during Louise's heart attack. Portia wonders what it would be like to be a guy with immutable metabolism—go to the gym, don't go to the gym, eat a whole pan of ziti, don't eat ziti—no matter what, you come out looking the same.

Portia used to go to the Greenwich Y with Patrick, but since he left her, Portia hasn't even taken a walk. She never liked going to the Y; the drive was a pain in the ass and never seemed worth the time. Portia would rather do a bunch of sit-ups and some leg-lifts in front of the TV. But Patrick went to the Y every night after work and if Portia wanted to see him in the evenings before she was too exhausted to speak, she had to meet him at the Y. The childcare center was open until nine o'clock. Portia would drop off Esmé, then follow her husband around the machines, or try to place herself on a Stairmaster next to him so she could recount to him her day with Esmé: where they went, clever things Esmé said, what they ate. It is only now that Portia realizes he probably wasn't even listening.

Buzzy normally walks, or hikes, every day but hasn't done so since the heart attack. Buzzy likes hiking. He considers it a form of meditation.

Today, on Day Eight, Buzzy decides he'll walk before going to see Louise, and Portia has agreed to go with him.

Anna is out on her run, Alejandro is still sleeping, Emery is sitting beside Portia, reading the *New York Times* and eating a cinnamon roll. Portia has been scanning the *Santa Barbara News-Press*, looking for people she might know from high school. So far she hasn't found any. Portia has noticed that every year she returns home she knows fewer and fewer people in town; she recognizes fewer and fewer names in the paper. She's starting to feel like a stranger.

"Are you sure you don't want to come with us?" Buzzy asks Emery.

"I'm going to wait for Alejandro to wake up," Emery says, and he folds the paper over and picks up a pen so he can do the crossword. He stares at Portia, like he wants to tell her something. Portia remembers when he was a kid and used to stare at Ace, his bird, trying to send him thought messages.

"Do you always do the crossword?" Portia asks.

"If I can get to it before Alejandro," he says.

Emery leans in closer to Portia. She tries to read his mind. She knows he wants to say something. Then he looks down at the puzzle and she thinks, *Fuck it,* if he wants to tell her something he can tell her later.

"Let's go," Portia says, and she puts down the newspaper. Her father could also have a heart attack. She should walk with him while they both can walk.

"Okay," Buzzy says. "I need to show you your inheritance."

"My inheritance forty years from now?" Portia asks.

"You never know," Buzzy says. "Louise made me get a portable phone so that when I'm out hiking alone I'll be able to call her if I run into trouble. Can you believe that? Can you believe that the property you're going to inherit is so vast that you need to take a portable phone with you on hikes?!"

"Why not just get one of those boat horns that lets out one huge blast of sound?" Portia asks.

"Yeah, why not get one of those?" Emery says, still staring at the puzzle.

"I thought of that," Buzzy says. "But Louise thought the phone would be better. It was her idea, the phone."

Step One of going for a hike is readying the backpack. Buzzy opens all the pockets and zippers and then inserts the portable phone (almost the size of a shoebox), a small box of raisins, and a thermos of water. He offers to take the scratched green aluminum canteen that he'd carried when they went for hikes as a young family, but Portia assures him the thermos is plenty.

Step Two is choosing a walking stick. Buzzy has been collecting them on his daily hikes, picking out sticks that are, according to him, the right length and width, many with a knob on the end or small tilt that forms a handle. He has sanded down the ones that aren't smooth and even made some primitive carvings along the handles of others: vertical rays, zigzags, his initials on the one he likes best. Portia is glad her sister isn't around. The prewalk rigmarole would probably drive Anna to an apoplectic fit.

The walking sticks are arranged by height against the head-high stucco wall that encloses the patio off the kitchen. Alejandro is up now. He and Emery are in the patio, watching

Portia poke through the sticks trying to find the perfect one. There is one the size of Portia's daughter, Esmé; Buzzy made if for her the first week he and Louise moved into the house.

"Can I carve one?" Alejandro asks. He is holding up a stick and rotating it in his fist. This is what everyone likes about Alejandro: he's a participator. Portia's soon-to-be-former mother-in-law always comments on who's a participator and who's not. Her other daughters-in-law aren't participators—they go off for walks on their own, won't play Trivial Pursuit at Christmas, and never eat dessert. She would approve of Alejandro. He never acts like an outsider.

"Yeah, you can carve one!" Buzzy seems excited by the idea. He flips the backpack off his shoulders, opens a pocket, and takes out his bone-handled whittling knife.

Alejandro takes the knife, sits on the wooden chair at the patio table, and immediately starts scratching out a design. Emery fetches the unfinished crossword puzzle from the kitchen table, brings it out to the patio, and watches Alejandro carve while he works on the puzzle.

Every now and then he looks up at Portia. He still seems intent on sending her a mind-message. Normally Portia would scratch it out of Emery, but she doesn't have the energy for that now—between her maybe-dying mother and her definitely divorcing husband, her curiosity about others is less pointed.

Instead of going down into the canyon, along the river where the bear died, Buzzy decides they should hike up the road that runs along the property. He wants Portia to see the view, the lay of the land. Portia is happy to have the heat of the sunshine radiating off the black tar road.

"So, sweetheart," he says, as they walk, "are you okay?"

"You mean about Mom? Or about my marriage?"

"Your mother's going to be fine," Buzzy says.

"So you're asking me about my marriage?"

"Yeah. Are you okay?"

Portia focuses on the dog, Jasmine, rooting through the scrubby brush that covers the ground like a thorny, long-sticked briar patch. If she looks at her father, she'll cry. She feels like Buzzy's question has opened up some creaky attic door that is about to let loose a pack of flapping bats, or an undulating sea of running rats.

"I guess," Portia says, and the safety trigger on her throat unlatches, releasing a choking sob that is too thick for words to break through. They keep walking. Buzzy holds Portia's hand, waiting for her to clear through the streaming mess of sadness. It seems like it won't end; the crying comes from some infinite part of her that is being refilled as quickly as it empties.

Just when Portia feels herself dog-paddling to breathe through her tears, Buzzy opens his backpack and answers his new portable phone, which Portia hadn't even noticed was ringing.

"Sweetheart," Buzzy says, almost whispering into his cell phone. And Portia knows things aren't right. She is shocked out of her own sadness, as if the phone call, the *sweetheart*, were a defibrillator paddle to her heart.

Portia walks on, her crying now a silent, spastic vibrato. She looks out at the ocean, takes deep breaths, and tries to simply *be* in the midst of the beauty. It looks like a postcard—the craggy, sloped mountainside leading down to the sensuously curvy Santa Barbara foothills and then out to the ocean, a shimmering blue-green framed by the blue-brown dashes of the Channel Islands.

I am here, Portia thinks. It is beautiful here. My mother is still alive. My daughter is healthy. Little else matters.

"That was my friend," Buzzy says, as he tucks the phone into his backpack.

"Your friend?" Portia sniffs and wipes her nose with the back of her hand. Her eyes sting from leaking mascara.

"Before the heart attack," Buzzy says, "things weren't good with your mother and me."

Buzzy hands Portia a clean, folded handkerchief from his pocket. She opens it, shakes it out, and presses it into her eyes. The handkerchief comes away with black-mascara Rorschach blots on it.

"Dad, do you have a Stinky?" Portia blows her nose and then hands the bunched-up handkerchief back to her father. Her entire life, Buzzy has always had a handkerchief in his pocket. Once, Portia had a fantasy of making a shroud of handkerchiefs and having her father mummified in them.

Buzzy puts the wadded handkerchief in his pocket, no mind that it now has her snot all over it. He doesn't answer the question.

"Dad! Do you have a Stinky?" Portia asks, again. Since she discovered Patrick's affair, everyone is a suspect. The only person she can be sure isn't having an affair, is herself.

"What do you mean, do I have a Stinky?! Who do you think I am? I'm not Otto or Jimmy-Don or Linus!" Buzzy pelts up the road, shaking his head as he goes. Portia keeps apace.

"You called her sweetheart," Portia says, quietly. It feels like there's gravel churning in her gut. She's a cement mixer.

Buzzy stops and knocks his walking stick against the ground as if he is summoning someone from below the paved road.

"She's only a friend," he says. "She's a really close friend and we talk on the phone a lot and she's wonderful. But there's nothing sexual. I swear."

"Does Mom know about her?"

"She's met her before. Your Mom hates her. She's the new attorney in my office."

"Oh, that's great, Dad!" Small light explosions flash in front of Portia's face as the sun hits the tears in her eyes. "Just like Patrick, some attorney from your office! I can't believe I married a lawyer! What was I thinking? Why would I ever marry an attorney who works with *attorneys*! You all love to fuck each other!" She is all-out crying again. Buzzy reaches his hand to her and passes off the handkerchief again.

"Sweetheart, come on! You're not being fair." Buzzy waits for Portia to blow her nose and wipe her eyes.

"My husband left me for an attorney in his office, Dad, you know that! It's sleazy! You're all sleazy!"

"Portia, just because your husband did it doesn't mean I'm doing it! She's only a friend."

"Dad! Mom is in the hospital with a heart attack! You shouldn't be talking to anyone you call 'sweetheart'!"

Buzzy says nothing. Portia sniffs up her snot and they start walking again.

"Your mother calls her 'Miss Shit-for-Brains' because Judy, at the office, told your mother that everyone has to help her write her briefs."

"And Mom has no reason to be suspicious of Miss Shit-for-Brains?" Portia sniffs.

"Not at all. She decided she's dumb and so she hates her. Don't tell her that we talk on the phone."

It is horrible for Portia to think that her father might be lying to her. That he might be a liar. She stays right behind Buzzy as he turns off the road, following the dogs. They head down a dirt path toward giant, glacier-sized rocks that slant toward the ocean. The farther Portia and Buzzy go, the quicker they go, leaping onto rocks and trotting downhill, hurtling across fissures that look like they drop straight to the center of the earth.

Portia stays in the hypnotic rhythm of the hike, her feet making a shuffling staccato, the dogs' nails clicking in beat, the sun like a hot hand on her face, her breath going in and out and in and out until she is exactly where she is: high on a mountain, running down a rock, safe from the invasion of cheating husbands, Stinkys, and unfaithful fathers.

Forty minutes later, Buzzy and Portia are alone in the kitchen. She is searching through the cupboards and the refrigerator, trying to find something to eat. Buzzy has his briefcase open on the dining room table and is looking over some papers.

"Do you want some cinnamon roll?" Portia asks.

"Sure," Buzzy says. He sticks his thumb in the waist of his pants and pulls it out. "You know, I've lost about fifteen pounds."

"You always look skinny, Dad." Portia doesn't look at him. She is putting cinnamon rolls on a plate.

"I've gotta make a doctor's appointment to make sure there's nothing wrong with me. I'm in a size thirty-two pants now!"

"Maybe it's old age."

"But it was so quick. And I don't think I've been eating differently."

"I have." Portia picks up the remnant of a chocolate-chip scone that has been sitting in a basket on the kitchen counter. She has picked from this same scone each time she passed it yesterday and this morning. By now it's the size of a cherry tomato.

When Portia brings her father his plate, she notices the edge of a photograph beneath the paper he's looking at. Portia reaches down and slips it out. In the picture is a girl. A woman. A girl-woman. She is in a bed with a kitten on her chest. Her hair is short, red, splayed across the pillow. The sheet is pulled up to her smooth, glossy neck. This is not the picture of oneself that you give to a friend. Portia's stomach drops, rises, shifts. There is a lava lamp inside her now.

"Oh, that's my friend I was telling you about," Buzzy says. "She gave me that picture."

"Awfully young friend, Dad." Portia feels sick.

Anna comes in the kitchen door. Her face is slick with sweat. Her hair is hanging in damp clumps. She has ropy legs that are no thicker at the calf than the thigh. They are like the slim trunks of the smooth-skinned manzanita trees that grow all over Buzzy and Louise's property.

"Dad's friend," Portia says, and she hands the photo to Anna.

"You told her?" Anna says to Buzzy.

Portia looks from Buzzy to Anna. She realizes that the affair is a fact, as true as her father's standing before her. And at that moment, Buzzy shifts in Portia's mind. It is like owning an expensive painting that you love and suddenly learning that it's a reproduction. You still love the painting, but it isn't the same painting you thought you'd had.

"Mom is in the hospital!" Portia says.

"This started months ago," Buzzy said. "Almost a year ago."

"How old is she?!" Portia takes the picture from Anna and looks at it again.

"She's a grown-up," Buzzy said. "A year or two younger than you." Portia remembers the man she saw a few weeks ago when she and a friend were out to dinner in Greenwich. She thought he was with his daughter; their features were vaguely alike. But then he leaned over the table and kissed her, deeply, on the lips. Portia and her friend laughed. They thought he looked ridiculous: vain, shallow, pathetic. And now here was her father; he is one of those guys who thinks a younger woman is going to keep him young somehow, give him her temporary youth.

"He didn't know Mom would have a heart attack when he started it," Anna says. She is busying herself with a glass of water and then a bag of frozen peas. She sits on the bench seat, stretches out her leg, and puts the peas on the knee that's twice had arthroscopic surgery. Portia thinks she looks irritated that Portia is asking about their father's Stinky and not irritated because of the Stinky herself.

"I haven't seen her since your mother went in the hospital," Buzzy says.

"You shouldn't even be thinking about her!" Portia's voice is screechy, like a teenager's.

"Love can be overwhelming," Anna snaps, and Portia knows she is on their father's side. "It's not something you can control."

"Sweetheart." Buzzy gets up from the table and tries to hug his daughter. Portia stands there, her arms dropped to the side.

"Well, doesn't this answer your weight-loss question?" Portia sighs. Truly sighs. With breathy noise and dropping shoulders.

"What do you mean, this answers my weight-loss question?"

"Everyone loses weight when they have an affair." She pulls away from her father, sits at the table, and eats her cinnamon roll. Portia wants to tell Buzzy that her husband, who also had an affair, with a lawyer from his office, lost weight, too. But she doesn't. She can't even look at him. She looks at her sister.

"Affairs have nothing to do with love and devotion," Anna says. She flips the bag of peas over, readjusts it on her knee. "I mean, look how devoted Dad's been since Mom's been in the hospital. Marriage is complicated."

"I know how complicated marriage is," Portia says. "I was married, too. My husband had an affair, too."

"Yeah, but you weren't in Mom and Dad's marriage. You don't know it. You shouldn't judge what either of them does." Anna is staring at Portia like she'd like to smack her. Portia feels like whacking the bag of peas off her sister's pathetic, swollen, lame-ass knee.

"And you *do* know their marriage?!"

"Girls." Buzzy sits at the table beside Anna. "I haven't seen my friend since your mother had the heart attack. At this moment, I am fully devoted to your mother."

"Oh, that makes you a great husband, Dad. Devotion at the necessary times!"

"Portia, you're being unfair," Buzzy says.

"You're being totally unfair!" Anna says.

Portia isn't going to argue. She doesn't have the energy for it. She is going silent again, like she did when Mrs. White died. At least for a while, so that she can separate her father from Patrick, her mother from herself.

Patrick was the last boyfriend Portia had in college, an Irish
Catholic from Stamford, Connecticut, with unhappily married
parents and a long heritage of alcoholics and storytellers. He was
funny, fun, and great-looking in that Irish way of thick black
hair, green eyes, and shoulders that looked like they had a two-
by-four running across them. There were six kids in Patrick's
family, four boys and two girls. His father, Regis, was a pink-
nosed silent worker who carried a briefcase out the door each
morning and carried it back in at precisely six p.m. each evening,
at which point he retired to the TV room with a beer and waited
for dinner in a chair that had molded to the shape of his body.
Patrick's mother, Sheila, ran the show at home. She loved her
sons, whom she envisioned would take over the world, or the
U.S. at least, Kennedy-style, before she died. Her two daughters
she ignored for the most part; their job seemed to be to help their
mother around the house and laugh at their brothers' jokes.

Portia saw Patrick's family twice a year. December, when she
flew home with him for Christmas, during which time she was
shunned by his mother and sisters because she didn't have the
sense to get up and help in the kitchen (at the time, she was
too in love with Patrick to abandon him for the chores, and too
enraptured by the manic fun he had with his brothers to leave
what always felt like a party). And April, when his family assem-
bled at an uncle's beach house near Los Angeles where the boys
and their cousins played hours of football on the sand while

their tall, sturdy mother stood by and cheered them on as if she were at the Notre Dame–USC game.

Sheila's two daughters did as she expected and married well-employed Catholic boys who fit in perfectly at the April football games. The four sons, however, each eventually disappointed their mother. The oldest, Sean, married a Spanish girl. She was the Catholic Sheila had wanted, but far too dark and ethnic for her tastes. The next son, Paul, remained a bachelor and volunteered at the church more than was considered masculine or productive (outside the family, he was thought of as gay). The brainiest of the brothers, James, married a Russian who Sheila was convinced was in the KGB, as she went to Yale with James, and how else could a Russian get into Yale? And Patrick fell in love with Portia. Portia was, perhaps, the biggest disappointment of all. Patrick was the youngest of the brothers, the last hurrah, the final hope. And there he was, senior year of college, and dating a Jew. "Be careful who your last college girlfriend is," Sheila had said, as he left home his final year, "as that's the one you'll marry."

When they moved into an apartment together second semester, Sheila stopped calling Patrick for fear that Portia would pick up the phone. Instead, she sent letters that instructed her son to call her every Wednesday and Sunday. He usually made the Sunday call after Portia reminded him. Wednesday eluded them both.

The best thing about Patrick was his lack of intense emotion. Here was a guy who neither complained nor praised. He didn't cry, didn't laugh at his own jokes (but would laugh uproariously at others'), and never said how he felt about anything. Patrick seemed emotionally uncluttered in a way that was a relief to Portia after the intense emotions and needs flying around her childhood house. Being with him, compared to being with her family, presented as stark a contrast as the cluttered coffee table at home compared to a shiny, empty slab of marble. Portia didn't have to tend to his psyche. She didn't have to think about him, or his needs, or his wants. She was free to simply exist. Peacefully. Quietly. Yet she wasn't alone. And she was laughing.

They had few conflicts. Patrick and Portia's first fraught moment came when she found herself pregnant the spring before she was set to graduate (she had stupidly believed that you couldn't get pregnant when you had sex during your period). Portia called Patrick at the campus bookstore, where he was working, the moment she got home from the Berkeley clinic. It took at least five minutes for him to come to the phone, which was near the cash register. Portia waited and listened to the clinking of sales and the murmuring banter of the cashier talking to the customers.

"Hey," Patrick almost whispered into the phone. He never liked when Portia called him at work and acted embarrassed by the calls, as if she were his mother checking up on him.

"So, you know how I didn't get my period?" Portia asked. She was sitting at their shared desk in the bedroom of their tiny two-room apartment. The kitchen was part of the living room. The bathroom was so small they couldn't stand at the sink together to brush their teeth. There were cockroaches, and neighbors who cooked cabbagey foods whose smells hung in the hallway like smog. The windows wouldn't stay open unless you propped a ruler or giant textbook in the sills to hold them up, and the bathroom door was too big for the doorway and always remained partially open. But it was rent-control cheap, only five blocks from campus. And in a city where it was nearly impossible to find a place to rent, they didn't have the luxury to turn it down when a friend of Patrick's left for law school and passed the lease on to him.

"Yeah?" Patrick said, and Portia thought she could hear him turning his head or shifting his focus away from the phone.

"So, I'm pregnant," Portia said.

"Okay." Patrick was using his social voice—the voice that left everyone believing that everything was great in his life. Simply perfect.

"Okay?" Portia asked.

"I'll go with you to that place," he said, and she knew he meant the clinic where they did abortions. "All right, I gotta go, I've got a lot of work to do here."

Patrick hung up quickly, leaving Portia listening to blank static and then the rhythmic, pulsating buzz of an empty phone line. This must be too much for him, she thought, a surplus of emotion for a guy who could say "I love you" only when the lights were out and Portia was too tired to respond. She forgave him for what seemed like a lack of sympathy—she forgave him everything, always. She was crazy about him.

Portia had wanted a baby since she was a little girl playing with Peaches, her doll. The only thing in her life that she was ever sure she would be was a mother. Portia knew Patrick's mother was right about his last college girlfriend; they would eventually marry. So, if they were going to end up together for the rest of their lives, why not have the baby now? Hadn't things turned out fine when Louise had Anna at twenty-one, a month after graduating from college? Although maybe, Portia thought, Anna's problems were due to the fact that she had popped out before their parents were ready to be parents.

Later that night, Portia lay on the bony mattress of their bed while Patrick sat at the desk beside her, studying for a physics exam.

"Don't even think about it. Don't talk to it." Patrick stared down at Portia as she absently swirled a hand in circles around her bare belly, her shirt pulled up to the bra line. Portia *had* been talking to it in her head, asking what it would look like, if it would have a good sense of humor, if it would have massive shoulders like Patrick, shoulders that in passing out of her body would work like a crowbar and rend her open.

Patrick repositioned himself in his chair, shifting as if his pants were binding him in the crotch. Portia tried to imagine him as a baby. And then she thought of a story he had told her. When he was eleven, Patrick had been sitting in his backyard, leaning against an elm tree while thinking about nature, God, and his mother when it hit him: Christ *had* returned, and Patrick was *Him*. He always got straight *Excellents* on his report cards, often helped his mother with chores, and was chosen first for every sports team. He had never tormented his sisters by amputating and burying their dolls or by trying to make them eat bug spray as his brothers had. He was clearly the favorite of his multiple aunts, who talked to him like he was a man, and especially preferred over his brothers by his widowed Aunt Patty whose lawn he mowed for free because she had no husband to mow it. Even his father, who didn't seem to speak to anyone in the household, spoke to Patrick, asking him to fetch a beer, or change the channel on the giant console TV whose brick-sized remote control his brother Sean had disassembled in an attempt to build a robot. Patrick could think of no one as good as himself, no one as kind as himself, no one as smart and talented as himself, no one as pure as himself. He was happy to stand by and wait for instructions from God.

If the baby were like Patrick, Portia wondered, would it, too, be so good that it might confuse itself for God?

Of course, the counter side to Patrick's stint as Jesus Christ

came when he was around thirteen years old and starting to phys-
ically respond to the girls at middle school. Within a matter of
days he went from believing he was Christ to believing he was the
devil, as he did the devil's work with his right palm full of hair
conditioner during forty-minute showers after school every day.

No, Portia thought. The baby would be neither Christlike
nor devilish. It would just *be*. Simply itself, utterly individual in
the universe with a wholly unique molecular makeup unlike any
that had come before or any that would come after.

"Stop thinking," Patrick said. He put down his pencil and
pushed his hand through his hair.

"How long did you think you were Christ?" Portia asked.

"About two years."

"Did you think you could heal people and turn water to
wine?" His Christ realization was her favorite story. She was in-
satiable for the details of those wondrous years.

Patrick looked up at the ceiling and thought for a moment.
"I don't think so," he said. "Or, at least, I never tried. I figured it
would all come to me as I got older. I mean, Christ, when he was
growing up, was just some kid named Jesus."

"Emanuel," Portia said. "Or Yushua."

"Yeah," Patrick said. He picked up his pencil again.

"That's not a bad name, is it?" she asked. "Emanuel?"

"Forget it!" Patrick said, and he looked down at his book
as if he were trying to block Portia out of the room. Portia lay
there peacefully, not angry or upset, her mind drifting back to
the possible outcomes of their cellular fusion.

Earlier that semester Portia had attended the abortions of two
friends. Cindy was the first, and she swore Portia to secrecy. They
went out to lunch every day the week before the abortion, eating
patty melts and shoving down fistfuls of French fries at a local

diner as Cindy claimed she had never been hungrier and Portia was happy to eat sympathetically with her. On the walk to the clinic, early in the morning on a Thursday when Portia had no classes, they talked about a guy Cindy had met at Henry's bar, and how she had scheduled her date with him for one week postabortion so she'd be sure she was no longer bleeding. The procedure seemed to take less time than having one's teeth cleaned, and after hanging around the recovery room and reading *Glamour* and *Paris Match* (which Portia had checked out of the French library on campus), they walked home as if nothing had happened.

The second abortion was a girl Portia barely knew, the close friend of her close friend Stacy. Portia and Stacy were at Café Roma one afternoon when Stacy said, "Can you take Kerri to her abortion? I was supposed to go with her but my father's going to be in town and I have to hang out with him."

Kerri was red-haired and near-silent. Portia held her hand before and after the procedure, then walked her to the apartment she and Patrick shared and let her sleep in their bed while Portia studied for an exam and Patrick was at class. Kerri and Portia never talked about the abortion after that day, but every time they ran to each other, their eyes would meet with a knowing flash, as if they'd had some messy affair that neither of them wanted to acknowledge.

"Can't we think of names for fun?" Portia asked Patrick. She lifted her foot and tapped his leg. The desk chair was that close to the bed.

"No way," he said. She didn't expect him to answer differently.

And really, honestly, she knew she'd never have the baby. Portia simply liked engaging in the fantasy of it, the fantasy of motherhood, and marriage. She'd have a clean, quiet house where no one threw furniture or walked around naked. And she'd be with this handsome man whom she imagined would age with the same slow, minutely perceptible changes as Paul Newman. And there would be the baby—a squeezy miniature human who smelled like vanilla and was as warm as fresh bread. Portia would dress it in cute clothes, lime-green maybe. And if it were a girl she'd put dandelion chain wreaths on her head and paint her tiny, gel-soft toenails pink.

Being pregnant then was like trying on a really expensive designer dress at I. Magnin on Union Square in San Francisco. A moment of reality (the dress is on, you exist, it exists on you) within the impossibility of the fantasy (you don't have three thousand dollars to purchase the dress, nor do you have anywhere to wear it—additionally, it doesn't even look good on you). Portia knew they couldn't have a baby. They didn't have real jobs, income, a decent apartment—they didn't even have their degrees yet. But she couldn't stop herself from feeling the dreamy hopefulness of maternity.

Portia expected her abortion to be as peaceful and quiet as Kerri's and Cindy's. She expected the same bovine-faced woman to hover over her and speak in silken, humming tones. Patrick went along. He was silent and uncomfortable, shifting in the plastic mold-form seat, not holding Portia's hand in the pre-op room, when she had held Cindy's and Kerri's hands. And then a pretty nurse with an anteater's long pointy nose took Portia away from Patrick and into a sterile, bean-green room.

The Slavic-looking doctor had various misshapen moles on his face and a pregnant woman's belly that pushed out under his blue surgical gown.

"You might feel a slight cramp, like a period cramp," he said, "and then it will be over and you won't feel anything."

Portia was on her back and couldn't see anything, but she heard a low rumbling machinelike noise, as if someone had turned on an old air conditioner.

"It doesn't hurt," the anteater-nosed nurse said, with the same tone as someone saying *Next in line* to a group of people at the complaint desk.

The doctor and nurse were wrong. It wasn't like a period cramp. It felt like an internal vise was gripping her insides and squeezing them until she couldn't breath.

Portia thrashed against it. She heaved against it. She tried to upend the table.

Portia had heard once (everyone has heard once) that you are never dealt a pain you can't handle. Wrong, she thought. Wrong! This was a pain her body refused to handle. She no longer felt human—she was a stringy car-wash rag being twisted into a tight, shredded rope with no room for the elements of life.

More people were called into the room and Portia battled against them. *To the death!* her uterus shouted. *Fuck you!* said her cervix! *No way, Jose!* Portia made sounds that came from somewhere deep inside her animal core, sounds that might be made by a creature that had no language.

And then someone put a needle in one arm and a mask on her face and she was down. They were down.

When Portia woke up, a couple hours later, Patrick was with her, staring out the window. He picked up her hand.

"Something went wrong," he said.

"Is it gone?" she asked.

"You're not pregnant anymore," Patrick said.

The nurse came in, the one with the strange nose. She was softer, slower now. Portia could tell she felt bad for her.

"You said it wouldn't hurt," Portia said. Tears swelled in her eyes as she remembered the pain.

"Yours was one in a million," the nurse said. "Your body didn't want to give it up."

"Wow." Portia's voice quavered. She felt strangely proud of her reproductive organs—insisting that they do what they were supposed to do, hanging on to the very end.

"They had to knock you out," Patrick said, and he lifted his eyebrows as if he were holding something in his forehead. Sadness, maybe. Or tears.

Portia understood then that her simple, uncomplicated boyfriend was as complicated and emotionally messy as everyone else she knew. But unless Portia cajoled it out of him, he wouldn't burden her with his emotional slop—and she, at the time, was happy to pretend that the surface was as clean as it looked.

They never discussed the abortion again.

DAY EIGHT

It is the evening of Day Eight. They are in the TV room watching cartoons again. Everyone but Anna is eating ice cream from the mismatched ceramic bowls Buzzy made years ago.

"Mom needs to get back to work," Anna says. "She needs to write and to paint and there's no way she can do it in that giant, stinky, cat-shit box of a studio."

"It's starting to smell upstairs," Alejandro says.

"What do you mean it smells upstairs?" Buzzy asks. He holds his empty spoon in the air as if he's conducting an orchestra.

"It smells like cat piss upstairs," Emery says. "The stink is rising." He had noticed but didn't think Alejandro had. Now that Alejandro smells it, too, the stink bothers him.

"She'll hate it if you go through her stuff. She doesn't like anyone in there." Buzzy lowers his spoon and shovels up some butter pecan.

"She never did," Portia says.

"Fuck her," Anna says. "She's in the hospital, her studio is a shithole, and we're going to fix it for her before she gets home."

"She has been wanting to paint it ever since we moved in," Buzzy says.

"Good," Anna says. "We'll paint it. And then if you ever have to sell the house, the studio will be ready."

"Don't talk about selling the house!" Portia says. "Mom's not going to die, there's no need to sell the house!"

"You know she threw out all the good stuff from the old house: photos, furniture, things we really could have saved. And she kept every piece of junk from her studio. It was like I paid movers to haul a goddamned dumpster." Buzzy's nodding his head, working up to one of his fits.

"We'll clean it out then," Emery says. He is flipping through the three hundred satellite television channels, looking for a different cartoon. He does not think his mother will die. His biggest worry right now is how to create a cartoon that's even better than *Pickle Man-Boy*.

"Do you know she got rid of the melodeon? That beautiful antique melodeon that she and Lucy spent months repairing when we lived in Ann Arbor. She gave it away to this pimple-faced kid who was loading the moving truck! Gave it to him! That thing was probably worth . . . I don't know, it was worth a lot!" Buzzy stands up, holding his empty bowl in one hand. He's so irritated now that he can't sit still. When Buzzy rants, his entire body becomes part of the process.

"I would have taken the melodeon!" Anna speaks with a piece of dental floss hanging from her mouth like two flaccid tusks. She looks furious. Emery wonders if she ever feels she has enough: money, things, men.

"We could have donated it and taken a tax credit!" Buzzy is pacing behind the couch. He steps over the golden lab, Gumba, who lies in the pathway. Gumba is splayed like he's been hit by a car. Emery gets up, crouches down beside the dog, and turns its head toward himself. Gumba licks Emery's fingers and he knows the dog's okay. He puts his empty ice cream bowl in front of Gumba's mouth so he can lick it. Gumba cleans the bowl without lifting his head. It is the laziest eating Emery has ever seen.

"Come on," Portia says, "let's go clean the barn. I'm so sick of cartoons."

Emery believes that there are two types of people in the world: workers and nonworkers. Workers work. They get things done. Nonworkers don't. It's quite simple. All of these people get along splendidly unless they're in a relationship, in which case the worker loathes the nonworker for not helping out and the nonworker loathes the worker for nagging and pestering the nonworker into working. Everyone in the family is a worker. Sure, Buzzy and Louise never worked on the house or the yard when Emery and his sisters were growing up, but they were both working on other things. They were always in the process of *doing* something. Emery and Alejandro are workers—together they retiled the bathroom in their apartment in New York, built a closet, and sanded all the floors. Patrick and Portia are both workers. Emery is surprised by their separation. He figured that two workers who are both calm and generally happy could keep going for a long, long time. Anna is a worker but her husband, Brian, doesn't seem to be. But Anna works faster and harder than most people, so maybe another worker would get in her way.

Emery explains his worker theory to Portia while they're in the garage searching for the paint and brushes to use on the barn.

"I wonder if Daphne Frank is a worker?" Portia says, and Emery feels bad for having brought it up.

"Probably not," he says. "So I'm sure they'll be miserable really quickly. There's no way it could last if she's not a worker." Emery thinks his brother-in-law was really, really shitty to his sister. He's glad he's not straight and doesn't have to deal with the whole affair business. It's different when you're gay. You might be slightly jealous, and there may be insecurities or issues of fidelity, but it's nothing compared to the earthquakes that are created by heterosexual affairs. Emery doesn't know why it is, but most gay couples he knows have a don't-ask-don't-tell policy. It's as if both sides get the purely sexual impulse of an affair, how the urge for otherness often has nothing to do with how you feel about your boyfriend. But in hetero marriages, Emery understands, these things are cruel, one-sided attacks that sever the victim's heart with the swift, clean cut of a wire thread.

Each person claims his or her job. Alejandro wants to paint, so he is given the white paint Portia and Emery found. There is enough paint to cover every wall in the studio and maybe even the ceiling. But there are rafters in the ceiling, and after much debate, everyone agrees that the ceiling should remain unpainted. Emery is organizing the art section of the studio—the canvases, paints, rags, brushes. He likes creating order. He likes lining things up. Anna and Portia are going through the writing area where Louise's desk is, along with files, bookshelves, and piles and stacks of papers, photos, and scraps that need to be identified. Buzzy is getting rid of the cat shit and the cats. One by one, he takes the three cats to the giant walk-in toolshed that is up the gravel road beyond the barn. With two scratched, old dustpans he picks up the shit. The rancid smell in the barn is so strong that they have all tied T-shirts and scarves around their faces. Emery thinks they look like bandits. It occurs to him they might be good cartoon characters: the Bandito Family, a bunch of weirdos who all disguise their faces with scarves. Maybe they'd live on another planet where exposing your face is like exposing your penis.

Alejandro has found a radio station that plays pop music: Madonna, Prince, Whitney Houston, Janet Jackson, Salt-N-Pepa. He and Emery know the words to every song. Portia knows some of the songs. Anna knows one or two. Buzzy has never heard any of them, but when they're all singing together he stops what he's doing and plays the bongos on his thighs with his head tilted up the way you'd imagine a cat dancing. There is something sweet about Buzzy's bongo/dancing. When Emery watches him, he guesses that this is probably what he'll picture when he thinks about his father after he's died. He's not sure what single thing about his mother would encapsulate her. But there's no need to worry about that now; Louise will be around to meet the baby he's going to have. Emery finds it strange to connect the living with the not-yet-conceived. It's odd how this child who isn't here yet pulses with the same power as the dead: an idea of a person, an image of a person, but not a person.

At one-thirty in the morning they are still at it. Buzzy has been hauling out the bags of trash, then arranging them in what is becoming a small hill behind the toolshed. He says he knows someone who can pick it all up in a truck and carry it away.

"Dad," Portia says, "you must call this guy tomorrow. If Mom comes home she'll start digging though all that shit and pulling stuff out. So it has to be done right away."

Emery looks at his sister and wonders if she has any idea the condition their mother is in. When she does come home, she will be no more able to sift and sort through a heap of garbage than Maggie Bucks could with her paws.

Emery has finished organizing the art supplies and is now shuffling through papers in Louise's desk, trying to arrange them in a logical order: bills, letters, receipts. He has made three tidy piles in his mother's desk drawer and is straightening them so that none of the piles touch. Emery reaches under the letter pile to scoot it down to the bottom edge of the drawer when he notices a corner of frayed red ribbon sticking out, as if caught between the bottom of the drawer and front of the drawer where the pull is. He yanks at the ribbon and the bottom of the drawer lifts up. A whole mess of letters lies in a secret compartment, swirled on top of each other as if they have landed there after a tornado. Emery looks up to see if Buzzy is nearby, but his father isn't even in the barn. He wonders if Buzzy knows about this secret drawer and then quickly decides he won't tell him in case Louise doesn't want him to know.

Emery unfolds one letter. It is written on nearly transparent onion paper, the stuff people used to use for airmail. There is no envelope. The small tight writing slants toward the right and looks, at a glance, like a series of shrunken bobby pins. It wasn't until Emery was around twelve years old that he was able to decipher his father's handwriting, and here it is.

My dearest darling love, the letter starts.

"Portia," Emery says, and he gets up and hands the letter to his sister, who sits where he was at the desk. Emery knows Portia will be interested in this. She is interested in everything having to do with emotions, relationships, love, people. Emery leans over her shoulder and they read the letter together.

Emery can't get much further than the first sentence. Reading a love letter from his father to his mother is almost as bad as catching them having sex. He scans the page, reads the date: August 10, 1990. His eyes alight on certain words: breasts, tongue, ass, fuck, love. Portia puts the letter face down on her lap. Emery goes to the ladder and helps Alejandro paint the window frames. He looks down at Anna, on her knees, scrubbing the cement floor, trying to wash away the sour, oaty cat-piss scent that remains so strong it beats through the smell of wet paint. Anna and Alejandro still have the T-shirts tied in front of their faces, though he and Portia have removed theirs.

Buzzy walks into the barn carrying a rolled-up rug on his shoulder. The batik-print scarf he had been using as a mask sits around his neck making him look like a foreigner, Moroccan maybe. Buzzy hoists down the rug, grunting a little. Portia folds the letter up, sticks it back with the pile, replaces the false bottom that was sitting angled on the drawer, and shuts the drawer. Emery hopes she doesn't say anything about the letters.

"Dad," Portia says. "How could you possibly have a Stinky?" Emery is confused. The love letter was from Buzzy to Louise. Does Portia somehow not understand that?

Anna stops scrubbing, tugs down her face scarf and looks up. "Will you leave Dad alone, please." And Emery feels a small jolt in his body as he realizes both his sisters know something that he does not know. He shouldn't be surprised, he thinks. That's the way it's been his whole life.

Emery climbs down the ladder, still holding a paintbrush, turns, and faces Buzzy. He cradles his left hand under the brush to catch any drips.

"Dad?" Emery says. "You have a Stinky?" He understands now the connection Portia made between the letters and the Stinky. Are the letters bullshit? Cover-up?

"I'm not seeing her right now," Buzzy says. "I haven't seen her since your mother went into the hospital." He unrolls the carpet on the part of the floor that's already been cleaned.

"Jesus Christ," Emery mumbles. He looks down at the ground. His sister is practically disassembled from her husband's Stinky. How could his mother, who's been with his father for decades and had three children with him, support the idea of a Stinky?

Alejandro has stopped what he's doing and is looking at each of them in turn. He slips his face scarf-down so it sits around his neck.

"I'm sorry, kids." Buzzy sits on the rug and drops his head into his hands.

"You didn't know she was going to have a heart attack," Anna says, and she sits beside Buzzy.

"Dad, you really fucking better not be seeing your Stinky while Mom's in the hospital. Really. That would just be so shitty. So, so shitty." Emery's voice quavers. It only shakes like that when he is bone-deep angry. He has never been in a fistfight before, has never punched anyone. But he wants to punch his father right now. In the heart.

"I love your mother," Buzzy says. "I love her more than I've ever loved any woman in my life."

"You've been with her since you were twenty," Emery says. "So how many women could you have loved?"

"Oy yoy yoy," Buzzy says.

"How long have you had a Stinky?" Emery rests his paint-brush along the rolling pan. "Does Mom know?" Maybe his father does overly romantic things like write love letters to his mother to compensate for his infidelities, to fill in the blank spots where he has removed emotion in order to give it to some-one else. Emery has never written Alejandro a love letter. But he truly loves him. Emery knows that Alejandro is the right person for him. When they have a baby together they probably won't even fight about who changed the last shitty diaper or who was the last person to wake up and give the kid a bottle. Or maybe they will, but it won't really matter.

"No, she doesn't know," Buzzy says. "Don't tell her. It would kill her."

"She should kill you," Emery says. He is surprised by his sudden allegiance to his mother. He never thought of himself as attached to her, as it was his sisters whose presence he felt as he grew up. But here he is, willing to do battle for Louise. Feeling ferocious in her defense.

"I love your mother," Buzzy says, again. He huffs out a breath.

Anna puts an arm around Buzzy, then looks down at the rug. "This is a nice rug," she says. "Where'd you get it?"

"I bought it for the guest quarters but it was too big, so it's been sitting rolled up in the garage."

"Is it real?" Alejandro asks. "It looks Persian."

"Yeah," Buzzy says. "Cost a fortune."

"Don't let the cats back in here," Portia says.

"I can't believe you have a Stinky," Emery says. He sits on the rug. He feels like he's exhaling blood. Everything is draining out of him.

"Emery." Buzzy looks at Emery, but says nothing more.

"Patrick doesn't love me." Portia leaves the desk and sits on the rug between her father and her brother. They are forming a half-circle.

"Of course he does," Buzzy says.

"No, he doesn't," Portia says. "It's not like you and Mom. It's not like we loved each other and then he fucked up and then I fucked up or we both fucked up. I loved him, and he never quite loved me, and that's how it went down." Portia seems calm, clear, certain.

"I'm sure it wasn't like that," Buzzy says.

"His Stinky's not the same as yours," Portia says. "He's not conflicted." Emery is surprised she's not crying. This seems so much worse than the Speedo fiasco at the club.

"He's an asshole," Anna says. She rolls onto her side so she is lying on the rug. Her folded arm is a pillow beneath her head. Emery thinks that Anna doesn't love Brian enough. This is why she is always having affairs. The difference between Brian and Portia is that Brian is willing to settle for someone whose love isn't equal to his.

Alejandro moves to the rug and sits beside Emery. Emery feels like his thoughts are splattering in his brain like spin art: his father's Stinky, his one sister's cheating husband, his other sister who cheats, his love for Alejandro, his sisters' eggs.

"It's weird, but I feel like maybe Patrick was only with me because I wanted to be with him. Like he went along with it until someone he really loved came along."

"Who wouldn't love you!?" Buzzy asks. He seems genuinely offended by the idea of someone's not loving Portia.

"He's like that," Portia says. "He doesn't make decisions, so things get decided for him. He didn't love me, he just never decided to do anything else. And when we got married, it simply happened. Or maybe I pushed it, and he didn't say no. Same thing with Esmé. He didn't decide with me that we'd have a baby; I told him I went off the pill, and he said okay." Emery thinks of his sister as a cored apple. Some center of her has been ripped out, leaving behind a hollow, tattered mess.

"Sometimes I think I don't love Brian," Anna says. *No duh,* Emery almost says aloud, but doesn't.

"There was never a time when I didn't think I loved Patrick," Portia says. "And I don't think there ever was a time when he was sure that he loved me. He never once wrote me a love letter. He didn't even sign refrigerator notes with 'I love you.' I always signed them with 'I love you.' Even if the note said, *Pick up vitamin C,* or *We're out of organic skim milk.*" Emery looks at his sister and sees how sad she is. He puts his hand on her back. Alejandro lies down and puts his head on Emery's lap. Emery looks down and feels lucky to have Alejandro. He knows that their love is equal.

"My love goes in and out all the time," Anna says. "A burning flame and then nothing. And then it lights up again."

"You're a revolving lighthouse," Portia says.

"Alejandro and I are going to have a baby," Emery says.

Portia looks at her brother and tears up. She's smiling.

"That's great," Anna says. She sounds like she doesn't believe it, like it's dreamy chatter.

"You adopting?" Buzzy asks.

"We've found this amazing woman who will carry an embryo," Emery says. Alejandro sits up and stares at Emery. Emery can feel Alejandro's anticipation on his own skin. He is catching it like a yawn.

"Is it expensive?" Buzzy asks.

"We can afford it," Emery says. "We've been saving."

"So where do you get the embryo?" Buzzy asks.

"We grow it in a test tube. We're going to use Alejandro's sperm."

"Where are you going to find a woman to give you an egg?" Anna says. "It's a brutal process. You have to take all these shots that fuck you up so you pump up your eggs. I swear, any woman who would voluntarily go through all that hormonal shit is going to be someone slightly out of her mind. And is that the kind of person you want to be the egg-half of your kid?"

"We were hoping you or Portia would give us an egg," Emery says. Fucking Anna. It's one thing if she doesn't want to give up her eggs, but now she's going to scare Portia off, too!

"Seriously?" Anna asks.

"You want our eggs?" Portia starts crying.

"Yes," Emery says. It would be fucking nice if his sisters would offer up their eggs like a few locks of hair (spread the remaining hair around and no one can even tell some is missing). He would love it if there were no thinking about the shots and the hormones, no wondering about what it might do to their psyches! If they were lesbians and needed his sperm to put in their girlfriends, he would give it in a minute! In a second! In as much time as it took to jack the sperm out! Christ! He'd give his sperm even if he had to shoot hormones into his eyelids for it!

"That's so sweet," Portia sobs. Emery wonders if these tears are a delayed reaction to her lack-of-love revelation.

"Portia's already such a mess she'd probably become completely psycho on the hormones," Anna says, and Portia cries harder.

"Well, why don't you guys think about it and let us know in a few days," Emery says. He feels edgy. Shaky. Anxiety is running from his toenails to his nose hairs. If Portia refuses, he'll blame it on Anna. If Anna refuses, he'll be, sadly, not surprised.

"But won't the girls be the mother of the kid?" Buzzy asks. "And then wouldn't the kid have a mother and father who are brother and sister?"

"Well, I would be the father," Alejandro says. "Emery would be more like the mother."

"The eggs are my proxy," Emery says. He wants everyone to shut up now.

"If it grew in someone else's womb I'd have no feelings of attachment for it," Anna says. "I think the only reason I love Blue is because it was so fucking hard to push him out of my body. He had to be worth the effort."

"I don't know." Portia's crying has slowed. "It would be really hard not to think of it as mine."

"Well, think it over." Emery tries to relax his voice. He doesn't want anyone to see how upset he is. Alejandro puts his hand on Emery's knee and he immediately feels calmer.

"That's a big thing to think over," Buzzy says.

Emery feels hope slipping from his mouth like air slipping out of a sliced tire. "Let's not talk about it anymore."

"Did you tell Mom?" Buzzy asks.

"No," Emery says. "I'll tell her tomorrow." He wants to cry a little. Or go to bed. Or drink from the bottle of absinthe he snuck home from a trip to France.

"Don't tell her about Dad's Stinky," Anna says.

"Of course I won't!" Emery's words are inflamed with spit and a surprising fury.

No one speaks for a moment. Then Portia snorts in some snot. "Does your Stinky have kids?" Portia asks Buzzy.

"Don't think about this stuff!" Anna says. "It's an affair. You don't need the details."

"Is she married?" Emery asks. He'd rather be talking about this than the eggs.

"I hope you all understand," Buzzy says, "that I think your mother is the most brilliant, amazing person I've ever known."

Emery pictures his mother in the hospital: a gray-and-white woman in a bed with a sheet tucked down at her armpits and rubber hoses snaking along her arms. It is hard to reconcile that image with his idea of her as a vibrant, forceful presence, the person his father wrote a letter to, the person Buzzy called *My Dearest, Darling, Love.*

"Yeah, yeah," Emery says. "You haven't answered our questions."

"She's not married. No kids." Buzzy takes a deep breath.

"Dad, did Mom have an affair with that poet back in the seventies?" Anna asks.

"What poet?!" Buzzy sits up straight.

"I read your diary a long time ago. When we were kids. And you thought Mom was going to have an affair with some poet."

"Oh . . . oh, yeah, I remember," Buzzy says. "I used to get jealous when we were younger. I worried about her having an affair."

"Do you think Mom had an affair?" Emery asks. He hopes she did. It would dull down the raspiness of his father's Stinky.

"I don't think so," Buzzy says. "She never admitted it if she did."

"Did you ever have an affair with Bitty Royce or Lompoc Lucy?" Portia asks.

"Or Tits-N-Ass McCoy?" Emery adds. Alejandro starts laughing.

"No!" Buzzy says. "I wasn't interested in any of them. Your mother was out of her mind to think about that shit."

"Apparently not," Emery says.

"What do you mean?" Buzzy jerks his head toward Emery.

"You've become a mystery," Emery says. "I'm not sure if we can believe you." Emery would like this to be the last he will say about the subject. He would rather walk away from a problem, let it dissipate or dissolve, than pick it up and face it.

"How can you say that?!"

"Dad," Emery says. "At this point the only thing we know for sure about you is that you're not gay." And one can never really be sure about that, either, Emery thinks.

"Or maybe you are gay," Anna says. "Maybe your entire life has been one long attempt to hide it."

"Yeah," Portia says. "You did let the rabbi suck you at your bris."

"What?" Emery asks. Alejandro starts laughing.

"What the fuck are you talking about?" Anna asks.

"Jesus Christ, Portia," Buzzy moans, "I didn't *let* him do any-thing. I was eight days old!"

"What are you guys talking about?!" Emery is relieved the

egg thing has shifted out of everyone's mind. He wants to laugh now, and he does.

"Dad had an orthodox bris," Portia says. "And in an orthodox bris, the rabbi puts wine in his mouth after he cuts the foreskin, then he sucks the wound and exchanges blood for wine."

"You're fucking kidding me!" Anna says. "Dad, is this true?"

"Our kid is *never* having an orthodox bris!" Emery says. Alejandro nods his head and grins.

"It's nothing!" Buzzy says. "The rabbi leans down and staunches the wound. You don't even notice it—it's done in a second."

"Not with you!" Portia taunts her father with a sing-song voice. "He did a whole lot more with you!"

Buzzy shakes his head and groans.

"Portia!" Anna says. "Tell the fucking story!"

"Aunt Sylvia told me that the rabbi went down and sucked Dad's wound. Then he came up, took more wine, and sucked it again. You're only supposed to do it once, but this rabbi did it, like, three times. And Bubbe was so upset that she went in the kitchen, stirred the soup, held a wooden spoon in her hand, and prayed for the rabbi to die and for Dad not to be gay."

Everyone, except Buzzy, is looking at Portia with some variation of a smile. All of Anna's teeth are showing.

"Who's Aunt Sylvia?" Alejandro asks.

"Bubbe's sister," Portia says.

"How did Sylvia know that Bubbe stirred the soup with a wooden soup and how did she know what Bubbe prayed for?!" Anna asks.

"I don't know. That's exactly how Sylvia told me the story. And she also told me to never bring it up with Bubbe because Bubbe would be upset."

"Why didn't you ever tell us this before?" Emery asks. Another family secret kept from him!

"Who even knows if it's true!" Buzzy says. "Sylvia was a madwoman."

"Was she?" Alejandro asks.

"Well, she claimed her dog Debby could answer the phone," Portia says. "And she said her hair had turned white instantaneously when she was raped by the Nazis. But she was in Trenton, New Jersey, during World War Two."

Emery hopes Alejandro won't look at his family history and reconsider the value of his sisters' eggs.

"When did Sylvia tell you this?" Anna asks.

"A couple years before she died, when I was in high school. You weren't talking to me then," Portia says to Anna. And then she looks at Emery and says, "And you were too young to hear something like that."

"So Buzzy got sucked by a rabbi," Alejandro says. His smile is enormous.

"I bet Sylvia was the one who stirred the soup and prayed," Anna says. "I always thought she was a lesbian. Maybe her fear of her own yearnings made her terrified that Buzzy was gay."

"She never did get married," Buzzy says.

"And she really, *really* loved that dog," Portia says.

Everyone, it seems, has temporarily abandoned talk of both the Stinky and the eggs. Emery thinks the two subjects are like naughty, wild children that have been tucked away in their beds, their absence giving a calm relief to those who are still awake. He wouldn't mind if the subject of the Stinky were never awoken. But the subject of the eggs will have to be pulled out again in the daylight. By then, Emery hopes, he will have rested and stored up strength to deal with it further.

Anna's wedding was fairly traditional—flowers, a meal, and at least a hundred people. She wanted to wear a dress like a normal bride, have Buzzy walk her down the aisle like a normal father, dress Louise in lavender with a corsage like a normal mother. Louise agreed to the lavender, but she refused to put on the corsage, claiming the pin would ruin her silk dress. Emery was in a suit that Buzzy had bought for him, and Portia was in a floral Laura Ashley dress that Anna had picked out. She looked sexless and earnest in the dress, like one of the multiple wives of an extremist Mormon hiding out in the mountains of Utah. Anna thought Portia could wear the dress over and over again, but by the time she got the wedding photos back she realized how deluded she had been.

She and Brian were married in a field out behind the flower and gift shop they owned near a covered bridge about thirty miles from Fulton Ranch in Vermont. It was a beautiful, warm day; the air felt as clean as sunshine. Brian was fifteen inches taller and ten years older than Anna (who was twenty-seven). He was a human longboard—as solid and stable as she was reckless. He spoke at half her speed, napped every day, and often sat completely still, meditating, while Anna spun around him like a whirling dervish. He calmed her and she invigorated him. Together they created a perfectly balanced energy.

Brian and Anna had met at a Narcotics Anonymous meeting in Santa Barbara. Brian had been going since he was fourteen years old—he was like a preacher at the church of NA. He went to meetings every day in Vermont, too, dragging Anna with him at least twice a week. There was no one in the family who wasn't grateful for the fact that Anna's variegated manias had been tamped down and diligently put to rest by Brian.

Seconds before the judge (Brian's friend from the Littleton, Vermont, chapter of NA) declared Brian and Anna husband and wife, a band of dogs began howling so loudly and intensely that the ceremony came to a halt. Everyone tilted their heads and tried to find the direction from which the invisible dogs were baying. And then the howling stopped, Anna and Brian kissed, and the crowd applauded, most people still looking off in the distance in search of the dogs. Sometime during the reception, while the three-piece banjo band was twanging out something no one had ever heard before, Louise told Anna that she was convinced the howling had been a message of some sort, as if the animal kingdom were aware of the importance of this particular human pairing.

"Why's this pairing more important than any other?" Anna had asked her mother.

"Because how many people would put up with you?" Louise laughed. "I mean, no one's allowed to make audible chewing sounds when you're in the room, you can't clink a spoon against a cereal bowl, you hate the way I exhale." Louise blew out smoke, making the popping sound that made Anna want to shed her skin.

"Mom! I get it!" This was her wedding. She was in a thick lace dress that trailed behind her and weighed about forty pounds. She wasn't going to fight with her mother.

Portia was married a month later; she and Patrick snuck off to the justice of the peace with a couple of friends as witnesses.

This seemed to thrill Louise, who couldn't help but mention to Anna on the phone how relieved she was that she didn't have another wedding to go to.

"Oy, *gut*," Louise had said. "The only thing I hate more than weddings are bar mitzvahs."

"Thanks, Mom. Glad we spent all that money throwing a wedding!" Now that Anna was married and settled, her mother seemed to protect her less from her spiky thoughts. Anna wasn't sure if it was because Louise knew Anna could handle it better, or if Louise was less able to censor herself the older she got. Her mother's little comments did sit with her, however, like little pebbles gathering in her shoes. It seemed to Anna that Louise approved heartily of every lame move Portia made (moving back east after Patrick passed the New York bar exam, buying an old house in Greenwich, Connecticut, staying home and fixing it up while her husband earned what appeared to Anna to be fabulous sums of money at a law firm in Manhattan, etc.), while she seemed to disapprove of Anna working her ass off in the flower and gift shop, fixing up her house that sat above the shop, and keeping her shit together through a combination of NA meetings, shrink appointments, running, and regular sex with her husband.

Anna called Emery at Haverford to complain about their mother and Portia.

"I mean, she acts like Portia gave her some huge fucking gift by running off to the justice of the peace instead of having a wedding!"

"Portia got married?" Emery asked. "Are you serious?!"

"Yeah, she fucking got married! But of course she had to outdo me, do it better than me, by not having a fucking wedding for Mom to groan and bitch about!" Anna was loading the dishwasher as she spoke, shoving in plates and bowls. She secretly hoped she'd break one.

"Wait. When did this happen?"

"About six days ago," Anna said. "Didn't anyone tell you?"

"No! No one tells me anything! No one told me when you were in the hospital for bulimia."

"Well, you seem to know now." Anna sniffed the sponge she was using, made a face, and tossed it across the kitchen to the giant open trash can that sat by the back door. She reached under the sink and got a new sponge.

"I found out way afterwards. And no one told me you were a sex addict."

"Emery! How the fuck could you say no one told you if you know all this shit?! Okay? You know! And now you know that Portia one-upped me with her non-wedding wedding that Mom thinks is so fucking wonderful!"

"What do you care which wedding Mom liked better?" Emery asked. "You had your wedding for you, right?"

"I gotta go," Anna said. She hated it when her younger brother was so wise. Things were much easier when she was the boss of him.

Anna dialed the numbers for Portia's house. The answering machine went off with Portia's grotesquely cheerful voice: "Hey! You've reached the answering machine of Portia and Patrick who are now officially Missus and Mister Portia and Patrick! Ta da!"

Anna wished there was some way to projectile vomit through the phone lines and have it come out in Portia's lap. "Hey, it's me." She spoke quick and stern, like she was giving directions. "I thought you should know that in your rush to have a non-wedding wedding, you totally forgot to tell your little brother that you got married. Smooth one." Anna hung up. And glared at the phone. She walked across the kitchen and replaced it in the receiver. "Fuck," she said.

Anna knew Emery was right. She had had the wedding she wanted and she shouldn't really care what Louise thought of it. She also knew that Portia hadn't done anything wrong. Portia had never even had a birthday party; of course she wasn't going to have a wedding. The irritation Anna was feeling now was the itchiness she got when things were too easy. After nine months of planning, her wedding had gone off as beautifully as she imagined. The store was doing fine, making enough money to support them. Brian was happy and content, made no demands, and let her run the show. (When she wanted to tear down the non-load-bearing walls in the house and make the downstairs a giant, open, loftlike space, Brian said yes. When she wanted to throw out the old furniture they had collected in the few years they'd been together, he agreed. When she wanted to paint the walls of the kitchen tangerine, even though Brian hated the color orange, he said sure.) Anna realized that maybe the problem was that she needed the chaos of these big projects (wedding, house renovation) in order to feel steady inside. When everything was calm outside, things started to storm in her gut and her limbs felt encased in cement. Anna wanted to shuck the cozy life that surrounded her and come out new again—wet, glossy, ready to slip through the cracks and escape.

During this period of itchiness, Anna woke up early from a dream one morning with an image stuck in her mind. She dressed in workout clothes and went out for a run. It was five a.m. and about sixty degrees. Anna liked these early runs because no one else was out, and the empty woods and dirt roads of Vermont were almost eerie. Frequently she saw deer and moose, and twice she saw a bear.

The image from her dream was of herself holding a gun. She loved the gun—the cold weight, the hardness against her palm.

In the dream she pushed it into her cheek and felt a rush of sexual energy.

Anna's footbeats made a wonderful chalky thunk. She ran faster, hurtling over a branch on the road as she thought about the dream, the gun. There were cows in the field beside her, a wooden slat fence holding them off the road. Anna envisioned herself lifting the gun and shooting a cow. She saw it crumple downward, like a falling cake. It would lie there, its giant ribcage heaving in and out, a pair of giant bellows.

Anna turned off the dirt road onto a smaller dirt road that led down along the other side of the farm and toward the pond where she had once seen a bear. She imagined shooting a bear, like her grandmother had done. It must have been wonderful to have felt the force of the bullet expelling from the gun. It must have been beautiful to watch that giant, warm animal collapse into a heap of blood and fur and weighty flesh.

Anna reached the wooden footbridge that crossed the end of the pond. She stopped for a moment and looked out at the water, where steam was rising in smoky little tendrils.

"I should be a cop," Anna said aloud.

Anna smiled the entire run back. She knew what she had to do and she knew that she could do it. She'd lie about the drug addiction. She'd lie about rehab. There was no federal record of who had or hadn't been in rehab. Besides, all that stuff was buried in California and Phoenix. She was in Vermont now. It was like another planet.

Anna figured out how to control her breathing, how to moderate her heartbeat, how to trick her body into believing what she was saying when she took the police academy lie detector test: no, she'd never smoked marijuana, no, she'd never tried cocaine;

no, she'd never stolen anything. And then she was off to academy training for sixteen weeks.

After the first week of training, Anna happily made the two-hour drive home for the weekend to be with Brian. But by the second week the drive felt like a transcontinental crossing. The academy life was like doing drugs in that Anna was continually living in the rush of the moment, fully present. There was no way to get through it, to survive the boot camp–like experience, unless you were entirely there. And when she wasn't there, when she was home with Brian, her head was still at the academy— Anna felt divested of herself, as if only her molded-skin form had come home.

Like being away at war, there was a nice intimacy between cadets that came from living in dorms, eating meals together, seeing each other sweat, cry, work, struggle. There were thirty-five men and five women in Anna's class. Anna was the odd-numbered girl who got her own dorm room. At first there was the usual division of guys versus girls. Fairly quickly, this changed into the ones who would make it versus the ones who wouldn't—and this division was gender-blind. Anna was in the top of the group who would make it. She felt almost obligated to be at the top, as her father had grumbled about Anna's reaching way below her potential. (Buzzy's statement, of course, infuriated Louise, who had been on the phone with Anna when she reported her new career plans. Louise had called Buzzy an asshole and classist, then insisted that being a cop was meaningful and great work and that she'd be proud of Anna if she were a cop.) Anna hated that, at twenty-seven, she still cared what her parents thought, but there it was, she couldn't help herself. And so she did more push-ups than anyone else in the academy, got nearly perfect scores on every test, and reported all of this and more to her parents in their weekly phone calls.

Anna had three best friends at the academy and they were all men, the four of them in a constant shift for the number one spot. It was a reality unlike normal life. There was a luxury in being removed from the endless, tedious bullshit like calling a credit card company, or doing the dishes, or putting away laundry. Yet there was nothing luxurious about it at all. Anna studied hard, trained harder, ate what she could, and slept in between. Until Milos.

Milos was the only black guy in the academy, and one of the few who, like Anna, had gone to a college where they didn't expect their graduates to come out as cops. Milos was beautiful, Anna thought, perfectly proportioned, skin as smooth and glossy as marble, a face that looked like it had been meticulously diagrammed—the nose exactly this far from the upper lip, the eyes just this far apart—before being created.

She had only been married a few months earlier, so it hadn't yet occurred to Anna that her marriage would include affairs. But after spending so much of her time with Milos, breathing in his exhalations, running side by side up mountainous roads, aligning even her thoughts with his as they studied together, quizzed each other, looked over each other's work, Anna came to the conclusion that 50 percent of love is simple proximity. You sniff in the molecules floating off a person's skin for long enough, and you will feel like you love him. Maybe that was nature's way of making sure people mated with whomever they were stuck with in the cave.

Anna stopped going home on the weekends and Brian accepted it as he always accepted her desires. From Friday to Sunday, Anna nestled in her dorm room with her academy husband

(Milos called Anna his academy wife; he, too, had a spouse waiting at home a couple hundred miles away). The sex was like alien sex, like sex from another planet with another species, operating in a way that was totally new to Anna. She had had fucked-up-on-drugs sex and addicted-to-sex sex, which had always seemed wild, like she was a cat in heat rolling around with tomcats (sometimes more than one at a time), trying not lose all her fur in the process. And she had sober sex with Brian: gentle, tame, like a visit to a pediatrician who had very warm, kind hands. But with Milos, Anna had found something completely new. She was in the best physical shape of her life, her mind was as sober and sharp as a scalpel, and she was mating with a guy who, totally sober, could keep the passion amped up beyond a cocaine high, beyond a sex-addicted obliteration. They fucked early in the morning before class. They often fucked during lunch break. And they always fucked late at night, soiling the sheets of one bunk in her room, then moving over to the other bed for sleep. Anna's life was both absolutely simple, consisting of only three things—Milos, physical training, and class work—and utterly thrilling: fucking, shooting guns, acing every test she took.

When Anna told her best woman friend at the academy, Julie, about the affair, Julie expressed such strong disapproval that Anna realized hers was a world unlike most others. Julie had been married around the same time as Anna and, like her sister Portia, she seemed to have a blindly romantic view of marriage, seeing herself as someone on the other side of dirty, or messy, or deceitful things. Julie's disapproval didn't bother Anna. She figured everyone would come over to her side eventually, one way or another. And in the meantime, she had to keep her private life to herself. This made for many distant and strained conversations with her old friends and her sister (she never spoke regularly with Emery, so he didn't count), none of whom seemed to have anything in their lives interesting enough to hide.

The end of academy training was painful, the return to normal civilization almost unbearable. But slowly, over time, Anna felt reconnected with Brian (thus reinforcing her belief that proximity is 50 percent of love), disconnected with Milos (they met in hotels two weekends postacademy, and neither time could they recreate the alien spirit they had had in the dorm room), and more accepting of the routine life of a cop.

And then, as soon as the itchiness was starting to return, when Anna found herself searching for another big project like a house to renovate, or a new store for Brian to run, Anna was asked to work undercover narcotics. She was small, appeared ten years younger than she was, and, most important, didn't look like a cop. It would mean dressing up like a girl who wanted to party, hanging out with people who loved to party, and buying drugs—all with a markedly greater possibility that she'd have to use her gun. Anna couldn't have been more thrilled.

Anna's first assignment was to enroll in high school and buy pot from the local dealers. She did such a great job she was sent to the junior college and then to the University of Vermont. Although most of the dealers were nonstudents dealing to the student population, occasionally a student would get sucked down with the bust, which always caused Anna tremendous roiling guilt. She knew it could have been herself a few years back, or Portia. Or even her mother buying pot before Buzzy started growing it. But Anna loved the thrill of being someone else on campus, playing the role of the eager party chick. And she especially, and surprisingly, loved being the party chick with her wits about her—the one who could see the way things were operating, as if she were floating on the ceiling looking down, rather than coiling in the inferno of her own body as she had done in the past.

Reggie Fish, the head of the narcotics unit, said he'd never seen a cop who was such a natural at buying drugs. He said it was like she'd actually been doing drugs her whole life. Then he suggested that Anna be put to better use: more complicated deals, larger buys, the big guys.

For the first time in their relationship, Brian didn't stand back and watch Anna move forward. He was worried she would be involved with people who had no problem shoving rocks down a narc's throat and dropping her in a murky backwoods lake. People who were busted for thousands of dollars of pot were angry. People who were caught with millions of dollars of heroin or cocaine were murderous. But there was no way Anna wasn't going to do it. As far as she was concerned, *she* was the only who had a choice in this.

John Domini, or Dom, as everyone called him, was Anna's partner. He looked like a cop: big, mustache, light brown hair, muscles bursting through his T-shirts. Dom was everyone's friend—cops trusted him, crooks trusted him (he had the most reliable informants), he made good arrests, and he would grind to the bone any asshole who messed with his people. When he and Anna were brought into an office together and told they'd be partners, her eyes locked into his like a button into a buttonhole. She knew he'd never let anything happen to her. She also knew they'd be fucking as soon as they could find the place and the time. Anna couldn't imagine anything hotter than sex with a guy who had a pistol strapped to his leg.

Their first assignment started out slowly: drinking at a cramped, musty biker bar, which had a collection of gas masks and license plates on the walls. Word had come in that cocaine traffickers were hanging out there. And although they weren't supposed to drink on the job (Anna had been instructed to order a beer, nurse it, take it to the bathroom, dump it, then order more), Dom sipped a couple of beers each night, and encouraged Anna to do the same. Their knees would touch under the polished wood bar counter, their cheeks would brush together as they whispered to each other. They'd concocted a story that they were a couple with a tumultuous but passionate relationship. Sometimes their faces would be only a breath apart as they pretended to coo at each other and Dom would crawl his massive hot hand up Anna's thigh. (She always wore a miniskirt, a teensy top, and heels that made her legs look like licorice sticks.) But they didn't fool around outside of playacting for the job.

And then after three weeks of showing up almost nightly with Dom, Anna came to the bar alone, as planned, her body wired with a Q-tip-sized microphone taped in her bra. She and her boyfriend had had a blowout fight, she told the regulars. They might be breaking up. Within two hours Anna was on the back of a rumbling Harley with an enormous grizzly bear of a man named Michael. They rode through the black Vermont hills on a lonely road with no streetlights. The stars in the sky were like a spill of glitter on a velvet blanket. Anna thought if she weren't so scared, she would have loved the sensation of being on the rushing bike as they cut through the still and quiet landscape.

After twenty minutes they pulled up to a farmhouse with yellow light glowing out every window. The house was so isolated, Anna was pretty sure you could unload a machine gun and no one would hear the rat-a-tat-tat.

Anna got off the bike with shaky legs. She pulled the helmet off and pushed her black hair out of her eyes. Her hands were trembling. Anna's gun, radio, and bulletproof vest were under the seat in her car, an old Saab with a new alarm. She had wanted to follow Michael to the farm, but he insisted that the only way there was on the back of his bike.

Breathe, Anna told herself. A lump of fear waited behind her heart; she felt it move into the shadows, like an animal that wanted her to forget it was there. A glint, like a shooting star, flashed off in the field beside the house. Anna hoped it was Dom, who was supposed to be following her. She hadn't wanted to arouse Michael's suspicions, and so, the entire ride out, had not once turned around to look for Dom. She had, however, quietly dictated into the microphone every shadowy landmark they passed. Now Anna feared that the wind had blunted out her voice, giving Dom only the crackly fuzz of static.

There was an army of people at the farmhouse—a rambling clapboard building that was decorated with hanging quilts and tables surrounded by Windsor chairs. It was past midnight, and yet someone was talking on the phone, the stereo was playing ZZ Top so loudly you had to lean in close to talk to anyone, and two dumpling-shaped women were cooking bacon and eggs in the kitchen. They both looked up at Anna, eyed her breasts popping out of her tiny shirt, and decided she wasn't worth knowing. Other than these women, the place had a firehouse feel to it: a bunch of bulky, bearded white guys hanging out, waiting for *something.*

Anna followed Michael through the kitchen and into living room, where four blue velour couches were arranged in a square around a low, pine-knotted coffee table. There was a framed mirror on the table with a couple of straws and a few small heaps of coke. Four guys were sitting there, each on a single couch, as if they'd contaminate each other if they sat too close.

"Scoot," Michael said, and one thick-thighed guy got up and moved to another couch so Anna and Michael could have the couch to themselves. Anna figured the body weight in the living room alone surpassed a ton. Even if she had had her gun, she couldn't have gained an advantage with this crowd.

When the coke was offered to her, Anna claimed she was getting drug tested soon for her job as an administrative assistant at Burlington Community College. For the first time since she'd been out of rehab, Anna wasn't even interested in coke. She was floating on being alert, on trying to figure out who was whom, how they were operating, why they were working in the middle of the night, and how she'd get to the back bedrooms where all the business seemed to be going down, as everyone who went in and out of that wing had either a telephone in his hand or a look of attentive concentration on his face.

Anna worried that getting out of sex might be difficult. Michael, who was drinking cans of Miller High Life, inched progressively closer to Anna over the night and continually cracked sex jokes that made his friends on the other couches lean over their bellies with laughter. Eventually he threw his hefty arm across Anna's shoulders and whispered in her ear that he'd like to show her the power a Harley man had between his legs. He smelled like wet newspaper and had pointed yellow teeth. Anna thought his hair looked like something might nest in it.

Anna tried playing coy and said, "But I already saw your bike." Michael laughed so hard he began wheezing.

"No, baby," he said. "This." Michael grabbed his crotch through his jeans. His stomach hung down over his forearm. Anna wished she had worn pants and had strapped a gun to her ankle.

"I've got massive creeping herpes sores right now," Anna whispered. "You know, the stress of fighting with my boyfriend." Michael pulled his arm away and told another joke. This one about a couple with matching sores on their lips.

It was after six in the morning when Michael drove Anna back to her car at the bar. She hadn't seen much, but she did have a location where they could begin clandestine surveillance. And she did seem to have Michael's trust. Anna would be invited back again, she was certain.

Anna sat in her car with her hand on the ignition and watched as Michael roared away down the road. Hers was the only car in the lot. And then headlights were beaming in her back window. Dom pulled up beside her, got out of his car, and stepped into Anna's. They looked at each other, their mouths open, almost laughing.

"Were you there?" Anna asked. She felt wild and electrified.

"If he had touched you, I would have shot him cold," Dom said.

Anna pulled the lever and scooted her seat back. She reached under her shirt and struggled with the wiretap.

"May I?" Dom rummaged his hands across Anna's breasts until the microphone was detached from the receiver that was tucked down the back of her skirt.

"You're free now," Dom said. He leaned into Anna and they fucked for the first time. It was inevitable. Everything that had happened earlier in the night had been their foreplay.

It took eight months for Anna, Dom, and their backup to bring down what was a multimillion-dollar cocaine ring. By the time they were ready to make the arrest Anna had befriended the two women, wives of the number two and three guys, and had grown to genuinely like Michael. Yes he was stinky, and he told jokes that only seventh-grade boys should love, but when you broke it all away, he was a genuinely sweet guy with whom she had enjoyed hanging out. And once it was established that they wouldn't have sex (Michael had, however improbably, accepted the story that Anna "wasn't ready yet" to be with another man), the friendship flourished. They loved the same TV shows (*Cheers* and *Kate & Allie*) and even shared a book (*The Bonfire of the Vanities*), passing it back and forth with each of them reading the same chapters each time so they could discuss them. Additionally, there was their joint love of bacon sandwiches, which Michael made for Anna and whoever was at the house that night: two pieces of white bread fried in butter with four strips of cooked bacon pressed between them. Most of the guys liked to put mayonnaise on theirs, but Anna and Michael ate them pure without a sauce. Anna felt a great pang of guilt every time she left Michael. She knew he'd be locked away for quite some time. No more bacon sandwiches.

The night of the bust, a rookie cop positioned outside the house thought he saw a gun pointed at him and let off a single bullet that whizzed past Anna's head in a buzzing rush of air (she thought about that bullet every day for weeks; it was like an encounter with a guy who was so scary, you loved him). Michael threw himself on top of Anna, then shoved her protectively behind the couch, her face pressed into the gritty, mold-smelling wood floor. Thick boots were running by, making the ground vibrate and quake. Floodlights fired up the walls like a laser show. Doors were broken open and bodies rushed into the house like a bull stampede as furniture was kicked aside and

Michael's gang was corralled. When it all played out, Anna was arrested with the rest of them, her cover never unveiled. And as she lay splayed face-down on the ground in a lineup, handcuffs cutting into her bony, hairless wrists, Anna couldn't remember a happier moment.

DAY NINE

On Day Nine Louise is moved out of intensive care into the cardiac wing on another floor. She has a regular room now, with a bathroom.

"I'm feeling a lot better," Louise says, after waking up from a nap. It is the afternoon. Anna, Portia, Emery, and Alejandro have returned from a walk to the secondhand store, Claire's Closet, down the street. Claire's Closet isn't one of those secondhand stores that smell like damp, used gym socks and mothballs, where the clothes seem to feel slightly gritty, as if there's salty sweat dried on them. It is a secondhand store with designer clothes, run by a woman with slick black hair in a model's bun and wearing a clingy dress that reveals just how narrow and tall she is.

"You look absolutely gorgeous," Buzzy says to Louise. "I'm so glad you feel better." When he leans over to stroke Louise's forehead, Emery groans in a quick hiccupping way. Anna thinks her brother's having a hard time letting the Stinky float off his skin; it's sticking to him like craft paste. She hopes he won't be stupid enough to tell their mother.

"What?" Louise turns her head toward Emery.

"Mom," Anna says. She wants to stave off any impulse Emery might have to out their father. "Did I show you the clothes I got?"

"Why'd you grunt?" Louise asks Emery.

"I was thinking about how hard it is to wake up with a baby

in the night," he says. Anna thinks he's lying, although earlier in the day he did tell Louise about the plans to have a baby. Louise seemed as uninterested as she was with Blue and Esmé when they were first born.

"You were not thinking about that," Louise says.

"I was thinking about Portia's marriage," he tries again. Louise jerks her head toward Portia. Today is the first day she's had the force to jerk her head.

"Sweetie," Louise says. "I forgot about your marriage. Can you believe that? This whole week I completely forgot."

"You've been on morphine, Mom," Anna says. She opens her purse and pulls out a pack of red licorice. "You forgot your own identity."

"Yeah," Portia says. "Our little brother, Schlomo, was here, and you even forgot that you gave birth to him. You sent him away telling him to go back to the kibbutz he came from."

"Yeah," Buzzy says. "And your Stinky came by, some twenty-year-old with a mustache, and you forgot that he was your lover!" Emery and Portia look at their father with the same snarling smile. Anna guesses they're disturbed that Buzzy, who has a Stinky himself, would make a joke like that.

"I think it's only a Stinky if it's a girl," Anna says, and she spins into thought on what the best name for a male Stinky would be. Stink Stick?

"Yeah, yeah," Louise says. "Seriously, Portia was heartbroken and I completely forgot."

"I think we all sort of forgot," Emery says. Anna wants to huff. Clearly he has forgotten that a moment ago he claimed he was thinking about Portia's marriage. And what about the revelation in the barn?! The entire family, save Louise, has devoted plenty of time to Portia's heartbreak, Anna decides.

"We didn't forget," Alejandro says, then he turns toward

Portia. "I think you're doing amazingly well. Considering." Anna disagrees. Portia has seemed about as comfortable and relaxed as someone who has red fire ants crawling over their skin.

"You'll meet someone else," Buzzy says to Portia. "You won't be single long. You're a beautiful girl." Portia shrugs and forks her fingers into her fine, brown hair.

"What if she were ugly like me?" Anna says. Anna believes that everyone in the family considers Portia to be prettier than she, even though her boyfriends have always told her that she is prettier than her sister. She agrees with her family, but thinks it would be nice if for once, in any arena, they preferred her to Portia.

"Yeah, what if I were ugly like Anna? Would anyone love me then?" Portia is laughing now.

"You're both beautiful girls," Buzzy says. "If Anna weren't with Brian she would meet someone else right away, too."

"She seems to meet them even when she's with Brian," Portia says, and Louise laughs. Anna hates how her mother always finds the blatant outing of Anna's compulsions funny.

"Okay, okay," Anna says. Licorice is sticking out of her mouth like a long, red cigarette. "I admit I've fucked up in the past. But never again." Even Anna herself knows this isn't true. Although, she has been faithful for almost a year now. As long as phone sex doesn't count as a cheat.

"Everyone's allowed one big fuckup," Louise says. She squeezes her eyes shut, as if she's in sudden pain.

"You okay, Mom?" Emery asks.

"I keep getting these shooting jabs down my arm," Louise says.

"Which arm?" Buzzy asks.

"Never mind! I'm sick of me. We were talking about Portia."

"I don't want to talk about me," Portia says.

"We can talk about me," Anna says. "I want to show you the clothes I got at the store."

"You should do a fashion show," Alejandro says, and he lifts his hand and does a little flip, like something a model might do.

"We should all do one," Emery says.

Louise smiles. "Yes. I want a fashion show."

A nurse comes in the room. She smiles and has curly hair that also seems to be smiling. The nurses on this floor are much cheerier than the nurses in intensive care. She wants to give Louise a bath.

"I came in early this morning and she didn't want it then," the nurse says to Buzzy.

"Why didn't you want a bath this morning?!" Buzzy asks. "Who wouldn't want a sponge bath first thing in the morning?!"

"I was eating!" Louise says.

"You ate?" Anna asks. Since the heart attack no one has seen Louise eat anything other than what one of the intensive care nurses spoon-fed her each night.

"Yeah," Louise says. "It was so good I didn't want to stop for the bath."

"What was it?" Anna asks.

"Cream of wheat and toast."

"Grain and grain?" Portia says.

"You kids go get dressed and take your time. I'll have a sponge bath, and when I'm done, you can do the fashion show."

Beyond the cardiac wing, down the hall, are men's and women's bathrooms. Anna and Portia go in one bathroom, the boys in the other. Anna is in one stall and Portia is in the stall beside her.

"What did you get?" Anna asks. She was in such a buying frenzy, she never even noticed her sister in the store with her. Anna loves shopping. It takes her out of her head in the same way as sex, or drugs, or being in love.

"I only bought the one dress," Portia says. Anna looks at her sister's feet below the stall divider. Her red toenail polish is chipped at the ends, as if her toes grew out of the polish. Anna thinks her own long, naked toes look better than that. Portia once told her that women's unpainted toenails remind her of testicles: a part of the body that looks almost foreign in how unappealing it is, like prehistoric insects, and albino deep-sea creatures. Anna totally disagrees. She rather have her prehistoric, testicle-looking toes than Portia's half-painted slatternly toes.

Portia's clothes are being flung over the beige panel that separates their two stalls. Anna wonders why she doesn't hang them from the hook inside the door. And then it is quiet and still beside her as Anna focuses on zipping the stretchy, short black skirt she bought and tucking in the shimmering glove-tight top that goes with it. Anna steps out of the stall and stares at herself in the mirror. There is a dusty white spot near the hem of the skirt. Anna takes a piece of sandpapery paper towel, wets it, and rubs at the spot. The towel crumbles into little brown ants on the skirt that she brushes away with her hand.

"I think there's a cum spot on this skirt," Anna says. Portia doesn't respond.

"God," Anna says, looking at her face in the mirror, turning from angle to angle. "Did I ever tell you about that time that I gave Randy Freeman a hand job in the janitor's closet at school and he came all over my black pants and I couldn't get it out? I swear, it was like there was an iron-on cloud on my pants."

The stall door opens and a stiff-haired woman in a pantsuit steps out. Her face is white. Her hands are shaking as she washes them. Anna looks over at the stall Portia had been in and sees that the clothes are no longer flung over the divider. She wants to laugh and she wants to leave the bathroom but she is somehow stuck in place with the glue of embarrassment.

"How do you know Randy Freeman?" the woman asks. Anna thinks this woman might be about to cry. Her wet eyes make Anna feel wobbly, like she's standing on the edge of a cliff (a feeling Anna doesn't really mind).

"We were in high school together. I'm really sorry if I offended you. I thought you were my sister. I didn't know anyone else was in the bathroom. I'm so sorry." Anna is already imaging how she'll frame this story when she tells her sister, brother, and Alejandro.

"Were you at Dos Pueblos Senior High?" the woman asks.

"Yes." Anna flips through the mental Rolodex in her mind, trying to find this woman's face. She must have been a teacher at Dos Pueblos, or maybe she worked in the office. "Do you know Randy Freeman?"

"He's my son," the woman says quickly, her lips as tight as stretched rubber bands. She walks out of the bathroom before Anna can speak. Once the bathroom door closes, Anna doubles over laughing. She waits a moment before leaving. There's no way she wants to pass Randy Freeman's mother in the hall.

Portia, Emery, and Alejandro are waiting in the corridor as Anna walks out. Emery is in a suit that makes him look like he's in the band the Talking Heads. Alejandro is in a fitted knit shirt that hangs so effortlessly you know it's well made.

"Oh, my God!" Anna is whisper-laughing. She grabs her sister's hand and Alejandro's hand, then pulls them down the hall and around the corner to a stairway. Emery rushes along with them.

"What?!" Emery asks.

"You won't believe what happened!"

"What?" Alejandro has already started tittering, even though he doesn't yet know what's so funny.

"I thought Portia and I were the only ones in there."

"Oh god," Portia says. "A woman walked in as I walked out."

"Yes, and I fucking started talking to her!"

Alejandro and Emery burst out laughing. Portia's eyes are wide and her mouth is half-open in anticipation.

"What did you say?" Portia asks.

Anna relays the story of the cum spot, Randy Freeman, the hand job, and the fact that the listener was Randy Freeman's mother.

"NO WAY!" Portia says, finally laughing.

"I swear!" Anna starts cackling. Tears are running down her face. This makes Portia laugh harder.

"No fucking way!" Emery says.

"Yes!" Anna says. It is the only word she can get out.

And just then, when they are euphoric and joyful, the social worker who had told on the family to the nurse, reporting that they weren't a caring enough family, comes down the stairs and pauses in front of them. Anna looks at her, her long rectangular head, and starts laughing even harder.

"How's your mother?" the social worker asks when they are quiet enough to listen.

"Do you know our mother?" Emery asks. He does not seem to recognize her.

"She's fine," Anna says. "She's been moved to the regular cardiac unit."

"That's very good," the social worker says. "That's very good news."

When she walks away, Emery leans in and asks, "Who was that?"

Anna, Alejandro, and Portia are laughing so hard they can't even get out the words to tell him.

Louise loves the fashion show. She applauds after each spin and even tries to whistle, although she doesn't seem to have breath enough to do so. Buzzy is even more enthusiastic than Louise. He grabs Portia after her exaggerated model's jaunt around the room, gives her kisses and a deep, rocking hug. Anna wonders if this is Buzzy's way of asking her to forgive him for his Stinky.

Portia tugs herself away from their father and Anna sees that there's a steel wall in front of her sister's heart. She won't even smile at Buzzy. Anna knows the wall is there to protect their mother, but, really, their mother doesn't need protection—she is, has always been, a fiercely independent woman. Portia needs to grow up, get over it, move on. Marriage isn't a charming little tête-à-tête between a couple in love. It's an arrangement in a tiny unified country of two citizens, with a constitution that is in constant negotiation. And an affair, Anna thinks, is not a declaration of war. It's not even an incursion. It's a mild uprising. An act of rebellion. An irritation. If her sister understood all this she could forgive their father. And maybe then she could forgive her husband, too.

By the end of his freshman year in college Emery had been with many girls, stacking them up like a string of pearls. And then his sophomore year, things began to change. Emery met a cologne-ad handsome guy named Joseph, and together they started the Bi-College Film Club (funding came from both Haverford and its sister school, Bryn Mawr). Joseph came up with the name when he and Emery were eating pastries at a bakery in town, and then, seconds later, told Emery that he was bisexual. Emery laughed. He loved the secret pun of *bi* referring to both the joint-college project and the sexual orientation of one of the founders. Joseph's bisexuality intrigued Emery. It seemed gutsy and cool and made Emery want to spend more time with Joseph and less time with his brown-haired, skinny girlfriend who had the name of a French writer (Anaïs) and a black belt in karate.

After the first two screenings (*Seventh Seal* and *8½*), one of the film club members proposed that prior to all future screenings the eleven members of the film club must take a few bong hits together. The movement was passed by a vote of ten to one, the one being Jenny Pepper, who claimed she loved doing bong hits but thought there was something wrong with making them mandatory. Emery voted in favor of the bong, not because he was for it, but because as director of the club he felt the need to be current, hip, contemporary. The truth was, in spite of the abundance of pot in his life, he had still never gotten high.

Joseph brought his bong to the next meeting and Emery brought the bag of weed he had purchased (with a portion of the membership dues) from a guy on his dorm floor who dealt on demand (he kept nothing on hand, but took and filled orders for any drug). The Film Club sat in a circle on the floor in front of the stadium seating of Stokes Auditorium and passed around the bong. Joseph was to Emery's right, their knees touching and hands brushing as Joseph handed him the packed bong.

Emery held the bong up like a torch and said, "This meeting of the Bi-College Film Club will officially come to order. All those in support of the club and tonight's movie, *Hiroshima Mon Amour*, must smoke the peace pipe as way of committing yourself to the experience of appreciating good movies."

Emery put the bong against his lips, then stuck out his palm, waiting for a lighter. Joseph placed a red Bic in his hand and Emery lit and inhaled. He knew exactly what to do; he had seen this act thousands of times. And although he had never before been interested in pot, there was something magical about Joseph—his open bisexuality, the black sideburns he grew at a time when no one had sideburns, the fruit-colored Izod Lacoste cardigans he wore casually thrown over his shoulders, and the fact that he only got A's—that made Emery feel like he was floating in a safe, happy world where pot was as wholesome as fresh-cut apple slices. This wasn't his mother's pot-smoking, where you lay on a couch in a dark room, watched Mary Hartman, and read *The New Yorker* during commercials. And this wasn't his sisters' pot-smoking, where you rub yourself out into a viscous smear of a human, then splatter yourself against any half-decent guy within range. This was thinking pot. Film pot. Joseph-who-always-smelled-like-spicy-soapy-aftershave pot.

Emery listened to the phlegmy gurgle as he inhaled, then passed the bong to Joseph. It made its way around the circle in relative silence, each person smiling slightly as he or she finished his or her turn. There wasn't much to it after the first hit. Emery felt slightly loose, like he'd been massaged or had just gotten out of the bath. And then, when the bong made its second round, he discovered the magic of being high. It was if the edges of his consciousness had been sanded down into butter-soft rounds. His daylong worry about the picture and sound quality of the reel he had obtained of *Hiroshima Mon Amour* dissolved. It was either of good quality or it wasn't. So be it.

There were smatterings of laughter about nothing in particular as everyone made their way to their seats. Emery and Joseph went to the projection booth where they sat in the sultry red light and threaded the film. When Emery pushed the play button, Joseph put his hand on Emery's and held it there.

"Hey," Emery said, his whisper so low it was more like a breath.

"Hey," Joseph said, and he leaned in and kissed him. It felt sparkly and clean and unlike any kiss Emery had ever had. Every time Emery kissed Anaïs he felt like he had when he was six years old and made the kid around the corner, Mary-Louise, ride her bike in circles in the garage naked: it was intriguing simply because it was so unnatural. When he kissed Joseph there wasn't the strange curiosity of the foreign. It felt perfectly normal.

They made out through most of *Hiroshima Mon Amour*, shifting between kissing and staring transfixed at the black-and-white screen on which alternated images of bodies shredded, gouged, and mutilated, like living zombies, and a man and a woman making love. At one moment, when Joseph and Emery were paused in a kiss, the woman on screen slapped her hand against the man's shoulder and declared, "I'm very fond of men!" Emery looked at Joseph and they both giggled. The statement, as she said it in French, *J'aime bien les garçons*, rolled around like a dime in Emery's head throughout the film.

The postfilm discussion was more animated and emotional than usual. Jenny Pepper started crying as she gave her analysis of *why* the filmmaker would choose to juxtapose images of love with images of war. Emery wasn't sure if it was the pot that had inflated the emotions or if it was the film. He didn't think about it long. He could barely hear what people were saying. The quaint little saying, *J'aime bien les garçons,* was still circling his head as if it were the only, lonely thought there.

That weekend Joseph invited Emery to a guys' night party at his friend Chase's house. Chase was from Villanova, a small country-club-feeling town about fifteen minutes from Haverford. His parents were in Europe until Christmas and the cleaning lady, Diamina, who was living there during their absence, had to visit her ailing cousin in Queens, New York, for the weekend. Chase had promised Diamina he would stay at the house for the weekend, feed the dog, bring in the newspapers and the mail.

Five boys packed into Chase's convertible VW Rabbit. Joseph was in the front seat. Emery sat in the back between Miguel, the green-eyed exchange student from Barcelona, and Larry, a New Yorker who dressed like a rock star in leather lace-up pants and shiny shirts.

Chase pulled the car into the circular driveway and parked it near the front door. Emery thought Chase looked exactly like his house: WASPy, stony, exclusive. Everyone climbed out and grabbed their duffel bags from the trunk. Inside, they dropped everything on the black-and-white marble floor in the entrance, and the four boys followed their host through the cavernous kitchen, then out the backdoor to the yard where the pool and attached Jacuzzi were covered with a black tarp on which flitted red and brown leaves.

Chase went to work uncovering the Jacuzzi while Joseph left for the kitchen to make drinks. Emery, Miguel, and Larry wandered the house looking into rooms that appeared to be set-decorated: everything colonial, horsey, smelling like furniture polish. When they made it to the backyard again, they found Chase and Joseph naked in the foamy Jacuzzi, each with a giant margarita in his hand. Emery, Miguel, and Larry grabbed the drinks that were waiting for them at the built-in stone bar, undressed, and joined them.

It was all bubbles. The alcohol bubbled up to Emery's head. The bong that Joseph had brought into the Jacuzzi bubbled. The frothy water bubbled all around them. Chase declared that he, like Joseph, was bisexual. Miguel claimed that he and all his friends in Barcelona were bisexual, that this was how they passed the time in between girls. And then Emery cracked open the piggy bank of his head and finally dropped out the dime that had been clanking in there since *Hiroshima Mon Amour.*

"J'aime bien les garçons," Emery said, and Miguel, the only one who understood French, laughed and threw his arm around Emery's shoulder. Miguel's skin felt slick and warm. His hands were the size of oven mitts. Emery didn't want him to ever pull away.

"What the fuck does that mean?" Larry asked Emery.

"It means I'm bi, too," Emery said.

"Well, fuck," Larry said, "I've never thought about dick before, but I guess if I get fucked up enough I could be bi for the night!"

It started out as a five-way—an octopi soup with elbows, knees, chins, and shoulder knobs bobbing around the roiling broth. Emery wasn't sure who belonged to what body part, but it didn't really matter: each thing he encountered was gorgeously slick over a dense, stiff base. It was as if he had been programmed to respond to this exact balance of hard and smooth flesh.

The idea of Anna's sex and drug addiction dropped in Emery's thoughts for a moment, but he pushed it away, rationalizing that he wasn't doing this every night to the detriment of his normal routine. This was one weekend, one moment, one hot tub. Emery got near-perfect grades and was involved in extra-curricular activities (intramural soccer, film club, French Club). And other than tonight, he didn't partake in boozy, marauding partying. In fact, he rarely drank. And when he did drink, Emery always preferred to follow his grandfather's advice and drink closer to home.

Eventually Larry hoisted his tall, skinny body out of the Jacuzzi and stumbled away into the house alone. Joseph and Chase went off to the rope hammock that was hanging between two giant elms on the other side of the pool. Emery thought they looked like they knew what they were doing, or perhaps they'd done this together many times before.

This left Emery alone with Miguel. That was okay with Emery. When they kissed, Emery felt like there was silver in his veins. His skin was electrified, his head was exploding with fire and light. The idea of love floated in front of him.

Being bisexual was like having the *E* ticket at Disneyland—it allowed you on any ride in the park. Emery told Anaïs about his fling with Miguel. He explained his newly blossomed bisexuality while convincing her that Miguel wasn't a replacement for her, but rather an addition—the mashed potatoes next to the turkey at Thanksgiving. Anaïs agreed to this arrangement. She was feeling a little bi herself and wanted to explore things with Leslie, the girl with whom she had made a short film for her Women's Studies class. The movie was about the tyranny of shaving, how women and girls senselessly abused themselves to appear childlike and smooth for the male aesthetic. When they were making the film, Anaïs told Emery, she and Leslie each undressed and showed each other all their hair in the various tucks and folds of their bodies. Emery wanted to cringe and shut his eyes as she spoke. Like the sexist tyrants Anaïs spoke of, he, too, found her abundant goatlike fur slightly repugnant (although he would never have let this be known). Miguel had less hair than Anaïs. He was like a beautiful piece of ocean-polished driftwood.

Within a couple of weeks Anaïs broke up with Emery to be with Leslie. This left Emery free to dispense all his emotional energy onto Miguel. They declared their love for each other without ever mentioning a future. Miguel would go back to Spain at the end of the school year and probably, he told Emery, go back to women. Emery agreed that he'd go back to women, too. But he wasn't sure it was true.

Still, it was easier somehow to just be in transition. Less to hide when he spoke to his family on the phone, or saw his sisters with their probing tentacles of questions. He never mentioned Miguel, but Anna and Portia knew the story of Anaïs—how she left him for a woman who wrapped her breasts in an ace bandage so as to appear flat-chested and more masculine.

When Miguel returned to Barcelona in May after his last final exam, Emery took to his bed for three days. It was his first heartbreak, although it didn't feel like a break. It felt more like a mutilation. Emery saw his heart like the bodies of those blown apart in Hiroshima: raw, bloody, unrecognizable. When he finally emerged from his room, he was officially gay. But it was a quiet gay, a gay that appeared only in the confines of campus. A gay that Emery didn't feel he had to carry home to California.

21

DAY TEN

On Day Ten, Louise is deemed strong enough for surgery. She seems almost normal when everyone arrives in the morning, although she is still attached to wires and tubes as if she'd float away were she untethered.

"You know, I woke up this morning," Louise says, "and I had this song stuck in my head that my father taught me after he came home from the war."

"Yeah?" Anna says. Emery can tell she isn't listening. There's a magazine in one hand and two pieces of red licorice in the other.

"What's the song, Mom?" Emery asks. He's at the chair closest to Louise's head. Buzzy is on her other side near her hip. Anna is sitting near the curtain door, and Alejandro and Portia are both standing up at the foot of the bed. There are never enough chairs and someone, usually Portia, always ends up sitting on the bed.

"Shut that curtain and I'll sing it," Louise says.

Alejandro walks to the curtain and drags it shut.

"Okay," Louise says, and she sits up straighter. Louise is smiling as she begins: *"There's a monkey in the grass, with a bullet in his ass, pull it out, pull it out, pull it out, pull it out!"*

Everyone applauds except Anna, who is engrossed in *The New Yorker.*

"How old were you when your father taught you that?" Alejandro asks.

"I guess it was about 1945, so I would have been six."

"You were allowed to say ASS?" Portia asks.

"No!" Louise says. "Otto sang it to me, and I was allowed to laugh at it. But I had to sing it in private. So I used to sing when I was walking to school. I also used to scrape black gum off the sidewalk and eat it because Billie never let us have gum."

"Who's the monkey now!" Buzzy says, and he whoops a little and pokes Louise in the side like she's a kid.

"What's the song?" Anna finally looks up from the magazine. Emery thinks she's interested now only because everyone else seems interested.

"Did you really eat old sidewalk gum?" Emery asks.

"Yeah! I'd sing the song, chew some black gum, sing some more. Sometimes I'd stop at this old woman's house along the way—she had a trough of water in her front yard with a tin dipper, and I'd get a drink."

"The olden days, Mom," Portia says.

"Sing the song again," Anna says. "I wasn't listening the first time."

"Mom, I can't believe you didn't get sick from eating black sidewalk gum!" Emery says. He tries to imagine his mother as a six-year-old. He can't even imagine his sisters when they were sixteen. All these people have always been older than him, hovering above him in the same way that the sky has always hovered above him.

"Let Mom sing the song!" Anna says.

"*Order in the court! Order in the court—*" Portia recites. Anna and Emery join in. "*The monkey wants to speak! The monkey wants to speak! Let the monkey speak! Let the monkey speak!*"

"What is that?!" Alejandro asks.

"No idea," Emery says. "My sisters used to say it sometimes."

"It started in Ann Arbor," Anna says.

"So let the monkey speak," Buzzy says, and he looks at Louise.

"Oh, the song, right?"

"Yes, Mom! Sing the fucking song! Let the monkey speak!" Anna says.

Louise begins: "*There's a monkey in the grass, with a bullet in his ass, pull it out, pull it out, pull it out, pull it out.*"

And then they all start singing: "*There's a monkey in the grass, with a bullet in his ass, pull it out, pull it out, pull it out, pull it out. There's a monkey in the grass . . .*"

Alejandro takes Portia's hand and they do a half-disco, half-tango dance. Buzzy begins drumming on his leg. Anna swings her arms as if she's marching. Emery holds his mother's hand, singing, with Louise doing harmony. He feels almost like a baby again, like he is connected to her. Or maybe, he thinks, as their voices vibrate together, it's that he's reconnected to her. Whatever she did—give him away to her sisters, never show up at his soccer games—it's finished now. It's all pure again. Solid. He is his mother's son.

They sing the monkey song over and over and over again, getting a little louder every time. Alejandro and Portia are now spinning around the room, like Cinderella at her ball, belting it out with the rest of the family.

And then the curtain rolls open, making the sound of distant thunder, and the doctor steps in. Everyone freezes. The doctor has a crooked Charlie Brown smile on his face.

"Why are we always getting busted for *something* at this hospital?" Anna asks, and they crack up. Nothing, it seems, could be funnier. And Emery knows it's weird and odd and strange and funny that they were singing, and that the doctor walked in on them. But he also knows that the reason they are laughing so hard is because Louise seems fine. She is here. She is alive. And it doesn't appear that that will soon change.

The doctor wants to talk to Louise about the surgery she will have tomorrow morning. She will be taken to another floor where the doctor will snake a tube through her thigh and toward her heart, clearing out her arteries as if they were clogged plumbing. It is a simple and common surgery, the doctor explains. The bigger risk is simply being put under anesthesia, and that's hardly a risk. Following the surgery, Louise will be returned to her bed in the cardio-care unit. The doctor is expecting a full recovery. Louise will be released to Casa del Viento Fuerte within the next three days.

Anna, Portia, and Emery each spend part of the evening on the phone with the airlines arranging for flights out of Santa Barbara. Emery knows Louise won't want them here when she gets home. If they stay, Louise will feel crowded, claustrophobic with their noise and their bodies and their things strewn about. And although none of them would ever ask her for anything, or make an emotional demand upon her, the simple fact that they are so needless floats in the center of the family like a sore that won't heal. This is why Louise seems to prefer the animals, Emery thinks: they don't make her feel guilty when she puts them out of the house. When you ignore an animal, it doesn't seem to notice. The animals have nothing to forgive.

Emery is heating milk in the microwave for coffee, while Portia is on hold on the kitchen phone (she sings along with a Captain & Tennille song). Maggie Bucks jumps out of the cupboard, leaps onto the table, and stares at Portia with misdirected eyes.

"Guess what," Portia says to the cat. "Smoker Lady is coming home soon."

"Then you leave!" she answers in Maggie Buck's Siamese accent. "Smoker Lady no want you! Smoker Lady like only cat and dog!"

"Oh, yeah," Portia says, in her own voice. "Well, fuck you."

The microwave dings; Emery pours the milk into his coffee.

"You talking to the cat?" Anna has walked into the kitchen and is standing at the open refrigerator door. Jasmine, the dog, approaches Anna; she stomps her foot to shoo the dog away.

"Scram!" she yells, when Jasmine doesn't budge.

"Bet they'll be glad to have Smoker Lady back," Emery says.

"Nah," Anna says, "deep inside, they'll really miss us. They probably even love us."

"Just like Mom," Portia says.

"Yeah, just like Mom," Emery says. Then his sister sings aloud with the phone again, crooning about the gluey and eternal nature of love.

22

Three years after Portia and Anna were each married, a year after Emery graduated from college, Buzzy and Louise rented a rambling shingled house on Fire Island in New York. The house was three homes in from the Atlantic ocean and seven homes in from the Long Island Sound (Fire Island is just that narrow—viewed from overhead, it looks like a baguette floating off the coast of New York). Ten cruiser bikes came with the house, each with a basket to carry back groceries from the markets, as there were no cars allowed on the island. Since Anna and Portia were already situated on the East Coast and Emery had accepted a job with a TV station in Manhattan, Buzzy and Louise thought it would be nice if there were a place not too far from all their children where they could meet up some weekends and for at least one week all together in the house. Also, Anna had recently had a baby boy, named Blue, and she and Portia entertained some fantasy of Blue belonging to all of them within the realm of the house. Portia was excited about spending time with her nephew, whom she'd seen only once, the week after he was born. Babies, pregnancy, and childbearing were all interesting to her. She was pregnant with her first child, due to deliver the end of August.

Of course it was much harder than they had imagined for everyone to get to Fire Island at the same time. So it wasn't until the end of July when Portia, Anna, and Emery could each spend a full week at the house. Patrick was in the middle of a big case and had to stay in Greenwich, and Anna's husband, Brian, needed to stay in Vermont to mind the flower store. So it was going to be what Portia thought of as "the Real Family," plus Blue.

Within seconds of boarding the standing-room-only train to Islip, New York, three people stood to offer Portia their seat. She was clearly expecting, as fat a toad, having gained weight from the tip of her chin down to her belly in one fell swoop. (Patrick told her she looked like a completely different person, a fact he claimed to enjoy because when they had sex it was like he was having an affair.) Anna and Blue had already flown down, arriving the day before Portia. Emery took the train from Manhattan and met his sister at the ferry station and they, and her protruding belly (which felt like luggage you could never check), took the ferry to the island together.

Within the first hour at the house, Anna and Emery went off to change into their suits. Portia hadn't seen Buzzy yet and Louise had barely looked up from her crossword puzzle to say hello. Portia held her four-month old nephew turned out from herself and walked him around the house, telling him what everything was called as if he were a foreigner (which he was, in a way) just learning English (which he also was).

"This is the laundry room," she said. "Where your mother, who does more laundry than anyone in the family, will do your laundry. And my laundry. And probably your uncle's laundry, too." Portia walked up the stairs to the main living area.

"This is the living room." She rotated the boy, one hand under his bottom, one on his back.

"Couch." Portia leaned him toward the nubby, orange, L-shaped couch.

"Coffee table." Flat, low, covered with magazines that Portia assumed had been placed there before Buzzy and Louise moved in: *Island Life* and *Us Weekly*.

"Ocean." She stood by the window and stared out at the blue-green sea. It looked endless, still, solid.

"What?!" Louise came up the stairs and walked into the kitchen. The house was reversed, with bedrooms and bathrooms downstairs and communal rooms upstairs, perched in the trees. There were no rugs to absorb any sound. From the first floor you could follow the tracks of someone on the second floor by their footsteps.

"I'm talking to the baby," Portia said.

"Do you want some coffee?!" Louise yelled.

Portia took Blue into the kitchen with its scratched linoleum countertop and creaky appliances. There was a dishwasher, but she imagined it only swished the water around like a lazy lake. The plastic dishes all seemed to have a dull smear of grease on them. When she first arrived, Portia got a glass for water and saw that it had a blot of Louise's lipstick on it.

"Do you have decaf?" she asked.

"Decaf? Decaf is for babies!"

Portia lifted Blue up and waved him around as if the decaf were for him. Louise laughed, then lit a cigarette.

"We better back up," Portia said to Blue, and backed away from the smoke toward the dining room, which was divided from the kitchen by a long open counter.

"What do you think of that baby?" Louise asked.

"He's pretty darn cute." Portia turned her nephew's face toward her own and smiled. Blue smiled back. He had the soft animal look of Emery as a baby. And he was a nice solid weight. A sack of warmth. As sweet-smelling as cake batter.

"Don't tell your sister, but I'm not really interested in babies until they can talk."

"I'm going to have one of my own in about a month, Mom. Are you not going to be interested in that one, either?"

"No," Louise laughed. "Unless it comes out talking."

"What about Dad? Is he into Blue?"

"You know, he sure talks about him a lot, as if he were interested. But he hasn't spent more than thirty seconds with the kid since your sister arrived yesterday."

"I haven't even seen Dad yet."

"Get on a bike and go find him. Who knows where he is. He's like Emery when he first realized he could leave the backyard. Gone. Bam. Disappeared."

"I hope I can balance on a bike."

Louise laughed and waved her cigarette around. "I'm surprised you're not tipping forward. You need a counterweight or pulley on your back to make sure you stay upright!"

Emery walked in the room wearing bathing trunks. He was tan, sculpted, man-sized.

"Mom's saying I'm fat," Portia said.

Emery laughed. "Well, do you think you look thin?!"

"Where'd you get those muscles?" Louise asked.

"I don't know," Emery said. "They sort of grew in my last year of school."

"Well, you didn't get them from your father," Louise said. "You got them from my side of the family."

"Do I look fat or pregnant?" Portia asked. Emery looked down at his sister's inflated belly and laughed.

"Fat!" Louse said.

Three of Portia's friends in Greenwich were pregnant, but they had each gained only a portion of the weight she gained. They maintained a cool chic in their regular-person clothes that they adjusted minutely (a shoelace tying a button to a buttonhole under a long shirt), or wore expensive maternity clothes that hung so well they didn't look pregnant from the back.

In her anxiety to properly feed her child, Portia burst out like the winning gourd at a 4-H meeting. She wore overalls and Patrick's button-down shirts. It was startling to see how differently people responded to a fat person in déclassé clothes. The saleswomen in Greenwich's shops showed little interest in helping Portia, as if they were certain she wouldn't buy anything. And men looked right past her, never making eye contact. She wondered if they were biologically programmed to ignore anyone who didn't appear to be a possible mate. The result was a quick loss of hipness, but vision and insight into the blur of Portia's yuppie self-centered self-righteousness of the past few years.

"You know, Patrick's been losing weight since I got pregnant, so sometime last week we actually weighed the same," Portia said.

"Christ," Louise said. "You're going to end up like one of those ladies in the grocery store who has to ride in a cart to get around."

"I have stretch marks on my *wrist*!" Portia held out her wrist. Emery leaned over, looked at the faint purple lines, and laughed.

"Let me see," Louise said.

"Don't come near Blue with that cigarette!" Portia said.

"Oh, for God sakes! You and your sister with the goddamned smoking. Why don't you just get over it!"

"Mom!" Emery said. "She's pregnant and Blue is a baby!"

"So what!" Louise stubbed her cigarette out in the sink and walked into the dining room. "I smoked when I was pregnant and when you were all little babies."

"Yeah, Mom," Portia said. "Thanks for the asthma." She had

developed a mild case of it in fifth grade that came and went according to the season.

"You know, I once dropped a cigarette ember onto your head," Louise said as she picked up her daughter's wrist and looked for the stretch marks.

"You dropped an ember on my head?!"

"No, on Emery's." Louise let Portia's wrist fall. "I felt horrible about it. And I tried not to smoke while I was nursing after that, but—"

"I sort of remember that." Portia looked at her brother and imagined his baby face, his brown button eyes, his little chimp mouth.

"Yeah, you were there," Louise said. "You held him while I ran to the refrigerator for some butter."

"Way to mother me, Mama," Emery said. He yawned and scratched his belly hair.

Anna came up the steps and into the dining room.

"Mom! You weren't smoking near the baby, were you?!"

"Don't worry! Your sister there wouldn't let me get near him with my cigarette!"

Anna was in a bikini that was no bigger than black censor marks on a nude photo. She was as lean as she'd been at fifteen—before the chain of chubbiness, bulimia, anorexia, and recovery.

"I can't believe you lost all the weight already." Portia nestled Blue onto her shoulder, stepped back and stared at her sister.

"I only gained eighteen pounds," Anna said. "I mean, I had to look like a druggie as long as possible." Anna only quit doing undercover narcotics when she could no longer properly fit into a bulletproof vest. She had told Portia that the day after Blue was born she suddenly realized she could never go back to being a cop. She had to be committed to staying alive for the baby's sake.

"What have you gained?" Emery asked.

"Fifty," Portia said, and her mother, sister, and brother laughed.

"No, seriously," Anna said.

"Fifty."

"Fifty fucking pounds?!" Louise asked.

"No, fifty stones, Mom. Yes, fifty pounds. Twenty-two kilos, or something like that."

"Well, tell people your kilo gain and pretend it's pounds," Louise said.

"Put on your suit," Anna said, and she took the baby from her sister's shoulder. "Mom, you coming?"

"I don't have a suit."

"You came to an island for the summer without a suit?" Emery asked.

"I've never owned a suit—you know that!" Louise said. And of course, they did know that; they had only ever seen their mother swim naked. "And the nude beach here is gay, which is fine with me, but your father won't go there and I don't want to go by myself."

"Well, we're here now, so go buy a suit and come to the beach with us," Anna said.

"I'm too old for a suit."

"But you're not too old for the nude beach?" Portia asked.

"Nude beach people are gross," Louise said. "They're fat and saggy and old and wrinkly. It's the bathing suit people who always look good, and I don't look good enough for a bathing suit."

"They're not fat and saggy at the gay nude beach," Emery said.

"True," Louise said. Then she snapped her head toward Emery and asked, "How do you know?"

"Mom," Anna said, "everyone knows that gay guys take care of their bodies and look great naked."

"Mom, why do you care how you look in a suit? You're not going to run into anyone you know here," Emery said.

"I told you already, I'm too old!"

"You're hardly old. And it's not like old age is some humiliating sickness or something," Portia said.

"Yes, it is! Old people are ugly. They shouldn't even leave the house. I hate looking at them."

"Mom. Come on. I hope I'm old one day." Since she had gotten pregnant, Portia had started worrying about things ranging from landfills that were overrun with disposable diapers to moles that could turn into skin cancer. And right then, she started worrying that she wouldn't know how to age and accept old age, that she'd be resistant and resentful of it like her mother. Portia made a mental note to find new friends who were old: old-age role models. She decided that she needed to embrace old age before it was upon her.

"The fuck are you still doing here?" Anna said to her sister. "Go get your suit on!"

Emery pulled the red wagon that came with the house to the beach, loaded with towels, chairs, an umbrella, and a canvas beach bag filled with water bottles, oranges, apples, a baguette Emery had picked up from the corner market, and a couple of Knudsen yogurts. Anna carried the baby and Portia waddled behind.

At the beach, Portia held the baby while Anna and Emery set up chairs and opened the umbrella to put over the towel where Blue would lie. Portia couldn't help but note the effort it took to do something that seemed effortless as a child. Growing up near the ocean they simply went. No food. Often no towel. Never a chair. It was like walking into another room. And now that they all lived on the East Coast, the trip was an excursion, a trek, even with home base mere yards away.

Anna and Emery settled into their chairs, faces turned toward the sun. Blue lay on his stomach on a towel, reaching for and examining a clunky plastic chain with a plastic monkey hooked on one end. The only other people sitting on the beach were too far away to see, but lots of people strolled by—dog walkers, couples, gay men in small black suits.

"I can't believe you two aren't wearing sunblock," Portia said.

"There are about three thousand things I'm more likely to die of than skin cancer," Anna said, and she shut her eyes.

Portia slathered her legs that had grown so thick and fatty they were touching from the top of the thigh almost to mid-calf. She was wearing a suit loaned by a neighbor who had recently had her third baby. It was the orange of a "Men at Work" sign, with a built-in bra that hoisted Portia's breasts up and out so her body resembled the bodies of the women in old postcards of Coney Island. She put sunblock on her face, arms, and chest, then threw her hair (newly thick since the pregnancy) into a Pebbles fountain on the top of her head. Portia's sunglasses had been missing since she arrived, so she wore the pair Louise had found in a plastic bowl on the kitchen counter: red, mirrored. Big.

Portia thought it was impossible to think of a way in which she could have made herself even less attractive. Boils, perhaps. Although she did have a flowering of pregnancy acne across her forehead and chin. Beneath the suit were the shimmering purple stripes, like fish skin, that decorated her belly from her navel to her pubic bone.

Anna nursed Blue until he was sleeping. She unsuctioned his mouth from her nipple, then laid his limp body, dewy with sweat, on the towel under the umbrella. Less than a minute later she, too, was sleeping. Emery and Portia sat and looked out at the calm sea, the sand that seemed chunkier and more yellow than California sand.

"So, I'm living with someone," Emery said.

"Yeah, Mom said you had a roommate. Some guy from Cuba."

"He's not my roommate."

"He's not your roommate?" Portia lifted her head and looked at Emery.

"He's my boyfriend."

"Really?"

"Yeah."

"Do you have a picture of him?"

Emery laughed, got up, and fetched his wallet from the beach bag. He pulled out a Pennsylvania driver's license.

"Doesn't he need this?" Portia asked, staring at Alejandro. He was dark-skinned, dark-eyed, square-headed, handsome.

"He's got a New York one now."

"Are you in love?" Portia wanted to kick her sister awake and say, "Guess what—he IS gay!" She wanted to phone up Patrick and tell him, too. The thrill in having been *right about it* all those years was almost too much to contain.

"Yeah, I'm really in love."

"I'm happy for you," Portia said. And she was.

Emery seemed thrilled to tell his sister everything about Alejandro, his work (graduate studies in architecture), his family (emigrated, father died in Cuba), and how they met (at a restaurant where Alejandro was waiting tables). It seemed strange to Portia that he had never told her any of this before, that he'd been living with Alejandro for a month and no one knew that he was his boyfriend.

"Are you going to tell Mom and Dad?" she asked.

"I guess." Emery looked at the ocean. He held a hand up over his eyes like a visor and watched a pelican dive into the water. "Or you could tell them."

"Do you *want me* tell them?"

"Yeah, maybe."

"What about Anna?"

"I would have told her if she were awake."

"Would have told me what?" Anna sat up straight and shook her head as if there were water in her ears. She was talking in her usual headlong prattle as if she hadn't just been sleeping.

"Emery is gay. His roommate Alejandro is his boyfriend."

Emery laughed. Anna smiled.

"Really?"

"Yeah," Emery said.

"Well, I can't say I'm really surprised," Anna said.

"His boyfriend's cute, check him out." Portia tossed the driver's license to her sister.

"He's totally hot," Anna said. "Does he have brothers?"

"Two."

"How's that marriage treating you?" Portia said, and Emery laughed. Anna raised her eyebrows and pursed her lips. Portia wondered if that was how old women got those lines around their lips, from pursing their mouths in disdain for so many years. Louise had lines around her lips, but they looked like smokers' lines—everything directed in toward the point of a cigarette-sucking pucker.

A soft thumping of sand came up behind them and they all turned to see Buzzy loping down the dune.

"Hey!" Buzzy said. He was wearing beige trunks with blue stripes on the side and a blue T-shirt. His legs were as white and thin as branches from a birch tree. His black wrap-around sunglasses looked like they'd been given to him after an eye exam. And his hat looked like it was older than he was—like it was something Zeyde would wear.

Portia and her brother and sister all stood up and hugged and kissed their father, who gave them each numerous kisses in a chain from ear to ear.

"When'd you kids get here?" Buzzy grabbed the extra chair that lay folded near the beach bag, unfurled it, and sat.

"I was here yesterday, Dad, remember?" Anna said.

"Oh yeah, I forgot I already saw you!" Buzzy laughed. "Do you have any food?" He was talking as quickly as Anna, feet jiggling, head rocking. It was like he was high.

"Portia and I got here about an hour ago," Emery said. "We caught the same ferry."

"How's the baby?" Buzzy leaned back in his chair and looked at Blue. The baby was on his back, arms and legs out as if he were sacrificing himself to the sky gods.

"Sleeping. Don't wake him," Anna said.

"You kids didn't tell Bubbe and Zeyde we're here for the summer, did you?"

"Your secret's safe with me," Portia said.

"Why don't you want them to know?" Emery asked.

"Because they'd show up here!" Buzzy said. "So when we call them on Sunday you all have to be quiet so they don't hear you in the background. And next time you talk to them, don't mention anything about having seen us."

"Don't fucking worry, Dad. We're not going to alert your parents to your whereabouts," Anna said.

"Where's your mother?" Buzzy asked.

"She said she won't come to the beach," Emery said. "Is that true? She really won't go to the beach?"

"Can you fucking believe it?!" Buzzy said. "We rent this house for the whole summer and she says she's too old to put on a bathing suit! What kind of bullshit is that?!"

"Take her to the nude beach," Portia said.

"How crazy is it that now that she's over fifty she'll only go naked?!"

"Fifty's not old," Anna said.

"I feel like I'm twenty!" Buzzy said. "And she's acting like we're some decrepit old couple. She wants to stay in her studio all day and paint or write. She doesn't want to go anywhere, she doesn't want to see anyone, and she won't go to the fucking beach!"

"Take her to the nude beach," Portia said, again.

"The nude beach is gay here. I don't want to go sit on the beach with a bunch of gays!"

"Dad!" Anna said. "Emery's gay."

Everyone paused. Anna, Portia, and Buzzy each turned their head toward Emery, who took a deep breath, his shoulders rising and then falling.

"You're not gay, are you?" Buzzy finally said.

"Yeah. I am."

Buzzy dropped his head into his hands. Portia, Emery, and Anna all looked at him, waiting for him to say something. And then his shoulders began to bounce a little and Portia wondered if he was getting angry, or laughing. When a noise burst forth, she realized he was crying. With hiccupping and snorting sounds. Choking gasps. His body was bobbing in beat with his sobs. Portia was stunned. Her father wasn't a crier. In fact, she'd only seen him cry once before, when she was about twelve years old. Buzzy had called a family meeting one night and tearfully told everyone he was depressed and hadn't been able to work for a couple months. Portia, Anna, and Emery had sat silently on the couch and watched as Louise pulled Buzzy into her shoulder, like a baby, and told him the whole family was there for him.

"Jesus Christ." Emery stood, picked up his T-shirt, and walked away toward the water.

"Dad, come on," Anna said. "You're going to wake the baby."

Buzzy lifted his head for a second, then dropped it again with a coughing series of sobs. Portia felt so bad for Emery that she had no sympathy for her father. Emery belonged to her as much as to their parents, and if *she* didn't care that he was gay, why should they? And why, Portia wondered, would this extremely liberal, Democrat-voting lawyer who did pro bono work for illegal Mexican immigrants and anyone of color who dared show up in his mostly-white town cry because his son was gay?

"Dad." Anna moved off her chair and sat on the sand next to Buzzy. She put her hand on his shoulder and rubbed it in inch-round circles.

"How could he do this?" Buzzy's voice cracked.

"It doesn't have anything to do with you." Anna's voice was sweeter, slower than normal.

"What about grandchildren?"

"What do you think that is?" Anna's sharp voice returned as she pointed at Blue. "And that!" She pointed to Portia's belly.

"It's a baby, Dad," Portia said. "I'm not that fat. And ugly. And pimply." She was ready to go tell on him to her mother. Louise would stand for none of this.

"The world will shit on him! He'll never have a great career! No one will promote him!" Buzzy banged his forehead into his palm. Snot and tears were smeared across his face. It was such an unusual sight, so foreign, that Portia didn't quite know how to react. Eventually, she leaned back in her chair, reached into the beach bag, and pulled out the cloth diaper Anna had brought to wipe up Blue after he nursed. Or vomited.

Buzzy took the diaper and wiped his face. He blew his nose into it.

"What the fuck is this?" Buzzy held the diaper out in front of his face.

"It's a diaper," Anna said.

"It's clean, right?"

"Yeah! I don't even use cloth diapers. I use it for a clean-up rag."

Buzzy blew his nose again.

"Where's your handkerchief?" Portia asked.

"I don't carry it in my bathing suit pocket," he said, and he stuck his hand in his pocket as if checking to see if this were true.

"You okay now, Dad?" Anna asked.

"You know he's a genius," Buzzy said.

"Yeah, Dad," Portia said. "You've always made it quite clear that he's smarter than us."

"I don't mean that," Buzzy said. "You girls are smart, but Emery's always had something that's more marketable than what you girls have. He was reading at three, for God sakes!"

"We know, Dad. We were there." Portia looked at her sister. Anna looked back with steady eyes.

"Dad," Anna said. "Emery has a great job. He'll be fine. There are gays all over the world who are quite successful."

"And what about AIDS?"

"I'm sure he uses condoms," Portia said. "And he's in a relationship. He's not out at some bathhouse mixing it up with a string of men."

"Oy!" Buzzy said, and he dropped his head into his hands again and quietly cried some more. Portia turned and looked in the other direction. This was more than she could abide, confusing in that it felt completely out of character. This man was a father she'd never even met before.

"I can't believe you'd be upset about this." Anna's smudge of compassion was turning to fury. "He's a great guy, he did well in school, he has a great job. He's never been to rehab, never been trouble, you've never had to bail him out of jail. He's kind, he's smart. He even fucking saves money! And you're sitting here sobbing over who he has sex with?!"

"I'm crying over his future!" Buzzy said. "Over the opportunities he won't have! The stigma."

"His eyes are fine," Portia said. "Astigmatism doesn't run in our family." No one laughed.

"Would you rather it were me, Dad? Since I'm always borrowing money from you, I've changed jobs three times since college, I was a drug addict for a while—"

"A sex addict, too," Portia said, and her sister smiled.

"I had bulimia—"

"And anorexia," Portia said.

"Yeah, and anorexia. And I'm on antidepressants right now, and if I weren't I'd probably be pretty fucking crazy. So would you rather I got all the disappointing stuff and Emery stayed pure?"

"Well, yeah." Buzzy lifted his head. "I mean, we're used to this kind of shit with you."

"What about me?" Portia asked.

"I never expected anything from you."

"What do you mean?"

"I mean, I've always expected that you'd meet a nice husband. And you did. And that you'd have a baby, which you're doing. And that you'd take care of your family."

"Glad I could fulfill your low expectations, Dad." Portia could feel her brain checking out, floating away the way it did when she was kid and her parents fought and she didn't want to be there.

"Well, I've got more disappointing shit for you," Anna said. "My marriage is fucked up."

"Eh," Buzzy raised his head. He had stopped crying. "That's what marriage is. It's fucked up and then it isn't fucked up and then it's fucked up again and then it isn't. You just wait through the cycles."

"Is it really fucked up?" Portia asked.

"I'm having an affair." Anna's tone was no different than if she'd told them she had filed her taxes.

"You have a Stinky?!" Portia could feel her mind zooming back into her body. She was suddenly fully aware.

"Oy," Buzzy said.

"I think I love him."

"Oy yoy yoy." Buzzy inhaled, then exhaled as if he were blowing out smoke.

"Wow," Portia said. "I can't believe you're having a real live affair."

"Well, I think I'm going to leave your mother," Buzzy said.

"Dad!" Portia said. "You just said that marriage is fucked up and then not fucked up and that you wait for it to get better!"

"I've done enough waiting," Buzzy said. "I'm done."

"Wait through the cycles!" Portia said. "You just said that you wait through the cycles!"

Anna seemed to have no reaction, as if Buzzy had told her all this before. Portia looked back and forth between her sister and her father; she felt poised like a spring. And then the three of them looked up, in unison, as Louise came tramping down the dune. She was barefoot, wearing a long batik skirt and a tank top. In her right hand was a pack of cigarettes with matches stuck behind the cellophane wrap.

"I decided, 'What the fuck!'" Louise yelled, and she laughed.

"Did you put on a suit?" Portia asked.

"No. But I'm here, right?"

"Great, Mom," Anna said without looking at her.

"What's wrong?" Louise sat in Emery's chair and looked at them, one by one. Buzzy lifted the diaper and wiped his nose with it.

"Emery told us that he's gay, and then Anna told Dad, and Dad burst out crying. Emery walked off. I think that's him way down there." Portia pointed to a dot on the shoreline.

"You burst out crying in front of him?!" Louise glared at Buzzy.

"Pretty much," Anna said.

"What a fucking asshole!" Louise leaned forward in her chair so that she could better face Buzzy beside her. "How could you do that to him? He is a wonderful person. An amazing person. And you're going to cry because he's gay? Who gives a fuck?!"

"You're not upset that your son is gay?!" Buzzy leaned forward in his chair. Their faces were inches apart.

"No. Not at all. Everyone's suspected it all along but you, Buzzy. You're too fucking blind to see what's right in front of your face."

"Astigmatism," Portia said, and her sister smiled.

"You're not upset that you're not going to have a daughter-in-law, or grandchildren?!"

Anna and Portia both lifted their arms and pointed at Blue.

"I have daughters!" Louise said. "I don't need daughters-in-law! And who gives a fuck about grandchildren!"

"Clearly not you," Anna said, pursing her lips in that old-lady way again.

"Where's Emery?" Louise asked.

"I told you," Portia said. "Down there." She pointed to the speck again.

Louise got up from her chair and marched toward the speck. Over the last few years, her hair had turned gray. She wore it shorter than she had when she was younger, but it was still silky and swished against the top of her shoulders when she walked. She moved youthfully, with grace. Anna, Buzzy, and Portia said nothing until Louise was well out of hearing distance.

"So, have you made your final decision?" Anna asked, and Portia knew right then that her sister already knew about their father's pending plans.

"I feel like I'm dying in this marriage," Buzzy said. "She's done with life. She stays in. She paints. She doesn't even want to drive to LA to visit museums or eat at a fancy restaurant. I don't want to finish my life like this. I mean, she won't even go to the fucking beach!"

"Wait through the cycles!" Portia said.

"If he wants to leave he should leave." Anna said. "It's not like they have little kids to take care of."

Portia glared at her sister, then pulled down her sunglasses and covered her eyes.

"Where would you go?" Anna asked. She seemed to be asking for herself, looking for permission to leave her own marriage.

"I dunno. I always wanted to live on the beach."

"Does Mom know you're thinking of leaving?" Portia asked. "Are you going to support her? I mean, what is she supposed to do?"

"I'll support her, but, you know. She's young. She could get a job. Your mother hasn't worked our whole marriage, I've been supporting her since she was twenty, maybe it's time she—"

"Dad! She was raising kids!"

"You raised yourselves, for chrissakes! The two of you raised Emery!"

"I did Emery," Portia said. "Anna cooked."

"I did Emery, too!" Anna said.

"But I did him more!" Portia said. "He was mine. You were cooking and busy with going to the shrink and to gymnastics."

"You both did everything," Buzzy said.

"I really think you should wait through the cycles," Portia said, to Buzzy. It was as if she had run out of words and could only repeat the platitude as she had first heard it.

"I think you'll be happier if you leave," Anna said. "No one should stay in an unhappy marriage."

"I can't believe you're going to leave Mom, and Anna's having an affair!" Portia didn't look at either of them. She felt queasy and hollow. Like storms were swirling in some empty cavern in her center. "And I did Emery! We didn't both do Emery!"

"We both raised Emery, and quit fucking judging me and Dad!" Anna said. "You'll either leave or have an affair eventually, too."

"I don't plan on doing either of those things."

"You're as flawed as we are, only in different ways!"

Anna looked at Blue to make sure he hadn't awoken. Buzzy was staring out in the distance, toward where Louise and Emery were.

"So are you getting divorced?" Portia asked her sister.

"Not until Blue's in college."

"You're going to have an affair for the next eighteen years?"

"If it lasts that long, yes."

"Everyone has to do what works best for them," Buzzy tuned back in, turning his head toward Anna.

It was clear they were aligning with each other in order to prove their rightness. In this crowd Portia was going to be deemed uptight, closed-minded, judgmental, limited. And maybe she was all those things. But more than anything, she was upset for her mother—that Louise would happily cook dinner for them that night, her husband included, while he was plotting an escape, planning a future for her that she would never choose. The imbalance was too great, the unfairness was too apparent. It was like not telling a dying person that they were actually dying and letting them fret about balancing their checkbook when you know they're not going to live long enough for the next bank statement. And she was sad for Brian, too. Although Portia had hardly seen him since he and Anna married and couldn't even imagine what it was like to live with him.

"What's your boyfriend's name?" Portia was curious in spite of her feelings.

"Roy. He's Hispanic."

Portia wanted to ask if he were dyslexic. Anna had a boyfriend in high school, James, who was dyslexic. Anna never brought James home because of the mess in the house, but one night when she had mentioned she was making spaghetti, James talked her in to having him over for dinner. Buzzy was going through a bread-making phase that year, baking a loaf every couple days. When Anna put the spaghetti on the table, Buzzy pulled from the oven a fresh loaf of his Portuguese sweet bread (the family favorite). James loved Buzzy's bread. As soon as he finished his first hand-sized hunk, he wanted more, but the bread was at the far side of the table from where he sat.

"Buzzy," James said (all the kids' friends had called their parents by their first names), "can you pass me some more of that porky-cheese sweet bread?" There had been a beat of silence as the family took in James's beautifully comical mispronunciation. And then everyone, except Anna, burst out laughing. Even James laughed. The word *porky-cheese* was too ridiculous not to laugh. But Anna was infuriated. She never brought James home again, and got up and left the table every time anyone asked to be passed the porky-cheese sweet bread (which they all did every time Buzzy baked it after that).

"Is he Mexican?" Portia asked.

"Nicaraguan," Anna said defiantly. Portia wondered if Anna thought they'd react to a Nicaraguan. She said it as though Roy were an actual Contra, or at least an illegal alien. Portia thought her sister would probably love having sex with a Contra—she'd be able to feel the danger on his skin, he'd vibrate from the violence brewing in his blood.

"What does ROY do?" Portia's voice was strained, screechy.

Anna rolled her eyes. "He drives a beer delivery truck."

Buzzy and Portia were silent. There was an unspoken rule in the family that you could tease anyone to any degree except Anna. She took it to heart, carried it around like a bitter seed in her mouth. There could be no delivery boy taunts.

"So are you going to go out and look for a natural-born Jew?" Portia asked Buzzy. Often when he was mad at Louise he would grumble that he should have married a Jew or a black woman. Portia wasn't sure why or how either of those would have worked out better for him, but he'd always been convinced they'd make more successful mates.

Buzzy shook his head, refusing to answer.

"Roy's Nicaraguan," Anna said.

"You already told us that!" Portia said. Her sister *definitely* wanted them to think Roy was a Contra.

"He's got these giant size-eleven feet," Anna said.

"Is knowing your lover's shoe size some sort of prerequisite before you have sex?" Portia asked.

"Roy's feet were large at birth. His nickname as a kid was Big Foot."

"In English or Spanish?" Portia asked. "Grande . . . how do you say 'Big Foot' in Spanish?"

"Emery will know," Buzzy said, and he winced and rocked his head as if someone were stepping on his toes. Portia thought he'd suddenly been reminded of Emery's being gay and his own wet, weepy reaction. Or maybe he was reminded of Emery's brilliance that he thought wouldn't come to fruition now that Emery was an out gay. Emery had studied languages in school. He was fluent in five of them already, which was a great source of pride for Buzzy.

"Does it matter that he speaks so many languages, Dad, now that he's gay? He's worthless now, right?" Portia asked. She was smiling. She loved catching Buzzy in this moment where he was stuck between pride and shame.

"Jesus," Buzzy shook his head. "I'm a schmuck, aren't I?"

"A schmegegge," Anna said.

"A schmendrick," Portia said.

"Not a mensch," Anna said.

"Not like Emery," Portia said. "He's a mensch."

"Roy's a mensch, too," Anna said.

"Don't let Roy get you pregnant," Portia said. Then she looked over at Blue and noticed his thick black eyelashes and his tiny pinned-back ears that resembled neither Anna's nor Brian's ears.

"I'm nursing," Anna said.

Portia rolled her eyes in disgust. "Gross." Surely her sister knew that she could still get pregnant. And, Portia wondered, who could have sex with some near-stranger when your baby's milk was pumping out of your breasts? It seemed against the laws of nature, upside down, perverted. Plain wrong.

Anna looked toward the water. Portia and Buzzy followed her gaze. Louise and Emery were approaching. Everyone watched silently as they grew closer.

"You better apologize," Anna whispered to Buzzy, before they were in hearing distance.

"It's really hard for me," Buzzy said. "It breaks my heart."

"You'll get over it," Anna said.

Buzzy stood as Emery walked up. His feet clunked into the sand as he went to Emery and Louise. He hugged Emery and held him. Louise looked at them for a second, then dropped down between her daughters on a beach chair.

"I love you. I'm sorry I reacted like such a schmuck," Buzzy said.

"It's okay," Emery said, and when he wiped a tear away, Louise, Anna, and Portia each started crying a bit. They all were plagued with an inability to control a sympathy cry. Portia cried once when a woman she barely knew told her, in tears, that her uncle had died. She cried when a stranger at the park in Greenwich admired her belly, then started crying because she'd been trying to get pregnant for years. Portia couldn't be within three feet of a crying person without crying herself. Unless, of course, the crying person was being an insensitive asshole, as Buzzy had been.

There was a lightness, almost an excitement, at dinner that night, as if the foul, tense air had blown away and everything was fresh and pure again. Anna and Louise prepared the food together— steak, salad, slivers of potatoes pan-fried in almost a stick of butter—while Portia played with the baby (who was looking more and more Hispanic as the night wore on) and Emery set the table. Buzzy got on his bike and went to the market for a bottle of wine. He returned about an hour later, even though the market was at the end of the block. Louise didn't seem to notice as he walked in right as supper was ready, seconds after Blue had fallen asleep in his stroller.

Emery opened the red wine, poured some in Anna's glass, then tried to pour some in Portia's glass.

"I can't," she said, and covered her glass with her hand.

"She throws up, remember?" Anna said.

"Well, yeah, and I'm pregnant. And, actually, I haven't really had a drink since college."

"I drank wine while I was pregnant," Anna said.

Emery poured wine in his own glass, then Buzzy's. Then he went for Louise's glass.

"None for me," Louise said, and she put her hand over her glass just as Portia had done. She turned to Anna. "I thought you stopped drinking after rehab."

"Mom, I was a drug addict, not an alcoholic." Anna lifted her glass and took a gulp.

"But I thought that you were supposed to stop everything. Even though you weren't an alcoholic."

"Mom!" Anna took another sip. "I've been drinking ever since I left rehab. You've had wine with me maybe three hundred times since then. Rehab was like ten years ago!"

"It wasn't ten years ago, it was seven or eight years ago," Louise said.

"Mom," Emery said, "she's been drinking ever since. I can't believe you haven't noticed."

"I guess I never thought about it until now." Louise sighed and then filled her plate with food. "Portia, what do you mean you haven't had wine since college?"

"I just stopped," Portia said.

"Did you have a problem?"

"Yeah, I had a problem," Portia said. "I couldn't drink!"

"Mom! It made her vomit, remember? She's allergic or something." Anna threw back a few more gulps of wine.

Emery chuckled. "I remember seeing you vomit!"

"There are few people who have not seen me vomit," Portia said.

"I've got one who doesn't have a problem and stops drinking anyway, and another one who has a problem yet continues to drink," Louise said. She was looking down at her plate, clearly working something out in her mind.

"I told you, Mom," Anna said. "I don't have a problem with alcohol!"

"Do you want to tell them?" Buzzy had started eating. A piece of lettuce hung from his lip.

"I'm an alcoholic," Louise said.

Portia looked at her mother, then started laughing. "No way."

Anna and Emery laughed, too. Buzzy and Louise smirked, as if to acknowledge that nothing was more charming than seeing their three grown children laugh. Even if it was at Louise's expense.

"You don't believe me?" Louise asked.

"Mom, since when are you an alcoholic?" Anna said. "I've never even seen you drunk."

"I've never seen you drunk either, Mom," Emery said.

"For the past few years, I've been drinking every night. I'm an alcoholic."

"You're a fucking pot addict!" Anna said. "Forget the alcohol! If you want to quit an addiction, quit pot."

"I did," Louise said.

"She had me chop down the plants and everything," Buzzy said. "And they had some of the most beautiful, pungent buds I'd ever grown. They'd actually stick to your hand, they were so fertile."

"When did this happen?" Portia asked.

"A few weeks before we left Santa Barbara. I go to AA meetings every day. They even have AA on the island here."

Anna, Portia, and Emery started laughing again.

"Why is this funny?" Buzzy asked.

"Because she's NOT an alcoholic!" Anna said.

"It seemed a little kooky to me, too," Buzzy said. "But who are we to decide? If she says she's an alcoholic, she's an alcoholic."

"All right, Mama," Emery said. "Whatever."

"Cheers to Mom being an alcoholic and going to AA!" Portia said, and she picked up her plastic water glass and held it out toward the center of the table.

"Cheers!" the family responded, including Louise, who clinked her plastic water glass with each of them in turn.

"So everyone has some secret they've blown open today. Except Portia." Anna turned to Portia. "What's your secret?"

"There's no baby in here," Portia said. "It's an hysterical pregnancy."

In truth, she had originally thought she was having an hysterical pregnancy. She and Patrick had stopped using birth control in the middle of November and about two weeks later, around the day her period was due, Portia knew she was pregnant. Nothing had changed; she wasn't nauseous and her breasts weren't sore. But she knew she was pregnant in the same way that she knew she was alive and awake. At the doctor's office the blood test came out negative and the doctor, a middle-aged Persian woman, insisted to Portia that she was not pregnant.

At home that afternoon, Portia sobbed—not because she wasn't pregnant, but because her sense of being pregnant was still so acute that she figured she was having an hysterical pregnancy. Twenty days later, she still hadn't gotten her period. Portia returned to the doctor, ready to have herself admitted to the psych ward of Greenwich Hospital. It had been a relief to find out she was not insane.

"What's *your* secret?" Louise asked Anna. She was swirling potato slices in the small pool of salad dressing on her plate.

"I'm having an affair," Anna said, looking down at her plate.

"Jesus Christ," Louise said. "You just had a baby! What are you thinking?!"

Emery stopped eating and stared at Anna with a half-smile on his face. Portia had forgotten that he hadn't been with them when Anna confessed her affair and Buzzy confessed his desire to leave Louise.

"Don't criticize me! You don't know my marriage!" Anna pointed her fork at her mother.

"Are you in love with the other guy?" Emery asked.

"He's Hispanic," Anna said.

"What kind of Hispanic?" Emery asked.

"A Contra!" Portia was excited to say it.

"Did I tell you about that?" Anna looked surprised.

"I don't want to hear about this!" Louise said. "You kids can discuss Anna's affair when I've gone to bed—I really don't want to know!"

"Is he really a Contra?" Emery asked Portia. She shrugged.

"Why can't you know about her affair? She's opening herself up to us!" Buzzy said.

"Jesus Christ, Buzzy!" Louise lifted her plate and walked it to the counter that looked from the kitchen into the dining room.

She sat on one of the painted black stools. "You have no sense of decorum! You have no shame! An affair is an affair because it's secret and WE should not know about it!"

"We're her family! We should be able to know about her affairs!"

"I don't want to talk about it anymore!" Anna said. "Please!"

Emery and Portia looked at each other across the table. He was five again and she was ten. Anna was thirteen, fighting with their parents—taking up all the noise and space and conflict.

"Okay," Louise shook her head. "Whatever."

"Don't sit there. Come on back." Buzzy talked with a cheekful of food in his mouth.

Louise looked at her family, stared down at her plate, and carried it back to the table.

"So we know Anna's secret, Mom's secret, my secret, and Portia's secret," Emery said. "But what's Buzzy's secret?"

"That he's freaked out by gays," Portia said, and her brother smiled.

"When your affair falls apart, don't even tell me about it. I don't want any details. None," Louise said to Anna.

"I already said, I'm not going to tell you shit," Anna said.

"Good, 'cause I don't want to know shit."

"Good, 'cause I'm not telling you shit."

"Fine. I don't want to know."

"Alcoholic," Anna mumbled, and Louise laughed.

"Mom, are you dying for a glass right now?" Emery asked. "Is it hard for you when we're drinking?"

"Not really," Louise said.

"You are SO not an alcoholic!" Anna said. "Alcoholics crave alcohol!"

"Did I ever tell you kids about Elbows Max?" Buzzy asked.

"I'm sure everyone knows the story but me," Emery said. He poured some more wine in his glass and took a sip.

"He was our great-grandfather," Anna said. "A professional boxer."

"Yes, but what you might not already know is that Elbows Max was an alcoholic," Buzzy said.

"Oh, please, Dad!" Anna reached across the table and took the wine bottle from in front of Emery. She emptied the bottle out into her glass. "Everyone knows there's no such thing as a Jewish alcoholic."

Portia found it funny that her addiction-prone sister appeared to be entirely serious.

"Look at your mother!" Buzzy held out his open palm directed toward Louise.

"I'm not a fucking Jew!" Louise said. "I quit being Jewish! So stop with your Jewish-wife fantasy!" She was almost-smiling.

"Yeah, Dad," Anna said. "Listen to Sarah!" Everyone cracked up at the use of Louise's Jewish name. Even Louise.

Portia let the chatter drift away. She rubbed her inflated belly as if her hand could communicate to the person floating in there. She wanted to tell the baby that everything would be okay. Yes, Portia was fat. And she had pimples, stretch marks, and gelatinous legs. But she wasn't an alcoholic (although, who really knew if the baby's grandmother was an alcoholic?); she couldn't imagine that Patrick was planning to flee their marriage (and hopefully Portia's father would stay put); and she wasn't about to push her milky breasts into the bristly face of a Contra (that was strictly Anna's domain). Additionally, if the baby turned out to be gay like its Uncle Emery, Portia wouldn't even have the urge to cry. For now, Portia was sweetly, happily, blindly content.

23

DAY THIRTEEN

It is early morning on Day Thirteen, the day they leave. Emery and Alejandro are in the barn packing up their things. Emery feels that although his mother is coming home, this trip is still hanging open. His sisters both said they needed more time to think about their eggs. And they wanted to discuss it together, as if the decision about how he should make a baby were more theirs than his. He is trying not to be angry, he wants to accept whatever they each want, but it is hard for him. Emery reminds himself not to let his fantasies get in the way of reality. He needs to remember that even his sisters, who used to delve into his brain as if it were a pot of soup, are unaware of how large this fantasy has been looming.

When he goes to the kitchen, Emery finds Portia sitting at the kitchen table eating a bowl of Grape-Nuts with one hand while fanning her wet toenails with the other hand. "Finally got your pedicure?" Emery asks.

"Did it myself," Portia says. "I want to do Anna's toes for her—they look so bald and ugly—but I think she'll be offended if I suggest it."

"She probably will be," Emery says. He wishes his sister were thinking about her eggs and not Anna's toenails.

Emery sits beside Portia and looks around the kitchen, at the things his mother has chosen to surround herself with. Along the wall above the stove is a procession of wrought-iron Pennsylvania Dutch trivets. One has an angry-looking woman molded on it; she wears a red apron and is raising a black frying pan in one hand. Above her are the words "Ach, don't talk so dumb!"

"Ach, don't talk so dumb!" Emery says. Portia laughs.

"That was my favorite trivet," Portia says. "Whenever I was setting the table, if we needed a trivet I always got the 'Ach' one."

"I don't even remember those trivets," Emery says. Sometimes he feels like he's seen only an edited view of his own life, while his sisters got to see all the footage.

The phone rings and Portia reaches to answer it, knocking it off the receiver and onto speaker. Louise is on the line. Anna has answered from the extension in the bedroom.

"Don't stop off to say good-bye," Louise says. "I'm going to be busy all morning and you've gotta get to the airport early."

"Mom," Anna says, "you're in a hospital bed—how busy can you be?"

"Busy," Louise says, "busy. You know, the doctor checking out one thing, a nurse checking out another; and then I've gotta walk a lap around the cardio unit before they'll even let me out."

"We're stopping by," Anna says.

"Please," Louise says, "I really don't want you to come."

"Mom?" Portia says. "You're on speaker. Emery and I are here."

"You're on the phone?"

"Hey, Mama," Emery says.

"Mom doesn't want us stopping by," Anna says. "She's *busy.*"

"Mom," Portia says. "I'm only going to tell you this once."

"What?"

"ACH! Don't talk so dumb!"

Louise laughs and so does Emery. Portia hangs up, leaving Anna to sort out the plans.

By eight a.m. they are in Buzzy's car speeding down the mountain. Anna has claimed the front seat, just as she did when they were kids. Emery is beside Portia in the back; Alejandro is on the other side of Portia. She believes that with Buzzy at the wheel, the back is probably the safest place. Emery doesn't disagree.

"Wouldn't it be funny," Portia says, breaking a silence, "if we all died right now in the car and Mom ended up being the one who lived longest."

"We're not going to die," Buzzy groans. "No one is dying." He takes an S-turn too quickly and Portia rocks against Emery and then away from him again.

At the bottom of the mountain Buzzy pauses, puts the car in neutral, and turns toward Anna.

"Well?" he asks. If he turns right, they go directly to the airport. Left and they'll be on the way to the hospital.

"Left," Anna says.

"She'll be pissed," Buzzy says.

"Fuck her. We're her fucking kids." Anna is obviously pissed.

"Don't upset her," Emery says. "Go to the airport." He can't understand why his sister won't respect his mother's wishes. If she doesn't want to say good-bye, she doesn't want to say good-bye. Let the woman be!

"I'm not sure what I'm more afraid of," Portia says, "Mom being mad because we've stopped off to say good-bye, or Mom dying before I get a chance to visit her again."

Emery wishes his sister would stop thinking about everyone

dying all the time and start thinking about her eggs and how they can help him have a baby!

Emery looks over at Portia. As the car accelerates, she closes her eyes.

Louise looks up when the family appears in the doorway. She is genuinely surprised. She is definitely not busy.

"What? What the hell do you want?!" Louise is scowling.

"The kids want to say good-bye," Buzzy says. His head nods like a spring-necked doll as if to say, "I knew you'd act like this." They, the kids, are huddled behind him. Alejandro is half-smiling—his face reveals an appreciation one can have for cantankerous souls only when not related to them by blood.

"So good-bye!" Louise says. "Go."

"Honey—" Buzzy says, and he goes to her bedside.

"They're acting like I'm about to die! I'm fine. I'll see them all this summer—they never stay away long."

"Sweetheart," Buzzy says, "say good-bye to them! I've gotta run back to the car—I parked illegally." Buzzy kisses Louise on the lips, then inches past everyone, waving his hands as if to direct them in, before he rushes down the hall to the elevator.

Emery, Alejandro, Portia, and Anna are still hovering in the doorway. It's as if no one has the nerve to enter.

"I cannot believe what a pile of spineless sea slugs this family is!" Anna whisper-hisses. She pushes in and goes to Louise's bed.

"Fine, Mom." Anna leans over and kisses Louise's cheek. "Good-bye, I love you."

"You too," Louise says. The exchange is quick: words, kiss, words, kiss. Anna backs away from the bed and looks at Emery with her hands open and head shaking. He gets it.

Alejandro goes to Louise's bed with Emery; they, too, have a quick exchange. The words sound like clucking, the kisses appear to be henpecks. Emery imagines they have been transformed into a herd of chickens.

Portia is waiting her turn to say good-bye. Emery steps back and makes room for his sister at the bed.

"Give me a kiss and get outta here," Louise says. "You're going to miss your flight."

"I think Maggie Bucks hates me." Portia perches on the edge of the bed as if they're staying for a while. As if Buzzy isn't waiting outside with the engine running.

"Why?"

"I don't know, she sits on her fat ass and glares at me every time I open the cupboard."

"She's not fat!"

"Mom, she's obese," Anna says.

"She's not obese!"

"She's seriously overweight, Mom," Emery says. "She's the size of a raccoon."

"She's a delicate little thing!" Louise says.

"Fine. She's zaftig," Emery says.

"Maggie is not zaftig. She's perfect. She has a perfect figure." Louise's tone is utterly serious.

"Well, she hates me," Portia says.

"Maggie Bucks doesn't hate anyone. She's a loving, kind cat."

"Did I tell you she came out? She's a lesbian, you know," Portia says.

Louise laughs.

"I've always had a strong gaydar reading on her," Portia says, "so it was really no surprise."

"We've all known she's a lesbian," Anna says. "It's like before Emery came out when we all really knew that he was gay."

"You knew before I came out?" Emery asks. He had no idea. He had thought he was so good at hiding it—all those girl-friends, the extracurricular activities, soccer!

Louise laughs harder. She is wiping laugh-tears from her eyes.

"I think she came out because she thought you were going to die," Portia says. "She was thinking, 'Ah-so, now I be true self; Smoker Lady dead, I fear no judgment.'"

"Smoker Lady?! Is that what she calls me?!" Louise is in full rolling guffaws.

"Maggie got everyone to start calling you Smoker Lady," Emery says, and Louise lets out one more laugh bark.

"All right, kids," she says, "get going."

Portia leans into her mother, working her hands under the tubes attached to her arms so she can hug her, and suddenly she is crying.

No, not crying. She is sobbing. Anna sobs, too. And when Alejandro wipes tears from his face, Emery cracks open and he, too, is sobbing. Just like their mother.

None of them can speak.

And that is how they finally say good-bye.

In the thirty-four years since Buzzy and Louise started dating, their parents have never met. Early this afternoon, Anna picked up Billie and Otto from the airport and brought them straight to the cemetery—the one in Santa Barbara on the cliff, overlooking the ocean, not the Jewish cemetery in Los Angeles that Louise hated sight unseen. Bubbe and Zeyde flew in last night and stayed in the barn. Anna, Portia, and Emery, along with their mates and children, crowded the house like a newly immigrated family, sleeping on couches, Louise's bed, and the floor.

It is a day where the air is so clear you feel like you're in an oxygen bubble. Before the service starts, Emery and Anna walk Portia's daughter, Esmé, to the cliff of the cemetery so she can see the ocean. It is a waxy blue, foamy, and alive. Esmé looks silently at the water; Emery watches her; Anna watches the sea.

"So," Anna says. "Do you still want our eggs?"

"Yes. Of course!" Emery looks at his sister. They haven't discussed the eggs since that night in the barn. He's been waiting for someone to bring it up.

"Are you sure you want *my* eggs?" Anna says. "I'm loony. I'm addicted to everything. I eat sugar all day long, I drink tons of coffee. I'm short."

"But there are millions of variations of you and they all come from Mom and Dad, and I come from Mom and Dad. And who knows what version of Mom and Dad that egg will have."

"I got the shitty version of Mom and Dad."

"No, you didn't."

"Well, between the three of us I did."

"No, you didn't. But your version is irrelevant, anyway. The baby is going to be half of Alejandro's family, too—Cubans who originally came from Spain and France."

"Think how dark this kid could be," Anna says. "Between me and Alejandro—"

"Dark is beautiful. There's nothing more beautiful than dark skin." Emery has never understood why his sister doesn't love her dark skin. Who doesn't love dark skin?!

"Didn't feel like that when I was a kid."

"That's 'cause we grew up in a beach culture, the land of Malibu Barbie."

"What are you guys talking about?" Esmé asks, and she tugs her uncle's hand.

"Eggs. I want your auntie's egg to put with Tio Alejandro's seed to make a baby for me and Tio."

"Oh," Esmé says. Emery can see she isn't impressed. He figures she can't even fathom the usual rituals that precede most egg/sperm unions.

"It would have part of Mom in it." Emery wipes a tear from under his eye with his index finger.

"Yeah, it would." Anna blinks, and tears run free down her cheeks.

"So?" Emery asks.

"You can have mine," Anna says. "Portia and I discussed it, and we think I can handle it better. But if for some reason I die before you get them, Portia will give you hers. We won't leave you eggless."

Emery starts crying. He leans in and hugs his sister in a way he hasn't done since he was about nine. Anna cries, too.

Esmé looks up at her aunt and uncle and watches them. They look down at her and cry more. Anna picks up Esmé and rocks her in her arms, then passes her off to Emery, who does the same thing.

"It's okay," Esmé says.

"Yeah, it's okay," Emery says, and he's fully crying now. Anna leans in, puts her arms around her brother, Esmé sandwiched between them. They stand like that, crying, for a couple of minutes while the sea wind wraps around them like a shawl.

"We're probably going to start soon," Emery says. He puts Esmé down and takes her hand. The three of them walk back to the family, winding around headstones that are shaded with oak and eucalyptus trees. It is as pretty here as any city park. Probably as pretty as any place in the world. It even smells good—the musky oak with the clean smell of salty ocean.

Aluminum folding chairs have been set up beside the hole where the coffin sits. As Louise once requested, only immediate family is here. It has been two weeks since Louise had her surgery. She was home, recovering, when she had a heart attack in her sleep. Buzzy didn't even know until late the next morning. He thought Louise was sleeping in.

No one is sitting yet except Buzzy. Portia has barely spoken to him since she arrived, and every time she has, all she could think of was his Stinky: if he was going to see her again, if Louise had found out. Portia sits next to her father.

"Dad," she says. "Mom would be so disappointed to know that you're wearing a yarmulke."

"You're right." Buzzy reaches up and pats the blue velvet skullcap, but doesn't remove it.

"I guess she won't know," Portia says.

"I'm sorry about my girlfriend," Buzzy says.

"Did Mom ever find out?"

"No."

"Are you seeing her again?"

"I haven't yet. But I probably will eventually. I'm not dead yet, and I'm not that old."

"Yeah."

"And I know it was shitty. And what Patrick did to you was shitty. People are shitty sometimes."

"Yeah, they are." Portia leans her shoulder in against her father's.

"I'm sorry, honey." Buzzy puts his arm around his daughter and kisses the top of her head.

"Were you and Mom getting along when she got home from the hospital?"

"We were getting along great! It was really a wonderful couple weeks. Much better than before the heart attack."

"I was worried that she died being mad at you for something."

"It was one of our nicest times ever," Buzzy says. "I stayed home from work. We played Scrabble. We watched movies. It was really good."

Portia imagines herself home recovering from a heart attack. There would be no Patrick with whom she could play Scrabble. And then she realizes that she wouldn't want him there. Not for Scrabble, and not even for a bad TV movie. He never took proper care of her heart before; he surely wouldn't treat it right after a heart attack. Portia takes a deep a breath, and when she exhales, she can almost see the ghost of Patrick leaving her. She knows he will soon be sweated out of her, excreted from her pores like too much garlic.

Following the service, where Buzzy, Anna, and Emery spoke in turn (Portia couldn't speak without crying, and so said nothing) the family is hanging around, with no one giving the signal or sign that they should leave. Esmé and Blue gather acorns and hoard them in their pockets. Anna is on a chair next to Billie, who is beside Otto. No one else is sitting. Bubbe walks toward them, audibly crying, wiping her nose and face with an embroidered-edge handkerchief. She has on a black nubby suit and a black hat with a veil over the front. Zeyde is standing near the edge of the hole looking up toward the tops of the trees. Anna imagines he's seeing how high they go, so he can tell his pals at the Golden Ages Club for Jewish Seniors what cemeteries in Santa Barbara look like. Every time Anna sees him he tells her what he's told his friends at Golden Ages. Once, years ago, he told Anna, Portia, and Emery how he had regaled the crowds at Golden Ages by explaining to them what a taco was. The kids didn't think he was serious at first; it seemed impossible to them that someone wouldn't know what a taco was.

Like Buzzy, Zeyde is wearing his yarmulke. In the Jewish tradition of mourning, Zeyde has a ripped piece of cloth pinned to his shoulder. Bubbe has one pinned to her shoulder, too, but it's smaller, more delicate-looking. "*Baruch dayan ha'emet,*" Bubbe says, and she picks up both of Billie's stiff hands. Anna leans forward in her chair to find her brother and sister. She wants them to witness what she is witnessing. She catches Portia's eye.

"Pardon?" Billie says. She frowns and looks toward Otto, who is sitting up tall as if to get a better look at Bubbe. Portia approaches and stands beside Bubbe. Anna gives her googly eyes.

"Oy!" Bubbe says, and she starts crying, clinging to Billie's hands. "Sarah, Sarah, Sarah! We will miss her so much!"

"Who the hell is Sarah!?" Otto says. Billie pulls her hands from Bubbe's and places them firm on each of her hips.

"Oy yoy yoy!" Bubbe daps the handkerchief against her face, then blows her nose and walks away.

"Who the hell is Sarah?" Otto is speaking to Anna. Anna shrugs. She turns her head away from Portia, because she knows her sister will make her laugh.

"Portia!" Otto says, and he stares at his other granddaughter. "Who the hell is Sarah?"

The only person Anna knows who would find this as funny as she and Portia is their mother. This exchange would have made her laugh so hard she'd have to stub out her cigarette and put down her cup of coffee before it spilled.

"It's her Jewish name," Portia finally says.

"What the fuck does that mean, her Jewish name? Since when does she have a Jewish name?!"

"Since she converted," Portia says. "Right before they were married." Anna looks at everyone but Portia. If they make eye contact it will all be over.

"Oh my," Billie says, and she shifts in her seat, pulling down the legs of her black pantsuit as if to adjust the fit.

"Louise goddamn converted to Jew?!" Otto's mouth is open. He looks like he can't quite breathe.

"Well, yeah," Portia says. "Remember? She had a Jewish wedding. Isn't that why you didn't show up?" Anna is stunned by how bold Portia is. She used to be so quiet around Billie and Otto.

"Oh, yes," Billie says. "I remember that she was planning a Jewish wedding."

"But that doesn't mean she converted to Jew! I fucking didn't know that she actually became a Jew!" Otto says.

"Well, you might be happy to know that she tried to unconvert later. She ended up hating the Jews," Anna says. A hiccup of a laugh hovers in her throat. She sees Portia's shoulders bounce and knows her sister is pinning back a laugh with the force of a barricaded door.

"So are we at a funeral for a goddamned SARAH or for my daughter LOUISE?" Otto asks.

"Louise," Anna says. "The only one who called her Sarah is Bubbe. Everyone else called her Louise. I swear."

Zeyde approaches in his black bow tie, his black yarmulke, his black sideburns that he seems to grow in thick to make up for the dearth of hair on his head.

"Oy!" he says, and he leans in and kisses Billie. Billie's back shoots straight up as if someone has goosed her. "Oy!" He kisses Otto and Anna has to turn her head so no one will see her laughing. Out of the corner of her eye, she sees Portia has turned her head away, too.

"You're not going to call her Sarah, are you?" Otto asks.

"Yetta called her Sarah," Zeyde says. "She loved her like a daughter. And let me tell you, there is no one on this side of the Mississippi who cooked better kosher food than your daughter!"

Anna gasps out a small chortle, then turns and rushes to Emery. Portia slips in behind her. The three of them cluster in a circle.

"Bubbe called Mom 'Sarah' when she was talking to Billie and Otto," Anna says. "And then Zeyde told them that no one—" She starts laughing so hard she can't finish the sentence. Emery is laughing, too. Portia is wiping tears from her eyes, crying as she laughs.

"Zeyde told them that no one—" Anna tries to continue but can't.

"Say it!" Emery says, still laughing.

"That no one cooked better kosher food than Mom!" Anna says, and she breaks open with full crying laughter. She doubles over, and Portia and Emery fold with her, holding each other up by the arms, tears streaming down their faces.

"God, I wish Mom were here," Portia says, as the laughing dies down. "She would have loved that."

"I know," Anna says. She looks around and sees everyone watching them: her husband, Brian, who is grinning as if he knows what is going on; Alejandro, whose eyebrows are raised as if to ask what's up; Billie and Otto, who both look like they are about to scold their grandchildren; Bubbe and Zeyde, who have their arms around each other and heads cocked together with curiosity; and Buzzy, who is smiling with so many tears on his face that his cheeks shine.

Back at the house they eat corned beef, turkey, rye bread, coleslaw, and sliced cheeses that Buzzy ordered and had delivered from a kosher deli in Los Angeles. Louise's aunts, uncles, and cousins call from Vermont and the phone is passed around as condolences are given to Buzzy, Anna, Portia, and Emery.

By the end of the night, after Otto has drunk some scotch with Zeyde, after Anna's husband, Brian, has fallen asleep in Louise's bed while reading to Esmé and Blue, and after Alejandro has fallen asleep sitting upright in the wing chair Louise had recovered herself with ticking stripes, Anna, Portia, Emery, Buzzy, and the four grandparents nestle together in the living room. On one couch, Anna sits between Billie and Otto; Emery sits beside Billie. On the other couch, Portia is between Bubbe and Zeyde with Buzzy on the other side of Bubbe. Everyone is thigh to thigh, shoulder to shoulder, tucked in like pack animals, a brood.

"That was a beautiful service!" Bubbe says, and she squeezes Portia's knee. "A beautiful service."

"It was what she wanted," Buzzy says.

"So Dad," Anna says, "does this mean you're going to forgo the Jewish cemetery so you can be buried next to Mom?"

They all look at Buzzy expectantly. He takes a slow, deep breath and lifts his hands open as if asking a question. Zeyde adjusts his yarmulke on his head.

"I've been wondering all day," Zeyde says, "why wasn't she in a Jewish cemetery?"

"She had a tattoo," Buzzy says. He had mentioned to Anna and Emery and Portia earlier that if Bubbe and Zeyde questioned the funeral location, he would tell them this lie.

"She had a tattoo?!" Otto asks. "She was a goddamned hippie, wasn't she? Where did she have the goddamned thing and what was it?!"

"Oy! A tattoo!" Bubbe says.

"Jews don't get tattoos!" Zeyde says, then he turns to Billie and Otto and explains, "You can't be buried in a Jewish cemetery if you have a tattoo."

"Will somebody tell me what goddamned piece of art my daughter had engraved on her body!" Otto says.

"A marijuana leaf," Emery says. His sisters seem to appreciate the imagery. Anna smiles and Portia winks at her brother.

"Oh, no," Billie says.

"Jesus Christ! She had an illegal drug tattooed on her body?" Otto says.

"Oy yoy yoy!" Bubbe lifts her handkerchief to her face and tamps her eyes.

"Isn't it illegal to tattoo illegal substances on your body?!" Zeyde asks.

"It was on the center of one ass cheek," Anna says, and Portia bursts open with a giggle. Emery and Anna laugh, too, and as quickly as it started, they all three begin weeping.

"She lived a beautiful life," Bubbe says, when the crying has stilled. "We'll forgive her the marijuana leaf on her *tuches*."

"Well, I have some good news," Emery says. He decides he might as well come out to everyone who hasn't figured it out already. He'll drop Alejandro and the baby on them in one clean detonation. Who could freak out about something like this when his mother has just died? Also, Emery has made an oath to himself that he'll keep in better touch with his grandparents. He imagines them as the tops of a circle that loops him to his mother. And his grandparents need to know with whom they're looped.

"Oh, yeah," Otto says. "What's your news? I haven't heard you say three words since you called me 'fucker' when you were a little sissy boy!"

Emery smiles. He stopped being afraid of Otto around the time he grew taller than him. "Alejandro and I are going to have a baby."

"Wonderful!" Bubbe claps her hands. "If it's a girl, you name it Sarah after your mother. If it's a boy, you name it Sheldon."

"Yetta!" Zeyde says. "Did you hear who he's having this baby with? His roommate! That Mexican boy who's sleeping in the chair over there!" Zeyde points with his thumb toward Alejandro, who is as still as Lincoln sitting in his stone memorial.

"Yes, yes, Emery and his friend are having a baby!" Bubbe claps her hand and actually bounces on the couch.

Emery wonders if Aunt Sylvia had told the truth about Bubbe praying for Buzzy not to be gay. Bubbe seems perfectly fine with the gay thing, as if she's been around gay couples the past eight decades.

"Wait a goddamned minute!" Otto says. "Let me get this straight. You and that Mexican are homosexuals?!"

"Oy," Buzzy says. "Of course they're homosexuals! They live together, they're in love!"

Billie has a sly smirk on her face and Otto is fully smiling. Emery thinks it's like seeing a machine gun smile.

"What are you going to do?" Otto finally speaks. "Pull a chocolate kid out of your asses?!"

"No." Emery grins. "We found a hospital in New York where they'll implant an already fertilized embryo into this woman we met who will carry it for us. The sperm will be from Alejandro and the egg will be from Anna."

Everyone turns and looks at Anna.

"Anna's eggs?" Buzzy asks. "I thought you were using Portia's."

"No, Anna's, Dad. I told you already that we're using Anna's." Emery wonders if his father has had a stroke. He told him he was using Anna's eggs about ninety minutes ago when they were alone in the kitchen getting out the sandwiches.

"You think Portia could handle having her body pumped up with chemicals that fuck you up for weeks?!" Anna asks. Emery hates when she puts it that way. Can't she look at the gentle, sweet side of this process? The simple fact that she's giving them eggs?

"Is there such thing as a Jewish Mexican?" Bubbe asks.

"He's Cuban," Emery says.

"They have Jews in Cuba!" Bubbe says, and she gets up from the couch and kisses Emery on the forehead. "Mazel tov!"

"You're having a goddamned baby with a Jewish-Cuban homosexual!?" Otto says.

"Congratulations," Billie says, and she nods her head as if to put an exclamation point on the end of the word.

"Alejandro's not Jewish, is he?" Buzzy says.

Emery shoots him a shut-up look. Let Bubbe think he's Jewish, it'll make her happy! Let Otto think he's Jewish, it will make his banter that much more interesting!

"He loves gefilte fish," Anna says. "He's the only one who will eat it with Dad."

Bubbe has tiptoed over to sleeping Alejandro. She pushes the black hair off his forehead and gives it one of her wet suction-kisses. Alejandro opens his eyes, widens them comically. Emery laughs.

"Mazel tov!" Bubbe says, and she returns to the couch.

"So you're going to have sex with your brother's homosexual, Cuban, Jewish lover?" Otto says to Anna.

"Of course." Anna winks at Alejandro, who's smiling. Emery thinks for a second that his sister probably would have sex with Alejandro, but it's way too creepy a thought—he shakes it away.

"They're not having sex!" Buzzy says. "They're going to take Anna's egg and mix it with Alejandro's sperm in a test tube. It's a test-tube baby."

"The miracles of modern science!" Zeyde says, and he lifts his pointer finger—his signature gesture.

"Jesus Christ," Otto grumbles. "I'm going to have a homosexual, test-tube great-grandson from my homosexual grandson and his Cuban, Jewish, Mexican homosexual lover!"

"A part of you will be in the child," Emery says. "My mother will be in the child." He swallows a walnut of sadness in his throat.

"Well, let's hope it's not the tattooed hippie side of your mother," Otto says. "The kid'll be lucky if he just gets the normal goddamned heterosexual white American part of me!"

"Yup. Let's hope he's normal like you, Otto." Emery shares a secretive smile with each of his sisters.

A few scotches later, Zeyde leans forward on the couch, his face pointing like a yardstick toward Otto and Billie. "Tell us," Zeyde says. "Tell us about my beautiful daughter-in-law—"

"May she rest in peace," Bubbe says.

"Tell us about Louise as a baby," Zeyde says. "Where did it all begin?"

"It began with a fuck!" Otto says. "A couple of scotches and a fuck! Like all the other people crowding this planet!"

Anna wonders if her propensity toward drugs and fucking comes from her grandfather. It might be a tremendous relief to grow old and outgrow all those self-destructive urges. Anna's looking forward to being abstinent when she's readying her eggs for Alejandro and Emery. The risk of pregnancy is so high (and she absolutely does not want any more kids) that she's been advised that even sex with a condom is too risky. It will feel good to force herself to be still, to stop running for a few weeks, to try to live in the most peaceful way she can find. She couldn't slow down like this for herself, to save her own life. But for her baby brother, she'll do whatever's necessary to get the best, ripest eggs. It's the biggest thing she's ever given him, Anna thinks. And it will make up for all the times she kicked him in the shoulder or thigh when he sat too close to her on the couch watching television. Maybe it will even make up for the time she promised to take him to Magic Mountain if he stopped clearing his throat for one week. It was difficult for Emery to stop, but he did (he had allergies and was feeling the continuous light finger of phlegm). Then Anna decided she didn't want to take him to Magic Mountain after all. Of course, she would have forgotten about this years ago (in the tome that held her crimes, this seemed like one of the smaller ones), but Portia and Louise wouldn't let it go. The two of them flung her offense back and forth like a smelly old dishrag, as if it were Anna's most heinous transgression.

"Seriously," Emery says. "Tell us about Mom as a baby."

"Well, I suppose she was normal," Billie says.

"Normal," Otto says. "Not a homosexual, Mexican, Jewish, Cuban, alien test-tube kid!"

"Normal, like you hope my kid will be!" Emery says. Anna watches her brother. It is obvious that he can't wait for the birth of his homosexual, Mexican, Jewish, Cuban, alien test-tube kid.

It is well after midnight. Alejandro has squeezed onto the couch next to Emery, his arm carelessly around him as if the grandparents have been in on this relationship from the start. Buzzy, slouched in a chair, has fallen asleep and awoken again at least three times. Portia wonders how he can sleep—her brain is twirling and flying with her mother's voice. She can feel Louise everywhere: beside her, across from her, in the kitchen, under her skin.

"I can't believe Mom's gone," Portia says. "I keep expecting her to walk in the room looking for a pack of cigarettes and some matches."

"She's here, she's here!" Bubbe says, and she claps her hands in some strange little applause. Portia actually glances around the room to see if her mother has wandered in.

"Yetta!" Zeyde says. "How is she here? She's not here, she's resting in peace."

"She's in the children," Bubbe says, and she picks up Portia's hand and covers it with her knobby, clawing fingers.

"Yeah," Portia says. "I guess she is here."

Portia is surprised that she has not faded and evaporated with the loss of her mother (or even with the less tragic loss of her husband). She understands suddenly that the stuff that fills her up is not the love or attention she might get from other people; it is the love she herself has for other people. We are, Portia decides, the people we love.

"You still haven't told us the story of Mom's life," Anna says to Billie and Otto.

"Ask your sister, the nosy girl." Otto points his cigar-sized finger toward Portia. "She asks so many questions she probably knows more about Louise's life than I do!"

"Portia asks a lot of questions," Bubbe says, and she bounces Portia's hand on her lap.

"I'd love to tell Mom's story," Portia says. "But when I get to the part after I'm born, where I'm a kid, I'm leaving out those times Otto accused me of going to dummy school."

"Ach, you can't leave that out," Otto says, waving his hand as if to eliminate some smell. "Dumb girl like you. Even if you don't say it, everyone will know you went to dummy school."

"No point in hiding it from us," Anna says.

"In New Jersey," Zeyde says, "there's no such thing as dummy school."

"Wait, did you really go to dummy school?" Emery appears to be asking in earnest. Portia wonders if her family truly does think she's dumb—or maybe they think she had a dumb period, something like Picasso's Blue Period.

"No, she didn't go to dummy school!" Buzzy says, awake again. "But the fact that Otto claimed she did is part of the story! That's why she has to tell it—because he really did say that."

"You're right," Portia says. "I'll keep in the part about dummy school, but then I'm putting in your coming out, Emery. And all of Anna's little—"

"Manias?" Anna says, and she lifts her wineglass to her mouth and empties it.

"Indiscretions?" Alejandro twirls his finger in Emery's hair.

"All of it," Portia says. "This has to be an honest story."

"Honesty," Zeyde says, with his finger in the air, "is the best policy!"

"Oy," Buzzy groans. His eyes are melted red dimes.

"And I'll also keep in the part about Mom as an infant in the snowstorm." Portia surprises herself as she speaks. No one has ever before mentioned in front of Billie and Otto the time Louise was left for dead in the open convertible during an early spring squall.

Portia looks toward Billie and Otto. They appear shriveled and lax, as if the air has slipped out of them as from two partially deflated balloons. She doesn't want to hurt them. She just wants to tell her mother's story. Or perhaps it's the family story—with Louise as the beating heart in the center of them—that she wants to tell. The living truth.

"We learned a goddammed good lesson that night," Otto says.

"Always go drinking closer to home," Anna says, and she pours a fresh glass of red wine for herself and Emery. The other drinkers are sticking to scotch. Portia is sipping at bubbly water.

"Amen," Emery says, and he clinks his glass against Anna's and then Portia's.

"Amen," Portia says, and that, she decides, is all that needs to be said.

(acknowledgments)

I am forever grateful for the brilliant Katherine Nintzel of HarperCollins and the ebullient Joanne Brownstein of Brandt and Hochman. Thank you for the support and guidance of early draft readers: Geoff Becker, Kit Givan, Michael Kimball, Madeleine Mysko, Ron Tanner, and Tracy Wallace. I am in great debt to the people who cheered on and tirelessly promoted my last book: Phyllis Grossbach, Sally Beaton, Fran Brennan, Larry Doyle, Bruce Fleming, Lindsay Fleming, Boo Lunt, Kindall Rende, Lynda Riley, Claire Stancer, Satchel Summers, Shiloh Summers, and many others too numerous to list but not forgotten. Thank you to Rachel, Poppy, and David Piltch for lending their immense talents to the Naked Swim Parties video. This book would not be possible without the immeasurable hard work and boundless creativity of Carrie Kania, Cal Morgan, Amy Baker, Erica Barmash, Carl Lennertz, Mary Beth Constant, Robin Bilardello, Alberto Rojas, and Meredith Rusu. Maddie Tavis and Ella Grossbach are the two great loves of my life. And my heart belongs to David Grossbach.

Insights,
Interviews
& More...

Meet Jessica Anya Blau

David Grossbach

JESSICA ANYA BLAU was born in Boston and raised in California. She studied French at the University of California, Berkeley, and didn't start writing until she was stuck in Canada without a work permit or a study permit. Once she started writing, she found it hard to stop, and eventually she went to graduate school at The Writing Seminars at Johns Hopkins so she could be around other writers and learn from them. Jessica had twenty-five short stories published before her first novel, *The Summer of Naked Swim Parties,* was published. *The Summer of Naked Swim Parties* was chosen as a Best Summer Read by the *Today* show, the *New York Post,* and *New York* magazine. The *San Francisco Chronicle,* along with other newspapers, picked it as a Best Book of the Year. ∾

The Truth Inside the Lie
Interview with the Real Family

ALTHOUGH *Drinking Closer to Home* is a work of fiction, I used the members of my family and some of the things that actually happened to us as a launching pad for the novel, so it only seemed fair that I let the "real" family speak up about our past and the book.

What did you think of the character who resembles you in the book?

Mom (Louise): I like her. She's me, and she's great!

Becca (Anna): I love Anna. Despite her craziness and her sharp, angry tongue, she is smart and good. I have a lot of compassion for her. I love her spirit and her fierce love for her family. She is very much like me in all of my many flaws and strengths.

Dad (Buzzy): I think I got off easy.

Josh (Emery): I don't know what to think. It was interesting to see some events put into fictional form.

Anything you want to clear up—anything you want people to know?

Josh: Not necessarily. It's fiction, based on me, but not *me*.

Mom: I'm not dead. And I'm not Jewish.

Becca: People who have read this book are shocked that I am not upset about the portrayal of my character, Anna. I, however, happen to love her. And while I am not a ▶

> 66 People who have read this book are shocked that I am not upset about the portrayal of my character, Anna. 99
> —Becca

3

The Truth Inside the Lie *(continued)*

coke addict or a sex addict, I possess both the recklessness and compulsiveness that Anna does. Also, this is my sister's story. I love it just as she tells it. Perhaps she remembers things that I don't.

Dad: Nobody in this book resembles any actual persons living or dead.

Mom told me once, in all seriousness, that she thinks she looks like Bruce Springsteen. Do you agree?

Becca: She does look like Bruce Springsteen, but also like Alice Cooper and Bob Dylan.

Dad: She looks like Anne Bancroft.

Josh: Yes, she looks like Anne Bancroft. Or Mia Farrow.

Mom: I look like Bruce with a touch of George Jones.

I think I look like Vincent Van Gogh. True or false?

Josh: Not like Van Gogh. Maybe someone from a Munch painting?

Mom: You look exactly like Vinnie. A dead ringer!

Becca: I think the portrait that Mom did of you at age twelve looks very much like Van Gogh's self-portraits.

Dad: You? (laughs) No, you don't look like Vincent Van Gogh. What kind of crazy talk is that? That's crazy talk. Maybe if you took off an ear!

Josh looks like Matthew McConaughey and Ralph Fiennes mixed. True or false?

Josh: False. I look more like Edward Norton.

> 66 I think the portrait that Mom did of you [Jessica] at age twelve looks very much like Van Gogh's self-portraits. 99
>
> —Becca

Mom: Josh looks like Bruce Springsteen and Mickey Rourke.

Becca: True—but also like Liam Neeson.

Dad: I agree with Becca. No, I think— Yes, I agree with Becca. He looks more like Ralph Fiennes than anybody. Who's the other one? Oh, I don't know what Matthew McDonaughey [sic] looks like.

And don't you agree that Josh looked like a turtle when he was a little guy?

Becca: Josh did look like a turtle though I can't put my finger on exactly why. He looked like a cartoon turtle . . . like the character Franklin.

Josh: I still have some resemblance to a turtle.

*Becca looks like either Batman, or Marlo Thomas back in the **That Girl** days. Or like that model Talisha Castro.*

Mom: She looks like Bruce Springsteen. Plain and simple.

Dad: Marlo Thomas.

Becca: Batman? If I'm Batman, you're the Penguin. I think I look like Michael Jackson. I am serious. Check out my comparison below. ▶

❝ I don't know what Matthew McDonaughey [sic] looks like. ❞

—Dad

The Truth Inside the Lie *(continued)*

Josh: Michael Jackson. But I suppose she did have a Marlo Thomas phase. Becca and Dad are the lovely dark ones. I remember when Becca was eighteen, someone came up to her on the street in NYC and asked her if she was black or white: "Yo, girl, you black or you white?"

Alan Alda reminds me of Dad. You too?
Mom: Nooo. More like that guy Larry David.
Josh: No. But I did meet his doppelganger once in Sicily.
Becca: I see what you are getting at with the Alan Alda comparison, but I would say you'd have to mix in Larry David and Woody Allen.
Dad: I'd like it to be Alan Alda. I'm afraid it's more Woody Allen and Larry David. And I also look like Joel Klein. He's the chancellor of New York City schools. He's in the paper.

Mom and Dad clearly always thought that Josh was the smartest, I was the dumbest, and Becca was the most trouble. Does anyone see it differently?
Mom: Nope. That's how it was, and that's why you went to Dummy School.
Becca: I was the most demanding. You were the sweetest and easiest to love. Josh was adored but never really "seen."
Dad: No, I didn't think Josh was the smartest. I think I thought Becca was the smartest. I thought Josh was the most like me in his thinking. And I thought you were most like Mom in your thinking. Which is just as smart but different.

> 66 I thought you were most like Mom in your thinking. Which is just as smart but different. 99
> —Dad

We had a downstairs bathroom that was wallpapered with New York Times *articles about the Watergate scandal. Mom graffitied it in places before she shellacked it. Anyone remember any headlines or graffiti?*

Mom: I wrote on Nixon's grinning face, "Why is this man smiling?"

Becca: Headlines: "Agnew Resigns. Nixon Consults on Successor." "Baseball Takes on Image of Ugly Japanese."

Josh: "Man Hit by Five Cars on Coast Freeway"—remember that one? What a great wall. We should have documented it!

Dad: I just remember what it was about. I used to read it when I was in the bathroom. There was nothing else to read. I do remember the "Agnew Resigns" headline.

What do you think Grandma and Poppop, were they alive, would say about the chapters where they show up as Bubbe and Zeyde?

Mom: I think Poppop would say, "In Trenton we don't have Dummy School girls writing about their family."

Becca: Poppop would probably offer to rewrite it for you.

Dad: I would never let them read it.

Josh: They wouldn't even realize it was based on them.

Everyone has different versions of the past. In this novel, the family home has bird shit on the back of the couch and the kitchen floor is like hard black sidewalk ▶

> " I would never let them [Grandma and Poppop] read [*Drinking Closer to Home*]. "
>
> —Dad

gum (even though it's a white floor). How messy do you think our house was?

Mom: It wasn't messy at all. I vacuumed and dusted and cleaned every day. I wore a doily on my head.

Becca: It was messy. Floors were filthy. There were dust balls everywhere. The kitchen had crud and crumbs everywhere. The stove and oven were black. We had worms in our cupboards and in our cereal and rice. We also had the worst scratchy little towels. My room was neat as a pin. I made my bed, vacuumed regularly, and sprayed Lysol to freshen the air. I made sure that my throw rugs were exactly an inch from the wall before I went to bed. That might have had something to do with my OCD.

Josh: It was very, very messy. When I was seventeen, some friends came over and cleaned the fridge 'cause it was so gross.

Dad: I don't remember it being nearly as messy as people tell me it was. But I think it was less messy than the house I grew up in.

Mom, did you really back the car into and knock down the neighbors' mailbox three times? Or am I remembering it wrong?

Mom: Yes, of course you are remembering it wrong. It was your Dad who knocked down their mailbox twice, as I recall. Ask him.

Dad: It's true. It was me. At least twice. Maybe three times.

When we first moved to California, we often gave the neighbors on our cul de sac

66 When I was seventeen, some friends came over and cleaned the fridge 'cause it was so gross. 99

—Josh

the excess lemons from our trees. Once, the college-aged son of one of our neighbors had a party while his parents were out of town. The party included a big dog who shit on our lawn. Dad scooped up the dog shit, put it in a brown paper bag, and told Becca to deliver it to the boy. The boy thought it was lemons and put it on the kitchen counter with a note that said, "The Blaus sent these over for you." Do you think this is why everyone on the cul de sac stopped talking to us?

Dad: It is why *those* neighbors stopped talking to us. They're the same neighbors whose mailbox I ran into three times. There is no connection between those two facts.

Mom: Truth is, it was the doily on the head that did it.

Josh: The neighbors could have hated us for many reasons. Apparently I called the family next door "fascist pigs" when I was, like, three. I didn't really understand what that meant until I was much older, in my twenties. Strangely, it's a word I use a lot now, mostly when speaking Spanish. *Fascista* or *facha* is current slang for anyone on the far right.

Mom: Josh *did* call the neighbors "fascist pigs" at age three. I had forgotten that. He also said "fuck you" to Mrs. Christenson. I guess he was a bit of a hellion. But he was a good boy, an angel, nonetheless.

Josh: Maybe they hated us because they knew that Mom used to get stoned and play basketball down in Isla Vista behind ▶

> " Josh *did* call the neighbors 'fascist pigs' at age three. I had forgotten that. "
> —Mom

The Truth Inside the Lie *(continued)*

her studio. [Isla Vista is the neighborhood where all the college students live.]

Mom: I was forty-two then, Jesus Christ, give me a break! I'm seventy-one now. No comment. Well, okay, it was a one-time tournament, best of three, two four-person teams. My team played twice and won. I probably was stoned.

Is there anything else you think I should ask in this interview?

Mom: No, you've caused enough trouble. Go to bed. ◡

Excerpt: *The Summer of Naked Swim Parties*

Fourteen-year-old Jamie will never forget the summer of 1976. It's the summer when she has her first boyfriend, cute surfer Flip Jenkins; it's the summer when her two best friends get serious about sex, cigarettes, and tanning; it's the summer when her parents throw, yes, naked swim parties, leaving Jamie flushed with embarrassment. And it's the summer that forever changes the way Jamie sees the things that matter: family, friendship, love, and herself.

AFTER ALL, it was the seventies, so Allen and Betty thought nothing of leaving their younger daughter, Jamie, home alone for three nights while they went camping in Death Valley. And although most girls who had just turned fourteen would love a rambling Spanish-style house (with a rock formation pool, of course) to themselves for four days, Jamie, who erupted with bouts of fear with the here-now/gone-now pattern of a recurring nightmare, found the idea of her parents spending three nights in Death Valley terrifying. Jamie was not afraid for Allen and Betty—she did not fear their death by heat stroke, or scorpion sting, or dehydration (although each of these occurred to her in the days preceding their departure). She feared her own death—being murdered by one of the homeless men who slept between the roots of the giant fig tree near the train station; or being trapped on the first floor of the house, the second floor sitting on her ►

like a fat giant, after having fallen in an earthquake.

Jamie's older sister, Renee, was also away that weekend, at a lake with the family of her best and only friend. But even if she had been home, Renee would have provided little comfort for Jamie, as her tolerance for the whims of her younger sister seemed to have vanished around the time Jamie began menstruating while Renee still hadn't grown hips.

"I invited Debbie and Tammy to stay with me while you're gone," Jamie told her mother.

They were in the kitchen. Betty wore only cut-off shorts and an apron (no shoes, no shirt, no bra); it was her standard uniform while cooking. Betty's large, buoyant breasts sat on either side of the bib—her long, gummy nipples matched the polka dots on the apron.

"I know," Betty said. "Their mothers called."

Jamie's stomach thumped. Of course their mothers called. They each had a mother who considered her daughter the central showpiece of her life. "So what'd you say?" Jamie prayed that her mother had said nothing that would cause Tammy and Debbie's mothers to keep them home.

"I told them that I had left about a hundred dollars worth of TV dinners in the freezer, that there was spending money in the cookie jar, and that there was nothing to worry about."

"What'd they say?"

> 66 They were in the kitchen. Betty wore only cut-off shorts and an apron (no shoes, no shirt, no bra); it was her standard uniform while cooking. 99

"Tammy's mother wanted to know what the house rules were."

"What'd you say?"

"I told her there were no rules. We trust you."

Jamie knew her parents trusted her, and she knew they were right to do so—she couldn't imagine herself doing something they would disapprove of. The problem, as she saw it, was that she didn't trust *them* not to do something that *she* disapproved of. She had already prepared herself for the possibility that her parents would not return at the time they had promised, for anything—an artichoke festival, a nudists' rights parade—could detain them for hours or even days. There was nothing internal in either of her parents, no alarms or bells or buzzing, that alerted them to the panic their younger daughter felt periodically, like she was an astronaut untethered from the mother ship—floating without any boundaries against which she could bounce back to home.

Allen walked into the kitchen. He'd been going in and out of the house, loading the Volvo with sleeping bags, a tent, lanterns, flashlights, food.

"You know Debbie and Tammy are staying here with Jamie," Betty said, and she flipped an omelet over—it was a perfect half-moon, and she, for a second, was like a perfect mother.

"Why do all your friends' names end in Y?" Allen asked.

"Tammy," Jamie recited. "Debbie . . . Debbie's I E." ▶

> Jamie knew her parents trusted her, and she knew they were right to do so—she couldn't imagine herself doing something they would disapprove of. The problem, as she saw it, was that she didn't trust *them* not to do something that *she* disapproved of.

13

"But it sounds like a Y."

"So does my name."

"You're I E," Betty said. "You've been I E since you were born."

"Yeah, but Jamie sounds like Jamey with a Y."

"There's no such thing as Jamie with a Y," Allen said. "But there is Debby with a Y."

"Well Mom's a Y—Betty!"

"I'm a different generation," Betty said. "I don't count."

"And she's not your friend, she's your mother," Allen said.

"Oh, there's also Kathy and Suzy and Pammy," Betty said.

"No one calls her Pammy except you," Jamie said.

"Too many Y's," Allen said. "You need friends with more solid names. Carol or Ann."

"No way I'm hanging out with Carol or Ann."

"They've got good names." Allen sat on a stool at the counter, picked up his fork and knife, and held each in a fist on either side of his plate.

"They're dorks," Jamie said.

Betty slid the omelet off the pan and onto Allen's plate just as their neighbor Leon walked in.

"Betty," he said, and he kissed Jamie's mother on the cheek. His right hand grazed one breast as they pulled away from the kiss.

"Allen." Leon stuck out the hand that had just touched Betty's breast to Allen,

'Too many Y's,' Allen said. 'You need friends with more solid names. Carol or Ann.'

14

who was hovered over his omelet, oblivious.

"Did you find some?" Allen asked.

"I stuck it in your trunk," Leon said.

"What?" Jamie asked.

"Nothing," Allen said, although he must have known that Jamie knew they were talking about marijuana. They rolled it in front of their daughters, they smoked it in front of them, they left abalone ashtrays full of Chicklet-sized butts all over the house. Yet the actual purchasing of it was treated like a secret—as if the girls were supposed to think that although their parents would smoke an illegal substance, they'd never be so profligate as to buy one.

"So what are you going to do in Death Valley?" Leon asked.

Allen lifted his left hand and made an O. He stuck the extended middle finger of his right hand in and out of the O. The three of them laughed. Jamie turned her head so she could pretend to not have seen. Unlike her sister, Jamie was successfully able to block herself from her parents' overwhelming sexuality, which often filled the room they were in, in the same way that air fills whatever space contains it.

"And what are you doing home alone?" Leon winked at Jamie.

"Debbie and Tammy are staying with me," she said. "I guess we'll watch TV and eat TV dinners."

"You want an omelet?" Betty asked Leon, and her voice was so cheerful, her cheeks so rouged and smooth, that it just ▶

66 It was a scene from a sitcom gone wrong. . . . 99

Excerpt: *The Summer of Naked Swim Parties* (continued)

didn't seem right that she should walk around half-naked all the time.

"Sure," Leon said, and he slid onto the stool next to Allen as Betty prepared another omelet.

Jamie looked back at the three of them as she left the kitchen. Allen and Leon were dressed in jeans and tee shirts, being served food by chatty, cheerful Betty. Wide bands of light shafted into the room and highlighted them as if they were on a stage. It was a scene from a sitcom gone wrong. There was the friendly neighbor guy, the slightly grumpy father, the mother with perfectly coiffed short brown hair that sat on her head like a wig. But when the mother bent down to pick up an egg shell that had dropped, the friendly neighbor leaned forward on his stool so he could catch a glimpse of the smooth orbs of his friend's wife's ass peeking out from the fringe of her too-short shorts.

Jamie wished her life were as simple as playing Colorforms; she would love to stick a plastic dress over her shiny cardboard mother. If it didn't stick, she'd lick the dress and hold it down with her thumb until it stayed. ❧